3 9082 14583 9901

D1507016

CURSE UNDONE

CURSE UNDONE

The Gold Spun Duology

BRANDIE JUNE

CamCat
Books

CamCat Publishing, LLC
Brentwood, Tennessee 37027
camcatpublishing.com

Hardcover ISBN 9780744306224
Paperback ISBN 9780744306330
Large-Print Paperback ISBN 9780744309034
eBook ISBN 9780744306095
Audiobook ISBN 9780744306194

Library of Congress Control Number: 2022937137

Book and cover design by Maryann Appel
Map illustration by Jaya Matteis

5   3   1   2   4

To Nicole, Dana, Jackson, Nina, Julie, Ayla, Leigh,
and the rest of the WestWord gang.
Thanks for being such an amazing and supportive part
of my writing tribe.

"Fly out into the world and make your own living," the wicked Queen told them. "Fly away like big birds without a voice."

But she did not harm the Princes as much as she meant to, for they turned into eleven magnificent white swans. With a weird cry, they flew out of the palace window, across the park into the woods."

—The Wild Swans (1838)
By Hans Christian Andersen, translated by Jean Hersholt

Prologue

"Is that natural?" Casper asked, staring out at the dense mist that spread through the trees ahead, filling the distance with a milky cloud. He had never seen a fog appear so suddenly nor so thickly, but he had never lived in the Biawood Forest, not the way Nor had. He wasn't going to tell her she was keeping them alive as they made their way home, but they both knew that her years as a swindler and thief living in the woods made her adept at surviving on their trek.

Casper was well aware that he would have poisoned himself the first day of their escape from the fay, had Nor not yelled at him to drop the wild mushrooms he'd gathered, the ones that to him looked so similar to the ones the royal chefs would sauté in butter and serve with garlic back at the Rose Palace. He had not thought to dig up edible roots, nor noted how the ground was littered with acorns and pine nuts. And until Nor pointed it out, he had not seen the wild asparagus, chicory, garlic grass, and clover that grew in abundance. All things Nor had noticed with familiar ease. He would have admired her skills, appreciated the protective way she watched out for him on their way back to Reynallis, would have loved learning this new aspect of Nor had he not walled off his heart to her. The sting of her trickery was still sharp as knives. It was easier to focus on their survival and escape. He could ignore the rip in his heart till they were both safely back at the Rose Palace.

Nor met his eyes for only a moment before she followed his gaze. She turned the way they had been coming, back toward Magnomel, land of the faeries. The air was clear, the bright sun filtering through the leaves, a reminder that it was still summer. Her brows knit in concern as she turned back to the gray fog.

"I highly doubt it." She bit her lip, sucking in air through her teeth, a habit of hers when she was trying to solve a problem. Casper had seen her do it countless times in his study, back when they were engaged and she was going to be his queen. He had loved watching her analyze a situation, loved the way her mind came up with solutions he would never have considered. But that was before she betrayed him. His heart ached at the memory, but he pushed it away. He had to focus on returning to Reynallis, returning to his country and his palace.

"Perhaps we should wait for it to disperse?" Casper eyed the wall of mist uneasily.

"We don't have time to wait," Nor said, pacing anxiously along the fog barrier, as though her quick steps could break up the mist. She kept glancing the way they had come, and he knew she was wondering how close the Faerie Queen Marasina and her soldiers were to catching up with them.

"Is this some faerie trick?" he asked. The word "faerie" tasted bitter on his lips.

"How would I know?"

"You might." Casper knew he was being harsh, but he couldn't help it. Every strange thing in the woods reminded him about the fay, and the fay reminded him that Nor had lied to him, chosen a faerie over him. He told himself that those details alone were enough. Though the fact that the faerie had been a handsome young man made him burn.

"I *don't* know." Nor sighed, running her hands through a tangle of her hair, getting even more frustrated as her fingers pulled on knots. She looked almost feral; her dress dirty, ripped shreds that had once been fine velvet. A ruined skirt of broken loops that had been gold embroidered spinning wheels only days ago. Her various cuts from the battle with the attacking fay had scabbed over to crusty scars, and several bruises had healed to a sickly greenish purple. Despite it all, she still looked beautiful to him, strong in ways he had only learned about, a survivor.

She lied to you. She worked with your enemy. Casper remembered lying on the cold stone floor of the cathedral, a faerie with gold hair and snake-like eyes holding a blade to his throat. He was the one Nor had called Pel or perhaps Rumpelstiltskin. The sickening moment when Casper realized she knew their attacker; was even friends with the creature. He had every right to be suspicious of her. But it would all be so much easier if he didn't find her so beautiful.

Casper watched as Nor stepped up to the mist wall, tentatively reaching her hand into the mist. He held his breath until she pulled her arm back, examining it. Tiny droplets of water dotted her hand, but she seemed unscathed.

Suddenly she yelped in pain, staring down at her wrist. The thin gold bracelet that Nor wore at all times was glowing a hot white, searing her skin. It only lasted a moment, the bracelet returning to gold even as an angry red line in her skin formed from where the gold touched it. Nor pulled at the golden thread, trying to yank it free, but despite how delicate the bracelet appeared, it held fast.

"We have to go. *Now!*" Nor looked over her shoulder, back toward Magnomel, as though the fay would be charging through the woods at any moment.

"What was that?" Casper asked, no longer looking at Nor's wrist, but rather staring into her eyes, eyes the color of polished wood.

Nor swallowed hard, meeting Casper's stare. She was tense with fear, like a rabbit catching the scent of a wolf.

"When I saved Pel from the bandits in the woods, he changed a strand of wool from his shirt into gold and gave it to me." Casper ground his teeth together, forcing himself to stay silent. "It was how I could contact him to . . . repay the debt."

The room full of gold, Casper thought. He knew about her debt all too well. He had not known about the significance of the bracelet she wore, and learning it was from the faerie caused another stab of pain in his heart.

"And you kept it?" Casper didn't bother to keep the disgust from his voice.

"Not by choice," Nor snapped, pulling at Casper's sleeve. "Pel cursed the Chace-forsaken thing, so it won't come off. But now he knows where I am."

Casper immediately understood Nor's panic. His stomach clenched in fear, knowing the fay would be able to track them even if a tiny piece of him was relieved that Nor had not lied this time.

"We should separate, it's safer for you. Please take care of my brothers when you get home." Nor turned to run when Casper grabbed her arm, his grip firm enough to hold her in place.

"We are getting home together." His words were hard, with the assured authority he used as a ruler, even when he was faking such confidence. Even with the war going on in his heart and the anger he felt toward Nor, he was determined to get her to safety.

Casper released Nor's arm and extended his hand to her. Tentatively, she took it. There was a familiar warmth with her smaller, calloused hand in his. He tightened his grip.

"We don't want to risk getting separated. We'll walk one foot in front of the other to avoid going in circles."

"Right," Nor agreed.

They stepped into the fog.

The mist immediately swarmed around them, making it hard to see farther than a few feet. Casper had been sweating in the forest, but now the air was damp and chilly, tasting vaguely of mint. The mist mingled with his sweat, cooling his skin. He would have been grateful for the refreshing sensation if the surroundings weren't so strange. Moments before, the Biawood had been vibrant greens and browns; everything now was muted to pale grays. The ghostly mist was so bright that his eyes hurt, but he forced them open, even as tears ran down his face.

He stepped slowly, one foot in front of the other, holding tight to Nor's hand, as their grip grew clammy. The world had gone silent, he noticed with a surge of unease. There was no birdsong, no falling leaves, or scurrying of woodland creatures. It didn't even feel like a true silence, rather that his ears were filled with cotton. There seemed to be a weight to the mist, the air growing colder the deeper they went. Casper ignored the goosepimples forming on his skin. Beside him, Nor shivered.

Something moved.

Casper froze, trying to make out the shadow in the gloom. He could feel Nor stiffen, her hand squeezing his. Something loomed to his right. He pointed, before realizing Nor couldn't see his hand in the thick mist. He tried to peer through the fog. Everything was once again a hushed stillness.

"What is it?" Nor whispered close to him, her breath warming his ear.

"I thought I saw something." Casper took a tentative step to the right, straining to make out the shape in the distance. Nor pulled his hand back, stopping him.

"We'll get turned around."

"Just a few steps. You stay here."

Reluctantly, Nor dropped Casper's hand and he took several more steps, his nerves alight, terrified that something would ambush them. Dimly, something large took shape in front of him, an ominous dark gray figure in the gloom. The figure stood still and silent. His heart pounded in his chest, and he instinctively got ready to fight, putting himself between the shadow and Nor. He reached for his sword, only to remember it wasn't there. Biting back his fear, Casper plunged ahead, ready to face this new monster head on.

His hand met moss-soaked bark. Casper let out a gurgle of a laugh. Where he had seen a tall figure with long limbs, he now viewed a tree, branches replacing the outstretched arms of his imagination. The spike of energy dissipated into giddy, self-conscious relief.

"It's only a tree, Nor," he said, returning to her.

Nor smiled at Casper, the tension in her shoulders relaxing. "Thank you."

"For what?"

"Your valor to put yourself in harm's way over any dangerous trees."

Casper gave a small smirk. "I am also feared in all the lands by enemy shrubs. And don't get me started on hedges."

Nor giggled, the first time Casper had heard her laugh since the fay attack. "We should return to our original path and get out of here. Who knows what other plant life may be plotting against us."

"Indeed," Casper said, but then he heard another noise. He stilled. "Do you hear that?"

"No need to mock me."

"Hush," Casper hissed, straining to make out the sound. It was growing louder, a soft song floating on the mist, dark and deadly.

"One dark night I'll walk into your dreams
And tear out your heart to hear your screams
Hey nonny nonny, hey nonny hey."

"Run!" Nor cried, and Casper heard pure terror in her voice. He reached for her, to grab her hand, but he was too late. Invisible hands reached out, pulling him backward, away from Nor.

"Nor!" he screamed. He could no longer see her in the fog, and for a moment any resentment he had for Nor vanished, and all he could think was how he needed to keep her safe. He fought against his attackers, but there were too many of them, faerie hands and faces coming into view as they pulled him to the ground, restraining him. He kicked and clawed, bit and punched, but he was no match to the surrounding faeries. The mist seemed thicker, slowing his movements, and almost suffocating him with cold, heavy, wet moisture that filled his lungs and stung his eyes. In the distance, he heard Nor call his name, but it was drowned out by another verse of the chilling song.

"I'll lock your heart in a crystal jar.
So never again shall you go far
Hey nonny nonny, hey nonny hey."

A face loomed over him, one with golden hair and green snake eyes.

"Chace take you," Casper swore at the faerie. It was the one that Nor knew, the one she had whispered secrets to and had chosen over him. Jealousy and rage ignited in Casper and he struggled again against the fay. The faerie was unconcerned, knowing Casper couldn't move as four or five other faerie soldiers had him pinned to the ground.

The faerie slowly pulled out a short, sharp dagger and held it to Casper's neck. Casper wondered if this was how he was to die. The faerie pressed the dagger further into his skin, a shallow cut, but Casper could feel the blood sliding down his neck.

"You shouldn't have tried to escape with Nor," the faerie said, his voice flat. "My queen might have accepted Nor's escape if she had left the kingling."

"If you hurt Nor, I will kill you," Casper said, staring into the fay's strange, green eyes.

"I think not," the faerie said, placing one palm over the cut on Casper's neck. Casper tried to flinch away, but more hands came, securing him in place. Casper waited for the faerie to tighten his grip, squeeze the air and the life from him. But the strange creature merely rested his hand there, covering the shallow cut.

"*Dormir sange*," the faerie said, his voice soft as a lullaby.

"What—" Casper started, but ice suddenly filled his veins, making every movement a struggle. His limbs grew too heavy to move and black spots bloomed in front of his eyes, eyes that were fast becoming too heavy to keep open. A calm settled over him, and he wondered if it was the feeling of dying. Far away, he heard yelling. Maybe it was Nor. Casper blinked, slowly, before his eyes closed, and the world slipped away.

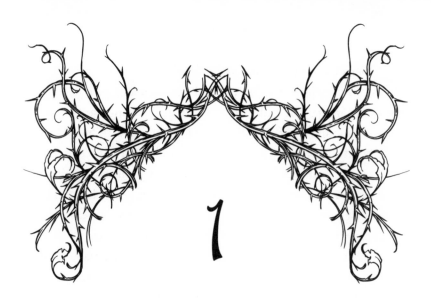

I opened my eyes to darkness. I was lying on the cold ground, staring up into a dark, clouded sky. Someone was calling my name.

"Nor. Nor, wake up!"

I tried remembering where I was. I heard lilting music and the murmur of voices, but my mind was groggy. My eyelids felt heavy, and I desperately wanted to fall back asleep. Deep exhaustion penetrated my bones; even yawning felt like too much work.

"Nor, please wake up."

It was Casper's voice.

The numbing bliss ended in an instant as the fight in the mist came back to me. Casper and I had been separated. I had been caught by Pel's brother, Elrik. He had pinned me to the ground before cutting my cheek, using blood magic to force me into an unnatural sleep. I sat up, desperate to find Casper. My vision tilted and a wave of nausea rolled over me. I stilled, closing my eyes and inhaling deeply through my nose, trying to get the world to stop spinning.

"Thank the Mother. Nor, you're alive."

A dozen steps away, Casper stood next to a long pole that stuck out of the ground. He and I were in a circular clearing, the perimeter marked by lit torches. By the flickering light of the torch fires, I could make out the tension in his face and body. And then I saw his restraint, a cruel faerie creation. Long, green vines grew from the top of the pole, hanging down the sides like ribbons, the structure resembling a village maypole. Except one of the vines was twisted around Casper's neck, a living collar of leaves that kept him standing, lest he choke.

I scrambled to my feet, fighting past the nausea and fatigue, and tried to run to him, to find some way to cut down the cursed plant. I only made it a few steps before I was yanked back, hitting the ground hard.

"Chace's chaos," I swore, examining my own bonds. I had been too preoccupied to notice that thin vines encircled my wrists. Instead of growing from a pole, these vines sprung up directly from the ground, giving me only a few feet of movement. I yanked at the vines, convinced I could dig up such slender plants, but they held fast, as strong as chains.

"I tried that," Casper said, pulling my attention back to him, his face pained. "These are not natural plants. But we are not in a natural place." His eyes lifted from me, taking in our surroundings. I followed his gaze, registering the laughter beyond the circle.

I stared past the torches, a black sea. I heard the murmur of voices, the eerie, musical laughter that sent shivers down my spine, as my vision began to adjust to the darkness. I saw the eyes first, catlike eyes that reflected the light of the flames. I could make out the forms of dozens upon dozens of faeries. I inhaled sharply, realizing we were surrounded, on display for them.

"Casper, where are we?" I asked, the horror rising in me.

"You are in my court." The voice was not Casper's, but that of the Faerie Queen herself, Marasina. She stepped past the ring of torches and into the clearing where Casper and I were imprisoned. I froze at the sight of the warrior queen. Queen Marasina had led the raid that destroyed the cathedral at the Rose Palace, killing nobles and taking us prisoners.

I could still clearly picture the imposing Faerie Queen covered in blood and mocking my trust of Pel.

This night, she wore a long silver dress studded with crystals, and it reminded me of her chain mail. Though she carried no sword, the hilt of a small dagger protruded from her braided belt. Her silver hair was loose under a crown of delicate strands of silver intertwined with living vines. Around her neck hung a glowing gold pendant that seemed to pulse, as though it were a tiny, beating heart.

"What are your intentions with us?" Casper asked, his voice firm, despite our predicament.

"To make an example of you, of course," the queen said, her musical voice incongruent with her cruel words. "You humans stole my firstborn, my beloved son, away from me. Your father's war killed my son, and that is a debt I will never forget. I should take your life for it." Marasina took several steps toward Casper, relishing the moment. Casper silently met Marasina's gaze, his head held high.

"No!" I cried, pulling with all my strength at the vines that imprisoned me, but they refused to budge.

She drew up to Casper, running her finger along the collar of vines around his neck. She was a head taller than him, and he had to look up to meet her eyes, but even then, he didn't flinch. "But I am more merciful than you barbaric humans." She turned from him, addressing the faeries beyond the clearing.

"Come, my loyal subjects, gather round for an evening's entertainment." Marasina's sweet, strong voice rang out, and the fay immediately responded.

Even more eyes reflected in the flickering light, as the fay crowded around the circle. In the dark, I could only make out shifting silhouettes, catching glimpses of sharp, grinning teeth or the glimmer of dragonfly-like wings in the torchlight.

"Dance for us, little kingling. And give us a good show," Marasina commanded, giving him a mocking smile.

Casper pressed his lips together, silently defying the Faerie Queen, as his hands formed tight fists by his side.

"I said *dance*," Marasina repeated, a sharp edge to her voice. When Casper remained motionless, she frowned. "I was hoping you would be more compliant."

"Sorry to disappoint you," Casper said through gritted teeth.

"If you wish to be difficult." Marasina gave a tiny shrug before she placed one long, elegant hand on the pole. "*Vive estringersi*," she commanded, not to Casper, but to the pole. The vines that sprouted from the top started shrinking, pulling back into the pole, including the one latched around Casper's neck.

"No!" I screamed.

Casper felt the tug around his neck, his hands flying up to his collar. He clawed at the vine, desperate to free himself, even as it stretched up, hauling him to stand on tiptoes lest he choke. His eyes were wide with terror, the horror I saw there mimicked in my own pounding chest. After a moment that lasted too many lifetimes, Marasina lifted her hand from the pole. The vines immediately stopped shrinking. Casper could breathe, but only as long as he kept his back to the pole, standing precariously on his toes.

"I said *dance*." Marasina's command was all threat.

Reluctantly, Casper began a court dance, though he had to remain on his toes, staying in place. He slowly raised one foot, twisting it in the air before switching to the other foot. The whole time his eyes burned at the Faerie Queen.

"Faster," she demanded.

Casper's steps became hops as he obliged. He stumbled, the vine collar choking him as he scrambled to regain his balance. The faeries laughed, an unnatural sound in the dark. I screamed, clawing at my own vine cuffs in a desperate attempt to free myself so I could get to Casper, but the vines held firm, chaffing my wrists.

Casper found his footing, coughing as he dragged in air. Queen Marasina stepped closer to him, patting him on the head as though he were a dog.

"What a pathetic creature you are, little kingling, without your army. Good sport only to amuse my subjects." More faerie laughter came from beyond the torches.

Casper moved before I could understand what was going on. Almost as fast as a faerie, his arm shot out, yanking Marasina's small dagger from her belt. He swiftly cut through the vine holding him hostage.

Freed, he brought the blade to Marasina's neck. The silver metal shone in the moonlight, Casper's face determined as he held the dagger to the Faerie Queen's throat. His other hand grabbed a fistful of her silver hair, pulling her head back to expose her neck as her crown toppled to the ground.

"How about now?" Casper's voice was rough, desperate. Though his eyes were wide, dilated with fear, his hands were steady. The dagger pressed into the soft flesh at the queen's throat, but not so deep as to draw blood, at least not yet. A hush settled on the watching fay, their eyes wide, reflecting the torchlight. There were no murmurs or snickering now.

I thought Marasina might scream or at least show some sort of fear. Instead, she laughed. The sound, silver bells and waterfalls, scared me more.

"Casper, what are you doing?" I was supposed to be the one with a rash temper and outrageous ideas.

"Getting us out of here."

"Is that your plan, kingling?" Marasina asked, her voice still full of mockery.

"I wouldn't argue if I were you," Casper told her, his voice hard. "Not in the position you are now in."

"And I suggest you release me now, little king. I might even show mercy. You are toying with powers beyond your meager understanding." The humor had left the queen's voice. I tried not to shiver.

"I demand you release us," Casper yelled. I couldn't tell if he spoke to Marasina or the fay court at large. No one moved. "Release Nor and clear a path for us or I kill your queen." Still, no one moved. Their strange cat-eyes stared at us from beyond the flames.

"And what leverage would you have then, little king?" Marasina's words were cold. Goosebumps rose on my arms. She was not worried. We were missing something.

"Don't think I won't," Casper said, pressing down on the blade. A thin line of golden blood slid onto the dagger.

"Release me now, or you shall regret it."

"Casper," I strained against the vines, desperate to get to him. "Something isn't right."

"Release my betrothed. Now!" Casper yelled, his voice shaking from anxiety. The faeries didn't move, continuing to stare at us with their strange eyes.

"I warned you." Marasina smiled, raising her hand.

Casper, his focus on me, didn't see her lips moving in an incantation. I was certain whatever magic she had in mind was as deadly as her grin, sharp teeth white in the moonlight. Her arm reached out toward the dagger.

Marasina instead gripped Casper's arm, her brutal magic flowing into him. Immediately, Casper's eyes bulged, and he clawed at his chest, as though he were trying to rip himself apart. I remembered the magic Pel had used on bandits in the woods, making them choke on their own blood.

Somehow, this seemed even worse. If Marasina continued, she would kill Casper.

"No!" I strained against my bonds, desperate to get to Casper. His eyes were rolling up into his head, his hands going limp as he dropped the blade, and a wave of panic crashed over me. Heat burned in my chest, as though Marasina's magic was burning into my heart as well. I pushed with everything I had against the vines, the fire spreading down my arms, through my fingers. At that moment, I felt the vines holding me snap. I raced to Casper, needing to get him out of Marasina's grasp. I collided with him, effectively freeing him from Marasina as I landed in a heap on top of him.

"Casper!" I rolled off of him, giving him space to breathe. He lay motionless on the ground. "Can you hear me? By the merciful Mother, be all right." I leaned over him. He was breathing, and the pressure around my own chest loosened. "You're going to be fine. Just breathe. It's all going to be fine," I promised over and over, having no idea how any of this would be fine. Casper's eyes cracked open, and I swallowed a sob of relief.

"Nor," Casper started, but even that one word was a struggle for him.

"Shh." I cradled him in my arms on the ground. Outside the torch ring, faerie eyes stared down at us. I ignored them. I had to ensure Casper would live. Then I would deal with the fay. For a few precious seconds, the world narrowed to only Casper in my arms. As his breathing steadied, I felt my own heartbeat return to normal. I hadn't realized how fast it had been racing.

"Well, that was quite the theatrics." I looked up to see Marasina staring down at us, her face serene, her silver dagger back in her hand.

"You tried to kill him." I had nothing to fight this queen, but my voice was fierce.

"Only after he threatened me." She wiped at the cut on her neck. Already her luminous skin was knitting together, leaving only a drizzle of shiny blood and a small scar. She stared at the blood on her finger for a long moment, as though making a decision; one I was sure I wouldn't like. "I don't appreciate being threatened." She nodded to a cluster of faeries outside the ring. "Take them to the Aqueno Prison."

Before I could react, several faeries stepped into the circle, guards or soldiers by the looks of them, wearing thick leather armor. Two of them yanked me up to my feet, ripping me away from Casper. Two more guards hauled up Casper, dragging him, as he didn't have the strength to stand on his own.

I struggled against my captors, tried to kick and claw, anything to break their hold, but it was useless.

"They say humans make lovely entertainment," the queen said, appraising us. "But I already grow weary of them." Marasina turned to her guards. "Take them away. There is no trusting their kind." She ran her finger along the small scar on her neck, which had healed to little more than a scratch. The guards started to drag us toward the torches.

"Wait."

Elrik stepped into the circle. The faerie guards' grip on my arms kept me from flinching away from the dangerous fay, the one who had tortured and taunted me in the woods. It was all I could do to stay silent. I dreaded the idea of a fay prison, but I also wasn't so foolish as to think Elrik cared at all for our wellbeing. I wondered if Pel had stood next to his brother, watched our punishment and humiliation. Marasina raised one elegant eyebrow at Elrik. I couldn't tell if she was pleased or annoyed at his outburst, but she let him continue.

"Elenora Molnár had nothing to do with the attack. That was all the little king. Perhaps it would be better if she stayed here."

"I'm not leaving Casper," I said, feeling a rush of defiance. If they took Casper somewhere far from here, I might not be able to find him.

"Nor, don't be so noble," Casper said. I turned to him. He was struggling to stand even as the faeries gripped his arms, ready to drag him to their prison.

"The Magia Sange brothers seem to have developed quite a soft spot for this female human. It's not becoming." Marasina stepped in the direction Elrik stood. Though he was tall, she was taller still, looking down at him with sapphire eyes.

I doubted Elrik would try to disobey his queen, not the way Pel had. In the moments after the battle at the Rose Palace, Pel had tried to allow me to go free. Instead, the queen had commanded him with his true name to take me prisoner. It was then that I also learned his true name, *Rumpelstiltskin*, and the power one had over the fay if one possessed such knowledge.

Use a faerie's true name, and one could force them to do anything.

"I would never disobey you, my queen, I only humbly request that you spare her, as she did not come at you with a blade." Elrik gave a deep bow, his golden hair falling over his brow.

"I would have if given the chance!" I snapped, but Casper shushed me. Not that anyone was paying the humans any attention. The full focus of the crowd was on Marasina and Elrik. I couldn't understand why he was risking her wrath for me. Only a few weeks ago he had tried to kidnap me to bring me to Queen Marasina.

"I have no wish for the paramour of this human king to sully my court. She can go to the Aqueno Prison as well." Marasina waved the guards off and they began to drag Casper and myself toward the darkness beyond the clearing.

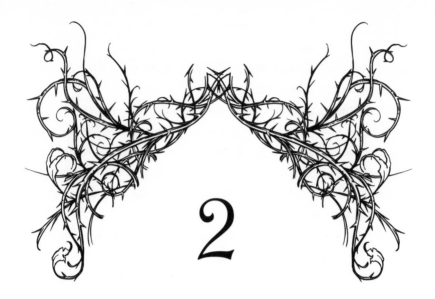

2

"**A**ctually, my queen."

Marasina turned her focus on Elrik, the start of a sneer marring her lips.

"Did I not make myself clear, Elrik?" The queen put a sharp edge to his name.

"Before she is taken away, I simply wish to take full advantage of the opportunity before us. I request permission to question the girl."

Marasina snorted with contempt. "There is nothing I desire to know from her."

"My queen, I have reason to believe that this human has fay blood in her veins." I heard several audible gasps from beyond the torches. *At least the faeries are getting their fill of entertainment*, I thought bitterly. Elrik's face was smooth as glass, his amber eyes focused on Queen Marasina, waiting for her permission. I wondered what he was playing at.

The guards leading us away paused in their steps.

"You go too far, Elrik. I tolerate much, but you insult our kind with such baseless remarks." Queen Marasina's words were harsh, her face paling in anger. I glanced at Elrik, but he was serene, almost smiling.

"My queen, I mean no disrespect. My theory is based on information I received. I know it sounds unlikely, but what could be the harm in allowing my little test?"

"Brother, enough." From outside the ring of torches, Pel stepped into the clearing. Deep down, I had known he'd be here, the beautiful faerie boy as pale as moonlight with golden hair and emerald eyes. But part of me wished it wasn't so, wished the faerie I thought had been my friend, the one who once had offered me freedom, might have been genuine. But I knew better. Pel and I could tally the times we had betrayed each other.

Elrik ignored his brother, pulling a small glass vial from a pocket. In it was an amber liquid, which seemed to glow in the firelight. "I ask only that I may interrogate the girl."

"Is that sitano?" Pel asked, his voice tight, his eyes growing wide as he stared at the vial. His actions did nothing to ease my growing alarm.

"Of course. Distilled to its strongest essence." Elrik held the vial up, appraising the color as though he were assessing a fine wine. I did not think that whatever was in the vial was such a treat.

"That isn't questioning her," Pel said, almost yelling at his brother.

"It is finding out answers," Elrik said, calm as ever, "in the only way that won't allow for the tricky human to lie."

"Is your evidence really so strong?" Marasina asked. The anger was gone from her voice, replaced by a cool curiosity as she stared at the vial in his hand.

"I'm not fay," I said, the idea ludicrous.

"And if you're wrong, you'll kill her!" Pel snapped, but Marasina waved away Pel's comment as though it was a trivial issue. My head whipped over to Pel. Sick dread welled up in my stomach.

"What do you mean, kill me?" I asked, louder than before. I dreaded a prison, but whatever Elrik was holding looked to be a swifter death.

"Don't you dare," Casper said, but again, no one was paying attention to what the humans said, even if the entire conversation was about murdering me.

The queen stared at me with her sharp blue eyes, but I couldn't read any expression on her marble face. "I think you are mistaken, Elrik."

"Then let it be my mistake to make." Elrik's eyes never left the queen, but I could see his hand tighten on the vial. "The sitano shall burn away whatever is not fay."

"Very well," the queen said with a dismissive wave of her hand.

Fear rose inside me. "No," I said, my voice no more than a whisper. Casper reached for me, but the guards pulled him away.

"Many thanks, my queen," Elrik said, a dark smile sliding across his face. At the same time, his brother called out, "No, you can't."

Pel stepped toward me in a way I could almost pretend was protective.

"She does not deserve such a fate!"

"What fate, brother? It would be the greatest of all blessings for her if she is actually fay," Elrik purred, gliding next to his brother.

"And what if you are wrong and it kills her?"

"Pel, stop now," the queen commanded, a dangerous edge in her voice.

I had grown still, icy dread slowing my movements and my mind. A prison might have locks that could be picked, guards to be deceived. But there was nothing I could do against a poison. Perhaps I could pretend to drink it, secretly spilling the drink down my neck.

"I'll drink it, if you insist on poisoning someone," Casper said. I turned, horrified to hear Casper's offer.

"Not a chance," I countered. *You'd probably drink the poison without even trying to fool these creatures*, I wanted to say.

Elrik winked at me, as though he and I were sharing a secret joke. "Don't worry, I won't let your little king be so noble." He turned to Pel. "Besides, brother, if you really didn't think she has any life magic, why would you tell me that delightful story?"

"What is he talking about, Pel?" I demanded. Even though I knew Pel was a royal spy, I felt a fresh stab of betrayal lance through me.

"A lovely tale," Elrik said before Pel could answer. "One about a fay prince and the human maiden who stole his heart." The queen snapped her attention to Elrik.

"That was nothing. Some folktale my father told me. It means nothing," I pleaded, hoping I could make them believe me. *It didn't mean anything, did it?* The fear that this dangerous fay wanted to risk my life over a bedtime story chilled me.

I cursed myself for sharing the tale with Pel back when I was locked in a tower with a room full of straw and an impossible task, summoning the faerie boy I had thought was my friend. To pass the time, I had told him a story about a fay prince who gave up his throne and his people when he fell in love with a human maiden. But it was only a silly story.

It certainly wasn't anything based on real life.

The queen turned her sapphire eyes toward me, her look keenly appraising. It did nothing to settle my fears. She focused her attention on Pel. "Is this true?"

Pel looked uneasily between Marasina and me, not willing to lie to his queen.

I resisted the urge to lash out at him, knowing I'd only be stopped by the guards. "She believed it was only a folktale."

Marasina looked at me and wrinkled her nose in distaste. "It's unlikely she is Soren's child."

"I don't know anyone named Soren. My father's name was Samuel, and I promise you he was human!" I said, desperate for the Faerie Queen to believe me.

"I'll allow the test. Elrik, this shall be your reward for recovering the human kingling and the girl. Ask for no further payment." The queen sounded intrigued, almost amused.

"No!" both Casper and Pel yelled out at once. I was surprised to see Pel denying his queen. I almost wanted to laugh. That is, until I looked at Casper, his face so determined and so sad, I was sure he would do something noble and stupid.

"Pel, you will stand down," the queen demanded.

"Please, my queen. Don't let my brother kill her." I marveled at Pel's sincerity, and even prayed the queen might listen to him.

"My patience for these disobediences wears thin. Stand down or I shall force you to."

Slowly, Pel stepped away from me. The fear I had felt for Casper's safety suddenly fell back on me, and I realized I was going to die. Terror washed over me. If they poisoned me, I would never see my brothers again, never free Casper, never make anything more of myself than a liar and small-time thief. I wanted to reach out and grab Pel, beg him not to abandon me, as though he had ever been a protection.

"I'm sorry, Nor," he whispered. The tears falling down his face scared me. But he held his place several feet away from me.

"Don't be so dramatic, brother," Elrik tsked. "She will be fine. *Probably.*" Elrik glided up to me, gleeful and deadly. "Drink this," he said, offering me the vial as though it were a costly prize.

"Don't drink it, Nor." The desperation in Casper's voice only intensified the dark fear that was flooding my senses.

Elrik held out the vial. I reached out for it, ready to hurl it on the floor. Whatever made him think I would willingly facilitate my own demise, he was mistaken. I would fight him. But before I could grab the vial, his other hand shot out, lightning-quick, and held my wrist. He leaned in, whispering so only I could hear him. "If you don't drink this, I will kill your king. Don't think that I can't or won't. I can slip some of this into his food. You might survive. He certainly won't. I promise you that. The choice is yours, my darling." And just as quickly, Elrik stepped back, releasing my wrist.

I paused, no longer ready to smash the bottle. I wanted to believe he was bluffing, but his words were a promise of retribution I couldn't ignore. I knew he would kill Casper, no matter what Queen Marasina ordered. Casper's blood would be on my hands if I didn't do exactly as Elrik asked. My hand shook as I reached for the vial, which Elrik now allowed me to take. I held a poison that would likely kill me. I could make it look like I drank it while letting it pour out. But then what? I had no idea what this poison would do, and if I failed to show the right symptoms, then Elrik would murder Casper.

I thought about Casper extending his hand to me in the Biawood Forest, after we had escaped the fay. He had learned about my many deceptions, learned how I had worked with a faerie; the royal spy. He learned how I had allowed for the fay to attack the Rose Palace, even if I hadn't known Pel would use everything I told him to plan an attack. And what Casper hadn't figured out from the attack, I later admitted in the woods. The confession that there was no crime I wouldn't commit if it meant protecting and feeding my family came tumbling from my lips as we waited in the woods, bloodied and bruised from the attack and the capture. And I remembered what he said to me.

"I don't know if I can ever trust you again, Nor. Not after all this. But I'm not going to leave you in the middle of the Biawood with a fay army so close. We need to get home. Then we'll figure out what to do next."

I had not had a home in a long time, and couldn't shake the idea that despite everything, I might still have a home with him. That somehow, I could make things right with Casper. It was a beautiful and delicate hope. Too delicate, I now realized. I wouldn't have a home with Casper, but maybe someday he could go home.

Casper was yelling at the fay, demanding they stop. When it was clear they would not budge from their plan, he started yelling at me, first screaming, and then begging me not to drink the poison. He would have ripped it from my hands if guards were not restraining him. My heart cracked from the pain in his voice, the utter desperation. Hating myself, I only shook my head, refusing to look at him, afraid I would lose my nerve. I failed to block out his frantic pleas. I blinked hard against a pressure behind my eyes, willing myself not to cry. I felt far away, almost outside myself. I prayed this numbing shock would stay with me.

"This is quite enough," the queen said, almost bored. "Guards, take the prisoner king to the Aqueno Prison. *Now.*"

I jerked my head up, half terrified to know Casper was leaving and half relieved he would not have to watch me die.

"I love you," I said, knowing those were likely the last words I would ever say to Casper. I doubted he heard; he was cursing and threatening the fay, fighting desperately to break free of the guards, but he was no match for two faeries. They dragged Casper into the darkness, his screams fading into the black of the night.

The clearing was eerily quiet after they left, the fay outside the circle of torches silently waiting for the next part of their evening's entertainment, for that was all my life was worth to them. Though I knew this was the end for me, a small warmth bloomed in my heart, knowing Casper still fought for me, tried to defend me. I wrapped myself in that warmth as I removed the cork stopper from the vial.

With shaking hands, I carefully lifted the small glass tube and tentatively smelled it. I expected something foul, but it smelled like wildflowers, fresh and floral, but with a bitter undertone.

"We haven't all day, my love," Elrik purred in his sickeningly sweet voice.

I held the vial, willing my shaking hand to still. *It's such a small vial*, I thought, trying to convince myself that it couldn't be as fatal as Pel believed.

The deadliest poisons require the smallest doses, a voice in the back of my mind insisted. But I didn't have another choice, not one I could live with. I stared at the vial. The amber liquid was thick, clinging to the sides of the glass like honey. I closed my eyes, refusing to look at Elrik's smile or Marasina's inquisitive gaze. I allowed myself one deep breath. And then I pulled the vial to my lips and tipped the contents into my mouth.

The liquid slid down my throat. It tasted of overly ripe raspberries, tart and sweet, with a sour aftertaste. After I swallowed, a coat of it stayed on my tongue, sugary yet bitter. For a moment, I felt nothing. I exhaled slowly. Maybe this had all been some elaborate ruse by Elrik, a way to terrify me before I was hauled off to prison, another one of his twisted games. I opened my eyes, the faeries inside the circle and those shadowy forms outside it all staring at me. The torches' light reflected in their strange eyes as they glared at me from all directions, waiting for something to happen. I almost smiled, feeling happy to the point of giddy to disappoint them. I opened my mouth, ready to tell them they failed, when my world shattered.

A fiery hot pain ignited in my stomach and flared through my throat and then inflamed my mouth. My tongue, where I had tasted sickly-sweet berries a moment ago, now was on fire, scalding and burning. I screamed, certain I would exhale smoke. The pain, the fire, spread through my veins, scorching me from the inside out. My knees buckled and I fell, too much pain inside me to notice if I hit the ground. I might have been on my knees or laying on the hard dirt. Everything was a white-hot agony, and I wished for anything that would make it stop. My insides were blistering. There would be nothing left of me.

Pain.

Pain.

Pain!

I couldn't think. I couldn't feel anything except the inferno that ran through me. I screamed again and again. Begged for mercy, begged for a stop, begged for death. I was being burned alive from the inside. I had no control of my body or my mind. Everything was pain.

Distantly, so very distantly, I felt hands hold me down. I struggled and squirmed, the touch alighting my skin with more fire.

I didn't feel Pel cut my skin. I barely heard his command of "*dormrir sange.*" But I did feel the cold that swept through me, slicing through and then burying the fire under his strong blood magic. In that moment, I was grateful that the fire stopped, even if Pel used blood magic, even if I was trading one prison for another. Tears coursed down my cheeks as I lay on the dirt, too weak to move. Pel was leaning over me, his hand pressed to a fresh cut on my hand, the source of his control over me. I didn't have the strength to care or even be afraid. I felt my blood at war with itself, the poison trying to ignite it and Pel's magic cooling it, slowing it. My eyes became heavy, and it was a losing battle to look into Pel's concerned face.

"Sleep, Nor," he said, the last thing I heard before I was dragged into blackness.

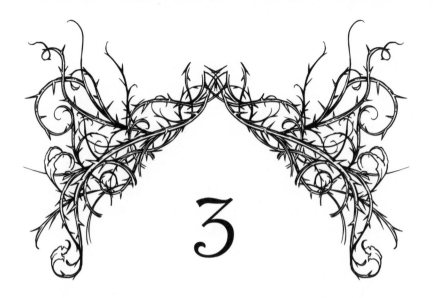

3

Consciousness came back in a wave of blistering pain. My skin was burning. I screamed. And screamed. I screamed until someone cut my palm and a chilly rush of magic flooded my veins, temporarily dousing the fire. I tried to focus on my palm, but the darkness was already creeping in.

It happened again.

And again.

And again.

I lost track of how often I woke to terrible agony, my flesh scorching from the inside out. Sometimes the cooling relief came quickly and I'd immediately fall into unconsciousness, but other times it took so long I thought I would die.

I wished I would die.

There were voices I couldn't understand over my screams and faces I couldn't focus on through the pain.

Eventually, by agonizingly slow degrees, the pain lessened. I opened my eyes, and my skin was hot, too hot, but no longer on fire. I didn't think there was anything left to burn. I stared up at an unfamiliar ceiling, one with a strange woven pattern.

"She's awake," a female voice to the side of me said. I wanted to turn my head to face the speaker, but the slightest movement shot pain down my neck, and my head throbbed.

"I'll fetch the Magia Sange," another voice said, light and airy.

"Elenora, can you hear me?" the gentle female voice asked.

I tried to speak, but my mouth felt swollen, my throat scraped raw from screaming. All I managed was a moan.

"Don't try to speak if it hurts too much." A damp cloth was placed on my forehead, providing a moment of relief from the burning. I heard footsteps approaching but did not bother trying to move.

"She's not screaming this time. That is an improvement." It was Pel speaking now. His voice sent a wave of anger through me, but also an unwanted yearning. I might not be screaming, but my skin felt hot, the burning sensation stronger the longer I stayed conscious. Weakly, I wanted him to make it go away.

"Indeed, but the recovery is slow," the female answered. "She's still burning with fever thanks to what your brother did." There was an edge of accusation to her voice, and I liked her for it.

"My brother can be a cruel creature," Pel said, his voice flat. "And you have my thanks, Lady Lorella, for tending to her." I heard Pel's voice coming closer. I wanted to say something or even simply turn to look at him, but movement was beyond me. I hated the feeling of helplessness, made worse by my craving for Pel's cooling blood magic. I needed the ice in my veins to calm the fire of the poison. The pain was getting worse again, and I bit my lip to avoid crying out. I kept it in, holding my breath until I felt a sharp bite of metal across my palm.

"Dormir sange." The cold was a welcomed relief.

I awoke to a smoldering burn. The fire was gone in my veins, burned out, or at least died to embers. There was a soft mattress supporting me, and I was no longer in my ruined gown, but wearing a simple shift dress, light and silky against my skin. I tried not to think about who might have changed my clothes as I stared at the woven ceiling. I noticed that the ceiling was not simply an interlacing pattern, but comprised of branches and vines intertwined tightly, with leaves growing out at odd angles.

As I studied the room, I realized the entire chamber had the same woven look, as though the branches had been convinced to grow in the shape of a room. A wide, oval opening formed a window, spiderweb curtains billowing in the slight breeze. My memories felt foggy as I tried to recall the last few days. I struggled to sit up, but every muscle ached and my skin felt bruised to the touch. A gentle hand supported my back, helping me to sit.

My head swam.

"You're awake." It was the same voice I had heard speaking to Pel. I scrapped my mind to remember her name.

When the dizziness lessoned to a mild swaying, I looked at the person who spoke, the same one who had helped me sit. She was a beautiful faerie with charcoal eyes that seemed kind, even with their strange cat-eye pupils. She appeared young, maybe my age, but with pale gray hair shot through with silver that was complemented by the elegant dress she wore, a garment the color of a pearl, that shimmered as she moved.

"Are you Lady Lore—" I started, recalling Pel's conversation with her. But my throat felt full of ash, and I coughed, a painful hacking that dug into my lungs before I got her name out.

"Shh, don't try to speak yet. Your throat is still raw from the sitano. Yes, I am Lady Lorella. Please, call me Lorella. I am here to help you."

"Why?" I managed to choke out. Though she seemed genuine, I had learned the hard way not to trust the fay.

"Pel asked that I care for you. He knows that I am the only Magia Viveralis that would." The confusion on my face supplied the question I didn't have the voice for, as Lorella explained. "Sorry, I imagine you would not know. The Magia Viveralis make up the royal family. We deal in life magic. It is similar to how Pel, a Magia Sange, works in blood magic."

I took in her words, wanting to ask more about the fay. I had assumed all faeries could do blood magic, the way Pel and Elrik could, but apparently I was mistaken. Life magic. I thought about Queen Marasina controlling the growth of the vine around Casper's neck. Memories of that doomed night came crashing back to me. Casper being dragged away to a prison as Elrik handed me a poison.

"Casper!" I croaked. I needed to get to him, to find out where the Aqueno Prison was and rescue him. I struggled, trying to get out of the bed, but the movement shot fiery heat across my skin and sent my world reeling again.

"Elenora, please stop," Lorella begged, her gray eyes wide with concern. "You're in no position to move around. Please, drink this, it will aid in your recovery." She plucked a small vial of green liquid from the table next to the bed and poured the contents into a goblet. She added water from a pitcher and drew the cup up to my lips, ready to help me down the liquid.

I stared at her in mute rebellion as the world steadied, but the horror of the situation washed over me. Casper had been taken away and I couldn't even stand, much less go to him. I pressed my lips tightly together. I didn't need to rely on the old folktales to know the dangers of fay drinks—Elrik ensured I experienced it firsthand.

Lorella appraised me with a keen look, acknowledged my resistance. "I doubt I would trust us after what happened to you. But we are not all brutes like Elrik. I only seek to help you. This elixir is safe, I promise. Here." She brought the goblet to her own lips and drank a sip. "See?" I stared at her, not sure what to make of her gestures. She took my silence as further reluctance. "You need to heal and regain your strength for when you face the court, and my mother has demanded your presence as soon as you are well enough to walk."

"Your mother?"

"Yes, Queen Marasina." Lorella smiled, almost sheepishly. "But I am her youngest child, so Pel thought it might not be beneath me to help nurse you."

Though I felt overwhelmed by her revelations, I noticed that the elixir was having no ill effect on her. And one way or another, I would have to heal. I would be no good to Casper or myself this vulnerable. And if my options were this strange drink or continue to rely on Pel's blood magic, I would take my chances with the goblet. I carefully nodded, and Lorella handed it to me. Even the minor weight of the silver in my hand made my skin burn and hands shake, but I refused to be helped to drink. I gripped the goblet tightly, my hands glistening, already coated in sweat.

Slowly, I lifted the chalice to my lips. The liquid smelled fresh and grassy, and tasted of rosemary and other herbs I couldn't identify. It was slightly sweet and musky, but cold, and the chill eased my throat as I swallowed. Almost immediately a slight numbness spread through me. It wasn't nearly as powerful as Pel's sleeping magic, but it dulled the burning pain and helped to steady the world. I ached all over, but it was a vast improvement.

"What was that?" I asked. My words came out rough, but I no longer felt like I was choking on ash.

"Choraka root, mainly. It's an elixir I created from the root, some juniper berries, rosemary, and a bit of other things. And of course, I infused it with some life magic. It should provide you with some relief and speed the healing process. But if the pain is too great, I can still fetch Pel."

"No!" I snapped, and my cry made my throat ache even with the choraka in effect. The pain was bad, but manageable. I didn't want to rely on Pel or his magic.

Lorella moved back at my sudden outburst, but then nodded. "This should help dull the pain enough for you to sleep."

"I have questions," I said, my voice raspy. Even as I spoke, my eyelids felt heavy. For the first time in what felt like forever, it was from my own fatigue, and not from blood magic. That knowledge let me relax as unconsciousness stole over me.

It was utterly silent in the Biawood Forest. Casper stood a few feet away, his dark eyes burning into me. His lips moved, but I couldn't hear him. I tried to go to him, but my legs gave way, and I fell to my knees, my skin suddenly scalding. I looked down to see vines snaking around my wrists. I screamed, pulling at the vines. Casper vanished, and Pel stood in his place. He didn't speak, but as I watched him, his features subtly melted into that of his brother.

"I will have you," Elrik said.

I sat up with a start, breathing hard. *Only a dream*, I thought, staring at the embroidered blanket as I waited for my heart to slow. The burn on my skin still felt real. The sun cast long shadows in my room, letting me know I had slept through most of the day.

"Sleep well?" Pel was in the room, sitting on a stool that looked more like a tree stump.

"Have you been watching me sleep?" I asked, unsettled by his presence. I glanced around the room, realizing we were alone.

A look of hurt flashed across Pel's face before he smoothed it out.

"Lady Lorella, her handmaids, and I have been taking shifts, in case you woke up in pain."

"I'm fine," I lied. "And I would be even better if your brother had not poisoned me." I could already feel the dull burn in my bones, but I would not waste this opportunity. It might be my only chance to use Pel.

"He should not have done that," Pel leaned toward me, but I threw my hands up, and he stopped. "I need to speak with you about that. In a way, he has given you a gift."

I scoffed. "I cannot believe you, Pel. The fay must be sick folk indeed to consider so much pain a gift." My mind raced, trying to best frame the command I would use. I needed to get free and rescue Casper. But I had to be careful. If I commanded Pel to take me to Casper, he might yell to summon guards while doing so. Pel sensed something, a frown tugging at his lip.

"Nor, I can tell you are plotting. But I need to speak with you about what you've become."

"Where is Casper?" I asked.

"Nor, you should forget about him. He cannot be a part of your life now." Pel's voice was gentle, but rage boiled within me, as though Pel had any right to tell me who should be a part of my life.

"*Rumpelstiltskin*, where is Casper?" I demanded, using Pel's true name.

The frown turned into a full sneer, his face glowing with anger as he was compelled to speak. I knew it was the gravest insult to command a faerie, to steal their free will. I didn't care. I would do anything to free Casper and myself.

"The Aqueno Prison," Pel spat out.

"But where is that prison?" I needled, frustrated with his lack of information.

"Nor, there is something you need to understand," Pel said, the urgency speeding his words.

He wasn't answering my question, but I realized I hadn't used his true name for the demand.

"*Rumpelst—*" I started, but Pel cut me off.

"Elenora Molnár, by all the sacred magics, stop it! Look at yourself!" Pel picked up a silver mirror, shoving it in my face. I was ready to try my command again, until I saw my reflection.

I didn't recognize the creature staring back at me. Gone was my straw-colored hair, for it was now as white as fresh snow. Instead of gold-flecked brown eyes, my irises were pure gold, the brown completely gone. Instead of round pupils, cat-eye oval slits stared back at me. My skin was still darker than the pale fay, but the luminous copper hue was distinctly inhuman. And I could make out the pointed tips of my ears.

I slowly reached for the mirror, hoping to find it was another cruel faerie trick. As Pel handed it to me, I truly studied my hands. I had thought they gleamed with sweat, but I realized now that they actually glimmered. My skin was no longer the sun-kissed tan I took for granted, but the same shimmering copper as the face in the polished silver and glass. I had become the enemy. My very skin betrayed me.

My world tilted as the horror of it washed over me. I dropped the mirror; the sound of it cracking seemed far away as a ringing grew in my ears. I stumbled out of bed and away from Pel. He might have been speaking to me, but I couldn't focus on him. My vision blurred as I tried to make it out of the room, needing to escape. As I reached for a chair, I felt unfamiliar muscles on my shoulder blades contract. Large dragonfly wings extended, knocking over the nearest chair, and I screamed, realizing the wings were a part of me. I sank to the floor, dropping my head between my knees, attempting to breathe through the panic. My bare feet stepped on broken mirror shards and my skin burned, but those pains paled compared to the disgust I felt at the abomination I had become. My breaths came out short and quick, as though I couldn't get enough air. Nothing in the long list of deceptions and difficult situations I had lived through came close to preparing me for this.

I waited to pass out, unconsciousness preferable to accepting the monster I had become. But I remained awake. After some time, my breathing slowed, the quick, sharp panic settling into something deeper, a horror rooted into my soul. The terror transformed into a depression. The adrenaline seeped from my system, leaving me utterly exhausted.

"I know this is a shock, but in time you may view this as a gift." Pel's words were soft, as though he were speaking to a frightened animal. I wanted to hit him.

I sat back on my heels, wiping my eyes with the palms of my hands. I felt depleted, my insides hollowed out.

"So, this is what your Chace-cursed poison does? Turns humans into fay?" I spat the word fay.

Pel grimaced. "Sitano is not *my* poison. I truly wished my brother had not forced you to take it." I scoffed, but he continued. "And no, sitano does not turn a human fay, such a thing is impossible. The sitano strips off any glamour, any part of you that is not fay. A harsh treatment, but one that is quite effective." Pel looked around the room, his eyes avoiding my own murderous stare.

"But now I'm fay," I argued. Realization tried to creep into my mind, but I desperately wanted to deny this new truth.

"Technically, you are only half fay." Pel slowly picked up the pieces of the mirror.

"But my father was Samuel," I said, stubbornly holding on to my threads of humanity even as I felt them pulled away from me.

"And doesn't Samuel sound an awful lot like Soren?" I shook my head, but Pel continued, "Nor, if you were truly all human, the sitano would have burned you to ash. You would be dead now." He stared at the cracked mirror, refusing to meet my eyes. In his utter sincerity, I felt the raw truth of his words. My last connections to humanity snapped as conversations about the queen's dead son started to make more sense.

"Which makes me a granddaughter to your queen." I had thought Elrik merely enjoyed torture, but his cruelty had another purpose. And I was certain Elrik had not been trying to reunite an estranged royal family out of kindness.

"That is most likely." Pel paused, weighing his words. "I thought you should know, before you see Queen Marasina tomorrow."

"What do you mean?" I asked warily. I was exhausted, and all I wanted was to forget everything in sleep.

"My queen has summoned you to attend her at court tomorrow morning."

I swallowed hard. I had no desire to see Queen Marasina, even if somehow it was true that she was my grandmother. I would never consider her kin. "And if I refuse?"

"There is no denying my queen. You are in her domain and her word is law. It will go better for you if you seem eager to please, lest she have to send guards to fetch you." There was no joy in Pel's tone, and I wondered if he felt some remorse for dragging me to his queen.

Trapped, I thought. I was trapped here in this room and with these fay. I was even trapped inside my own body, transformed into something I didn't recognize. I looked down at my hands, glowing copper skin reminding me I was no longer human.

Will Casper even want to see me after what I have become? And as fay are prohibited in Reynallis, how will I ever see my brothers again? Despair threatened to overwhelm me again.

"Pel, I think you should go," I said, refusing to look at him.

"Very well, Nor." I heard him rise to his feet. He paused before adding, "I shall see if Lady Lorella can escort you to court tomorrow." He waited, but I didn't respond, didn't look up. Finally, he left me alone.

I continued to stare at my hands long after his footsteps faded.

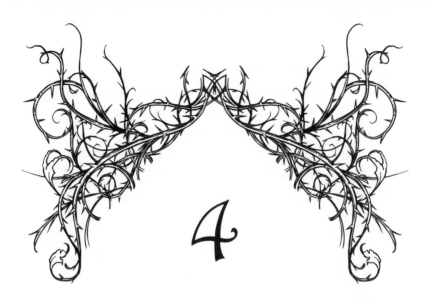

"Elenora, you must wake up."

I opened my eyes. Everything hurt. Lorella was leaning over me, her wide, gray eyes staring at me. She was flanked by two faeries, delicate, tiny things, one with shining green skin the color of fresh buds and the other a pale lilac.

"Go away," I grumbled, closing my eyes again. The few blessed hours I had slept were a welcome reprieve from my situation. Seeing Lorella and the strange faeries with her was a sharp reminder that I was no longer human.

"I cannot," she insisted, her voice gentle. "Mother has insisted on seeing you during the morning's court, and there is no refusing her."

Recalling Pel's warning of the queen sending guards if I did not come on my own, I struggled to sit up. It was more of an effort than I wanted to admit.

"Oh Elenora, you look awful." Lorella pursed her lips.

"Thanks," I said, nearly flopping back down onto the bed.

Lorella looked immediately contrite. "I didn't mean it like that. You must have . . . did you have a bad night?" Her voice was softer as she pressed the back of one hand against my forehead.

"They are all bad nights," I muttered.

"You're warm, maybe you had a relapse with some of the sitano." She turned to the lilac faerie. "Corine, go to my quarters and fetch a draft of choraka root elixir. Mix five drops in a glass of wine. Make haste."

"Yes, milady." The lilac faerie dipped into a quick bow before leaping out the window.

I stared, open-mouthed, momentarily forgetting my own pains as I struggled to watch the faerie spread her wings—deep amethyst butterfly wings with intricate black patterns—and easily fly up the side of the palace. I heard the green faerie muffle a snicker at my blatant wonderment as Lorella shot her a look.

"Can you all fly?" I asked, gesturing to the window. I had seen Pel fly before, but maids jumping out of windows unsettled me.

"Any of the fay with wings can, and that would be most that live within the Forest Court. But it is considered polite to use a door with guests," she said with a sigh.

"Can't you fly?" the green faerie asked.

I turned to her, and she blushed a deep jade. She was even smaller than the lilac faerie and seemed younger. She was staring at my shoulders. *At my wings*, I realized.

"Drusia!" Lorella snapped.

"I'm sorry, milady," the faerie said, now hiding her face in her hands and backing up against the wall, as if she could make herself smaller than she already was.

"Apologies," Lorella said to me. "Drusia is young and not always able to keep her questions in check."

"It's no matter," I said, self-consciously reaching back to feel my own wings. They were smooth and I could feel the veins along them. "I

forget I even have these. Maybe someday I'll learn how to use them."
And that would give me another option to escape, I thought, but didn't
mention. Experimentally I tried to flutter my wings. They opened in
opposite directions, one banging against the bedframe as the other
nearly smacked Lorella.

"I'm certain you will," Lorella said, taking a quick step back to
avoid my erratic wings. I forced the muscles in my shoulders to relax
until my wings dropped down. "But until then, it is best that we walk.
But you must get up. Mother is eager to find out if you are indeed
Soren's child."

I wanted to protest that the very notion that I was somehow relat-
ed to a Faerie Queen was absurd, that my father could not have been
anyone other than the gentle, humble miller I knew growing up. But
as I threw off the blankets, the strange truth was undeniable, written
in my skin, the way it glowed like a new coin, the dragonfly wings I
could feel brush against the pillows. Instead, I asked Lorella, "You
knew Soren? He was your brother?"

Lorella smiled, but I sensed a touch of sadness. "He was always
kind to me. Never partook in the crueler pranks my other siblings
played on me."

"Not even a faerie princess is safe from 'pranks'?" I retorted. If their
sense of humor was anything like Elrik's, I did not want to find out.

"I'm not a princess."

"But . . . your mother is the queen."

"My father was not the king." She took in my shocked expression
and continued, "It is no secret that I was born long after the death of
King Velario. I have no idea who my father is, but everyone knows it
was not our late king."

Realizing my mouth was again hanging open, I quickly closed it,
not sure how to respond. "Why are you telling me all this?"

"Better you hear it from me since I'm sure you shall hear rumors
of the royal bastard at court. And in case you decide you would rather

not be seen with a bastard, I can leave you now and find you another escort." Though she tried to make the comment light, there was a decided tightness to her words.

"I guess spreading rumors is a popular pastime no matter the court," I said, thinking back to the whispered insults I endured as a commoner in the Rose Palace. I tentatively reached out and squeezed her hand. "But by Chace's chaos, I don't care who your parents are. You are the only one who has shown me any kindness here."

Lorella seemed surprised at my touch, but quickly collected herself. "Very well. Now, we really must get you ready."

Remembering the summons made fear coil in my stomach. I was not inclined to see Marasina, nor any of the rest of the fay court. A protest was forming on my lips when the purple faerie flew back in through the window.

"Corine, you could use the door," Lorella scolded.

"That would take longer. I returned as quickly as I could," Corine said, handing the goblet to Lorella.

Lorella offered me the goblet. "Drink this, it will help cool your fever."

I took the goblet and swallowed. It tasted like a fine wine, smooth and rich, with a slightly herbal smell. The effect was subtle, a slight cooling, but it helped get me moving.

Drusia went to work brushing my hair and braiding in small, yellow flowers. Corine helped me dress in the fresh clothing they had brought, a long carmine dress of a delicate silk that shimmered and swirled with my slightest movement. The back of the dress was cut low so as not to hamper my wings, useless as they were. Corine used long matching ribbons to lace up the sides of the dress. The effect was elegant, but light.

Such airy garments appeared to be standard fashion for the fay court. Lorella was in a gossamer gown of pale gray that reminded me of foggy days, which set off her silver-gray hair and coal-colored eyes.

Even Corine and Drusia wore delicate clothes: purple Corine in wispy silks and violet petals and green Drusia in similar silks woven with leaves and vines. Despite myself, I had to admit I felt freer in this fine-spun gown than the constricting corsets and heavy satins and velvets I had worn in the Rose Palace. *Not that such comfort is worth the cost* I reminded myself, my movements still slow and awkward from the poison.

"You look lovely," Lorella said as her handmaids added the finishing touches to my appearance. Drusia offered me a silver hand mirror, but I shook my head. I had no desire to see the creature I had become. I felt a sharp stab of longing for the days in the Rose Palace when my maid, Annabeth, would do my hair and I would see myself a future queen in the mirror.

All of that was shattered now.

Lorella offered her arm in support. Seeing little alternative, I took it, allowing her steady strength to lead us to the faerie court. Little green Drusia flitted behind us, but Corine fussed about the mess of my room, and that she would join us as soon as she had tidied up.

As we left the room, I couldn't help but stare at the strange surroundings. Instead of hallways and stone walls, we walked out into bright sun. I squinted, trying to get my bearings. The smooth wooden path turned out to be that of a winding branch, wide enough for several people to walk side by side.

"We're in a tree," I breathed. Above us branches and tree limbs, larger than any tree I had ever seen in Reynallis, stretched toward the sky. The path we stood on circled around the tree. Beyond the path, the drop to the ground was dizzying. Various twisting branch off-shoots from the path led around the tree, some veering inward, where other rooms were nestled into the tree. It was as though a tree had grown into the shape of a palace. I was so surprised I nearly tripped, a fall that would have meant my death, but Lorella kept hold of my arm, keeping me on my feet.

"You shall want to be careful on these pathways, at least until you are able to use your wings," Lorella warned.

"How is this possible?" I whispered, in awe of the wood and leaves around us. Beyond the massive tree, there was a green meadow, and all was surrounded by a wide, crystal blue lake that glittered in the sun, making this strange place appear as a small island.

"Welcome to the Forest Court," Lorella said.

We wound our way around the strange path till we neared the ground. Vines curled up to form intricate window frames and doorways, leading into rooms and hallways inside the tree. I glanced into a few of the rooms as we passed. Some opened into huge ballrooms decorated with gold and emerald chandeliers while others led into tiny hole-shaped pockets that seemed too small for anyone to fit inside. Finally, Lorella turned into one of the pathways that led into the tree.

Dense woodwork replaced the loose branches as we continued inside, into the heart of the tree. Smooth wood walls set with glowing crystals illuminated the hallways. Every so often I would see a stray vine wrap around a doorway or leaves peeking out from stairs, reminders that this place was something wild. There was a feral beauty to it.

We eventually reached the ground, gentle grass meadow beneath my feet in place of tree branches. I realized that the center of the tree was hollow, creating a massive courtyard that was open to the sky, but surrounded by the walls of the tree. The open ceiling let in bright sunshine, and the air smelled of fresh green leaves and new wood.

Stepping into the clearing, I took my first look at the full fay court. It was a magnificent and terrifying sight.

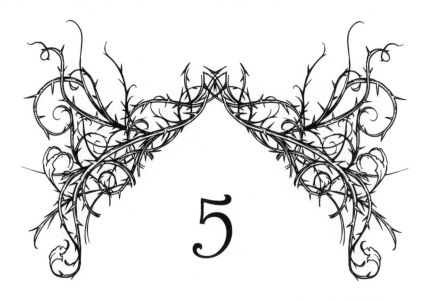

5

Here were the faeries. Tents of shimmering silk provided shade for the fay who lounged on plush cushions and jeweled chairs. Others sat on the grass under flowering trees or played near a crystal waterfall that ran down one side of the tree, winding into a small pond. Many of the fay looked similar to Pel and Lorella, tall and willowy with luminous skin and dragonfly wings. But there were other fay as well; fat, blue imps with webbed feet by the pond; tiny pixies, like Drusia and Corine, with skin ranging from purple to green to pale pink. Wrinkled brown creatures with bark for skin. Bright orange fay that appeared to be made of fire and smoke.

But it was the center of the courtyard that drew my eye. An enormous willow tree, its branches dotted with cerulean blooms, formed an enclosure, under which more faeries reclined, all of them now turned to stare at us as we crossed the meadow. Two massive thrones sat in front of the trunk of the tree. *No*, I realized as we approached it, they weren't in front of the tree, *they are part of the tree.* Glossy white wood twisted and grew into the seats of power. One was empty, but in the other sat Marasina. Though she was not garbed in chain mail, her presence was none the less imposing for it. She wore an elegant white silk tunic and trousers. The fabric was so like the tree, she almost seemed part of it. A crown of crystals adorned her braided hair, and the glowing golden amulet rested around her neck on a thick silver chain, her only ornamentations.

Her sapphire eyes fixed on me as we slowly made our way toward her. The courtyard was uneven underfoot, and I had to be extra careful. Twice, Lorella had to hold my arm to prevent me from falling when my legs nearly gave out. I silently cursed Elrik and the sitano still in my veins. But I kept striding forward, determined to meet the queen with my head held high. We passed the strange creatures of the court, and they stared at me with their catlike eyes and too-sharp teeth. I knew I was not truly safer in my room, but still felt painfully exposed to the dangerous creatures out here in the open. Even if I was now one such creature.

Stools, chairs, and tables made of stumps, vines, and branches provided ample seating for the rest of the court. The fay spread out around the queen, adorned in a variety of fine leathers, earthy silks, and cobweb laces. As we drew close to the queen, I noted the faeries that were likely her other children, stunning creatures with silver-white hair and sky-blue eyes. Seated to Marasina's immediate left was a faerie with snow-white curls that fell around a handsome, cold face. His eyes glowed with hatred as he watched me approach. Something about him struck me as familiar, but it was no comfort.

When we were right in front of the queen, Lorella gave a small bow. I had no idea what to do in front of the queen, so I opted for a curtsey. It was a shallow thing, as I wasn't sure I could dip any lower without the risk of losing my balance. The queen's stare was unreadable, but many of the faeries snickered and giggled behind long-fingered hands and fans made of leaves.

"You wished to see Elenora Molnár, my queen," Lorella said, breaking the silence.

"I did, indeed," Marasina said, her sharp gaze still examining me. "Is this truly the same creature that took the sitano?"

"Yes, my queen." Lorella gave me an encouraging smile. "She is one of us now."

"It appears your theory was correct, Elrik," Marasina said, turning to where Elrik was lounging on a cushion.

"I am only too delighted to assist in returning a child of Soren's." He smiled, a predatory twist of his lips.

Marasina stiffened, a tightness to the commanding queen. "We shall see if she is truly his." She directed her attention back to me. "Come here."

Lorella gave me a reassuring squeeze on the arm before releasing me and joining the white-haired faeries I assumed were her half siblings. Seeing no alternative, I advanced the last few steps to the Faerie Queen. The whole time, she focused all her attention on me, as if the truth would be clear to her if she only looked hard enough.

"Did you know you had a faerie for a father?" Marasina asked.

"No." I saw no advantage to lie, but neither did I offer any additional information about my parents.

"Then you know nothing of your family's history. We shall test you to see if you are a Magia Viveralis." Marasina plucked a silver pear from a crystal tray. "Give me your hands."

For a moment I stood frozen in place. I had no desire to be tested by her, remembering the cruelty she inflicted on Casper. But I was surrounded by her fay and had no escape. I forced myself to comply.

She thrust the pear into my hands, clamping her hands over mine and squeezing. I had assumed it was a silver statue of a pear, the way it gleamed in the sunlight, but I realized it was an actual fruit, the soft silver flesh smashed into my fingers. Sticky juice ran down my arms. She tightened her grip, the pear core digging into my palms.

"*Vive swindle*," she said, force infusing her words. Her hands grew hot against mine, and then something in my palms tingled. It reminded me of the prickling I felt right before the vines snapped the last night I had been with Casper. Marasina repeated the strange words again and again; each time heat rushed from her hands into mine, and the pins and needles feeling increased. I tried in vain to struggle against her fay magic, tried to pull away, but my strength was nothing compared to her grip.

The prickling sensation became a throbbing force, stronger than I thought possible. It shot through my hands, and I could sense the pear seeds. Their promise of future life called to this new feeling in my hands, begging the sensation to flow into them. And I let it, the full force of the strange power shooting into the small seeds.

As soon as I did, the feeling stopped. Marasina released me, and I stumbled back, gasping for air. I put my sticky hands on my chest, desperate to catch my breath.

"What did you do?" I asked when I could muster sound. Marasina wasn't looking at me. Instead, she was carefully cradling something in her palms, staring at it with wonder.

"You do have it." I couldn't tell if she was speaking to me or the object in her hands. Faeries began to buzz with excitement, craning necks and flying above us to see what treasure the queen held.

"Have what?" I asked, frustrated with the lack of answers.

"I had to be certain," she said as she opened her hands. In her palm was the crushed pear. As I looked closer, I saw that the seeds of the pear had sprouted. Long, thin stalks shot out of the core, already tiny leaves budding from the young stems. But unlike the natural green of new growth, these stems were white as the moon.

"What did you do?" I repeated dumbly.

Marasina looked up at me. Her eyes shone with unshed tears. I had never seen the Faerie Queen as anything other than a warrior and a monster, but the emotion she wore now was a deep crack in her hard veneer. "I didn't do this," she said, a twisted smile pulling at her face. "I merely ignited your powers. You did this."

"What? No. I didn't do anything. You did that through my hands," I insisted, my mind refusing to believe the queen's accusations.

"Elenora, you have life magic in your veins. This proved it. You truly are Soren's child." She held the baby pear tree as though it were a priceless jewel. "My Soren."

"Mother, you can't be serious!" The faerie with the white curls jumped to his feet and yelled, silencing the court. His face took on a bright, burnished hue that I associated with a faerie flushing with anger. Upon hearing his voice, I was able to place him. He had slashed my arm during the battle at the Rose Palace.

"Valente, my son, I am indeed serious," Marasina said. Her voice still sounded delicate, yet it carried across the court, easily heard by all. Though she didn't rage like her son, the command in her tone was unmistakable.

"You cannot possibly believe this half-human thing is Soren's child," Valente protested. He stared at me with angry eyes. I tensed as I noticed his hand slipping down to the dagger sheaved on his belt. "Only days ago you had her in vines. She is an ally to our enemy."

"Enough!" Marasina said, effectively silencing Valente. "Her imprisonment was a mistake that I would be hard put to make again," she said, but her voice had gone cold. "And how she was raised is unfortunate, but nothing can be done about that. What is important is that the child of my beloved eldest son has been returned to me."

"I will not be supplanted by half-human filth!" Valente lunged toward me, his blade now in his hand. On instinct, I leapt to the side. Valente missed my heart, his intended target, but he managed to slash my arm as I jumped out of his way.

Desperate for any sort of weapon, I reached for the crystal platter where the pear had rested. The rest of the fruit on it fell to the ground as I swung the heavy platter at Valente's head. I heard a satisfying thud as the crystal connected with its target. My aim had been off and my timing a hair too late, so I only managed to connect with the side of his cheek, but it had the faerie staggering backward. I readied for another attack, though my legs were already shaking from the effort combined with the familiar and terrible burn of the sitano.

"Stop!" the queen yelled. Guards immediately materialized beside us. Valente and I were forcefully separated, a guard taking hold of each of his arms and two taking mine. I cried as one clamped his hand on the fresh cut on my arm. Noticing the blood, the guard quickly dropped my arm, though his companion kept hold of the other.

"I will kill you," Valente swore at me, even as the guards pulled him away from me.

"Not if I kill you first," I said, though I knew my threat was hollow. I felt ready to collapse. The cut wasn't so bad, but the brief fight had sapped my meager strength.

I didn't have the energy to struggle against the guard, too focused on standing. I felt the blood on my arm, soaking into the sleeve of my dress. I glanced down, the sight so shocking, I lost my breath. My blood was a golden liquid instead of the normal red. If my cut didn't sting so badly, I would have had a hard time believing it was truly mine. My golden blood was darker than fay blood, with a russet hue. I hoped that meant my blood was more human than the other faeries'.

The guard loosened his grip but didn't release me. Valente's guards had let go of him. They were standing close by, but I didn't find it re-assuring.

"Valente, by all the sacred magics, must you always act so rash? She is your kin." All Marasina's wrath was directed at her son.

"That thing is no kin of mine," Valente said. He spat on the ground, and I was gratified to see some blood leave a golden trace around his mouth as he wiped his face.

"Valente, you will keep a civil tongue in my court," Marasina said, her voice brooking no argument. I could sense the power behind her words. The whole court stared at us expectantly. "And if you cannot control yourself, I will command you." At that, there were gasps and murmurs.

I remembered when she commanded Pel, used his true name of Rumpelstiltskin to force him to take me prisoner. Pel once told me that Queen Marasina knew every faerie's true name. I wondered if even I had a true name now that I was fay. But I pushed aside my musings as Valente strode toward the queen.

"Mother, would you truly disgrace the court by making some half-human thing heir?" Valente made no move toward me, but there was murder in his eyes.

"What is he talking about?" I asked Marasina.

Marasina studied both of us for a long time before speaking. "Our laws pass the crown of Magnomel to the oldest child of the monarch, and from them to *their* oldest. That is how it has always been done."

My face crinkled in disbelief. There was no way my father had been a faerie prince. No possible way he had been heir to Magnomel. I still could not connect my father, the warm man with strong, calloused hands and laughter in his eyes, as a member of the faeries of Magnomel. One glance down at my own shimmering skin, that of a faerie and not a human, was enough of a reminder that I had not truly known my father. Though he had been dead for almost seven years, I felt betrayed by him.

"But that would . . ." I started, but clamped my mouth shut. I had almost said that would make my older brother heir, but if Marasina and her court did not know about Devon, I would do everything to keep him from harm's way. Fortunately, no one noticed my slip.

"If you claim her as heir, then I shall demand a challenge at the next revel," Valente said. I wanted to ask what this challenge meant, but the courtyard was alive with excitement as faeries chatted enthusiastically amongst themselves.

Marasina raised one slender hand, and quiet descended back on the crowd, everyone eager to hear her response. "There has never been a succession dispute within the Magia Viveralis line, but perhaps that would be the best way to sort out this unusual situation." Marasina's sharp blue eyes appraised me, but I couldn't tell if she found the sight of me wanting. "Very well. I claim Elenora as heir, as daughter of Soren. Valente, it is only two weeks until the next revel, and you may challenge for the title then. Thus, the strongest fay shall be my heir."

"As you command, Mother," Valente said through clenched teeth. Before Marasina could respond, Valente turned from her and stormed back into the palace. The guards looked questioningly at Marasina.

"What if I don't want to be heir?" I asked. I didn't need this target on my back. Marasina turned to face me, along with every other fay in the courtyard. She looked less like the formidable warrior from the attack and more like a tired monarch.

"Even if my father was your son, I can't imagine you want me to someday rule Magnomel." My instincts told me to lay low until I could figure out an escape plan. Marked as the future queen of the faeries was not laying low.

Marasina pursed her lips, as if this was a conversation she would rather avoid. Finally, she spoke. "It is because you are Soren's child, of course. It matters not that you grew up in the human lands, nor that your mother was human, though I'll admit that I would have been far happier if those conditions had not been true. Had you remained in your human form, even half-human, it would have been easy to deny you your birthright. But the sitano has burned away your human side, leaving you fay enough for this court. You are his child, and as he was my eldest, you now bear the responsibility of his inheritance since he no longer can." She said the words smoothly, though I saw pain flash in her blue eyes as she spoke of my father. While the court murmured in low whispers, she added, "It also matters not whether you or I or even Valente wish for succession; it is the law and tradition of our people. So long as you live in Magnomel, you are heir."

"As long as I live in Magnomel," I repeated.

Marasina nodded. "You are fay. You are my kin. You are no longer my prisoner." Her keen eyes studied me. "You are free to leave if you wish. If you know of another land friendly to a faerie." Her lips twitched slightly, the only indication that she knew she had won. She was right. All the human lands considered fay their enemies. I no longer had a home in Reynallis. And even if I found a way to disguise myself, I could never leave Magnomel until I rescued Casper from the Aqueno Prison.

"If I had not taken the sitano, I would not be the heir?" I asked, my thoughts sticking on that.

"Yes. You were too human."

My brothers are safe from the fay court, I thought, silently tucking away that knowledge. It was a relief to know that at least Valente would have no reason to seek them out, should anyone at this court discover that I was not an only child.

Nonetheless, I sent a quick prayer to the Holy Mother that none of the faeries learn of my brothers.

"You need time to accustom yourself to your new life, but it shall come," Marasina said, misunderstanding my silence. "And you shall need to train well if you are to defeat Valente at the challenge. He is a strong Magia Viveralis," she paused, her eyes glassy for a moment, "though Soren was much stronger." Her eyes readjusted, and her lips tugged down to see me, perhaps instead of Soren, in front of her. "You look tired. Sitano is an effective, but cruel drug. Perhaps you would like to retire for the time being. There is much you will need to accomplish. Best to take rest when you can."

"Yes," I agreed, giving a small curtsey before leaving the faerie courtyard. Lorella offered to escort me back to my room, but I shook her off. The walk on my own would be longer, my legs already shaking, the burn in my bones flaring up after the exertion from my short fight with Valente. But I needed space to think. My mind was brimming with too many new, strange changes to my circumstances. I was so focused on the morning's events, that I nearly ran into a faerie as I rounded the final bend in the path to my room.

6

"You bow, not curtsey." Elrik stepped in front of me. "No one curtseys. That is a silly human thing."

"And I'm a human thing," I retorted, trying to step around him. "Now will you leave me alone? Preferably forever."

Elrik maneuvered to block my way. "I brought you a crown. You should be grateful."

I gritted my teeth as irritation bubbled up in me. "Are you honestly going to tell me you poisoned me to help me?"

Elrik tsked. "Come now. It's not as though you died."

"And if I *had* died?"

He frowned slightly, as though the idea of my death was a minor inconvenience to him. "Then you would not have been very useful at all."

"Leave me alone!" I screamed, wishing I had a knife to throw at him. The scream burned my throat. I tried to shove him out of my way, but he was immovable.

Elrik's frown pulled into a sneer as he loomed above me. There was something feral in the way he looked at me that sent unwanted shivers down my spine. "Elenora, I can see why you're upset, but you mustn't let it come before your own desire for self-preservation."

I wanted to fight, but I was already exhausted, nearly collapsing from the exertion. Elrik chuckled. "You are a pitiable creature. Here." He offered me his arm, but I shook my head. My legs were quivering, but I forced myself to remain standing.

"I don't want you anywhere near me, or I swear by the Mother's maids, I will kill you."

Elrik was merely amused by my threat. "Be careful what you say, my dear. You need me."

"I most certainly do not."

He raised an eyebrow. "I think you do." He snatched a short dagger from his belt and, with inhuman speed, slashed at his own hand, a shallow slice across his palm, which he pressed to the twisted branches that formed the door of the room.

"*Visali sange.*"

A thin stream of golden blood ran down his hand, glowing from the magic. As if it possessed a mind of its own, the trail of blood veered toward the vines, delicate streams wrapping around the leaves in a thin, shimmering sheen. Not a drop fell to the floor.

"What did you do?" I asked, staring at the lacework of blood and leaves. It was such a strange sight I had to fight a manic urge to laugh, wondering if Elrik was trying to impress me by using blood magic to open a door.

Elrik didn't look at me, still focusing on the door. "You think you don't need my help little bird? There is spell work here, and I doubt it was made with a kind intent," he said, but his words were thick with concentration. "*Rimvere sange.*"

Immediately, the branches and vines exploded, the wooden frame of the entrance bursting into shards. Elrik staggered backward from the force of it, nearly thrown into the hallway wall. I shielded my eyes from the splinters.

I cautiously looked up, seeing a hole that used to be a door, the rough edges of the surrounding tree branches blackened as though singed from a fire. The air smelled of smoke and I could taste metal and ash on my tongue.

"By Chace's den, what did you do?" I cried at Elrik. I stepped away from him, but he grabbed my wrist, pulling me through the wide hole and into my room. He released me as we both surveyed the damage. The door was ruined, but much of the rest of the room was untouched.

"Saving your ungrateful life," he said. A sheen of sweat shone off his forehead and he was breathing hard. "Someone left you a nasty piece of magic, hoping you would be your normal foolish self and walk into it. And I can only imagine who would have done that."

"Valente," I whispered. Seeing the shards of broken wood scattered from the doorway and the scorched branches made me shiver to think what would have happened if I had tried to open the door.

Elrik looked at me coolly. "Still certain you don't need my protection, little bird?"

I made my way over to the bed and allowed myself to sit on the edge. If I wasn't careful, my legs would start shaking uncontrollably. I had always taken care of myself, taken care of my brothers, but then I knew the rules of the game. Here I could be killed simply by walking through a doorway. "Why offer me protection? What are you playing at?"

"You were worthless to me as a human." Elrik's eyes were bright with an inner frenzy, as though he had discovered some great prize. "But now you are heir. And a pretty one at that," he said, carefully looking me up and down. The leering way his eyes raked over me turned my stomach.

"Don't touch me." The words came out as a rough whisper. I tried not to show the fear I felt, knowing I was no match for him.

Elrik's lips twisted into a grimace before he smoothed out his features. "Being with me would not be as repugnant as you seem convinced it would be." He licked his lips, and I repressed a shudder. "Ally yourself with me, and you need not fear the Forest Court."

"Ally?"

"Marry me, and I can promise you that I shall always keep you safe." His voice was warm as honey, and it took me a moment to process his words. I stared at him, dumbstruck. He misread my silence as indecision. "You shall find no better offer of protection."

"But you tried to kill me! You don't like me, and I despise you," I finally managed, my anger boiling over my shock.

"Oh no, Elenora. I like you very much. I have a fondness for fragile things." The sincerity in his words chilled me. "And being bonded to the Magnomel heir would be compensation enough for me to overlook your many flaws. You would be getting the aid of the most powerful Magia Sange in the kingdom."

I noted that he didn't mention Pel. "There's one problem. I hate you. I find you repugnant, cruel, and spiteful. I could never marry you."

"My heart," Elrik said, mockingly placing his hands over his chest as though I had stabbed him, which sounded rather appealing. He then dropped his hands and his act of sweetness. "But you need not like me to find me useful. I could be critical to your survival. Think about it."

I wanted to tell Elrik that he was delusional if he thought I would ever work with him, much less marry him. But what if he was right about being useful? Pel had refused to answer my questions, but maybe his brother would. It was a long shot, but I needed information. And I didn't need to agree to marry Elrik so long as he believed I was considering it.

"Take me to see Casper."

Elrik's brows shot up in surprise. "The human kingling? You'd best forget him."

"If you want to form a partnership, then I need to know you can get me what I want."

"You mean besides your safety? Your very life?"

"Can you take me to him or not?" I pressed.

Elrik sneered. "I don't like you fawning over the little kingling."

"And I don't like you. We're well-matched there. Prove to me that you want an alliance, and not to simply keep manipulating me." I had no doubt that Elrik would do anything to get the power he craved, would never be an ally to me, but I would play the fool if it got me the information I needed.

Elrik studied me for a long time. Finally, he nodded. "Very well. I shall take you to the captured king. I'll meet you tomorrow at midnight."

"Why not go now?" I felt so close to seeing Casper, I didn't want to lose any more time.

Elrik scoffed. "You think we can enter the Aqueno Prison in the middle of the day and not be noticed?"

"Why not, where is the prison?"

Elrik laughed then, his voice filled with condescension. "My dear Elenora, the Aqueno Prison is below the lake. If the water parts in midday, some faerie is certain to notice." He smiled then, all sharp teeth. "You have so much to learn."

"Then I will see you tomorrow night," I ground out. I desperately hoped he would leave.

But he remained where he was.

"I demand my payment."

I should have known Elrik would never give without getting more for himself in the bargain.

"What about our new alliance?" I deadpanned.

"You will allow me the honor of escorting you to the next revel."

"Fine," I retorted. I would have agreed to almost anything if it meant I could see Casper.

"And you must appear to be madly in love with me," he added. In response to my silence, he said, "If you are serious about our new alliance."

I grimaced, the very idea of feigning any affection toward Elrik making me ill. "Very well, if that's what you require."

"That is hardly the way to speak to your love, little bird." I snorted. Elrik's eyes darkened, a terrible gleam in them that I did not like. "I need proof that you can do this. I require a kiss."

I gaped at him. I wanted nothing more than to spit in his conniving face. *But I need to survive*, I reminded myself. "One kiss," I ground out, ready to give him the smallest peck on the cheek.

Before I could deliver a chaste kiss, Elrik's hand wrapped around my chin, pulling my lips toward his. His fingers were tight on my cheeks, the pressure making the sitano in my blood burn my face. His lips were on mine, taking away my breath and my voice. I tried to push back, but I was no match for his strength. He kissed me deeply, as though trying to devour me, and I wanted to scream. A sharp pain shot through my lower lip, and suddenly Elrik released me, stepping back with graceful ease. As I touched my lip with my tongue, I tasted blood.

"You bit me."

Elrik only licked his lips as though savoring the flavor. "I told you before, you taste so sweet." And without waiting for a reply, he strode out of the room.

It was a long time before my heart stopped racing. But it was much longer before the fear and the rage subsided enough for me to focus on forming a plan. Elrik had said the Aqueno Prison was under the lake. I had no idea how one could get to the bottom of the lake, but perhaps I could find out on my own. I laid down in bed, knowing I would need to rest if I was going to venture to the lake this night.

As I tried to find sleep, my thoughts flickered to Casper. My heart ached to think about him imprisoned under the lake. I wondered how my brothers were, thankful they were still in Reynallis and not part of the mess I was in, no matter how greatly I missed them. I was so deep in my concerns, that it wasn't until dusk that I noticed the cut on my arm had already healed to a faint, white scar.

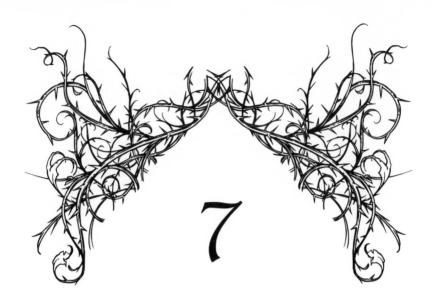

7

As the afternoon melted into evening, every footstep outside my room sent me into high alert, wondering if Valente was returning to finish me off. Though my body ached with exhaustion, I could not find sleep, even as I knew rest would help restore some of the strength I desperately needed. Once the sky turned black and stars dotted the night, I gave up all pretense of trying to sleep.

I pulled myself out of bed and walked to the window. The spiderweb curtains fluttered in the breeze. Outside, the field by the tree palace looked silver in the moonlight, and the lake glowed with the reflection of the moon. Giant swans nestled on the banks, soft white boulders with heads tucked deep into their plumage. Glass boats were docked, gently bobbing on the smooth surface of the lake. I scanned the meadow, searching for lingering fay. I couldn't detect any movement.

Beyond the lake, the thick forest was too dense for me to see past the first few branches of the nearest trees.

The height from my window was too great to jump. *But what if I could fly?* A long and strenuous hike down to the lake would be only a few seconds of gliding through the air.

I tried flapping my wings. I squeezed my shoulder blades, tightening new muscles that connected to my wings. Both wings shot together, unbalancing me as I fell forward, barely catching myself before faceplanting on the floor.

"Chace's chaos," I swore under my breath as I clambered to my feet. Disappointment killed the burst of excitement, as I acknowledged the truth. I might look fay, but I lacked their gifts. I carefully relaxed my shoulders, taking care not to flap my wings again. I crept to the hole that had been my door, as quietly as I could. I held my breath and peeked through the opening. No one was on the other side. I exhaled softly and tiptoed into the hallway. "Hall" was a loose definition for this walkway, with branches and leaves forming a knotwork of walls and floors, leaving the top open to the sky, which was clear and bright with an almost-full moon.

I started to the right, my bare feet silent on the thick branches. The design of the tree palace was as beautiful as it was strange. Every so often, I could see paths diverging from the main walkway, leading into other rooms, either deeper into the tree or external rooms supported by thick tree limbs. I held my breath each time I passed by a vine curtain or a wooden door, praying the occupants would not hear me. Some of the chambers were silent and dark, but others glowed with light, voices audible on the other side. Sometimes the voices were low murmurs, and other times they were loud and exuberant, singing and yelling, and I wondered what sort of dangerous festivities were taking place.

Chace was on my side as I made my way down the tree branch trail. I could almost see the ground when I heard a voice nearby. The owner of the voice was singing, and the song grew louder, signaling the approach of the creature. I looked around, desperate to find a deserted room or hall I could hide in. To my left was a dark offshoot, full of loose branches and thick with leaves. I leapt in, right as the faerie approached the main path. I crouched low, hidden by leaves.

"My love was lost at the sea. And so hence I foreswore she who calls herself the sea."

Through my hiding place, I could see the creature, a short, stocky faerie with deep blue skin, thickly webbed fingers, duck feet, and gills on the side of its neck. It wore drapings of seaweed as clothes, with more seaweed and pearls sticking out of its hair. The faerie wove back and forth slightly as it sang to itself. I was certain it was drunk.

"But now I have no mistress of my heart or my sea. How lonely is me, oh my, oh me."

The creature wobbled past me. It reeked of something too sweet, like fruit that fermented badly. But it kept on going, singing to itself of loss and the sea. I stayed hidden a while longer, making sure it was long gone before I emerged. When I finally rose, my limbs felt painfully stiff, as though I had been crouching for hours instead of minutes. I had to use branches along the walls to pull myself up, and a flush of uncomfortable heat ran across my skin. I hated how weak I was, but I forced myself to keep going. I skittered past the lit hallway that the creature had come from and moved as quickly as I dared until I reached the end of the path. The branch that comprised the main pathway turned into a thick root that sunk into the soft dirt of the ground. I stepped off the tree path, feeling cool, wet grass beneath my feet and nearly wept with relief.

I allowed myself a few minutes to rest, leaning against the massive root of the palace tree, summoning the strength to keep going. I stared out across the meadow of grass to the shore of the lake. As the Forest Court was an island in this lake, I had no idea where to even begin looking for an underwater prison. Off to my left were the scattering of sleeping swans, and to my right were the glass boats. I decided the glass boats would be as good a place as any to start my search.

I kept close to the tree until the boats were directly across from me, with only the large, grassy meadow between me and the lake. It would be a quick run if I was in better condition, but I already felt unsteady from my exertions. I closed my eyes, summoning any reserve of strength. I rubbed my fingers over Casper's signet ring, wishing he was by my side.

I would find a way to free him, and then I would figure out how to get to my brothers. Somehow, I would fix this. I opened my eyes and forced myself to head to the lake's shore. I could only run for a few seconds before I felt shaky. I slowed to a brisk walk, and while even that made my body scream in protest, I willed myself to continue. I made it as far as the small beach where the lake met the land.

I was so close to the glass boats; I could see the moonlight reflected in their perfectly smooth hulls. They were only a few feet into the water, gently floating on the dark lake.

I was mere steps away.

"I had hoped to find you here."

I whipped around to see Queen Marasina standing behind me. I hadn't even heard her approach. She stood tall and imposing, her silver hair illuminated by the moonlight. She wore a pale gold dress of delicate fabric that floated with her every move. She wore no crown, though the golden pendant still hung around her neck. In one hand, she held a long white cane.

The queen stepped toward me, and I inadvertently took a step backward, the water coming to my ankles. Without a word, she beckoned to one of the elegant glass boats, which silently floated toward her. She gracefully entered the craft, barely making any waves as she did so. I kept my eyes locked on her, though she didn't look at me as she settled herself in the boat. I looked around, trying to determine how I could get away from her. The grassy mounds stretched in all directions till they led to the lake. There was no cover and no way I could outrun the faerie warrior queen.

"Soren used to come to the lake at night. He said the quiet helped
him think," she said, sounding wistful. She finally looked up at me, her
sapphire eyes piercing, even in the dark. She seemed to contemplate
me for a moment before she added, "Come here, the lake is lovely at
night. And there are fewer listening ears here." She gestured to the
other seat in the glass boat.

I hadn't known what to expect from the queen, but not an offer
for a boat ride. Even though she acknowledged me as kin, something
I still was not ready to accept, I doubted I could trust her.

"I'd rather not," I said stiffly.

Marasina smiled, but it was forced. "You are impertinent for one
of my court."

"I'm not one of yours," I snapped before I could think better of it.
I took a quick step away from the boat.

"You are now, child," she said, but her voice sounded weary. "You
are fay, something you must learn to accept."

I couldn't help glancing down at my hands. Even in the moonlight I could see the skin looked inhuman, glowing from the fay blood
that now ran in my veins. It made me sick. "What do you want with
me?" I finally asked.

"I told you." But her tone suggested she was dealing with a petulant infant instead of a hated enemy. "Come here. We shall go
for a short ride. I have things to tell you. And a gift. You are in no
position to refuse me. Come now, you are shaking. I can sense your
fatigue."

I shook my head, taking another step back, but my legs were indeed trembling, and the movement caused me to stumble.

"Sitano is a drug with deep roots, and you will not be at your full
strength for some time, if ever. Truly, you should consider yourself
lucky it didn't kill you. If Elrik hadn't asked it as his boon, I should
have punished him for using it on a member of the royal family."

That stopped me. "I'm not a member . . ." I started.

"Don't," she said, her voice harsh. "You are all I have left of my son. I promise you I shall do you no harm on our little ride. And you have nowhere else to go. I have eyes and ears on the grounds too."

I looked around, half expecting to see faerie spies and guards, but I saw no one. *Doesn't mean they aren't there*, I thought. And I would have to wait to search for the prison now that Marasina was here. Maybe if the queen wanted to talk to me, I could learn something useful. Any knowledge would be power for me in this unfriendly court.

Cautiously, I approached the glass boat. I didn't have Marasina's grace and nearly fell into the glass vessel, causing it to wobble and rock on the waves before smoothing. All the while, Marasina studied me, not saying a word or offering help. I sat as far from her as I could, but the boat was small, intended for only a few people to take pleasure rides around the lake. It was a relief to sit. I rested my hands on the cool surface of the boat. Marasina clapped her hands once, and the boat suddenly moved on its own, away from the beach and onto the main portion of the lake. I tried to grip the seat, but my fingers were damp with sweat and could find no purchase on the slick glass. Fortunately, the boat's movement through the water was smooth and slow. I gazed down at the glass bottom of the boat hoping to make out something that might indicate where the Aqueno Prison was, but the water was black beneath us. I eventually gave up, realizing I'd never find it without Elrik's help.

For a long time, Marasina simply stared at me.

"What did you want to tell me?" I finally asked, unable to stand the silence.

"You do look like him," she said, more to herself. "I didn't see it at first, not when you were human. Not with such gross features. But now . . . now it's impossible to miss."

"Like who?" I asked, but my heart sank even as I asked.

"Soren. My son. Your father."

"I always thought they were only bedtime stories," I said.

"What did he tell you?" For the first time, there was a desperation in Marasina's voice. It was a familiar yearning that I recognized in the schemes I used to run. She had the need of someone who wanted something fantastical to be true. I heard that same need in those who used to ask me if the miracle elixir I was selling really would cure their ills or if the fortune I "read" for them was true. Marasina wanted to believe that I could tell her about her son. It was a strange realization. And it gave me a tiny advantage.

"If I tell you, I want you to tell me something," I said, forcing myself to be daring.

The queen smiled, almost amused. "You have my cunning. You certainly didn't get it from Soren. My son was too noble and sweet."

"Yes, he was," I said, remembering my father, loving and kind, teaching us children to read books and telling us stories late into the night. My parents had been tender and good-hearted. They had not given me my talents for conniving and cunning. I hadn't needed those skills when they had been alive. But if my father had also been her son, had been Soren before he was Samuel, then he had lied. He had deceived me my entire life.

"How about a trade, Elenora Molnár?" Marasina asked, quirking one elegant eyebrow at me.

"A trade?"

"Tell me about the stories your father told you, and I will give you this." Marasina picked up the white wood cane from where it rested at the bottom of the boat. It was an elegant thing made of carved white branches that twined together, the veins of the wood almost silver. Without my dagger, it would be the closest thing I would have to possessing a weapon here.

And so, I told the Queen of the Faeries a bedtime tale. I told her a story I had heard countless nights as a child, one I used to beg my father to tell. I told her about the faerie prince who fell in love with a human maiden, of how their love was pure. I described their journey to the faerie palace, and how his parents, the King and Queen of the Faeries, spurned them. And though I wanted to believe I was only telling a folktale, I felt acutely uncomfortable when I came to the part where the Faerie Queen declared the human girl too far below the prince and demanded her death. I wrapped it up, quickly describing how the young lovers escaped.

"And then the prince disguised himself as a human to spend the rest of his life with his true love . . ." my words trailed off, the weight of the truth hitting me. My father had told me his story and lied to me in the same tale. And I would never be able to ask him why.

Marasina sat perfectly still, a marble statue, the only sign of life a tear that silently slid down her face, her pale skin ashen. "I banished him. I forced him to leave. I could have let him stay, even with his human bride."

"What happened?" I asked, suddenly needing the truth, to know what was real.

Marasina let out a small laugh that came out as a choked cry. "Soren told the tale almost true. Though I doubt he met Eva in the woods."

I startled at her use of my mother's name. "You knew my mother?"

Marasina grimaced, as though the memory of my mother pained her. "Yes, though I have no praise for her." She sighed then, seeming far older and weary. "My court used to be open to any humans who would risk the journey. They sought to escape their old lives. We offered them safe refuge, often employing them as musicians, servants, or artists. I never doubted their inferiority to our kind, but I found them useful. The humans in our court were grateful for our hospitality. I never imagined that a mere maid, a *human* maid, could steal my son's heart. I was horrified when I found out, humiliated that my eldest son, heir to Magnomel, would debase himself by choosing a human as his bride." I scoffed at her insults, but Marasina kept going. "When Soren left with Eva, I thought it would be a passing phase. He would grow tired of her, weary of the human lands, and return home. Fay have far longer lives than humans, and I was ready to give Soren the length of one human life before fetching him home. I thought it would only be a matter of time. I never imagined that he was leaving me forever."

As Marasina spoke, I felt strangely tied to this faerie. Before tonight, I had nothing but hate for her. She led an attack on the Rose Palace, imprisoned Casper and nearly allowed my death. But she was also mourning my father.

"I didn't think he was leaving me forever when he left for the war," I confessed.

"How did my son die?" In this moment, Marasina was not a warrior or queen. She was a mother, and as much as I distrusted her, hated her for what she had done, I pitied her. "My sources could only determine that he died in the humans' war."

My mouth went dry as I remembered Thomson, the baker's son, returning from the front lines of the battle. He had survived but lost a leg and could no longer fight. He limped to our house, bringing the news to Mother that her husband had lost much more than a leg. She was inconsolable for weeks. Her cries echoed in my head. "I never asked for details. I was only ten. Knowing Papa wasn't coming home was all I needed to know."

"To die in a human war . . ." Marasina trailed off, lost in thought. "I will never forgive humans and their petty disputes, their deadly wars. But I blame myself, too. I often wonder how things might have turned out if I had not cast out my son. If I could have swallowed my pride, then I could still have my beloved son with me." Coming back to the present, she stared at me, as though looking for her son.

"I've been told I have his eyes." I did not know if that was still true. I had his eyes when my eyes were brown, flecked with gold, and entirely human.

Marasina smiled with heartbreaking sadness. "You have the shape of them, if not the color." She swallowed hard, then handed me the cane.

I took it, examining it by the light of the moon. It smelled faintly of pears. Set in the top of the cane was a large moonstone, round and smooth, and the size of my fist. It glowed in the dim light, reflecting blues and whites in its shimmering interior.

"I confess, I was hoping to find you out here this night. I thought perhaps you took after my son in that way. I created this for you."

I looked up from the cane, suspicious once again of the Faerie Queen. The cane was stunning, the moonstone worth a fortune. No one gave such presents for free. "Why would you do that?"

"Consider it a welcome home gift," Marasina said. I wanted to argue that this was not my home, but she continued. "The wood is from the pear tree you sprouted. It seemed only fitting."

"But that was a sapling." The tiny white stalk sticking out of the pear had been the length of my thumb.

Marasina laughed. "You have much to learn of our magic, Elenora. Us Magia Viveralis can not only spark life, but with time and learning, encourage it to grow at our whim. How do you think the Forest Court was created?" She gestured back to the tree palace.

"I had no idea," I admitted. I did not tell her that I used to believe all faeries performed blood magic, such as Pel and Elrik. Apparently, there was much about the fay I did not know.

"Soren was one of the strongest Magia Viveralis. He would have made a wonderful king one day." Her voice was again wistful as her eyes settled back on the cane. "That moonstone is from the crown he used to wear. It seemed only right that you have it now."

I looked back down at the moonstone that topped the cane. I hadn't owned anything of my father's for years; everything of his that hadn't been destroyed when our village was burned to the ground we sold for a few coins to buy food, and even that hadn't lasted long. I tried to imagine my gentle father, a mere miller, as a faerie prince, but it felt too strange. Nonetheless, I rubbed the smooth surface of the stone, trying to feel closer to him.

Marasina sniffled once before collecting herself. "You have so much to learn, Elenora Molnár. But the hour is late." She clapped her hands, and the glass boat began to head back to shore. "Meet Lorella at the docks tomorrow morning. I shall instruct her to begin your training. You must be able to draw on your powers without assistance."

We rode the rest of the way to shore in silence, my thoughts crowding around me. Tomorrow, Lorella would teach me magic. Tomorrow night, Elrik would show me the Aqueno Prison. Freeing Casper was still my first goal, my only goal. But as I rubbed my hand along the smooth wood of the cane, the pear wood slightly warm to my touch, I wished I had more time to learn who my father had been before he became Samuel.

8

Though it was still early, faeries were already out on the grass. Some were eating picnic breakfasts, packed in reed baskets. Others slept outside, content with their pillows of moss and cobweb blankets. Many grew quiet as I made my way past them, turning to watch me with their strange cat-slit eyes. They would nod their heads slightly, even as they continued to stare at me through long lashes. I gripped my cane tightly as I made my way to the cluster of glass boats, ignoring the whispers.

"She's the heir now."

"Funny, doesn't look human."

"Valente will surely kill her."

I kept my head high, trying to look like my deliberate strides were intentionally slow. In truth, if I tried anything more than a dragging, stiff walk, a burning pain shot up my legs. Lorella had left food and clothes for me outside my room, along with a note to meet her at the docks. I had changed into a blue-gray tunic the color of a stormy sea and a matching skirt trimmed in silver. The fabric was soft and fine, shimmering like a delicate silk under my touch. I was grateful that faerie garb did not require a maid's assistance to dress, though I missed Annabeth.

I ate the provided breakfast, fresh berries with honey and cream. I was feeling surprisingly refreshed when I left my room, but after the climb down the palace path, even with the assistance of my cane, a dull ache was seeping back into my bones. It was a relief to see Lorella sitting in one of the boats, her feet dangling over into the cobalt water. Corine sat beside her, holding a basket. Drusia fluttered overhead, the tiny, green faerie hardly ever able to stay still.

Around them, the delicate glass boats bobbed gently in the water as large swans floated by.

Lorella patiently watched me approach. A smile illuminated her pale face and she rose to meet me. She fluttered her dragonfly wings, carrying her from the boat to the beach.

"Elenora, I'm so delighted you are here." Her bare feet left wet footprints in the sand as she ran up to meet me. She wrapped her hands around mine with a warmth that surprised me.

"Queen Marasina said you would teach me magic," was all I could say.

"Yes, yes, of course. Come, I thought we could go somewhere a bit more private," she said, leading me back to the glass boats.

Once we were seated, she turned to the bow and added, "Far north shore, please." The boat began to move of its own accord. It was still such an odd feeling. Seeing my shocked face, Lorella smiled kindly. "It's always best to show respect to magic even if you can't see it." She winked. "Especially if you can't see it."

I nodded, taking in the sights. The ride away from the island palace was pleasant, the boat smoothly gliding across the lake. The further we traveled from the fay palace, the more I felt myself relax. I absently ran my fingers through the waters.

"Be careful," Lorella said, seeing my hand in the water, "there are creatures in the lake whom you are not familiar with. Not all are kind."

I yanked my hand out, inadvertently splashing Corine, who yelped in protest. "But you had your feet in the lake."

"Yes, but they know me," Lorella said with a smirk.

I kept my hands in the boat till the glass skiff reached the far shore. I stepped onto the sandy shore of the Biawood Forest. There was something comforting about being surrounded by actual trees, growing straight up instead of transforming into palaces.

"This way," Lorella said as Corine picked up the basket and Drusia flew above us. I followed them down a small path into the Biawood.

I inhaled deeply, enjoying the smell of the trees and the sunlight that dappled the path between the leaves. We had not gone far when Lorella stopped in front of a small clearing, a ring of tiny mushrooms forming the perimeter. I wondered if it was safe to walk into a faerie ring, village stories coming back to me about humans that did just that and were never seen again. *But I'm not human*, I reminded myself before I followed Lorella into the circle.

"Do you know how to summon your magic?" Lorella asked, settling down in the center of the clearing. She pulled several cloth bags out of the basket.

"Do I look like I know how to do magic?" I asked as I set down my cane and joined her on the ground.

"You look like a noble fay, so I would say yes," Lorella said, giving me a rueful smile as she continued to sort the bags she brought.

"I tend to forget," I admitted. I looked down at my hand. "I keep expecting to look at myself and see me, but I see someone else." I bent and flexed my fingers, still uneasy with the slight glow that came off them.

"I cannot imagine how one could forget they are Magia Viveralis," Drusia said, flying low to play with my hair, but Lorella waved her off.

"You are yourself, Elenora. No glamour placed on you or taken off can change that. Besides, appearances are too easily deceived. Corine, how about you demonstrate?"

"Yes, milady," Corine said. She murmured something I couldn't make out and closed her eyes in concentration. Her skin slowly lost its purple hue, fading into beige as her sharp edges softened into human shapes and her purple and black wings disappeared. She opened her eyes, her pupils round. Corine looked exactly like a human child. My jaw dropped open, and I gasped. But in the space of a breath, the illusion shattered, her skin returning to its lavender hue and all her faerie features returning.

"Can all fay do that?" I asked. My mind was already whirling. If I could create the illusion of looking human, that would be enough to go home safely after I rescued Casper. I could return to my brothers.

"Of course not, silly," Drusia said, giggling. "Only the Magia Illustraia."

"The what?"

"Magia Illustraia," Lorella repeated. "The fay with the power to create glamour magic. Just as the Magia Sange work in blood and we Magia Viveralis deal in life, the Magia Illustraia wield illusion."

"Oh," I said, my heart dropping. "I would have liked to learn how to do that."

Corine scoffed, "As if life magic isn't enough for you."

"Each Magia family possess a different magic. And even then, most magic lines are weak." Lorella turned to Corine. "How long can you maintain that glamour?"

Corine frowned. "That was as long as I can keep it."

"I illusioned myself to look like a fish for twenty-three seconds one time," Drusia boasted, momentarily adding scales to her green skin. When the illusion vanished, she rolled over in the grass, laughing.

Lorella smiled indulgently, "Yes, well, with few exceptions, only the noble fay possess magic with lasting change. Here, hold this." She pulled a small acorn from one of the bags. After a moment of hesitation, I held out my palm and took the acorn.

"What is a noble fay?" I asked, examining the tiny acorn. It appeared perfectly ordinary.

"The strongest magic in our world is performed by the noble fay, which is why they are in power. Some lesser fay can do small things, but mostly they rely on magic-imbued tokens from the noble fay. The royal family, the Magia Viveralis, has the power of altering and enhancing life itself, arguably the most potent magic. I could go on to the other magias, but we'd be here all day. Perhaps another time."

"Like the crests of the nobility," I said, thinking back to when Flora taught me the different noble crests to help train me to be a proper princess when I was betrothed to Casper. It seemed like a lifetime ago.

Lorella looked at me. "We have no need of crests. Our magic stands on its own. Come now, let's practice. Mother believes that as Soren's daughter, you will be strong enough to beat Valente at the challenge, but he is not one to be underestimated."

"I will be certain not to make that mistake," I said, thinking about the hole blasted in my door, the one intended to kill me. "But what exactly is this challenge? What will I have to do?"

"You don't know? You are as good as dead if Prince Valente challenges you," Corine said, but Lorella shushed her.

"I supposed it could be considered a duel of sorts," Lorella explained. "As a member of the royal family, Valente is allowed to make a claim to the throne as heir of Magnomel. Or at least he will be able to in a fortnight, at the next revel. And if he does, as the defender, you will have the right to decide the type of challenge. He will declare himself heir if he wins. If you win, then your position as heir cannot be challenged again by him and he would be forced to swear allegiance to you."

"What do you mean I choose the type of challenge?" I asked, trying to wrap my mind around so much new information.

"Combat, of course. You would pick the form it could take, such as a sword fight or a duel of magic."

"Are those the only types of combat allowed?" I asked, wanting to know the full parameters of this unwanted duel.

Lorella furrowed her brow. "Not technically, but I cannot recall anyone suggesting another sort of combat. Was there something else you had in mind?"

"Not really," I admitted. I wasn't skilled in sword fighting, and I doubted I would learn how to master magic as well as Valente by the next revel. I would have to ponder another way to best him.

"Valente is an expert sword fighter," Lorella continued, "so I would recommend magic."

"I recall," I said, remembering facing off with him at the Rose Palace. "And if he wins, then I would no longer be the heir? Is that all?" I would not mind stepping aside for Valente. I had no desire to rule Magnomel.

"Not being heir would be the least of your concerns. Valente will probably kill you," Corine said, but after a sharp look from Lorella, she ducked her head, becoming intensely preoccupied with sorting bags from the basket.

"Then what if I concede the win to him?" I asked, my thoughts racing through different scenarios that didn't end with my death.

"That isn't done," Lorella said, shaking her head. "Valente would still fight you at the revel."

"And if I didn't show up to the revel?" I wasn't above hiding in my room if it meant avoiding the challenge.

"Valente would still find you. He's an excellent tracker," Corine said, sounding almost chipper about it.

"I haven't told you what you gain if you win," Lorella said, forcing cheer into her voice.

"You mean besides not being killed?" I deadpanned.

"Corine exaggerated. Not everyone who loses a challenge is killed." I was about to protest, but Lorella kept going. "You get to request a boon of the reigning monarch. Mother would give you a token or a favor."

"But I don't know how to do magic," I complained. A favor from Queen Marasina would be useful, but I was as likely to win as Valente was to invite me to tea.

"And that is why we are here to practice," Lorella said, all matter of fact. "Magic is a part of you. It is something inherently inside all noble fay. You simply need to summon it and direct it to your will. Some magic only needs intent, but usually words help direct it." Lorella picked up another bag, withdrawing a small black seed. "*Vive swindle*," she whispered to it, her voice encouraging, yet gentle. Moments later, a tiny sprout poked its head out of the seed, a soft green stem that let open a tiny leaf. Lorella smiled and handed me the sprout. "Vive swindle is what we use to encourage a life force to amplify. It brings seeds quick growth, and is the easiest life magic to start with."

"Must make feeding people easy," I said lightly, but I felt a pang of longing. I recalled the long years spent scavenging in the woods and running small cons to bring in enough coin to survive.

"It does," Lorella said, and smiled. "No one goes hungry here."

"I'm hungry. We should have lunch," Drusia said, landing next to us.

Lorella sighed, "Drusia, you ate your weight in apples and sweet tarts this morning."

"But that was hours ago," the little green faerie whined.

"You are always hungry. We will break for lunch after Elenora has time to practice. Go find some berries if you are so starved." Drusia fluttered off, and Lorella gently took the sprout from my hand and pointed at the acorn. "Now you try."

I held the acorn in my palm and visualized it sprouting. "*Vive swindle*," I told it.

Nothing.

"*Vive swindle*," I repeated, this time louder.

Nothing.

"*VIVE SWINDLE!*" I yelled.

Nothing.

"I can't do this," I said, overcome with frustration.

Lorella clasped her hands over mine. "And you are ready to give up after three pathetic attempts?"

I groaned. "My attempts were not pathetic; they were as good as I can manage."

"You need more intention."

"I am full of intention," I insisted. "I imagined the sprout and everything."

"Is that all you thought of?" Lorella asked, her gray eyes studying me.

"What more should I be thinking of? I don't exactly have much experience with magic. Now if you wanted me to steal the seed and re-place it with a sprout, that I can do." My criminal background seemed to be sadly little help in the faerie world.

"I don't even know what you are talking about, Elenora. But think about it like this. Your goal is not to simply create a sprout, you are creating an entire life. Don't limit your thoughts to a tiny stem, but know that you are creating the entire tree. There are roots and leaves, and a new life. Try to imagine all of that and let your magic flow into it."

"New life," I repeated, holding up the acorn. I closed my eyes, imagining a large oak tree, with a thick, gnarled trunk and deep roots that reached out throughout the forest floor. I saw dark green veined leaves, shading the ground with their cover. I squeezed the acorn harder, the sharp tip poking into my palm and the rough cap rubbing into my fingers. I imagined something in my core, my very being, flowing into the acorn, encouraging it to become the tree in my mind. I tried to see not only a fresh green sprout, but roots, first tiny, stringy white protrusions then thick, weighty appendages that would spread out and support the tree. I imagined a thick trunk, one I could easily climb, and long, sturdy branches.

"*Vive swindle*," I whispered to the acorn. I could swear there was a flutter of heat in my chest, something pulling toward my palms.

Slowly, very slowly, I uncurled my fingers, hoping to see signs of life. The acorn looked the same. I turned it over in my hands, desperate to notice any change, even a crack on the surface of the shell which might indicate I had done something.

"Nothing." I sighed defeated, and dropped my hand, letting the acorn fall to the ground and roll away. "Maybe because I'm only half fay, I can't do magic on my own."

"I don't think that's it," Lorella said, picking up the acorn. I arched an eyebrow, ready to argue, but she continued. "I'm only half royal fay, and I can perform as well as any other Magia Viveralis." She held the acorn up to the light, as though she might spot something too small to see in the shade. "I think you almost have it. Here, give me your hand." She reached out for my hand. On instinct I jerked it back. She looked up at me, clearly surprised.

"I'm sorry. I don't want to be helped." I thought back to the afternoon prior when Marasina made the power flow through me. It was a strange feeling of helplessness too close to the control Elrik wielded with his blood magic.

"It won't hurt, I promise," Lorella said, misunderstanding my reluctance.

"It's not that," I said, still fumbling for words. "I don't like feeling controlled by someone else."

Lorella nodded and lowered her hand. "I understand. I am confident you will be able to summon your own magic eventually."

I sat back, a new royal face in my mind's eye, one with angry blue eyes, white curls, and a vengeance against me. "But I don't have eventually. I have a fortnight until the revel."

"Valente is not invincible, but he is strong."

"Very strong," Corine agreed.

Lorella frowned at her maid. "But Soren was stronger."

"Fine," I relented, choosing the lesser of the two evils. I held out my hands to Lorella. "Please help me."

Lorella smiled softly and placed the acorn back into my palm before wrapping her long fingers around my hands, her skin pale against my burnished fingers. "Now remember, this is coming from you. I'm only aiding your magic. Helping you to draw it out. Wait till you feel something, then direct it toward the acorn and say the words."

I closed my eyes, directing my focus inward. At first, I felt nothing. I sensed the acorn in my palm and Lorella's soft, warm hands over mine, but nothing more. I was almost about to say so when I felt a soft surge of heat in my chest. It did not burn the way the sitano did, but rather created a sense of alertness within me.

It was delicate pins and needles that made me aware of a force inside myself. It was a warmth and a vibration that seemed to spark in my heart, and with each heartbeat it expanded within my chest, before spreading into my arms and my legs. The feeling crept up my neck and into my feet and my hands, a steady buzzing, like a persistent fly. I almost jerked my hands away, but sensing my unease, Lorella leaned in close.

"You are doing well, Elenora. And I am here with you," she said, and her hands tightened slightly on mine, sending a stronger jolt through them. "Imagine the tree."

I thought about the tingling sensation melting into the acorn, filling the shell with this strange force. Instead of an acorn, I imagined that I was holding a tree, ready to flourish. I thought about the potential of the tree and that I could bring that potential to reality. When the feeling reached my fingers, I pressed on the acorn, trying to direct the pulsing into the seed. At first, nothing changed.

"Say the words," Lorella reminded me.

"Oh, right," I said, distracted. The pulse faded, but as I concentrated on the tingling feeling, it rose once more into my fingers. "*Vive swindle*," I said, my voice firm and commanding, pushing the pulse into the acorn, instructing the acorn to become the tree it was meant to be. As if breaking through a wall, the sensation flowed over my fingers and my palms and flooded into the acorn. I kept pushing the peculiar feeling through my hands and into the seed, trying to get all of it to seep into the acorn.

Blooming tree. Tree. Tree, I repeated over and over in my mind. *Stems, leaves, roots, branches. Tree. Tree. Tree.*

And suddenly, the acorn exploded.

I felt the hard nut burst open, splintering the shell and dislodging the small cap. Surprised, my concentration broke, and the magic fell away. Lorella released my hands and I carefully opened my fist, revealing my prize. The dark acorn shell had split nearly in two, and a slender, pale green stem with two small, serrated leaves unfurled.

"I did it," I said, staring at the oak sapling.

"I told you that you could," Lorella said, sounding pleased.

"I made a tree," I cried, louder, almost laughing. "A tiny, tiny tree, but a tree! By Chace's den, I made a tree." I examined the small sprout. It looked like a normal sapling. I wondered if it would now grow faster than normal trees.

"Do you want to try on your own?" Lorella asked after giving me a few minutes to admire my miniature tree.

I nodded, buoyed from the success. I dug a small hole and planted the seedling, covering the broken acorn in dirt until only the stem and leaf sprouts were visible. Lorella pulled out another acorn and passed it to me. Again, I focused on the idea of a tree. I gripped the acorn and waited for the tingle of energy. When nothing came, I concentrated harder. I imagined a full tree, large and sturdy, and thought about how much life would have to be poured into the small seed to create such an imposing oak. I pulled hard inside myself. Finally, I felt a small stirring in my chest, a tiny pulse that radiated no further than a hand's width from my heart.

I pushed harder, thinking of not only one tree, but a forest of trees, of rows and rows of trees, but the buzz was no stronger than before. No matter how hard I tried to force it, I couldn't get the feeling to move beyond my chest. My heart felt warmed, but there was no tingling pull down my limbs and out my fingers like last time. I recited the magical incantation, but the acorn stayed the same small closed-shelled object in my palm. I repeated the words, but the magic remained weak, stuck in my chest. Eventually, I released my grip and opened my hand.

"Nothing," I said, looking at the acorn as if I might find a small crack or any trace hint that my magic had reached it. "I don't know why it didn't work. I did everything the same."

"You simply need more practice."

"And then maybe I'll be able to grow a tree at Valente. Certainly that will keep him from killing me." The defeat of my last attempt drained away my elation from my earlier success. I was a novice at something Valente had been perfecting since before I was born. It had been foolish to even think I ever stood a chance.

"Growing plants is not the only thing we Magia Viveralis can do, but it's the best place to start learning. And tell me, how do you feel?"

"Like I've failed," I said, unable to be rid of the cloud of disappointment. Now that I was no longer concentrating on the acorn, I sat back, realizing the extent of my exhaustion.

Lorella noticed my fatigue, because she started to collect her bags of seeds, packing them back into her basket. "I imagine you are tired. All magic comes with a cost, and you are very new to it. Let's return to the Forest Court. You could use a rest." Corine picked up the basket and called out to Drusia, who came flying back, berry juice staining her lips.

"It doesn't help that Elrik poisoned me," I grumbled, pulling myself to my feet with the support of my pearwood cane. I bit my lip at the dull rush of hot pain that merely standing caused.

Lorella waited patiently for me, a look of pity on her kind face that tore at my pride. "It is odd that there was no better way to remove the glamour, strong as it was."

"What do you mean?"

Lorella's brow furrowed in thought. "Corine, isn't your great-great-great-aunt a noble fay of the Magia Illustraia?"

"Yes. Great-great-great-aunt Alverdine got all the gifts. She's one of the few noble Magia Illustraia." Corine wrinkled her nose. "Magia Illustraia is fickle. It only runs sporadically in our family."

"Most of us have only enough magic for an illusion of a few seconds," Drusia added, popping a wild strawberry into her mouth. "It's not enough to infuse a token or assist anyone." Drusia held up another strawberry to her face, puffing out her cheeks. Her shimmery green skin took on a red sheen, making her face appear like a large, round strawberry. The effect was so comical I laughed, a bright, unexpected sound. After a few seconds she let out her breath, giggling, and the effect was broken. Her skin melted back into new-leaf green, and she winked at me.

"Not good for much of anything," Corine added, sounding bitter. "Alverdine is one of the very few who can create long-lasting glamours."

"Corine, how about you see if Alverdine will have us over sometime? Perhaps she can tell us more about the glamour initially put on Elenora." Lorella looked at Corine, who nodded.

"Yes, milady."

I brightened, hoping their aunt could provide me with some answers. "I would appreciate that. I know so little about my faerie self."

Lorella took my free arm, leading us back to the boat. "I will help you find answers about your past, if I am able."

I studied the faerie next to me. She looked young, but I had no idea how faeries aged. She was my aunt. But also Valente's sister. "Why are you helping me?"

Lorella paused her steps, considering her answer. "I like to think we have become friends. And we are family."

"But Valente is also your family," I said. "Isn't this going against him?"

Lorella's face soured. "Valente believes he has a right to rule, but that doesn't mean he does. And besides," her eyes got a faraway look as she added, "I know how difficult it is to feel alone at court. To not know about one's own father."

I remembered Lorella telling me that she was a bastard, that she didn't know who her father was. At least I knew mine. I felt a new kinship with this faerie. In response, I squeezed her hand and smiled at her as we resumed walking back to the lake.

"Please, call me Nor. My family calls me Nor."

A bright smile broke out on Lorella's delicate face. "Very well, Nor."

The lightness I felt only lasted till we reached the lake. Though we had been gone all morning, it didn't feel long enough as the delicate glass boat made its way back to the palace. The anxiety that had abated came back full force as we approached the shore of the Forest Court.

Sensing my nerves, Lorella said, "You did well for your first day." She pulled out the bag of tiny black seeds from her basket. "You can use these to practice. You will improve with time."

"Time is in short supply if Valente plans to challenge me at the revel, assuming he doesn't kill me first." The glass boat docked on the sands of the Forest Court, the strange tree palace looming ahead of us.

Lorella climbed out of the boat, staring ahead. Her expression suddenly lightened. "Perhaps a visit to the Dusk Market will provide what you need."

"Yes, we should take Nor to the Dusk Market. There will be so much to show her." Drusia flew around in excitement.

Lorella smiled. "I'll send Drusia to fetch you from your room at sundown and take you to the market. I think we should be able to find some token that can assist you."

"What is this market?"

"You shall see. And you will love it." With that, Lorella kissed my cheek before running back to the palace.

9

The sun was low in the sky, casting long shadows across the floor when I finally took a break from attempting to sprout seeds. Tired, but needing something to do with my hands, I began palming the seeds. The familiarity of the motion was reassuring, and for a moment I could pretend that I was back with my brothers, practicing for a con job, not trapped in a strange faerie world.

See? Here's the seed. Now it's gone. Now it's here again. If I challenged Valente to a sleight of hand contest, I might have a chance. However, he would probably use magic to make something actually disappear, and then where would I be?

I sighed, letting the seeds fall to the bed. It was all about misdirection. *Make them watch the spinning wheel as I slip straw up my sleeve, replacing it with gold.* There had to be something from my past that I could use against Valente. Someone knocked on the wall outside my room.

"Yes?"

"I am here to take you to the Dusk Market," came a tiny voice. Drusia stood in the hole that had been my doorway, waiting for me to allow her in. I beckoned her to enter, silently noting that I needed a new door.

The little green faerie fluttered in and skidded to a stop. "Are you ready? Lady Lorella and Corine are already at the market. They shall be cross if we don't meet them soon. The market doesn't stay open for long. Otherwise that would be a night market, and how silly would that be?" Words flowed out of Drusia like a rushing a river as she twirled around the room, radiating excitement. At a loss, I had to put a hand on her shoulder to slow her twirls and chatter.

"Drusia, you're making me dizzy watching you and I only understood half of what you said."

The small faerie stopped moving long enough to stare up at me with her large emerald eyes, the slitted pupils unblinking as she took me in. After a moment she burst out in a large grin, happy, sharp teeth splitting her tiny face. "Now come! My lady should not be kept waiting." The faerie pulled at my hand, and I grabbed my cane before allowing her to lead me from the room.

"Shall we fly there? It would be much faster," Drusia said, looking hopefully at my wings.

"Sadly, I have not quite mastered how to use these," I said, self-consciously touching the dragonfly wings at my back. In truth, only the extra weight on my shoulders reminded me I even had them. Anytime I actively tried to engage the new muscles, my wings flopped back and forth haphazardly, nothing close to lifting me from the ground. "I'd feel better if we walk down the path."

"Very well," Drusia conceded, though she looked disappointed.

I had no coin for the Dusk Market but that had never stopped me in markets before. I took the descent slowly, careful not to stumble on upturned roots. My limbs ached more than I cared to admit, and I held tightly onto my cane, the moonstone head gripped tightly in my hand. My faerie guide was clearly frustrated at my sluggish pace, constantly fluttering up ahead before reluctantly walking back to me. This repeated until my feet finally hit the grass of the courtyard.

The clearing had been completely transformed. No longer sunny and open, the bruise-purple sky cast soft shadows on a new market that seemingly had appeared out of nowhere.

Instead of wide-open fields, there were billowing silk tents in jewel hues, each with tables of curious wares. Stranger still were the fay that sold the wares, a vast collection of creatures with skin of scales, feathers, stone and more. I stood, transfixed, while Drusia scanned the crowd.

"There she is, come on," Drusia said, interrupting my awe. The faerie led me past several tents, though I longed to examine each. A burnt orange tent containing tall sunflowers was guarded by a creature with tree bark for skin. A silver faerie stood under an iridescent, oil slick black tent selling a collection of the most ornate mirrors I had ever seen. Other tents had unusual foods with delicious aromas, trinkets made of glowing crystals, spider silk cloth that shimmered in the last of the evening light. Drusia pulled at my skirt every time I slowed to examine the variety of goods for sale until we reached a stall by the waterfall at the edge of the courtyard, the tent a blue silk the color of the pond during the day. There, Lorella stood, examining the merchant's wares, Corine by her side.

"Sister," Corine said to Drusia, "it took you long enough. Lady Lorella has been waiting since the market opened."

"It's not my fault, this one cannot fly," Drusia pouted.

"It's no matter," Lorella said, looking up from the stall. She smiled when she saw the awed look on my face. "Do you like the market?"

"It's unlike anything I have ever seen." I remembered the market from the Spring Faire in Sterling. The merchants made their stalls out of wooden crates or the back of wagons, some with rough spun, beige tents. At the time, I had found the goods, coming from all over

Reynallis, to be a vast selection. Looking back, everything at the market in Sterling was mundane, but also familiar, in a way that brought a pang of homesickness. It was difficult to believe it was only at the last Spring Faire where I met both Pel and Casper. It was at the faire where I convinced people that I could "transform" straw into gold, using the golden thread Pel had gifted me. Mindlessly, I tugged at the gold thread around my wrist.

"Nor?"

I snapped back to the present. Lorella was staring at me, and I realized I must have missed a question, as she clearly waited for an answer.

"What?"

"You looked so far away. Where was your mind?" Lorella asked. She was fingering a smooth piece of turquoise sea glass. It glowed under her touch.

"The market from my home," I said absently.

"Was it similar to here?"

I let my gaze travel down the table where the merchant was displaying his wares, all pieces of rounded sea glass, in shades of violets, dark blues, grass greens and pale grays. I looked up, glancing at the merchant, who was waiting patiently for Lorella, but kept sliding curious glances my way. His skin was seaweed green, scaled, like that of a fish. He stood like a human, but flapping gills protruded from his neck. His bulbous eyes never blinked.

"No, this market is rather different," I admitted.

"Oh well, no worries, you'll get used to the one here soon enough." Lorella said. She was only half paying attention, her focus fixed on the piece of glass in her hand.

"How strong are your magics today, Peseltine?"

The green creature looked down at the turquoise glass in Lorella's hands. "They are infused with solid Magia Acqueal spells, Lady Lorella, if that's what you're asking. I never bring less to market."

Lorella smiled, picking up a piece of robin's egg blue glass, weighing it in one hand and comparing it to the turquoise glass. "I would never accuse you of such, good Master Peseltine, but I need something that has been strongly infused with the pull of the tides. And I wouldn't say that I was disappointed with the piece that my sister Rosertina purchased from you last month. It wasn't your best work."

The green creature, Peseltine, flapped the gills on his neck. "You wound me, milady. I would never sell a noble fay anything but the best."

"You don't need to play coy with me. I spend more time working than my sister. I won't tell, but you need to do better."

Peseltine sighed, small bubbles escaping his thick lips. "Fine, it wasn't my best, but she didn't notice or mind. Besides, the token she traded for it failed me during its first attempt at growing a seaweed bed, and now I have nothing but stunted things."

Lorella smiled slyly and pulled out an acorn, like the one we had been working on before. *No*, I thought, looking closer at the seed, this one was somehow different than the acorns in the forest. This acorn pulsed with a faint gold light. Peseltine took the acorn from Lorella and held it up.

"And you infused this one? Personally?" Peseltine asked, before bringing the acorn close and smelling it. He inhaled deeply, and let out a small, contented sigh that sent his gills fluttering.

"Indeed. I wouldn't trust anyone else to create my tokens," Lorella said, giving the merchant a wink.

"A token from the royal family," Peseltine said, still examining the acorn. I could tell he didn't want to fully admit how much he desired it. I saw the same act from bartering human merchants back in Reynallis.

While Lorella and Peseltine bantered back and forth, sometimes complimenting each other's work and other times negotiating prices, my attention turned to the sea glass on the table. The smooth glass was lovely, lustrous in the evening glow. My hand was already brushing over the pieces before I realized I was falling back into my old habit of petty theft. Unlike the years I had stolen to feed myself and my brothers, I didn't need to steal a piece of glass, but the action felt so familiar that I suddenly wanted to. I slipped my hand over a purple piece, dark as the midnight sky, easily palming it. Lorella and Peseltine were still bantering and didn't notice.

I knew I should drop the glass back on the table. Rule one of a successful thief was not to con someone who knew you, and Peseltine now knew me clearly. I had no need of the trinket, but I wanted to know that I was still the person I was before being dragged to this strange world, even if that person was a thief.

"You know you need to buy that," a voice whispered. I turned to see Corine, her wide, dark eyes staring at me, pointedly not looking at my hand.

I silently cursed myself for being so careless. "I was only looking at it," I whispered back, dropping the purple glass on the table. Heat rushed to my face. Refusing to look at Corine, I deliberately began to inspect all the pieces of glass, trying to look like I had simply been examining each one, not trying to steal it. I picked up another piece, rubbing my fingers over the smooth surface and holding it up to the fading light to better see the color.

When I touched a piece of gray glass, I gasped. There was a tingling sensation that ran up my fingers and shot into my heart. It was faint, but undeniable. I felt a tug from it, some force that pulled at my own magic.

"What is this?" I asked.

Peseltine and Lorella stopped mid-conversation and turned to me. Peseltine gave me an appraising look, his buggy eyes intense.

"Ahh, so the broken princess does have a gift," he said, a knowing smile splitting his scaly face. I squirmed, seeing his needle-sharp teeth.

"She isn't broken," Lorella hissed, her demeanor suddenly stern.

Peseltine took a long look at my cane before finally saying, "My apologies, Princess. I must have been misinformed."

I couldn't form words. Until he spoke, I had not considered myself a princess or broken.

Lorella cut in on my behalf.

"You were. Princess Elenora is as whole and royal as any of my brothers or sisters." Lorella's words were a command.

"Again, my apologies," Peseltine said, giving a short bow. I couldn't tell if he was apologizing to Lorella or me.

"Understood and accepted," Lorella said, but she sounded stiff.

"But yes, that token is quite special," Peseltine said, eager to change the topic.

"It feels," I started, trying to put into the words the odd sensation I got from holding it. "I can feel it reaching out to me," I finally said, uncomfortable talking about an inanimate object as though it were a living thing.

"Yes, that one was most strongly infused with tidal magic," Peseltine said.

"May I?" asked Lorella, holding out her hand. I didn't want to let go of the glass, the buzzing a pleasant reminder that there was magic inside of me, but I forced myself to let it slide out of my grip and into her waiting palm. The moment the glass left my hand I felt a hollow emptiness as my magic went silent.

"Oh," she breathed, and I could tell that Lorella felt the pull as well. She held up the token, studying it. Between her fingers the glass looked so ordinary. All the other pieces were lovely colors, but this piece, while not ugly, was a dull, dove gray.

"It looks so plain," Drusia blurted out. As everyone turned to look at her, she covered her mouth with her hands.

"Hush," Corine scolded as Drusia fluttered around.

"Indeed," Peseltine said. "It is often the plainest pieces that will pick up the most magic."

"Very well, Master Peseltine. We will trade you my acorn for it," Lorella said.

"But—" Peseltine started, but then he thought better. "Of course, milady." He gave a stiff nod as he pocketed the acorn. Lorella turned to me and handed me back the gray glass. I immediately felt the pull of my power as soon as its smooth surface touched my skin.

Lorella bid farewell to Peseltine before taking my arm and leading me away from the blue tent. We passed an apple green tent manned by a willowy faerie wearing a wreath of buttercup blossoms and a midnight blue tent speckled with stars that displayed what looked like floating icicles, each illuminated with some light source I couldn't see. I was so distracted by the wares in the tents and the pulsing feeling from the sea glass that Lorella had to drag me along; at one point, I nearly tripped when my cane hit a rock. I would have fallen, but both Corine and Drusia were standing next to me, quick green and purple hands holding me up.

"Careful, Princess," Drusia scolded me. Like so many of the faeries, she and her sister were surprisingly strong despite their small size.

"Are you feeling unwell?" Lorella asked, as I took a moment to steady myself.

"Maybe I could use a brief rest," I said, frustrated with my weak body. I *wanted* to see the strange and wonderful wares in the stalls, but all this walking was more than I had done since being poisoned, and it was taking a toll. I had to lean heavily on the cane for support as the burn reignited in my bones.

Lorella slowed her pace until we were on the edge of the courtyard, a good distance from the tents and near the wall of the great tree that made up the palace. There, we rested on a large stump. It was a relief to sit down, though I hated how much I needed a break after so short a walk. In my previous life as a thief and even as a lady betrothed to a future king, I could run and walk and ride all day without a problem.

"Thank you," I said after I had taken a moment to catch my breath. Lorella wasn't looking at me but staring out at the market. There was a faraway look in her eyes.

"Things aren't going to be easy for you," she said. There was a sadness in her voice I hadn't heard before.

"I've been in difficult situations before," I immediately said. I wasn't sure why I wanted to reassure this faerie. Perhaps it was because even if I didn't fully trust any fay, Lorella was the closest thing I had to a friend here.

Lorella turned and looked at me, her dark gray eyes searching my face. "I imagine you have. Pel said he met you when you were living in the woods, stealing to survive."

There was no malice in her words, but I stiffened at the mention of Pel. I had thought him a friend, and that mistake had cost me everything. "I'm used to disasters," I said, a sharp edge to my voice.

Lorella took in my tone. "You know, he asked me to look after you. Make sure you would recover."

I went cold with resentment. "If he's the real reason you are helping me, then don't bother. I don't want anything from him ever again." I started to rise, but Lorella gripped my arm, her strong, slender fingers immobilizing me.

"Nor, stop. Pel was only doing his duty to my mother by reporting on Sterling."

"He lied to me. He betrayed me," I spat out. I remembered the moment when he turned from his battle with Casper, when he had Casper at sword point, the merest breath away from killing him. I felt the sick shock of it all over again.

"You know that's not the only reason I want to help you," Lorella insisted, changing tactics. "I told you, you're kin now. And I know firsthand how cruel the court can be."

I laughed, but it was a humorless sound. "You? A faerie? You're one of them. You have no idea what it's like." I knew I was being cruel to the one person at court who had gone out of her way to be nice to me, but in that moment, I didn't care. Thinking of Pel had me bitter.

"I may not know what it is to have been human, but I can tell you all about being thought of as inferior at court, and it's not a position you will want. You must be stronger than that. As a bastard, it was a lesson I had to learn firsthand. Don't let anyone, much less a simple water faerie merchant, talk down to you. Broken is not a nickname one can easily overcome."

For a moment I wanted to argue with Lorella, tell her that I *was* broken, so it did not matter who knew about it. My cane was all the proof one needed. And beyond my physical weakness, there was the part of me inside that was broken, the missing piece of me that used to be human.

And yet. I was touched by her kindness, even more so when she reached out and clasped my hands in hers. I expected many terrible things in the court of the fay, but I never expected a friend. And maybe there was something to what she said.

"People love to believe what they want to be true," I finally said, thinking back to my days of schemes and cons. "I used to convince people all sorts of things were true." And in a moment of honesty, I told Lorella a bit about my past, about who I was before I met Casper and went to the palace. Instead of disapproving, Lorella seemed impressed. In a strange way, her reaction made me feel proud.

"You already know the importance of a good story. That will be a good skill for you to have here."

"I hadn't thought of it that way, but I suppose you're right. This whole time I've been so convinced about what I can't do, I've forgotten what I can," I admitted. A small fire reignited in me, one that had gone out the moment I had drank the sitano. Elrik might have poisoned me, but he hadn't killed me.

"It seems my niece was a master of disguise even before coming to court," Lorella added.

"Niece? Right. I keep forgetting that you're my aunt, you don't look much older than me."

"I was born much later than my siblings."

"Do you have many?" I asked. "It feels strange to think I have family I don't know about." I recalled the cluster of white-haired, blue-eyed faeries that had stood near the queen during my audience with her.

"Five," Lorella told me. "Two girls, the twins Rosertina and Fabritsa, and my brothers Cosimo, Pietrael, and Valente." Lorella frowned. "It was six, of course, before Soren died. And I am sure they will want to get to know you."

I let out a short laugh. "You are the only one here who has been at all interested in getting to know me." I didn't mention my evening with Marasina.

Drusia snorted. "What about me?"

I smiled. "My apologies. You, Corine, and *Drusia*," I amended.

A slight golden blush rose to Lorella's cheeks. "My brothers and sisters will come around . . ." She stared at the ground, uncomfortable. "I believe they are waiting to see if you make it through the challenge first."

"Ah, so they are waiting to see if I am worthy of knowing?"

Lorella gave a helpless shrug. "I can see if they could be convinced to meet sooner. Though to be honest, as the youngest and a bastard, they really prefer not to have much to do with me either."

I shook my head. "Don't bother." I reached out for her hand. "True family is there for you no matter what. They don't make you prove yourself worthy of their love."

Lorella smiled at that. "Come, let us look at the rest of the market," she said, rising. I followed, feeling slightly better from the short rest.

"You still haven't told me what this does," I said, pulling out the gray sea glass. "Or why it feels so . . ." I searched for the right words but couldn't find anything adequate, "strange."

"Sorry, I forget you are unfamiliar with tokens," Lorella said as we headed back to the tents. The night was growing darker, and I noticed small floating lights moving around the courtyard overhead, adding a soft illumination to the creatures below. The smell of jasmine permeated the evening air. It felt like something out of a dream.

"That glass is infused with tidal magic. It will help you to summon your magic. Tidal magic calls to other magic."

"What do you mean infused?"

"Princess doesn't even know of infusing? But how does she pay for things?" Drusia, who had been walking behind us with her sister, interjected, and started tittering till Lorella gave her a sharp look which silenced her.

"We use such tokens as our currency."

"Your money?"

"I guess you could say that. I've heard humans trade metal coins because they don't have magic," Lorella said, sounding incredulous at the concept. "But in the fay realms, we trade tokens that are infused with magic; they can be traded for goods or services or other tokens. As part of the Magia Viveralis, you and I can infuse tokens with life magic."

I was intrigued with the system, my desire to summon my magic even stronger knowing I would practically be able to create my own money. I could see why Lorella would think it strange that humans traded coins, but almost immediately I saw a problem. "But what about fay without magic?" I asked, darting a look back at Drusia and Corine behind us. "You said only noble fay have magic, or at least they have the most of it."

"That's true, and we can make the most powerful tokens. But a lot of lesser fay have some level of magic, and even those that have none can earn boons of their own."

"Boons?"

"If a fay does a job for the higher fay, works in the palace or goes on a quest, they will be given boons, or favors. Many take the form of infused tokens." Lorella glanced up. "We need to hurry. The market will be closed soon."

I followed her gaze to see that the evening sky had darkened significantly, only a pale lightness in the west remained of the sunset. "And then what happens?"

"Evening dances. If there is a revel, it will begin at sundown."

I thought about the upcoming revel and grew quiet. That was when Valente would challenge me for a throne I didn't even want. I was about to ask Lorella for details about what happens during such festivities when she grew still, staring at someone in the crowd of bustling fay.

10

"Pel!" Lorella waved to get his attention.

A tall faerie in an oak-brown cloak and golden hair stilled, before slowing and turning around. Pel's sharp, green eyes slid past Lorella to land on me. A war of emotions kept me rooted in place. For an instant, I relived my last encounter with Pel, taking the mirror from him to see what his brother and the cursed sitano did to me. I pressed my thumb against Casper's signet ring till I felt the rose engravings imprint into my flesh.

Remembering that Casper was still locked in a prison filled me with a fiery desire to hurt Pel.

Ignorant of my struggle, Lorella ran up to him, wrapping her arms around him in a warm embrace before releasing him. Her smile radiated joy, though Pel barely seemed to acknowledge her, so often did he glance back at me. Lorella persisted in chatting with Pel, words that I couldn't hear this far from them. I turned away, walking as fast as I could manage.

I hadn't gone far before a hand wrapped around my shoulder, pulling me around. I turned, seeing Pel's eyes searching my face.

"How do you fare, Nor? Do you need anything for the pain?"

I sneered. I didn't want his false kindness. "I am surviving, despite you and your kin," I snapped. I gritted my teeth together, flushed with hatred. "You are a monster and you've made me into one."

Pel's eyes went cold, and he suddenly resembled his brother. "I offered you so many chances. You could have chosen me."

"I think everyone is a bit tense—" Lorella started, but I waved her off, stepping closer to Pel.

"Get your hand off me, or I swear by the Holy Family I will use your true name for something dreadful."

Pel jerked his hand back, as if my skin burned him. *Good*, I thought, though I felt a pang of guilt thinking about the first time I had used his name, when I had forced him to burn down his own camp. *He deserved it*, I reminded myself. If not for him, I would still be human and Casper would be king, safe in Reynallis, not a prisoner of the fay. I stepped away from Pel.

"I should have seen you for the selfish creature you are that first day in the woods," Pel said, grimacing.

"And I should have let the bandits murder you," I shot back.

"Then I wouldn't have had to save your hide in the tower."

"And I should have let you rot in the dungeon!" Somehow Pel and I had gotten closer during our yelling match. I stood a breath away from his face, beautiful, but radiating with fury. I wanted to smack him.

"I should never have contradicted my queen on your behalf."

"Both of you stop!" Lorella cried, getting between us and pushing us apart. I let Drusia pull me away from Pel as I tried to calm my rapid breaths. "You are causing a scene." And indeed, faeries around the market were staring at us. "Maybe you two should go somewhere you can have a civilized conversation."

I scoffed. "I have no desire to speak with spies." I turned and stormed back into the market, desperately needing space away from Pel. I allowed myself to get lost in the sea of multicolored tents, trying to distract myself with the strange wares, but they did not hold the same fascination for me that they had earlier in the evening.

"Princess, we should go back to Lady Lorella."

I spun around to see Drusia, trailing my skirts. "Go away."

Drusia pulled a face. "Lady Lorella asked me to watch after you."

"I don't need watching like some helpless child," I snapped, plowing deeper into the market. In truth, I wanted to be alone, back in my room, but I would have to pass back by Pel and Lorella to reach the entrance to the interior of the palace, and by the Mother's maids, I was not ready to see Pel again.

"On a mission, little faerie?" A tall, slender faerie with dark crimson skin stepped in front of me. His features were mostly masked by his hooded cloak, but he raised one deep red hand to stop me.

"It's no business of yours." I tried to step around him, but he mirrored my steps, blocking any escape.

"But I don't think you've found what you want at the market yet." He gave a small bow. "Are you still looking, Princess?"

"I'm not looking for anything." I started to turn, ready to face Pel and Lorella if it got me away from this unnerving creature. His interest in me was gnawing on already frayed nerves.

"So the princess does not wish to be human again?" His words were barely more than a whisper, but they rang in my ears, freezing me to the spot. I turned back to him.

"What do you mean?"

He glanced around, as though wary someone would overhear us. "Come." Then he was walking away from me, his steps quick and silent. Despite an uneasy feeling in the pit of my stomach, I followed, keeping sight of his black cloak as he swept into a small cove of trees away from the bustle of the market.

Alarm bells rang in my head. I should not be alone with an unknown fay, but I was not far from the stalls. If I screamed, the faeries at the market would hear me. I smothered my anxiety. What if he knew of a way I could become human? I would pay any price to be myself again.

"For the most discerning customers." He held out his hand. In his palm were three dark green berries, round and glossy, each no bigger than a blueberry.

"What are those?" I asked, leaning in to study the fruit.

"Piro berries. Very rare. Very precious. Found only on one plant that grows at the bottom of the Duset Sea. They will turn you back to human."

I wanted to believe him, wanted to believe there was a way out of Magnomel for me and back to my home. But I had acted rashly before, and it had nearly killed me. I pulled my gaze away from the berries and up to the faerie's face. His eyes were entirely black and impossible to read.

"And how do I know you are telling the truth? If they are so valuable, why don't you have a tent in the market?"

The faerie laughed, a dry sound like crushed leaves. "Do you truly think this sort of magic would be allowed at the court? I would expect the broken princess to know the hate Queen Marasina feels toward humans."

I ignored the broken princess remark. "How do I know I can trust you?"

Again, the brittle, dry laugh. "I know enough to know that you would give up the Magnomel throne to become human again. My source told me that you might be interested in my piro berries. They will take away your fay features. Erase the effects of the sitano."

The idea of becoming my human self again, whole and healthy, was so strong that I didn't realize I was reaching out for the berries until the faerie yanked his hand back, his arm and the berries hidden in the folds of his cloak. I felt an almost physical pull to get the berries from him. I had not checked myself as I should have, the need reading plainly on my face.

"But, if you cannot trust me, I shall take my wares elsewhere." He started toward the market when I grabbed his arm, holding him back. I was not going to give up my one chance to be human again.

"I'll take them," I said, desperate to hold the piro berries.

The faerie smiled, his thin lips stretched over sharp teeth, as he held out an empty hand. "Payment," he demanded.

I was about to object, tell him I didn't have any coin, when I remembered the sea glass trinket. With some hesitation, I pulled the gray glass from my pocket and handed it over. The pull I felt from the glass left me the moment I dropped it in the faerie's waiting hand. The faerie held up the glass, examining it for a long time. I started to worry he wouldn't deem it enough, but eventually he nodded, slipping the glass into his cloak and holding out the three berries. I snatched them from him.

"Eat them soon. Kept out of seawater for too long, and they will lose all their power," the faerie warned. He gave me a short bow. "Pleasure to trade with you." And before I could respond, he had slipped back into the Dusk Market, disappearing into the crowd.

I examined the small berries. They were soft to the touch, reminding me of fish eggs, and they smelled of salt and seaweed. Already, they were starting to dry out on my fingers, their glossy emerald surfaces beginning to dull into a matte green. How long did I have? The safest thing to do would be to wait till after Elrik showed me how to get to the Aqueno Prison. I could take them once I was alone and return to the Aqueno Prison and free Casper. But what if they were too dried out by then and no longer worked? I couldn't give up my one chance to be human again.

I popped all three berries into my mouth. They squirted a salty-sour liquid when I bit into them, their skin bursting between my teeth. I swallowed quickly, the tart aftertaste lingering on my tongue. I closed my eyes, trying to detect any difference in myself, but I felt none. Opening my eyes, I studied my hands, but they still had the copper sheen that marked them as fay. I wished I had asked the faerie how long the berries took to work. Then again, maybe I had just been swindled, my desire to be human so great that it made me an easy mark.

Frustrated, I started back down to find Lorella, hoping she was no longer with Pel. I felt dread having to explain that I had bartered away the token she had acquired for me. I had only taken two steps when a sharp pain speared through my side. I doubled over as another spasm twisted my stomach. I tried to cry out, but another stab of pain brought me to my knees and had me retching on the ground. I vomited my last meal, but the heaving didn't stop, even when I could only produce foamy spittle. I cried as my stomach again contracted, the sharp pain feeling like a knife in my gut.

My breathing became choked, and I tasted blood in my mouth. I tried calling out, but I had no air. My throat was closing up, even as my stomach shook with the need to vomit again. My jaw locked shut and my eyes bulged. Black spots dotted my vision as panic set in. I clawed at my throat as I went blind.

I was dying.

Hands closed around me. Long arms held me down, even as I convulsed against them. Strong fingers pried open my mouth and I heard a pop as my jaw was forced open. A tangy, thick liquid poured into my throat before the hand closed my mouth, keeping it closed despite my body's need to wretch again.

"*Annullaris sange.*"

My throat loosened as the liquid tingled in my mouth, easily slipping down into my stomach. The spasms of pain ceased, my body limp and desperate for air. The hands released me and I gasped, sucking in the cool evening air. All I could do was breathe, greedy for air that had been denied to my starved lungs. My vision returned, and I found myself lying on my back, staring at the darkening sky.

Four heads stared down at me. Lorella, Drusia, and Corine wore matching concern. Pel stared at me hard, his lips pressed into a tight white line with barely suppressed anger. All my energy had seeped out of me, leaving me depleted on the ground.

"Nor, how are you feeling?" Lorella's voice was soothing, soft with worry.

"What. Happened?" Pel's words were clipped, each one pulled from his grimace.

"Piro berries," I whispered, my throat raw from vomiting. The stinging heat of the sitano was again burning in my bones, but the pain felt like nothing compared to what I had just endured.

Lorella gasped, putting her hand over her mouth. Corine shook her head, and Drusia flew in nervous circles above us. Pel was now radiating fury.

"You stupid, ignorant girl! Why would you try to poison yourself?" Bits of spittle flecked out with his words.

I struggled to sit up, feeling too vulnerable lying on the ground. Lorella and Corine helped me, supporting my weight. "I wasn't trying to poison myself. I was told they would turn me human."

"Oh Nor," Lorella said, her voice thick with pity.

A range of emotions played across Pel's face as he flushed russet and his hands fisted tightly by his sides. He looked like he might explode. It was almost comical to see the cool, calm faerie I knew so overwhelmed. Almost.

"Do you have any idea how toxic piro berries are?" Pel spoke slowly, emphasizing every word as though speaking to a child.

"I do now," I grumbled. My relief at not dying was being quickly eaten away by the irritation at myself for being so foolish. I should have known better than to trust a strange faerie with a promise that sounded too good.

"Let's get you back to your room," Lorella suggested, her gaze darting around the market. I noticed that every faerie had paused whatever they were doing to stare at us, their feline eyes and sharp teeth making me feel like hunted prey.

I nodded, and Lorella and Corine helped me to my feet while Drusia picked up my cane. Pel marched behind us, his ire taken out on every step. None of us spoke till we were back in my room. Lorella made sure I got to my bed before examining the hole that used to be my doorway. Drusia tucked me into bed as though I were a child, and I let her, too tired to bat her away. Pel silently stood off to the side, his arms crossed and his expression angry.

"What happened here?" Lorella asked, tentatively brushing the scorched wood around the doorway with one finger.

"I believe Valente booby trapped my door."

"Why don't I fix this for you?" Lorella said, reaching for the doorway and muttering fay words I couldn't make out.

"And now he is sending assassins after you." Pel glared at me as though I were to blame.

"Excuse me?" My bed was soft and inviting, and my exhausted body wanted to rest.

"No one accidentally barters piro berries. They are deadly and forbidden here. You are lucky Drusia was following you."

I looked over at the nervously flying green faerie. I did not relish the idea that I had been watched, but I would be dead if not for her quick action.

"I guess I did need minding. Thank you," I muttered. Drusia landed and bowed quickly to me, her skin turning a shade of darker jade. I heard rustling from the doorway. Lorella was summoning branches and vines, which were growing over the hole, forming a door.

"Had she not alerted us so quickly, I would not have—" Pel's words were harsh, but as I faced him, he quickly wiped his palm over his eyes.

"What did you do?" My recollection of the events was blurred with the panic I felt from dying.

"Blood magic to nullify the poison."

The taste of his blood in my mouth came back to me, coppery and thick, but mixed with the relief from being able to breathe again. The respite from my body battling against itself. I laid back against the pillows, my stomach still sore from all the heaving. I didn't want to think about the implications, that I had tasted Pel's blood, that I had come so close to death, but above all, that Pel had again saved my life.

"Thank you." The words were little more than a whisper. When Pel's face softened into something akin to relief, he reminded me how stunningly beautiful he was, the strange yet sweet faerie I had rescued in the woods so many months ago. But I would not be swayed by his pretty face. He had betrayed me, used me to spy on Casper, and ultimately, to wage a battle on the Rose Palace. But I was too weary to manage the conflicting feelings toward the faerie boy in front of me.

"Nor, you cannot ever be human again." Pel advanced toward the bed, kneeling so he was eye level to me. There was desperation in his voice.

"I won't try piro berries again," I croaked. His sincerity was unnerving.

"I need you to know that there is no way for you to become human again, because you never were human." Pel's words sliced my heart, but he continued. "You were glamoured to look human. That doesn't mean you were human. The sitano revealed your true form."

"Are you mocking me?" I demanded, indignation bubbling up in me. "I nearly died this evening. No need to pour salt in the wound."

Pel reached for my hand, but thought better, pulling his hand back. He stared at me with earnest eyes, a naked plea in his voice. "No Nor, I wouldn't do that. But I don't want you taken in again. I don't want to see you wasting your life and risking your safety looking for a way to be human. You need to know and accept what you are. This is your life now." Pel's eyes bore into me, and I realized that he knew me well enough to know that I would do anything to get home.

"I can't abandon Casper." The words so true I didn't even think about them. More than turning myself human or escaping Magnomel, I owed Casper his safety and freedom.

Pel closed his eyes for a long breath, some internal struggle pulling his lips into a frown. Finally, he opened his eyes. "Nor, I think you could be happy in Magnomel. We can make a good life for you here." He said the last part so quietly, I almost missed it. This time he did reach for my hand. I wanted to correct him, tell him I had no plans to make Magnomel my home, when Lorella came back into the room. Her bright eyes immediately landed on Pel's hands wrapped around mine, and something in her dimmed. I pulled my hand away, shoving it under the covers.

"I fixed your doorway," Lorella said, her voice a bit strained.

"Thank you," I said, turning to look at the doorway. Indeed, fresh branches had grown over the blackened limbs, forming a sort of door of rough bark and young, green shoots.

"It was nothing," Lorella said, though her eyes were fixed on Pel. He didn't seem to notice, still waiting for my next response.

"No, I mean it," I said. "I cannot tell you how much I appreciate the security of a door."

"One can never be too careful in this place," Lorella agreed, her eyes meeting mine. I wondered how dangerous the life of a royal bastard was if she so quickly could make doors and barriers.

"You all have helped me so much," I admitted. "But I need rest." And it wasn't a complete lie. But more than relief from the physical pain, I needed respite from the conflicting emotions about Pel swirling in my head. It had been easier to hate him before he saved my life. And most importantly, I needed them gone before Elrik showed up.

"Of course," Lorella said quickly, "you must be exhausted. Corine, Drusia, we should leave the princess to rest." Lorella lingered by the doorway as the green and purple faeries went to join her.

"I can stay while you sleep. Make sure you are undisturbed," Pel said, his strange eyes intense, but unreadable.

"I think you should go too," I said, but I tried to soften my words. "I have a lot to process."

Pel nodded, and I ignored the flicker of sadness as he stood. "Nor, you are beautiful like this." He said the words so softly I nearly missed them, giving me a small bow before joining Lorella by the door. "Lorella, tonight's feast has only begun judging by the sky. May I escort you down?"

Lorella beamed as she accepted Pel's offer and took his proffered hand. After promising to have food sent up to me later, she left arm in arm with Pel, her faerie maids following behind them.

Finally alone, I sat on my bed, watching the door and waiting for Elrik. Soon, very soon, I would see Casper. I would figure out a way to set things right. It was enough to push away thoughts of Pel, of how he had surprised me once again.

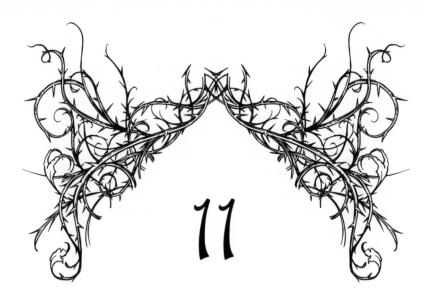

11

It was well past midnight when Elrik arrived. I had begun to wonder if he would arrive at all. When he finally appeared at my door, dressed in black and wearing a cloak of deep forest green, he tossed me a second cloak of the same hue before pulling the hood of his over his golden hair.

"Come with me, my dear," he said with a wink before turning on his heel, down the winding pathway. I quickly donned the cloak, camouflage from prying eyes, before hurrying after him into the dark.

Elrik led me out of the palace, down an unfamiliar path of twisted branches, one that became narrower as we reached the base of the tree. He moved like a shadow, and I did my best to match his silent steps. Once or twice my cane hit a bump in the branch path and I nearly fell, swearing under my breath. He only chuckled, a quick, breathy sound. The thief I had once been would have been ashamed.

Once outside, the path wrapped around the mammoth tree, seamlessly becoming a gnarled walkway of roots that led to the lake.

I started toward one of the glass boats when Elrik grabbed my shoulder.

I jumped away from the touch, a jolt of fear coursing through me. Elrik smiled, drinking in the power he had, letting his hand linger a moment longer before slowly releasing me. All he said was, "This way."

I was about to ask what he meant, but he already was dropping something small into the water. I caught a glimpse of a pale piece of sea glass, but it was soon swallowed by the lake.

"What's going on?" But as soon as I asked, I saw. Where the glass had fallen into the water, it had started to churn, a ripple at first, but soon a vortex that formed a hollow, dry pathway down into the lakebed. The root trail continued into the lake path, winding steeply downward.

My mouth hung open as I stared at the strange magic before me. Elrik walked down the root road, into the newly formed path inside the lake as though it were nothing new. A few paces in, he turned back to me.

"Are you coming?"

I had a momentary vision of going far down the path only to have the water flood over me. I shivered, hating the next steps I had to take. But I thought of Casper, trapped in some dark cell underground, *under the lake*, and I followed Elrik.

"Nothing is ever simple or ordinary here, is it?" I grumbled.

"Then it wouldn't be the thing of myths and legends to mere humans," Elrik said, not turning back to me, but I heard the amusement in his voice. "You don't have to do this, little Elenora."

I ignored him, gritting my teeth and walking down the trail cutting into the lake.

The path continued downward, so narrow I had to walk behind Elrik the whole time. The air grew cool and moist as we descended, leaving a bitter, briny taste on my tongue. To either side of the trail were walls of dark water, smooth as glass. I wondered how these uncanny walls would look in the light of day, if one could see the fish and turtles and whatever other creatures resided in the lake. I resisted the urge to touch the water walls, terrified of doing anything that might disrupt the spell and send inky waves crashing over us.

The steep steps made my legs ache and burn. Though I wanted to stop, to take a moment to rest, I knew better than to show any weakness in front of Elrik. I gripped my cane tighter and continued following him down.

The light from the bright moon and illuminated windows of the Forest Court penetrated only the top of the lake, a blurred illumination that created eerie, moving shadows through the water. By the time we reached the bottom of the path, the light from the Forest Court had been completely swallowed by the water.

I nearly tripped when the root ended, not expecting flat stone beneath my feet. I landed hard, my cane hitting the rock with a thump that echoed loudly. I inhaled sharply, the air cold and musty in my chest.

We had reached some structure, though it was too dark for me to see more than a large door, quarried of thick, gray stone that still shone with droplets of water. Elrik pulled out a short dagger, making a shallow cut in his palm, murmuring words too soft for me to hear as he pressed his palm to the door. It swung open to a black void. We walked in.

Squinting in the darkness, I surveyed my surroundings. The walls were dark stone, but I couldn't make out much more in the poor light, even with my keener fay sight. The stones were slick with wet moss when I reached out to them. Elrik pulled an unlit torch off the wall, which immediately ignited in his hand.

"Hurry up," Elrik said, not looking back as he walked further into the gloom. I followed the glow of the torch, the light from the outside completely gone. I focused on Elrik's back, his gleaming dragonfly wings, and not the distorted shadows we cast on the walls, grotesque forms that moved and flickered with the torchlight.

The corridor came to an abrupt halt in front of a large, metal door. It radiated a deeper cold, which settled into my bones, making me shiver. Elaborate etchings covered every inch of the door, including a large lock that held it closed. Elrik pulled out a key from around his neck.

"No magic to open it?" I asked, surprised that the prison was protected by something so mundane.

"This door is made of iron," Elrik said, the key clicking in the lock. "There have been fay prisoners before. My queen ensured no magic could be used here."

"And Queen Marasina gave you the key?"

Elrik snorted. "I am merely borrowing it."

The door swung open, and I gasped. I had expected cells similar to the dungeon at the Rose Palace, but this was far from that. There was only one room, and it was vast, an underground chamber, dimly lit by several glowing orbs. Stalagmites rose from the floor and stalactites dripped from the ceiling, which itself was as impressive as it was strange. Where I expected a ceiling of stone or even dirt or roots, there was a clear dome, as though made of glass. I could make out sleek schools of silver fish and large black rays swimming above us. The entire cavern was cast in a sickening greenish sheen. I felt a mix of awe and dread at the terrible splendor before me.

I wanted to ask how it was possible, but at that moment I saw Casper. Wrapped in a tattered blanket, he was in the far corner of the cavern, sitting on a large, flat stone. He was staring at Elrik and me, his expression wary, not saying anything.

"Little kingling, I bring you a visitor." There was cold glee in Elrik's voice. Before Elrik moved aside, he added, "Now, remember our deal." I heard the threat in his words, though he was staring at Casper instead of me.

"I know," I said, pushing him away from me so I could get to Casper. "Casper, it's me," I blurted out, unable to stop myself as I made my way toward him.

Upon hearing my voice, Casper rose, straining to see me and rubbing his eyes as though he couldn't quite trust them. "Nor?" My name sounded uncertain on his lips. He started toward me. Ignoring the pain, I raced across the stone floor. My heart was pounding so hard I thought it might burst. I was almost at him, when he halted, a horror filling his face. "What did they do to you?"

I froze.

"So, the rumors are true. You're not human," he said, stepping back, putting distance between us.

For a moment, I could only stare at Casper, too shocked to do anything, the joy at seeing him seeping away. Hurt and resignation warred within me.

I reached out to him, only to watch him flinch back. His face was chalky in the dull light, his chiseled features now gaunt, with dark circles under his eyes. I looked down, my own hand glowing slightly from the faerie blood in my veins.

"I'm still me," I insisted, but the words felt more like a plea. From the door, I heard Elrik laugh.

Casper took a tentative step toward me. He reached his hand out, gently brushing my cheek. His fingers were so cold. I placed my hand over his, hoping to warm him.

"Careful now," Elrik said behind me. I ignored him, but Casper yanked his hand away, leaving me aching for his touch.

"This is what the poison did to you?"

I nodded, unable to speak as tears pricked behind my eyes. I blinked hard and bit my lip.

Casper frowned, as though seeing something especially unpleasant. He looked away from me then, stared at Elrik with sharp, dark eyes. His hands clenched in fists by his sides, and I could feel the resentment radiating off him. "Elrik told me that you are a faerie princess now, a great fortune and destiny ahead of you."

I whirled on Elrik, who remained motionless by the door, a statue of a faerie in a forgotten, underwater world. His eyes glowed in the gloomy light, reminding me of something predatory. He stared at Casper with blazing amber eyes, but did not say a word.

"What did you say?" I demanded.

Elrik shrugged, slowly looking away from Casper, focusing on me. "You see how he feels about who you are now. About who you truly always have been." Elrik's voice was soft and dark. "Your little king looks at you as though you are a monster."

Elrik's words hit my heart, harsh because I had thought the very same thing. I wanted Elrik to be wrong, wanted Casper to contradict him, to convince me he still loved me, still wanted me, but Casper said nothing.

"Do you see a monster?" I finally asked Casper, bracing myself.

"Your home is here, Nor." Casper's words ripped out a piece of my heart. Last time he spoke of home, it was the Rose Palace, and it was the two of us going back there, together.

"I don't belong here. I don't want to be a faerie princess. I want to be with you." The words spilled out of me. But stuck in my throat was what I really wanted to say, *tell me you still love me, even as I am now. Tell me it doesn't matter and that we will find a way together.* I silently pleaded with him, praying my eyes could say what my mouth could not.

"I can't be—" Casper trailed off, scrunching his eyes closed as though in pain. "I no longer wish to be with you, Elenora."

"I don't believe you." But even as I tried to convince myself, tried to push away this new truth, I knew it was too late. Here was the terrible reality that I had feared from the moment Pel handed me a mirror, showing me what an unnatural thing I had become.

"It's for the best," Casper stared at the floor, unable to meet my eyes.

I swallowed hard, feeling the sharp pain sink into my heart, more agonizing than anything the sitano could ever do to me. But I owed Casper his freedom, and that was not contingent on his love.

"I'm still getting you out of here. Let's go."

"No," Elrik said.

I turned to him, my feelings out of control. I was desperate and scared, and I knew Elrik would take advantage of that, use that against me, but I was out of options. I had no brilliant plans, no clever deceptions. All I could do was pay my debt to Casper and get out of his life. I no longer cared about the consequences. I no longer had a home to return to.

"Let me free him. What is it to you if he rots under your lake or if he is gone? I will offer you another trade." The words were bitter on my lips, but I didn't take them back.

"I would love to make another deal with you, little bird, but you have not even fulfilled our first bargain." The corner of Elrik's lips lifted in the hint of a smile. "And besides, it is not necessary. The little kingling has already been promised his freedom. If you were to release him now, my queen would certainly think treachery was at work, and likely drag the kingling back here."

"Is that true?" I spun back to Casper, feeling suddenly lightheaded. Had Casper been promised his freedom this whole time? Was he already counting down the weeks and days till he could leave Magnomel? Till he could leave me?

Casper continued to stare at the floor, though his jaw was clenched tight. "Everything Elrik says is true. I will leave Magnomel in the winter. Alone. Please Elenora, if you care for me, do not get involved."

I stepped back as though hit. I felt my pulse in my ears, though I was sure my heart was broken beyond repair. I wanted to fight, to tell Casper that I needed him, that I loved him, that I wanted to build a life with him. But the devastating truth was that he did not want any of that, not with me. I was a liar and cheat. I had betrayed him and cost him his freedom. And now I was a broken monster. He had every right to despise me.

I pulled his signet ring off my finger. The gold was warm, the only piece of home I had in this strange world, but like Casper, it was not mine to keep. I offered him the ring, but he only stared at the floor, refusing to take it. I wanted to scream, to yell at him that he had no right to refuse this ring if he was taking away everything it represented. Instead, I gently set it down by his feet and turned away.

In several hasty strides, I was out the door of the Aqueno Prison. Pain flashed up my legs as I forced them to move quickly, but I refused to slow down. I was keeping myself together by the barest thread, so close to the edge, but not wanting to lose my composure in front of anyone, least of all Elrik. I started through the watery pathway, no longer caring about the danger. I heard the lock click, and Elrik's steps beside me. I refused to look at him.

"I am much better for you than him."

I turned, pulling my arm back to slap Elrik when his own shot out, grabbing my wrist.

"We are liars Nor, both of us. We lie and steal and cheat, but we can be honest with each other. You don't need someone who will be so cruel to you. I see you and I want you exactly as you are. I know your lies and your deception, and I know what it's like to deceive for a living. I understand you in a way he never could."

"Let me go."

"You will come around to my way of thinking." And to my relief, Elrik released my wrist.

I ran the rest of the way out of the water pathway, only stopping when the pain made it impossible. I stumbled up the Forest Court hallways to my room, tripping as tears blurred my vision, and falling as the sitano burned in my bones. I tried to focus on my throbbing limbs, wishing my physical discomfort was enough to block out the agony in my heart.

I threw myself onto my bed so my face was deep in the pillows, their stuffing of leaves and moss muffling my screams. I screamed till I was hoarse. The pillow was soaked with tears and snot and my silent screams.

Long after my voice had left, I continued crying into the pillow. Every time I moved my hand to wipe at my face, I saw my glowing fay skin and sobbed again, cursing my body for betraying me, for becoming something that wasn't human. I cursed Elrik, the sitano, Pel, Marasina and the whole fay court. Casper telling me he no longer wanted me was a pain that ate me away from the inside, breaking me in a way even the sitano had not managed. I had lost my brothers, Casper, my home, and even my humanity. I felt empty. I had lost everything.

I awoke late the next day feeling sick and dehydrated. I had cried most of the night, unsure when unconsciousness finally took over. Even sleep had not been a relief. I dreamed of Casper, his charming smile turning into something cruel as he told me I was no longer human, all while I begged him to say it wasn't true.

Drusia flew in through the window around midmorning, but I scared her away quickly enough, screaming for her to leave until she finally did.

Lorella stopped by briefly, knocking on my door, but left without much fight when I yelled through the door, demanding to be left alone. I admitted no one that day, though Drusia must have had the courage to return, as there was a plate of fruit and cheese outside my door. But I had no appetite. I laid in bed, my mind racing for a solution, a way out, a fix. I had always found an answer before, but this time my mind drew blank after blank. I was finally facing a problem I couldn't scheme my way out of.

By late evening, I felt resigned to my fate, or perhaps simply numb with exhaustion. I could almost feel grateful that Casper would be all right, even if I could never see him again, though thinking about that made pain surge in my chest. At one point, I considered asking Casper to relay a message from me to my brothers, telling them I was fine, even if it was a lie. But when I thought about what I would say to Casper, tears pricked at my eyes, even long after I thought I was too dried out to cry.

I pushed the thought away.

It was late into the night, well past midnight, when a knock came from my door. I hadn't been able to sleep. When my yells for them to go away didn't stop the *tap tap tap* on my door, I finally forced myself to get out of bed and see who was there.

I rested my fingers on the branches of the door. "Who is it?" I had no desire for another visit from Elrik.

"It's me." I heard Pel's voice on the other side. "Can I come in?"

"And if I tell you to go away?" I asked, but there was no force in my voice. I was too worn out.

"Then I shall wait here till you change your mind."

Too tired to argue, I opened the door.

"It's late."

"Late enough to discourage prying eyes. Most of the court is still at tonight's feast. May I come in?" He smiled then, a tentative, hopeful smile that I'd seen on him before, back when he wanted me to run away with him, away from the Rose Palace. Back when I thought him a friend who might one day be more. It reminded me how exquisitely handsome he was. I carefully opened the door and gestured for him to come inside.

He settled into one of the elegantly carved chairs and tension radiated from him. Not bothering to pull up a chair for myself. I leaned on my cane, meeting his summer-green eyes.

"My brother told me he took you to the Aqueno Prison."

"And Casper wants nothing to do with me now that I've turned into this." I gestured at my face, thinking about how my brown eyes were now gold, with strange, catlike pupils, my teeth too sharp, and my skin strangely glowing. I missed everything that made me human, even my straw-colored hair, now turned white. "I'm a monster." The heat had left my voice, leaving only the bitter ring of truth and resentment.

"Your king is a fool if he does not want you now."

I let out a small laugh, devoid of humor. "And yet I still love him."

Pel studied me a moment longer, but finally he said, "I want to show you your father."

For a moment I was at an utter loss for words. I flashed back to a time long ago, a memory of my father as he said his goodbyes to us before leaving for the war. Had he actually returned to the fay realms, living here in secret this whole time? Sensing my confusion, Pel clarified.

"There is a portrait of him in the royal gallery. I thought it might help you feel . . ." he trailed off before finding the right words. "Maybe if you saw your father from when he lived with us, you would feel less like a monster. And perhaps you can start to see the Forest Court as your home."

The brief burst of hope within me withered and died, the pang of losing my father feeling cut afresh. Torn between wanting to send Pel away and a new curiosity to see this part of my father's life, anything to feel a bit closer to the family I used to have, I gave in.

"Show me."

Pel said nothing as I threw on a cloak, patiently waiting for me by the door. We headed down the hallway, our progress slow.

"My brother was wrong to do that to you," he said, looking at my cane, his usually soft voice made hard by something fiercer.

I stopped. "Are you upset that now I am one of your precious fay?" I asked.

"No. Sitano is a dangerous drug. It could have killed you, even with you being half fay."

"I know," I said in a tone that I hoped would end this line of conversation. I tried to avoid thinking about the blur of time after Elrik had forced me to take the drug. The time when the fever burned so brightly I was sure I would ignite and there would be nothing left of me but ash.

But I did survive, I reminded myself.

We walked in silence after that, down several hallways made of branches and roots, the walls a patchwork of leaves and vines. I was again struck by how different this place was from the Rose Palace, all marble and glass and stone. Despite the name, the roses were a motif, where here, plants *were* the palace. I tried to keep track of where we were going but didn't think I would be able to find my room again by the time Pel led me into a large chamber, high above the ground.

"Here it is," he said, gesturing that I should go inside. The room was large and long, lit by glowing crystals embedded into the vines that clung to the walls and ceiling, bathing the room in a cool, bluish glow. As I entered, I noticed that portraits hung along the walls in ornate frames. Stepping closer to the first one, I realized that the paintings were not hung, but rather the walls themselves had grown branches in intricate patterns that formed the frames for the paintings, holding them close to the walls. I reached out and gently touched the closest branch frame, my fingers running along the smooth, winding wood of the interlacing branches.

Though the light of the glowing stones was dim, I could clearly see the faeries in each of the portraits thanks to improved vision with my new fay eyes. I focused on the faces staring back at me. There were dozens of portraits in the room, each majestically staring ahead. It reminded me of the royal portraits in the Rose Palace, but those paintings all depicted the royals of Reynallis, humans with jet hair and dark eyes. Men and women holding roses and looking somehow both delicate and fierce. And there was the one of Casper, his handsome face seeming to smile at the onlooker. I remembered the way he smiled at me, a humor lighting up his eyes.

Don't think about him, I reminded myself.

He was as lost to me as my dead father. I focused on the faerie images in front of me. All the royals had a sharp beauty. I would have thought the artist was being generous had I not seen the living fay. I walked down the aisle of royals, their luminous skin glowing from the strange rock light. At the beginning of the hall, I recognized no one, though snow-white hair and sapphire cat eyes were common even with these ancestors.

"Can fay die of old age?" I asked.

"Indeed," Pel answered. "Though our lives are so much longer than humans, it can seem as though we are immortal."

"I see," I said, still staring at the portraits. A part of me felt relieved by his answer. I didn't want to die, but somehow knowing I would made me feel almost more human. But then again, I wasn't entirely fay. "What about half fay?"

Pel studied me for a long time before answering. "It varies. Some live as long as the fay, and others have short, human-like lives."

"How will I know which I am?"

Pel shrugged. "There is no way to know, at least not until decades have passed. Both fay and humans age at the same rate until their third or even forth decade. Aging for fay slows down at that point. You shall just have to live your life and let time tell."

My lip twitched up. Strange as it sounded, I liked his answer. If I didn't know, I could hold out hope that I was still somewhat human.

"Besides, if we fay never died, there would be no need for succession," Pel added, almost as an afterthought.

"I hadn't considered that," I admitted, walking between the portraits of royal fay.

Pel chuckled softly, but without malice. "Then you are the first heir who never has."

"It's not something I asked for," I said, but was only partially paying attention to him. I was reaching the point where I recognized the faeries on the wall. Marasina was there, painted in her silver armor, shining and fierce. In a portrait next to her was one of a faerie I didn't recognize, but its proximity to her made me certain it was her late husband. Unlike her, he wore no armor, but a cloak of forest green and a doublet underneath it of sunflower yellow. There was something familiar in his face.

"She replaced her portrait after King Velario was killed. She wasn't in armor in her original painting."

I was about to ask Pel more when I spied the next portrait. Displayed between the paintings of King Velario and Valente was my father. Though he looked so different from the man who raised me, I could tell it was him. My breath hitched as I felt my heart squeeze tight. His skin was paler with the illumination that came from golden fay blood, his ears reached up to points and his eyes were not round pupils, but slitted cat ones, but it was still him. His teeth were sharper, but his smile was still warm, as though he had a joke or a tale he could not wait to share.

I stared into his eyes, eyes that were the same deep blue I remembered. These were the eyes I gazed upon as a child, when he would tell stories by the fire, stories of strange and magical creatures. Stories of his own childhood, I now knew. I could almost hear him calling me to come inside after a day of riding our mill horses, his voice caramel and love.

"My little Nor, whatever shall I do with such a wild child like you? Can't you be sweet like your sister?" he once asked when I came home muddy from playing by the river.

But there was so much love in his voice that I simply beamed with pride and said, "No Papa. You need a wild child in case the faeries come for you. I will scare them away." Then I growled, pretending to be the mud monster I looked like.

My father didn't say anything for a moment, before he scooped me up in his strong arms, holding me close despite the mud. "I will never let that happen, my wonderful girl," he promised, holding me tight.

"Nor?"

I turned to Pel, but at his concerned expression I quickly pivoted away. I hadn't realized I was crying but now wiped furiously at my cheeks.

"I'm sorry, Nor. I thought seeing him would help you feel more at home here." Pel's voice was contrite, and I felt guilty that I ruined his kind gesture.

"I miss them. I miss them all so much," I confessed, thinking of everyone I had lost. My parents and sister were dead, my brothers unreachable and Casper gone as well. Even my own body was a stranger to me. I started crying harder, sobbing as I stared at the portrait of my father. Missing him and angry he kept all this from me, my heart crumbled from the loss.

Long arms wrapped around me, Pel pulling me close. I let him draw me in, crying into his chest until I was spent, until I had emptied as much pain as I could. As my tears dried, I felt calmer, a bit lighter for having let it all out. The whole time, Pel held me, not saying a word. This close, I could feel his heart beating in his chest, reminding me of the golden blood that ran in his veins. The same kind of blood that now ran in mine. I tried to inhale, wanting the forest smell that was Pel, but my nose was clogged from crying. I pushed back slightly, feeling very vulnerable after such a display.

"Here." Pel held out a handkerchief and I accepted it, rubbing at my eyes and blowing my nose.

I looked up at my father's painting. "The people I love the most keep leaving me." I thought again about Casper, staring at the floor as he exiled me from his life, my misery almost making me cry again. Instead, Pel reached for my hands, slender fingers intertwining with my own.

"This can be your true home, Nor. You are your true self now. And I won't leave you."

I focused on Pel's bright green eyes, staring so intensely at me. I closed my eyes, but I saw Casper's face, dark eyes and easy smile. *He doesn't want me*, I reminded myself. I couldn't shake the image of him, nor how much my heart ached. I was suddenly hotly angry at Casper, furious he would abandon me. I wanted to forget, wanted to be wanted, even if I wasn't loved. I leaned toward Pel, until he was a mere breath away. I took a deep breath, thinking how sweet it would be to get lost in a kiss, for a blissful moment of forgetting. I moved to close the space between us, but my lips met his fingers.

I opened my eyes. Pel gently lowered his hand but stepped away from me. Hurt and humiliation washed over me.

"I'm sorry, Nor—" Pel started.

"No, I misunderstood. I thought you wanted—" but I couldn't finish my sentence.

"I do want you, Nor."

I stared at Pel, bewildered.

"But it's clear your heart is elsewhere." There was no malice to his words, only a tinge of sadness.

"Casper doesn't want me," I said, hating the words.

"That is his loss," Pel said, his words gentle. "But I am not a distraction."

"That's not—"

"It's all right, Nor. I know you are hurting. And I will be here for you, as long as you want me by your side. But for now, I can only be your friend. At least that is all I can be until your heart doesn't long for someone else." With that, he reached for my hands, squeezing them in his.

We stood like that for a long time. Eventually, the humiliation and the anger drained from me, and I was left feeling exhausted, but also relieved. I hadn't truly wanted to kiss Pel, I had wanted to forget Casper, to get back at him for hurting me. But here, I had a friend, and that made me smile, even if it was a weak and watery one.

"Thank you, Pel."

13

Over the next week, I practiced my magic and waited to find out if Corine and Drusia could convince Alverdine to meet with me. Progress with my magic was painfully slow. I could call on my magic without assistance, but I could do little more than sprout a seed. When Lorella came by my rooms to tell me Alverdine would see me, I jumped at the chance to leave my rooms and take a break from the tedious practice of magic.

We took one of the glass boats across the lake to the forest beyond. The walk to Alverdine's cottage was not far. Afternoon light danced through branches, breaking onto the forest floor in patches of space between leaves. The trees were heavy with green leaves, and I wondered how long it would be till winter, till the leaves dropped and Casper was set free. I focused intensely on the path ahead, forcing myself to not think about Casper or the tear in my heart. I must have been on edge, because the sound of a twig snapping behind me made me jump. I whirled around, but only saw the path and the trees. After some time, the sisters stopped in front of a boulder off to the side of the path. It was a huge piece of stone, big as a small house and flecked with bits of moss.

"Here we are," Corine said, appraising the large stone.

"Your great-aunt lives in a rock?" I asked, feeling that was a stretch even for the fay.

"Our great-great-great-aunt," Drusia corrected me. "And of course she doesn't live in a rock. Don't be so foolish!"

"Drusia!" Corine snapped. Drusia pouted but didn't say more. Instead, she approached the boulder, hands out as though not sure where the stone lay. As she got closer, her hands passed right through the stone. I gasped, but Drusia kept feeling around. After a moment, she seemed to grasp something inside the stone. She pounded her hand against that internal wall before she turned back and smiled at us. "I found the door," she declared.

When nothing happened, I wondered if this was some fay prank. I was about to question Drusia when a creaking came from within the boulder. Materializing from inside the stone, a large door swung outward, gray stone on the outside and polished wood on the inside. My mouth dropped open as warm light poured from the interior of the boulder, which I saw was a room of a house. An old fay woman stepped out of the doorway.

"Who comes to my door?" the woman asked as she hobbled toward us. Her movements were slow and shaky, her gaunt frame bent with age.

"Auntie!" Drusia cried, and fluttered over to the woman, wrapping her in an embrace so tight that I feared for the frail woman.

"Drusia, love, what a pleasure to see you. And you, Corine," the woman said, disengaging herself from the green faerie. She did not seem in the least bothered by the crushing hug, rather she stood taller. "And you have brought me company," she added, noticing Lorella and myself.

"Alverdine, it has been too long," Lorella said as she took the woman's hand. "Your charms are clearly as strong as ever."

"You flatter me," Alverdine said, but she laughed lightly. Her laugh reminded me of the current of a river.

"We've brought you a princess, Auntie," Drusia cut in, pulling Alverdine's attention away from Lorella. "The newly established heir of the Forest Court."

Alverdine appraised me, and her studied gaze made me feel oddly exposed. "So you are Soren's daughter." I nodded. "You look like him, but with something human about you. You have much of Eva in your look, too."

My chest tightened. "You knew my mother?" I asked, my voice little more than a whisper.

Alverdine gave me a warm smile, one that made her face appear years younger. "Yes, I knew your mother. Your parents came to me for a glamour to keep your father safe in the human realm after they were expelled from the Forest Court. And I met her again each time she was with child," Alverdine added, giving me a meaningful look. "Did my magic hold in the human realm?"

A memory came to me. Right before my little brother Jacobie was born, my parents left us for several months and we were in the care of our grandfather, my mother's father. We were told that my parents were visiting distant relatives, though they offered little information as to whom those relatives were.

When they returned, my baby brother was with them. Being only nine at the time, I never thought much of it. But now, I understood that my parents must have come here.

With a jolt, I realized I must have also been born here.

"Your charms were strong in the human realm," I confirmed. "They are still strong," I added, thinking of my brothers.

"They should be. It was strong magic. I am surprised you were able to remove your glamour without my aid."

"Elrik forced her to take sitano. It burned it off," Drusia said before being shushed by her sister.

"No!" Alverdine said, horror written on her face as she came closer to examine mine. "That rash fool, he could have killed you."

"I know." I forced my voice to remain calm, though there was heat behind my words.

"I could have taken off that glamour. I have ways that don't involve such drastic damage." Alverdine focused on my moonstone cane, and I could feel her pity.

Sharp resentment bubbled up in me. I knew Elrik well enough to understand that not seeking out Alverdine was likely intentional on his part. He preferred me crippled if it meant I needed his protection. I gripped the handle of my moonstone cane tighter, my knuckles turning white.

"Well, come in, come in. I expect you wish to know about your parents." Alverdine took my free hand, carefully leading me into her home.

As I stepped inside, everything shifted. The area I was standing in was much larger than the boulder should have allowed. It was a vast chamber that felt more akin to a laboratory. Large windows were carved into the stone walls, shining light on the row upon row of shelves that lined the walls. Each shelf was piled high with bottles of every shape and color. There were tall, slim glass bottles in jewel tones, and there were short, fat bottles made from shells, some bottles of clear glass with strange liquids that shimmered and moved on their own. Bottles made of cut crystals sparkled in the light.

"Incredible," I breathed, taking in the room and its trove of treasures. "How did you—" I started to ask Alverdine, but surprise wiped away the rest of my question. Alverdine was no longer an old woman with deep lines; the faerie now had the smooth, eternal look that I saw in Marasina and the older court fay, though her skin glowed an icy blue. Her hair, no longer shot with gray, was a deep cobalt, and seemed to float around her. Her eyes, still kind, but without any clouding, stared at me. The corner of her mouth twitched in a smile, and I heard Drusia giggle.

"Do I look different to you, Princess? Be wary of believing your first sight in Magnomel. Your mother learned that quickly, and I'll reckon it saved her life more than once before she and the prince found their way out of the woods. Magia Illustraia is perhaps the simplest magic to see through if you know what to do. Other magics can be trickier to unravel." She began rummaging through various bottles and potions.

"Your parents came to me over the years for three boys and two girls. Now, are you Rilla or Elenora?" Her tone was casual, conversational, but hearing my sister's name stopped me midstep and squeezed the air from my lungs.

"Elenora," I said, my voice flat.

"How fares your sister?"

I shook my head.

The pain of losing Rilla, of losing my parents, was always ready to pierce my heart, no matter how many years passed. I could swear I smelled smoke, but it was only in my mind. The fires of the war were never far enough away. "My parents and Rilla died in the Southern War."

Alverdine frowned and I heard Lorella gasp. I turned away from them, from all the faeries, and pretended to study some bottles. I didn't want to see their looks of pity.

"Do you know what your parents paid for your father's glamour? For your glamour?"

The question was so unexpected I turned to Alverdine. "I hadn't thought about it," I admitted. "My father was a prince, the heir, so I guess he was wealthy." I paused, remembering the fay did not use coins, but that the nobles possessed most of the magic. "Wealthy in magic, I mean. Did he offer you a token with life magic?"

Alverdine chuckled. "Now what would an old faerie like me want with some silly life magic?" The reaction to Alverdine's comment was almost comical. Lorella looked horrified and the maids giggled.

"To grow some plants?" I offered feebly.

Alverdine laughed again, but the sound was warm, like a grandmother. "No child, my garden does plenty fine on its own. What I care about are memories of true emotion. Those keep my magic warm on cold nights and ensure that my gifts are bestowed to those most worthy."

"I don't understand."

"I will show you what your parents paid," Alverdine said, her back to me as she picked through more bottles. I looked over at Lorella, who shrugged, clearly at as much of a loss as I was. I studied the shelves of bottles and potions. The light shifted, and I thought I caught movement out the window, but saw nothing but the forest beyond.

"Ah, here!" she said, triumphantly brandishing two small, dusty purple bottles. There was parchment attached to each bottle, but the labels were too yellowed and old to read. Stepping closer to her, I noticed that the glass wasn't colored, as I initially thought, but rather there was something deep violet inside, like a liquid, that moved and swirled on its own.

"What is that?"

"Watch." Alverdine took the first bottle, deftly pulling out the cork stopper. The violet contents inside began to float, rising out of the bottle and into the air, where it dispersed into a cloud of amethyst smoke that smelled faintly of baking bread. At first, all I saw was the cloud, but soon particles within the cloud began to take shape. The cloud formed shapes, strange, undulating, and moving objects that looked like cotton candy. The shapes slowly became solid, particles coming together till small figures stood in the cloud.

My breath caught in my throat. The figures had transformed into my parents. It was clearly them, as though I were seeing them through violet-stained glass. My mother grinned as my father wrapped her in a loving embrace. With a start, I realized my father's ears were pointed, his teeth too sharp when he smiled. He was the faerie from the portrait hall.

"Promise to love me forever," smoke Soren said. Hearing my long-dead father's voice, crystal-clear in Alverdine's home, sent shivers down my spine, a stab of longing in my gut.

"Ever and always." My mother's voice was warm and sweet.

"And how do I know you won't change your mind when you find someone more charming?"

"You don't," smoke Eva told him, but she was smiling broadly as my father pulled her close to him.

Trapped in his embrace, Soren tickled Eva, causing her to laugh and yelp, pleading for him to stop between fits of laughter as she squirmed in his arms. Eventually, they fell to the ground, both laughing so hard tears streamed down their cheeks.

They sat for a long time, panting to catch their breath, snuggling close to each other. Eventually, Eva turned to Soren. "Tell me a story."

"What would be a worthy story for the most beautiful maiden in the world?" Soren responded, nipping her ear playfully as he contemplated what tale to tell her. She shrieked, but still rewarded him with a kiss.

"How about the story of how we met?"

"Eva, my love, I think you already know that story. You were there."

"Yes, but you tell it so beautifully. I think you shall have to tell it to our children someday." My mother beamed at my father as he acquiesced to her request.

"Once upon a time, there was a maiden who lived in a faraway village. She was the most beautiful maiden in the entire village and had a voice like a nightingale. She would go deep into the forest to forage for nuts and berries. All the while she would be singing her beautiful song."

My heart seemed to stop in my chest as I watched my father tell my mother the same story he had told me countless times when I was a child. The story of the beautiful maiden and the faerie prince who fell in love with her. It was the same story I had told Pel when he was transforming straw into gold for me in the tower.

Memory Soren finished telling Eva about the prince's plans to marry the beautiful maiden. Eva wrapped her arms around him, pulling him in for a kiss. They were still kissing as the purple mist started to dissolve, the image of my parents becoming insubstantial smoke that floated in the air for a heartbeat before funneling back into the glass bottle from which it was held.

All too soon, nothing was left of my parents. I stared at the shelves on Alverdine's walls, blinking hard. No one said anything for a long time.

"What was that?" I finally asked when I could control my voice.

"The memory your parents shared with me to buy your father's glamour charm. It was a strong one. Only the strongest memory of their love would have worked." Alverdine busied herself corking the bottle, but her voice was gentle. "They loved you very much."

I raised an eyebrow. "And how would you know?" My voice was sharper than I intended. "Sorry," I immediately added, not wanting to offend the powerful faerie. Especially after she had just given me a gift, albeit a painful one.

"This is how I know," Alverdine said, pulling the stopper off the second purple bottle. Again, the liquid inside flowed out and formed the smoke that became the image of my father. Soren appeared fully human, no fay traits that I could detect. He paced back and forth, a nervous energy pulling him along. At the sound of a door opening, he jerked his attention forward. Instead of seeing an image of my mother, I saw the spectral image of Alverdine. She smiled at my father, though her face gleamed with sweat and she looked tired.

"How is she?" Soren asked.

"She is well. Your wife is strong for a mortal. She did wonderfully, same as the last two times."

Soren grinned, but only for a moment before worry again clouded his face. "And the child?"

As if on cue, a loud, baby cry sounded. "Also healthy. A girl. Come in, Prince, come meet your second daughter."

My heart stilled as the image swirled around, dissolving before reforming into a new room. My mother lay in a bed. She looked exhausted, her damp hair plastered against her face, but she smiled down at a small bundle in her arms, cooing at a screaming baby. *That's me*, I thought distantly.

"Eva!" Soren cried, rushing into the room. He ran over, embracing Eva, and stared down at the babe in her arms.

"Meet your daughter, Soren," Eva said, her voice weak with fatigue, but she beamed at him as she held up the bundle to him.

Reverently, Soren took the bundle, treating the child within, *treating me*, as though it was the most precious thing he could have ever asked for. "She is beautiful," he said, mesmerized by the child. "Welcome to the world, Elenora Astira Molnár." He leaned in, kissing the baby, the movement making the blanket slip off the baby's head. I saw a tiny face and slightly pointed ears. Translucent wings poked out from the baby's back before Soren rewrapped the child, murmuring to her the whole time. The baby stopped crying, delighted with the attention from her father.

"Oh little Elenora, I promise I will do everything to take care of you. You are so loved." And he kissed the baby's forehead once again before that image also dissolved into smoke.

I fought the urge to call out to them, to beg the images of my parents to stay as they melted into smoky shadows that were swept back into the bottle. An aching feeling washed over me, that I lost them again, that I was again an orphan. I dug my nails deeply into my palms.

"The memory my parents shared to buy my glamour?" I guessed, once Alverdine corked the bottle.

"Indeed. As you saw, I was there, so it wasn't truly a fair trade, but their love was so pure, I allowed it."

I took the faerie's hands in mine. Her long fingers were dry and warm, and they wrapped around my calloused hands. I forced myself to meet her eyes, her violet irises the same color as the purple smoke.

"Thank you."

"It was your right to see that."

I didn't know what to say, afraid I might start crying if I thought too hard about what I had just witnessed. I focused on the lines of the stone in the floor, forcing myself to calm my breathing.

"Let's give her some time," I heard Lorella whisper, before gently shooing out the others. "We'll be right outside when you're ready," she said to me. I nodded.

Alverdine pulled up two wooden stools, placing one next to me and seating herself on the other. I sank down on the stool, still staring at the floor. In my mind, I wasn't seeing cracked stone, but my family, alive and whole and together.

"I'm sorry, my dear."

"For what?"

"For causing such pain."

I looked up, meeting her eyes, which seemed filled with despair. "I'm reminded that I'll never see them again. My parents and Rilla are dead. I have lost so much of my family. I don't even know if I'll ever be able to get back to my brothers," I confessed, expressing the fear I had not confided to anyone. "And if I managed to make it back to them, would they even recognize me? I don't recognize myself." I examined my fingers, not as long as most fay, but longer than before. They glowed slightly, my sun-browned skin now a burnished copper. "I'm supposed to take care of them."

"Give me your hand."

Numbly, I extended my hand, my thoughts still wrapped around my family. But I was immediately pulled back when I felt a sharp pain in my finger.

"By Chace's den, what did you do?" I snapped, yanking my hand back. A small bead of blood welled up on my finger. I looked over to see Alverdine holding a small pin, the tip covered in golden blood.

"It's no more than a pin prick dear, don't overreact," Alverdine said, as nonchalantly as if she was offering me a cup of tea. "Now look at it."

"At my finger?"

"Yes, *look*," she insisted.

Deciding to humor her, if only to avoid another prick of her pin, I pulled my finger close, examining the small bubble of blood.

"What do you see?"

"A bloody finger thanks to you." For a cold moment I wondered if Alverdine could do blood magic, and if this was some trick, but she hadn't moved any closer to me.

"And what color is that blood?" she finally asked, exasperation creeping into her voice.

"It's gold," I admitted, feeling a strange sense of loss. *Not red, like it should be*, I thought.

"Are you so sure?" Alverdine asked, something mischievous in her voice. And before I could ask her to clarify, she stabbed her own finger with the pin. A drop of blood welled up on her finger, mirroring my own.

Except it wasn't the same.

Her blood was lighter, a gold so pale and luminous it was almost silver. It was the same color I had seen when Pel cut his hand to use his blood to heal me when I first rescued him in the woods. It was the same color of the blood of the fallen fay I had seen in the battle at the cathedral when the fay army attacked Casper's coronation. Side by side with my own finger, it was apparent that my blood was definitely gold, no longer the deep red of human blood, but it also wasn't the luminous shade of Alverdine's blood. Instead, mine was a bright rose gold, far lighter than human blood, but not nearly as close to silver as pure fay blood.

My lips pulled into a small smile.

"For such a clever girl, you can miss what is right in front of your face," Alverdine scolded. "You have always been half fay, but you have also always been half human. No glamour, no matter how strong, can ever change who your parents were or who your family is."

"Can you change me back? Even if it's only a glamour, I'll take it. Can you make me as I was before?" I pleaded with her, grabbing her hands in desperation. "Please, I'll give you anything."

Alverdine held my hands but shook her head. "Alas, I cannot. Such a strong glamour can be used only once on a soul. And the sita-no still burns in your bones, does it not?" I nodded, reluctantly. She frowned, but continued, "It will most likely stay in your body your whole life. It would tear apart the type of glamour I used."

Words deserted me. It was all I could do to nod. Revisiting the loss of my family and discovering that I could not even appear human again filled me with despair.

"But perhaps I can provide you with some small comfort. Give me that drop of your blood and I'll give you a gift."

"Why do you want it?" And thinking practically, I added, "What will you do with it?" Despite all she had shown me, my habit was to be wary around strangers, and doubly so if they were fay and asking for blood.

Alverdine laughed, a light sound that made me feel a bit more at ease. "You are a wise child, Elenora Molnár. I give you my word that no harm will come to you or your loved ones for this gift. I simply want to keep it as a memory. A reminder that the humans and faeries are not quite as different as they like to believe."

I nodded, holding out my pricked finger to Alverdine.

She smiled and pulled out a tiny glass vial, seemingly from out of nowhere. The vessel was smaller than my thumbnail, but she deftly scooped up a single drop of blood into the vial, corking it before it disappeared again somewhere in her robes. "Now child, give me your cane."

"I need it," I said, pulling my cane closer to me. Even though I was resting on a stool, I could feel the dull burn in my legs.

The faerie shook her head. "It's not for me, it's how I shall give you the gift." And before I realized what she was doing, she swiped my cane. Despite her age, she was strong. Before I could protest, she was speaking some sort of spell.

"*Nascondee con monstra.*" Alverdine's eyes were closed in concentration, her long fingers spread over the moonstone. As the words left her lips, the stone glowed, a brilliant, white light illuminating it from within. For a moment, it became so bright I had to shield my eyes. After several seconds, the glow faded, the stone returning to normal. Alverdine opened her eyes.

"May your journeys help you find your path, in whatever form you wish that to take." She extended the cane to me. Tentatively, I reached for it, the stone slightly warm when I took it back, but otherwise it seemed unchanged.

"What did you do?"

"I gave you a glamour charm. It is in the stone."

My gaze fell back to the stone as I took in her words. A glamour, that was what my father had used, and it had worked his whole life when he was in the human realm. I moved my hand over the stone, but Alverdine placed her hand over mine, stopping me. I looked up, confused. "But I thought you said I could not be human again," I started.

"This charm won't be as strong as the one I bestowed on your father, or even on you when you were but a babe. But here is a temporary one for you. The moonstone is the token for the charm, so keep it safe." She gestured to the stone. "If the vessel is damaged, the charm will be broken."

"I will protect it," I promised. "How do I use the glamour?"

"Tell the stone your true name. That will activate the glamour." Alverdine looked serious. "And the next time your true name is spoken, that shall break the glamour."

"My true name? The fay have true names, but I—"

"You are a faerie with a true name." Alverdine gave me a sly smile. "Have you not figured it out? The name your father gave you."

"Oh," I breathed, putting the pieces together. "Elenora Astira—" Alverdine put her fingers to my lips.

"Yes child, but don't say it before you are ready for the glamour."

I clamped my lips shut and nodded, considering the possibilities as I held my cane. I had a great gift, a secret weapon at my disposal. So long as I kept the moonstone safe, I could resume my life as a human, assuming I figured a way out of Magnomel. My heart still ached knowing that Casper had cast me aside, but if I could reunite with my brothers, then at least I would be with family. I stood up straighter and thanked Alverdine.

"Your parents would be so proud," she said, gently kissing both of my cheeks before I stepped out of her cottage.

14

As soon as I was outside, Alverdine's home once again appeared to be merely a boulder. I marveled at how strong her magic must be to create such a large and lasting illusion. I turned to the group, where they were waiting a few paces away. Lorella was speaking with Corine in hushed tones as Drusia flew amongst the higher branches of nearby trees, collecting leaves she then braided into her hair.

As we walked back through the forest to the lake, I felt something bounce off my shoulder. I turned, but saw no one, only the depths of the forest beyond. Looking down, I spotted a small, white stone in the dirt. I knelt to pick up the stone when another hit me on top of my head. I yelped. Another white stone dropped into the dirt. I looked up.

Several feet above me, my brother Finn straddled a branch. He gave me an impish grin and waved. I let out a muffled gasp, causing Lorella, who was several feet ahead of me, to turn around.

"Nor, is something the matter?"

"No, nothing," I said, struggling to my feet. "But I feel like this would be a good place for me to practice magic. I can sense a lot of life here . . . since we're surrounded by trees. Living trees."

Corine raised an eyebrow, but Lorella beamed at me. "Excellent idea, Nor." Lorella settled herself on the forest floor. "Begin anytime you feel ready."

"No!" I almost yelled. "What I mean, is that I would like to practice by myself." Lorella's face fell in disappointment, and I quickly added, "I've been feeling so self-conscious. Maybe I could try on my own for a bit."

Lorella stood. "Nor, you don't need to lie to me."

"What? Why would you say I'm lying?" *Had I lost all my skills as a thief and a liar?*

To my surprise, Lorella embraced me. I stood rigid.

"I understand, Nor," she said, finally releasing me.

"You do?" I asked, wishing I understood.

"It must be very emotional having seen those images of your parents." There was warmth in her words, and she patted my arm.

"Oh, yes," I agreed, nodding. "Very emotional." I kept my eyes on Lorella, resisting the urge to look up, to see my brother.

"Corine, Drusia, come on." Lorella gave me another embrace. "We will meet you back at the boat. Take all the time you need."

I watched the three faeries make their way down the forest trail till they were out of sight. As soon as they were gone, Finn jumped down from the branch, landing on the ground with the ease of a cat.

"It's really you, isn't it?" He inspected me with critical brown eyes, eyes that rarely missed anything.

I nodded, preparing for the fear and disdain that Casper displayed when he saw me. Instead, Finn lunged at me, wrapping me in a hug with so much force the two of us toppled to the ground. I started laughing, relief and joy at seeing my brother, as I squeezed him back.

When we finally disengaged, I sat in the dirt, picking leaves and branches out of my hair as Finn studied me. There was no disgust, not even trepidation in my brother's face. Instead, he seemed keenly interested, like the scholar I knew he should be. I gave him time, waiting for him to speak.

"Did you do something different with your hair?" he finally asked, smirking at me. I playfully shoved his shoulder. But then his eyes clouded, his face going solemn. "I heard what they said. Why did they call you Soren's daughter?"

I braced myself before telling Finn everything that had happened since I was captured by the fay. I told him about our father and our fay lineage. Finn took in every word I said, letting me share the whole story. We sat in silence for a few minutes after I finished.

"Does it hurt?" he asked, breaking the silence.

"Only when I move." I tried to laugh, but it was a hollow, brittle thing, my words too close to the truth.

"We shall find you the best healer in all of Reynallis."

I shook my head. "There is no fixing me, Finn. I can't be human again." The words stabbed through me, but it was better he understood now.

"For your pain, you fool," Finn said. "By the Mother's maids Nor, I didn't mean you need to be fixed. I think it's incredible that you're fay now."

"How can you possibly think I'm incredible?" I hated the way my voice broke.

"For being such a clever schemer, you can be pretty dense. I've always thought you extraordinary. And learning that you're half fay," he paused, "that *we're* half fay, doesn't change that. If anything, we can learn so much more about the fay. Can you see better with those eyes? I wonder why the pupils are different from ours. And can you fly? Those wings are so thin." Finn examined my wings, while continuing to volley me with questions.

I couldn't help but laugh in relief. "I was afraid you would be scared of me. Wouldn't want me home now that I'm so changed."

Finn sat back, his brow furrowed in concern. "You really can be an idiot, Nor. You are my sister. Nothing will ever change that. Of course, we want you to come home."

Pressure built behind my eyes, and despite trying to blink back the tears, a few slipped down my cheeks.

"How did you find me?" I asked, afraid any more talk of being a loving family would have me sobbing like a baby. "And where are Devon and Jacobie?"

"Slow down, big sister. One question at a time. Devon and Jacobie are in a cabin at the edge of the Biawood in Reynallis waiting for us. After the fay attacked the Rose Palace, Princess Constance began to muster the Reynallis army. She is reaching out to Faradisia and Glavnada to get them to join forces with Reynallis. She wants to ensure the fay are defeated when she attacks. Devon and I wanted to follow you immediately after the attack, but Jacobie wouldn't stay in the palace without us. And you know we couldn't take him here. Too dangerous."

I nodded, taking his story in. At eight years old, Jacobie believed he could do anything the rest of us could. I was grateful Finn and Devon had managed to keep him out of Magnomel.

"So the three of us found a cabin near the edge of the woods. We've been keeping watch over the forest. Princess Constance tasked us to report daily, in case the fay return. She promised we would get you and Prince Casper back once she could back up the military force, but I couldn't keep waiting."

"And Devon let you venture here on your own?" I couldn't see my older brother allowing my thirteen-year-old brother to be the one to take the risk.

Finn looked sheepish. "Well, I might not have told him."

"Finn!"

"What?" He raised his hands in defense. "I left a note. Wrote that I'd be back as soon as I found you." He smiled. "And now I've found you. So come on, let's go." Finn got to his feet, pulling me up with him.

"Wait, stop," I said, digging my heels into the dirt.

"What?"

"I can't leave now."

"Are you worried about how you look? We are masters of disguise Nor, we'll figure out something. We can buy you a lot of hats, that will take care of hiding those ears—"

"It's not how I look," I interrupted Finn. I thought about the gift from Alverdine. "I have a plan for a disguise, but I can't leave yet."

"Why not?"

"For starters, three faeries are waiting for me not far from here. They will notice if I don't return."

"Then how about you come back here tonight? I will wait for you."

Looking into Finn's bright, hopeful face, I desperately wanted to agree. There was no place I would rather be than back with my brothers, with the people who loved and accepted me no matter what. But I could not forget Casper. I would never be able to forget him. Absently, I rubbed the point on my finger where his ring used to sit. I still owed him a debt.

"Because Casper is here. He's held prisoner." I didn't add that he never wanted to see me.

Finn grabbed my hand, squeezing it. "And as soon as Constance musters forces, they will invade and get him back."

I shook my head. Marasina might be content to free Casper in the winter if she thought the humans had learned a lesson, but if Constance brought an army to Magnomel, if more fay were killed, then Marasina might take her vengeance out on Casper, the same way she had ordered Elrik to assassinate King Christopher, their older brother.

"We can't let them battle," I said, my mind racing for a way to escape and get Casper out. I bit my lip, sucking in air through my teeth as I tried to figure out a solution. If I returned with Finn now, maybe I could convince Constance to hold off on attacking until winter, after Casper was freed. But what if Marasina heard about the planned attack, the mustering of forces? She might decide not to release Casper. She might even kill him. If only I could figure out a way to rescue Casper, then I could return to my brothers with a clear conscience.

"What could you possibly do Nor? Reason with the enemy?"

"No . . ." but maybe there was another way. I remembered Lorella describing the challenge to me. If I won, Marasina would offer me a favor. I could use that favor to have Casper released early. That only gave me two days to practice my magic or discover another way to beat Valente. A slight thrill mingled with anxiety, but it was a chance I had to take.

"No, but I have a plan."

Finn crossed his arms. "You always have a plan."

"Meet me here in two days. It will be late, long past midnight. I'll return with Casper. And then we can all go home."

"Is there anything I can say to make you give up on this plan and come back with me now?"

"I'm sorry, Finn. I owe Casper this much." I didn't add that it would be the last time I would see Casper. Once freed, I was certain Casper would want nothing to do with me. "And don't tell our brothers that I'm fay, not yet." I felt that was news that I had better deliver in person.

Finn shook his head, looking sadly resigned. "Then stay safe." Finn gave me another crushing hug. "I will see you in two days." In the next moment, he had slipped back into the woods, disappearing amongst the trees.

My excitement ebbed as I followed the path back through the Biawood, my heart feeling heavier with each step closer to the Forest

Court. The anxiety of returning to the center of the fay kingdom darkened my mood. I dreaded Valente's wrath and Elrik's machinations. The revel would be held in only two days. By then I would need to find a way to beat Valente. I had no other choice.

15

I practiced my magic every waking moment for the next two days.
I improved. I could call on life magic and send it into an object. I
could grow leaves or encourage buds to flower, but it was not enough.
And before I knew it, it was the evening of the revel. I sat on a stool in
my room as Drusia braided small white flowers into my hair, or maybe
knotted them in, I wasn't sure.

"Will I ever be able to get these out?" I asked, examining one
intricate braid studded with tiny blossoms. On close inspection, the
flowers were not a plain white; each petal coated in a pearlescent sheen
that made them shimmer in the evening light. They matched the white
of my hair so perfectly, I could almost imagine them growing out of
my braids. I plucked out one of the flowers, summoning my magic
into it. The familiar surge of heat pulled through my heart and into the
flower. It grew several inches, unfurling leaves and wrapping around
my finger. But there it stopped, a far cry from the impressive powers
of the Magia Viveralis.

Drusia snickered. "What does that matter? They are for luck. And stop that." A green hand smacked my own away. In my anxiety, I had started to pull out the petals.

"I don't know how I'm going to get through tonight," I admitted. My magic was no match against Valente. Forcing myself not to touch my hair, I stayed busy with the flower in my hand, palming it, then releasing it. Palming it, then releasing it. The old trick from my conning days was a familiar comfort.

"I'm certain you shall find a way," Drusia said, patting my head. "You are very clever, especially for one raised as a human. That is a neat trick," she added, watching me make the tiny flower appear and disappear.

"Thanks," I muttered, but felt no better about the situation. Palming small trinkets was hardly defense against an angry faerie determined to destroy me. Maybe if I had more time to prepare, I could think of a con that would fool even Valente, but in all the time since my introduction at court, nothing had come to me. Elrik promised me he had a plan, but I couldn't trust the faerie to do anything that wasn't in his own best interest. *But keeping me alive is in his self-interest*, I reminded myself, trying to feel some reassurance from that. I focused on breathing, on making the flower appear. Now disappear. Appear. Disappear.

A knock at my door broke my spiraling thoughts. Startled, I crushed the flower as Drusia flitted over and opened it.

"Hello Nor." Pel stood on the other side of the door. I flushed, remembering the last time I had seen him, I had tried to kiss him. He seemed as embarrassed as I felt, becoming very focused on studying his boots.

"Do you want to come in?" I asked, swallowing down my humiliation.

"Yes, thank you." Pel shuffled in. We stood in awkward silence, neither of us saying anything as Drusia watched us. Several times Pel cleared his throat, about to speak, but then would look away. I couldn't decide if I wanted to apologize for the night in the portrait hall or pretend it never happened. I settled on staying mute.

"The flowers look nice in your hair," Pel finally said.

"I told you they would get you noticed," Drusia said. When we both turned to her, she added, "But don't mind me. Carry on."

"Lorella said she had a dress for me to wear to the revel tonight, perhaps you could go and fetch it."

"As my princess wishes," Drusia said reluctantly, but she fluttered out the window.

"Did you come here to check on my coiffure?" I asked. In truth, I was desperate to know what Pel was thinking.

"I wanted to make sure you were all right."

"Never better," I lied, giving him a bright, fake smile.

Pel frowned. "Actually, I wanted to make sure *we* were all right."

"We?"

"After that night—" Pel started, but I waved my hand for him to stop.

"Please don't remind me. I don't know what came over me." I could feel my cheeks burning.

"I do want to be your friend, Nor. We have such a tangled history, but maybe we could start over." The look he gave me was so earnest, it was hard for me to deny him.

"I wonder if we could ever be anything as simple as friends. At this point, I don't know if we've saved each other more often than we've betrayed each other." Pel's face fell, but I kept going. "But maybe we can start with a truce?"

Pel considered my words before nodding. "A truce then, Elenora Molnár."

I smiled, but part of me wondered if he would feel so friendly toward me if he knew I planned on running away that night.

"And another thing, Nor. I want to speak with you about the revel."

"Ah, is that tonight?" I tried to joke, but Pel did not even crack a smile.

"Nor, you cannot attend the revel. Valente *will* issue a challenge." His bright green eyes met mine, and he refused to look away. "I will find a way to hide you from him."

I scrubbed my hand over my face. I couldn't tell Pel how much I wanted to avoid the revel, how I had no interest in being Marasina's heir and the idea of facing off against Valente was terrifying. But despite all that, I needed to win, needed to assure Casper's freedom before I made my escape.

"I can't do that."

"Nor, you're many things, many incredible, wonderful things, but you are no match for a vengeful fay who has been practicing magic and swordsmanship a century before you were even born."

I stumbled for a moment, surprised by his compliment, but forced myself to focus. If Valente challenged me and Elrik didn't stop him, Pel was probably right. "Elrik has a plan," I finally said.

Pel went very still at the mention of Elrik. "My brother," Pel said slowly, his hands curling into tight fists by his sides, "should not be trusted with your life."

"Now brother, what an uncourteous thing to say."

Both of us turned to the door to see Elrik casually leaning against the doorframe, meticulously dressed and totally at ease. In place of embroidery, his moss-green tunic was embellished with actual vines, accented with sparkling citrines that brought out the amber of his eyes.

"Nor is not going to the revel," Pel said to his brother.

"She most certainly is," Elrik said, sauntering into the room. "She already promised me the pleasure of escorting her." I groaned, remembering the deal with Elrik—a visit to Casper in exchange for going with him to the revel. Elrik picked up the hand mirror by my nightstand, examining himself and smiling with satisfaction. "Besides, our queen is expecting her."

"Are you trying to get her killed?" Pel's words were cutting and his face was taking on a golden glow, blood rushing to his cheeks in anger.

"I would never do that to my little bird. She is far too precious." He put down the mirror. "You seem to think me careless," Elrik said. His lips lifted into an easy smirk, as if daring his brother to argue.

"I am right here," I finally yelled. Both faeries turned to stare at me, startled at my outburst. "Stop talking about me like I'm some helpless creature."

"But I think you're charming when you're helpless," Elrik said. I raised my hand in warning, trying to hide the cold, sick sensation of fear at his words.

"Nor, please, I'm begging you not to attend the revel tonight," Pel said. There was a desperation in his voice, one that alighted my already on-edge nerves.

"What's your plan?" I asked, turning to Elrik.

"This," Elrik said, spreading his hand out in front of me. Large gemstone rings glittered on his pale, luminous skin.

"Will you be accessorizing him to death?" I asked, frustrated that the fay were never direct.

Elrik gave a laugh, a musical sound tinged with something cold and sharp. "Not quite, dear Elenora. Here." He moved his thumb to slide along the side of a large, rough-cut amethyst set in a silver ring on his pointer finger. Something clicked and the stone swung back on hinges so tiny I hadn't noticed them before, revealing a small compartment filled with a chalky white powder.

"Put that away," Pel hissed.

"What is it?" I asked, but a dangerous feeling settled in my stomach.

"Ground up fangs of the crab-eye viper. A most potent poison." Elrik's grin was sharp, eager. I wrapped my hand around my stomach, remembering the agony of the piro berries. I hated how fond the Forest Court was of their poisons.

"You can't possibly be thinking of killing our prince," Pel demanded, his voice a low, urgent whisper.

Elrik coolly flicked his thumb back over the ring, securing the amethyst back in place. Despite myself, part of me admired the workmanship of such a ring. It was a beautiful piece of illusion, of misdirection. I palmed and released the crushed flower in my pocket, thinking about misdirection. I had a niggling sensation, as though I was close to figuring something out, but it was still a bit out of my reach. There. Gone. There. Gone.

"And what would you have, dear brother? That Valente kill Elenora?"

"That's not—" Pel started.

"Because that's what would happen. She can't win a duel of sword or magic or anything else. And at least one of us has promised to protect her."

With surprising speed, Pel pulled back his arm and punched his brother. There was a hard crack as his fist connected with Elrik's face, sending the latter to the floor.

"Stop it!" I screamed, pulling on Pel's arm. I didn't like Elrik, but I needed him if I couldn't think of a way to defeat Valente.

As if only belatedly realizing what he had done, Pel let me pull him away from his brother, almost surprised by his own actions. He turned to me, gripping my hands tightly.

"Don't go," he said, his fingers digging into my palms. "Stay here tonight and you'll be safe. I'll stay with you."

I looked between Pel and his power-craving brother. Pel had deceived me, and Elrik frightened me, but I knew I would rather spend the night with Pel, away from Elrik, Valente, and the rest of the dangerous court. And unlike Elrik, I knew Pel's true name, had that protection against him. Thinking about his true name gave me an idea.

"And do you suppose tonight will be the only problem?" Elrik said, standing back up. A line of golden blood ran from a cut in his lip, which he wiped at with his fingers. "For all your valiant gestures," he paused, bringing his fingers to his lips and licking off the blood. "For all your violent, valiant gestures, you can't keep her safe. Valente will find a way to get to her. At least my way takes care of him."

"What about using his true name?" I asked, breaking into the brothers' argument. Pel stiffened, dropping my hands, but I continued. "If I learned Valente's true name, I could command him to leave me alone or to lose the challenge."

Elrik gave me an appraising look, one made more poignant by the shine of blood on his lips. "It is so easy to underestimate you, dear Elenora, raised a human, so weak, and with pitiful magic. But you have a clever mind. Not that it would work, of course, but a novel idea."

"And why wouldn't it work?" I shot back, annoyed by his condescension. "It must be written somewhere."

"It doesn't work like that," Pel said softly. I noticed his face was flushed gold. *He's embarrassed*, I realized.

"Elenora, we fay guard our true names with the utmost secrecy. He wouldn't have it written anywhere. Only a faerie and his or her closest kin and the queen or king know a faerie's name. A true name is ultimate power over a fay. It is the gravest insult to use that name. No one does so lightly." Pel spoke quietly, staring intently at the floor.

I shuddered, and almost jumped when Elrik put his hand on my shoulder. "Come now, Elenora. Pel may want to stay and pout, but you and I have a revel to attend." I was still looking at Pel, which annoyed Elrik, his grip tightening on my shoulder. "Don't forget our agreement." I didn't miss the threat in his voice.

I turned to Elrik. Being forced to pretend to love him disgusted me. I despised the entitled way he touched me. The joy he took from making me weak. Elrik would do anything to get more power, and right now that meant keeping me from getting killed, even if it meant murdering Valente. After tonight, after I left the Forest Court, I was certain Elrik would turn his cunning mind on ways to find me, to drag me back here. But I would deal with that once I escaped Magnomel. I could only handle one murderous fay at a time.

I dropped the crushed flower, mashing it into the floor with my foot. I hated relying on Elrik's help, but he was right about one thing: I couldn't fight Valente in a fair fight, not of magic or swords. *But didn't I fight best when I was not following the rules? When I could tilt the odds, make someone look at what was in my right hand while I picked their pocket with my left?* I recalled what Lorella had said, that the duel didn't have to be of magic or swords.

Perhaps I could demand a fight that gave me the advantage.

"As soon as your maid arrives with your dress, we should get going," Elrik said, tapping his foot as he stared out the window, searching for Drusia. "Don't forget you're in love with me."

Love. Names. Misdirection.

"Nor, you don't have to do this," Pel finally spoke up, though he still refused to look at me.

Love. Names. Misdirection.

"She does if she wants to survive the night."

Love! Names! Misdirection! Things finally clicked into place.

"I've got it!" I cried, startling both faeries. Elrik raised a questioning eyebrow, and Pel turned toward me. But I didn't care. My mind whirled with a new scheme.

It was a risky idea, but it was my plan. That small sense of control invigorated me in a way I had not felt since I had been brought to the Forest Court.

"You've got what?" Elrik finally asked.

"A plan," I said, this time I was the one with the sly smile. "If it works, I can defeat Valente without murder." I had no love for my uncle, but I would rather win on my terms than have Elrik kill for me. I bit my lip, sucking in air as I mapped out the details in my head.

"You don't need a plan, little dove. I have one for us," Elrik said, touching his amethyst ring in a gesture full of meaning.

"No, I've not agreed to that."

"Agreed?" Elrik's face grew hard with barely suppressed fury, but I didn't care. For the first time in weeks, I felt the thrill that came with every new con. Elrik was almost shaking with anger. "I don't need your approval on my decision. You only have to do as your told."

"No," I said, my voice firm.

"I don't think you understand what's at stake," Elrik started, taken aback by my stubborn response. His hand twitched, and I was sure he would have hit me had Pel not been in the room. Elrik loved causing pain almost as much as he loved control. Knowing how much he wanted to hurt me strengthened my resolve. It was finally time for some payback.

"I don't think *you* understand," I cut in. "Either you play along or I will express my true feelings for you in front of the entire court." My lips curled into a smirk, one that I hoped looked half as dangerous as Elrik's. If my plan worked, not only would I defeat Valente, but Elrik as well.

"You don't know what you're playing at," Elrik hissed, stepping toward me. I saw him reach for his dagger at the same time Pel did. I jumped back right as Pel leapt toward his brother, grabbing at the knife.

"Stop it!" I yelled, forcing myself to be heard over the sounds of their struggle. "Killing me won't get you anything."

Pel wrestled the blade away from Elrik, who finally took a step back. "Don't you dare hurt her. Or I swear brother, I will kill you."

Elrik raised his hands in a mock surrender, though his eyes stayed cold. "I wasn't going to kill Elenora. I'm rather offended either of you would think so. But better that she stays here tonight if she refuses to be reasonable. Even if I need to use magic to make it happen."

"You were going to cut me so you could get to my blood," I said, my enthusiasm drenched by the memories of him forcing my blood to slow, forcing me to sleep. The cold chill that spread in my veins. But there was a fire in me now, and I would not cower to his threats. I would never allow myself to be his helpless victim again.

"You are the one being unreasonable," Elrik said, his cool veneer cracking.

"If you ever use magic on me again, I will make you regret it." The edge in my voice forced Elrik to take a long, appraising look at me. This time, I was the one who stepped toward Elrik, whispering in his ear, "Accept my scheme if you want any hope of getting closer to the crown through me."

"Fine," Elrik finally said, letting out a frustrated sigh. But there was something else in his tone, something that almost sounded like respect. "What is your magnificent strategy?"

But at that moment, Drusia flew in through my window, carrying my dress for the evening.

"All I need you to do is act wildly in love with me," I instructed Elrik before shooing him and a reluctant Pel out of my room so Drusia could help me dress. The gown was a pearlescent white, the skirt layers and layers of spiderweb-fine fabric that shimmered in the light and billowed out on the slightest breeze.

"Princess, do be careful," Drusia said as she secured silver clips in my hair.

"I'm only careful when I can't be clever," I said before picking up my cane and heading to the door. I took a moment to steady my breath, feeling the familiar mix of excitement and nerves that came with a new scheme. I opened my chamber door. Both Elrik and Pel were on the other side, Elrik leaning against the wall, his arms crossed, while Pel paced. They both looked so petulant that I almost laughed.

"All right, come on, lover-boy," I said, grabbing Elrik's arm. His mouth dropped in surprise at my gesture, before he collected himself, smirking as he pulled me closer to him. I fought the urge to flinch away.

This is my plan, I reminded myself.

"Nor," Pel started. Elrik shot him a look. For a moment I wished Pel would stop me. But he only said, "Are you certain?"

"Completely," I lied. "Come, Elrik. We have a revel to attend," I said, letting Elrik lead me down the hallway toward the courtyard. I forced myself not to turn back.

16

The courtyard was transformed. Tiny balls of light floated in the air, reminding me of stories about will-o-the-wisps. Above them, the vast, clear sky sparkled with stars. Thousands of crystals hung from the branches of every tree, glittering from the fay lights. Flower petals carpeted the soft grass, making the air fragrant with lavender and gardenia.

And the faeries. I was used to their earthy attire, but tonight they turned out in glittering jewels and gems. Blue-skinned faeries with gills, similar to Peseltine, were swathed in emerald and turquoise silks accented with shimmering shells and scales. They clustered by the waterfall; every now and then one of them dove into the pond or emerged from it, shaking off glistening droplets. Faeries I recognized from the Forest Court flittered around on their dragonfly wings, glowing in shades of amethyst, forest greens, and deep sapphire blues. Large creatures with mossy hair and stone-like skin that I imagined were the source of village stories about trolls and ogres, towered above the others in sharp blacks. Spindly creatures with bark-like skin and bird nests for hair sang in harmony with the small birds on their heads. Members of the royal family wore shimmering silvers, whites, and grays, similar to my own fine gown.

"Close your mouth or you'll start drooling," Elrik murmured in my ear.

"It's . . . different," I said, searching for the right word. A tiny creature no bigger than my thumb flew at me, landing on my cane. I looked down. It was a gray-skinned faerie that looked like a miniature human with moth wings, two big orange eyespots on each wing. "Hello," I said to it.

The creature blinked at me before flying back into the melee of the revel. I followed as Elrik led me along the side of the courtyard. We passed long tables piled high with tempting delicacies. There were roast ducks and geese in rich gravy, soft white breads dipped in cream, tarts of root vegetables and roasted chestnuts. Another whole table was dedicated to fruits. Rosy apples, ripe peaches, slices of oranges in honey, and sugar-glazed strawberries were piled next to fruits I did not recognize—bright green berries, a lilac pudding that smelled of violets, tiny lemon-like fruits the size of marbles, and many more. My eyes lingered on a display of sliced pears, their skin the same strange silver as the one Marasina used to make me sprout a tree. As we passed the food, the aroma of the feast mixed with the floral scents in the air and my mouth watered.

"Care for a drink?" Elrik asked as we walked by a table of libations. Crystal carafes of pale yellow wine glowed. Large casks were full of a deep amber liquid that fay poured into polished oak mugs. A platter of tiny cups as small as my thumbnail were filled with a purple liquid that smelled strongly of berries. Next to it were bottles of red wine, dark as blood. *As my blood used to be*, I thought.

"No. But don't let me stop you from partaking." I knew better than to accept food or drink from Elrik.

"As you wish," Elrik said, and I detected a hint of disappointment. He delicately lifted one of the small cups with the purple drink, downing the contents in one sip.

"When will Valente issue the challenge?" I asked as we passed by piles of discarded shoes.

"Impatient, dear one?" Elrik asked, his words slightly slurred. "We have some time yet. He would want the whole court to witness. Probably midnight."

"Wonderful." More time would be good to set the stage, but it also meant more time close to Elrik. I reminded myself what was at stake as I gripped his arm tighter, forcing myself to walk right beside him, as though I couldn't stand for even the smallest distance between us. He gave me a loose grin, pulling me along.

We made our way to the center of the courtyard. A massive circle, framed by soft gray mushrooms, created a dancing area. Inside the ring, a variety of faeries were moving to the music. Off to one side musicians played the lively songs that floated through the air.

I stopped when I saw the two massive wooden thrones. Queen Marasina watched the dancers from her seat of power, her silver gown complimenting her silver hair, both strewn with sparkling diamonds. She wore a crown of crystals and moonstones, her only other jewelry the thick, silver chain with the golden pendant. The other throne was empty, in honor of the late king, but she was not alone. Surrounding her were members of the royal family, lounging on cushions or standing nearby, drinking and talking amongst themselves. Lorella saw me and smiled. She rose and headed toward me. I waved but kept searching till I spotted Valente as he returned from a dance. His face was stony, as though he were at a funeral, not a celebration, and his eyes narrowed when he noticed me, his lips pulling into a sneer. Though a coldness snaked inside me, I didn't let my smile falter.

Now. Swallowing my disgust. I turned to Elrik and seized his tunic, grabbing handfuls of velvet and vines, and pulled him in close, kissing him firmly on the mouth with closed lips. He smelled of the forest, the way Pel did, but his lips were cool on mine. He stilled, surprised, but then kissed me back as he wrapped an arm around my waist and his other hand twisted in my hair, holding my head in place with a firm grip. He kissed hard and rough, as though trying to devour me. His tongue pried my mouth open, even as I tried to keep my lips together. I was no match for his strength. My skin prickled in fear and loathing. Just the smallest bite with his sharp teeth and he would have complete control over me. I forced myself to keep kissing him. If he used blood magic, it would ruin the illusion.

Bile rose in my stomach as I thought of how I was betraying Casper in this moment, even if he wanted nothing to do with me. But it was too late to stop now. I allowed the kiss to go on for a few more seconds before I tried to break away from Elrik. When he only pulled me in tighter, his fist almost yanking out my hair, I broke out in a cold sweat. His lips remained hard on mine, his grip on my waist unrelenting, and panic spiked through me as I grabbed at his arm, digging my nails in until he finally released me.

"What was that for?" he asked. I couldn't tell if he was referring to the kiss or my nails. His eyes were glossy, a bit dazed as he stared at me with dilated cat-eye pupils.

I risked a glance over his shoulder to confirm every member of the royal court was staring at us. Lorella had stopped mid step, her brow deeply knit in concern. Marasina raised an eyebrow in surprise, but Valente took it in with a smug expression. *Probably pleased he has discovered another of my many weaknesses*, I hoped. I focused again on Elrik, noticing something else in the languid way his amber eyes took me in. It was the same look I saw in any mark who wanted something they didn't deserve to have. He stared at me with undisguised greed.

"Because I am wildly in love with you," I replied, forcing my voice to be light. Giggling, I leaned in closer to him, so my lips almost brushed his ear. "And because I am excellent at deception."

I pulled back, a sweet smiled carefully arranged on my face. Elrik's eyes flashed in anger, but it was gone in an instant. Then, his lips curled up and he had his mask back on, one of a handsome hero who would do anything to protect the helpless princess.

"I will ensure that you will never be able to live without me, my darling," he responded. I kept the smile, refusing to be intimidated by his threat. He slowly licked his lips before adding, "I wonder if my brother knows how delicious you taste." My smile stayed in place, even as I ground my teeth together. I would show him soon enough what I thought of him.

"Shall we dance, my lovely?" Elrik asked, pulling me toward the mushroom circle.

"I don't know this dance," I admitted as we approached the circle. The dancers' large, wild gestures were unlike any dances I had ever seen, either at the Rose Palace or at simple village celebrations. I stared at them for a moment, a jolt of shock running through me as I noticed that some of the dancers were humans. There were only a few, none looking older than I, and each was dancing closely with a faerie. I wondered if they had once been stolen children.

Elrik smiled, "All you need to do is let the music guide you."

I paused when we reached the ring of mushrooms. In my village, old legends warned that nothing good would come from crossing a faerie ring.

Well, nothing good was coming from any of my dealings with the fay, I thought as I lifted my foot to step over the ring. My toes were brushing the grass inside the ring when a strong hand grabbed my wrist, yanking me away from Elrik and out of the circle.

"What are you doing?" a voice snapped at me. Pel had hold of my wrist, keeping me from the faerie ring. His face was a mix of concern and anger.

"About to go dancing," I retorted. I did not need Pel complicating my plan.

"Nor, why didn't you take off your shoes?" Lorella had reached us, her anxiety matching Pel's.

"My shoes?"

"If you can't feel the grass beneath your feet in a faerie ring, you'll be completely lost to the music. You won't be able to stop. It's probably worse for someone half human. You didn't know?" Lorella asked.

"No." I studied the dancers, noticing they were all barefoot. The piles of discarded shoes made sense. "And my escort didn't think to warn me," I added through gritted teeth.

"You're more fun when you're out of control," Elrik said, not even a hint of remorse in his voice.

"How come you kept your shoes on?" I asked, pulling free of Pel's grip and going up to Elrik. He still wore his soft leather boots.

"I thought you would become suspicious if I took mine off, so I modified them." He lifted one foot, revealing that the sole of the shoe had been removed, leaving the bottom of his foot bare.

"Chace take you," I swore, using all my self-control not to smack the cursed faerie with my cane. "We should pay our respects to my grandmother," I said to Elrik. Looking back at Pel and Lorella, I noted how Pel was staring at me, oblivious to the way Lorella gazed at him. I needed Pel not to interfere. With some guilt, I added, "Lorella, perhaps Pel needs a dancing partner. I no longer feel inclined to dance."

I didn't miss the way Lorella's face lit up nor the reluctance in Pel's stance as he slowly got to his feet. "Nor, are you certain you want Elrik by your side tonight?"

"Completely," I said to Pel, hoping he believed me.

Pel turned to Lorella, and I was relieved to see that he was at least a gentleman, as he bowed to her, saying, "Shall we dance?"

As Pel and Lorella headed to the dancing ring, I turned back to Elrik, twining my arm with his, forcing myself not to stiffen as he yanked me closer, inhaling the smell of my hair before leading me to the royal pavilion.

All the royals were fixedly staring back at us. I kept glancing at Elrik, ensuring they all noticed my attachment to him. He and I bowed low in front of Marasina.

"My queen," Elrik said, his voice smooth and pleased. "This is a beautiful night for a revel."

"Indeed," Marasina said, her gaze appraising. "And how do you find it, granddaughter?"

I moved in closer to Elrik. "I could not imagine a more lovely celebration."

"And how does it compare to the human ones?" Valente asked, his eyes hard on mine.

"No need to discuss such history," Marasina started, but I dared to cut her off.

"Oh no, my queen, I insist that I tell you tonight is stars and moons above anything I ever experienced in the human realm. Even balls in the Rose Palace taste dull and drab compared to the splendor of tonight," I said, gesturing around. After a pause, I added, "I still cannot believe how fortunate I am to be the heir to such a realm."

"I am pleased to see you appreciate your position," Marasina said. My words brought a smile to her face, one that made her beautiful features even more stunning.

Though her words were meant to encourage me, I noticed Valente's lips pressed into a fine line, and he was nearly shaking with rage behind Marasina. I bowed again, saying, "I shall take care to treasure my position."

I smirked at Valente, and that broke him.

He reached for his sword, not pulling it out, but tightly gripping the hilt. He strode toward me, his face splotchy with rage.

"I challenge you for title of heir of the Magia Viveralis throne and future ruler of Magnomel."

A collective gasp rose in the crowd. I allowed some of the fear I felt flicker on my face, nervous wringing of my hands and a worried glance at Elrik before I slowly took a step toward Valente, all the while leaning heavily on my cane. Valente's grin grew wide and wolfish. He expected no fight from this weak half human. I stared up at him, making my eyes big, playing into his notion that I was a pathetic creature.

It's showtime, I thought.

17

"Would anything persuade you to reconsider?" I asked, forcing my voice to crack.

"Nothing will dissuade me. Now pick the battle."

"Very well," I said, pausing to give the impression that I was considering my options. I slowly glanced around the courtyard.

"You must choose the nature of the contest," Valente snapped, impatiently tapping his sword hilt.

"I'm thinking," I said, allowing a few more seconds of mock contemplation. If Valente was irritated, he would be distracted. And a distracted mark was the best kind of mark. I let my eyes lock on Elrik, lingering there till Valente finally burst out.

"Your love can't save you now."

I whipped my head back to Valente, as though I had only now made the critical connection. "I have decided on our contest."

"About time," Valente said, his bright blue eyes eager. "And what do you choose?"

"A battle of wit," I said, allowing a small smile to lift the corners of my mouth.

Valente's look of confusion soon shifted to irritation. "Battles are of magic and swords, not words."

"A challenge is not limited to swords or magic. Even if fay have not been creative enough to pick other weapons." My smile widened. "But please let me know if you do not think yourself up to such mental taxation. I will happily accept your forfeit now," I added, baiting him.

Valente grumbled. "I doubt very much that a filthy half human can outfox one of the fay. I have been in these woods for centuries before you were even a babe in arms. What is this battle of wits you propose?"

"A riddle."

Valente let out a snort of derisive laughter, but I held his stare. "You, little human, think you can outwit me?"

"I do," I said, forcing my voice strong and cool. "That is the challenge I propose."

"And if I win, if I solve your riddle, then you will relinquish the title of heir back to me," Valente said. His eyes shone with greed. "And you will fight me in a proper fashion," he tapped the hilt of his sword, "with blades."

My mouth went dry. I knew if things went south that he'd become heir, but I hadn't expected to sword fight him. If I lost, he would kill me. I swallowed hard.

"And *when* I win, you will swear your loyalty to me as the rightful heir. Never again will you try to harm me nor knowingly allow harm to befall me." I hoped I was explicit enough. I did not plan to stay in Magnomel past this night but figured I might need the support once Elrik learned of my deception.

Valente didn't hesitate, so certain of his win. "Agreed."

"Agreed," I echoed. Something simmered in the air between us, as though fay magic was sealing our deal. Goosepimples broke out on my arms.

The details of the contest were quickly worked out. Valente insisted I write the answer down to keep the challenge honest. I conceded to do so, and a servant handed me parchment and ink, along with a long white quill made from a swan feather.

"Very well, what is your riddle? Show me how clever you are."

I bit my lip, running my fingers up the silky edge of the quill, looking for all the world like an anxious child. Valente raised an eyebrow, "Sometime before sunrise."

"What . . ." I started, then faltered. I quickly scanned the crowd, my gaze settling on Elrik. He smiled at me. I hoped it looked like that of a lover instead of the predator I knew him to be. I beamed, scribbling on the parchment then blowing it dry before folding it up. The same faerie servant returned it to the queen, but I paid them little mind, my attention back on Elrik.

I stared at him like an enamored fool until Valente cleared his throat in frustration.

I turned to face Valente. "What has no weight, being carried on the air from the lips, yet has the greatest pull in the world? What, when truly known, can cause one to do anything, whether one wills it or not?"

Valente would have had to be dead to miss the infatuated looks I kept shooting Elrik. Valente grinned, a victorious smile that showed his sharp teeth. "Oh, you little half-breed, don't you think you're clever? I fear you inherited your human mother's wit, for Soren would never have been so plain."

"Do you have an answer or are you stalling for time?" I prodded, refusing to be baited about my parents.

Valente stepped toward me, and though I wanted to flinch back, I refused to move. "You will be sorry when this is over," he said, soft enough that only I could hear.

"Your answer, *Uncle*?" I felt a perverse satisfaction at the way he stiffened when I referred to him with such familiarity.

"Love," he said, his voice carrying to all of the watching fay. "The answer is love." He didn't even look to Marasina for confirmation, so certain he was right. Instead, he pulled out his sword, long and gleaming in the fay lights. I backed up, not wanting to be cut down because he was too eager for a fight. "Who is the clever one now?" he asked, raising his sword in the air.

"You're wrong."

Valente stopped dead in his tracks. Sword still raised, he turned to where Marasina sat, disbelief etched on his face. "What did you say?"

"You are wrong, my son," Marasina repeated, the parchment unfolded in her hands. "You lost." Her face was serene, though I detected amusement in her voice.

Valente finally lowered his sword, still looking too confused to speak.

"Swear loyalty to me, Valente. You have failed the challenge."

Valente spun around, rage flaring in his eyes. "I will not. You cheated!"

I snorted a laugh. The exhilaration of pulling off a successful scheme ran through me, like lightening in my veins. "Are you such a sore loser? I won."

"Prove it."

His voice was icy and sharp.

"One wills what they do for love." I thought about Casper, a sharp pain in my chest that I shoved down. "One can even betray the person they love the most. But even love has its limits."

"You cannot challenge with a riddle that has no answer," Valente growled.

"It has an answer. Queen Marasina has the proof."

All eyes turned to Marasina, and I swore she was trying not to smile. "A faerie's true name," she read off the parchment.

Valente stood perfectly still, his lips moving with no sound as he ran over the riddle again in his head.

"A faerie's true name has no weight, but once known, can compel a faerie to do anything," I said. Valente's irritation melted away as the blood drained out of his face.

And though I won, I feared Valente might still attack me, his stillness reminiscent of a viper about to strike. But his next movement was not to leap at me; rather he lowered to one knee in a swift, fluid motion. And though his voice rang with disgust, the words were clear. "I, Valente, son of the Faerie Queen Marasina, Prince of the Magia Viveralis family, do swear my loyalty to Princess Elenora, heir of Magnomel. From this day forth, I shall never allow harm to her, not by my hand, not by my knowledge, not by my directive to any other creature. By the magic in my blood, this I swear at the revel with the court to witness."

"I should require your name, your *true* name." I said the words lightly. The watching faeries broke out in nervous murmurings, but all my attention was fixed on Valente. He stayed immobile, still kneeling in front of me, but the rage left his eyes, his catlike pupils growing almost as round and wide as human's. *He's scared. No, he's terrified.* With his name, I could possess him like a puppet, strip him of all his autonomy. I wanted to feel justified to do so, vindicated after his treatment of me. But seeing him helpless in front of me, a slight tremble in his body he couldn't quite hide, I wondered if I was ready to be as ruthless as he had been.

"Kill me instead, your majesty." His words were soft as the rustle of leaves.

I closed my eyes for the length of a breath, deciding what kind of person I wanted to be.

"I will not ask you for your true name," I declared. His shoulders sagged in relief before he rose to his feet. "But remember, you swore your loyalty to me," I added.

His face was a blank mask, but he nodded once in acknowledgement. I wondered if I was expected to dismiss Valente, but without saying a word, he rose, gave a reluctant bow before turning and striding away. He did not stop at the royal family but continued walking till he left the courtyard entirely.

An excited buzz rose from the faeries, eager chatter that I could not make out. Elrik looked furious, humiliated. But I didn't care. I had dealt with Valente, and soon I would be gone, away from this court and away from Elrik. Relief washed over me, lightness I had not felt in weeks. For the first time since arriving in Magnomel, I was able to overcome using my skills, instead of being rescued by a faerie. I felt giddy with relief. But with the relief also came the chronic fatigue and ache that I had been able to ignore in the presence of Valente. I leaned on my cane, wanting to slump over, or better still, to lie down on the cool grass.

Instead, I forced myself to stand tall, not wanting the waiting crowd to see me as anything other than victorious.

"Granddaughter, you held your own well this night." Marasina's voice cut through the chatter, silencing the fay. I turned to her, watching as she gracefully rose from her throne, her silver hair floating behind her. As she approached me, I could not help but think of how her eyes were the exact same color as Valente's, but this pair shone with respect. I bowed as she drew near.

"You did well. You are clever like your father, like a faerie heir should be. And that deserves a boon from your queen. Ask of me what you will, and perhaps I shall grant it."

"You are most gracious," I replied, wanting to show proper respect. I was so close to my goals. Soon, Casper would be free and I could return to my brothers.

"My queen." Her eyebrows raised, but she said nothing, even as her lips turned up in a pleased smile. *Good*, I thought. "I would ask that you release King Casper now, instead of waiting till winter comes to Magnomel. Send him back to his home in Reynallis as a sign of good faith."

A thick silence filled the air. The smile on Marasina's face froze, hardened, and then broke. Her brows knit in confusion before her lips puckered in distaste. "Our magic prevents winter, granddaughter. It's always spring in Magnomel. And I have no desire to release the human kingling, now or ever. We keep him to teach the humans a lesson, to avenge my late husband. You would do well to remember where your loyalties lay, *heir*."

Her words hit me so hard that I took a step back, all the air leaving my lungs. I had no ready response. Casper had seemed so certain of his release. Had he lied to me, or had someone lied to him? And why would any of the fay promise Casper's release if there were no plans to let him go?

"I am sorry my queen," I said, desperate to get my mind working again. By Chace's den, I had screwed up, and needed to fix things immediately. Otherwise, I would never be able to help Casper. "I was misinformed." I bowed again, hiding my face as I set my features in a mask of calm. But my mind was whirling, running through the possibilities. I straightened. "I was thinking that such an act would strengthen the fay, protect the fay. I was wrong." The words tasted bitter on my tongue, but I didn't take them back.

Marasina stared at me, her eyes two cold crystals, before her features softened. "You are young Elenora, so very, very young. I forget how naive you are." I swallowed back the retort that came to mind. "But you have much time to become accustomed to our ways. I'm sure you shall soon come to understand why all of this is for the best."

"Thank you, my queen," I said, making my words sound true. I desperately wanted this exchange to be over. I could do nothing while all eyes were on me.

Marasina smiled at me then, looking magnificent and benevolent, but I heard the condescension in her tone as she continued, "But you have proved yourself capable and worthy," she added, gesturing to where Valente had stormed off. "So I shall be kind and offer you this boon instead, a more appropriate reward for winning the challenge, one that you will surely see the value of."

Marasina carefully lifted the golden pendent from around her neck. I heard gasps and exclamations amongst the watching faeries. The thick, silver chain glittered as she held out the necklace to me, the pendant pulsing with the golden glow. She reached her hand over my head, allowing the necklace to encircle my neck, dropping it with a weight that rested against my chest. A warm, pulsing sensation radiated from the pendant, giving me the eerie feeling that it was somehow alive.

I tentatively reached down, touching the orb. I sucked in a sharp breath as I felt the pull of magic, similar to the sea glass token at the Dusk Market, but magnitudes stronger. I stared at the amulet, seeing small flickers of green light wrap around the glowing gold like tiny shots of lightning. "Thank you, Queen Marasina," I finally said, meeting Marasina's stare. I might not know what I held, but I could tell it was something powerful.

"That is the Regalia Vive Amulet. Queens of ages past have all imbued this token with life magic, passing a part of themselves on to the next queen. It is a symbol of the Magia Viveralis and the rulers of our realm. You could have no greater gift than this."

I would rather know Casper was free than have a pretty piece of jewelry, no matter how much life magic was in it, I thought. Instead, I only repeated, "Thank you." I tried to convey gratitude, but felt like the ground was shifting underneath me. I was so busy playing Valente, so set on humiliating Elrik, that I hadn't noticed the game played on Casper. What faerie would gain an advantage from Casper believing he would be freed if he behaved? Another thought came to me—what if I was wrong? What if Casper was not the mark, but rather a pawn?

"Very good," Marasina finally said. She stared at me a moment longer with an appraising look. As if on cue, her features shifted to one of a benevolent ruler, a delighted woman, her blue eyes sparkling and a gracious smile lighting her lovely face. "We should celebrate this joyous victory. A challenge well met, a great gift bestowed, and hours still of the revel to enjoy! Come, heir, sit awhile with your family."

The last thing I wanted was to spend another minute in her presence, but there was a hint of steel in her request that I didn't miss. And if I was with her, I could put off dealing with Elrik. My mind ran over possible culprits as I followed Marasina to the cluster of royal fay, all with silver-white hair and deep blue eyes. The other royals stared at me, a range of surprise and interest on their faces. Perhaps my aunts and uncles now found me worthy of knowing. Not that I cared to know them.

I was the only one here who would care what happened to Casper, could I have been the one meant to be duped?

Marasina gestured to the right of her throne, the seat Valente had formerly been occupying. Feeling the eyes of all the court on me, I delicately sat down, ensuring my smile did not falter. Marasina nodded, then waved her hand at the musicians, who immediately began to play a beautiful, upbeat tune. Barefoot faeries, and even a few humans, began to trickle back to the dance floor, their bodies carrying around in graceful circles to the rhythm of the song.

I silently puzzled out Casper's lie as I ticked off those who would like to do me harm. Valente would have loved to hurt me, but such a well-placed lie seemed too subtle for him. Pel might no longer wish me harm, but he had pulled away from my botched attempt at a kiss. Maybe he reasoned that if I believed Casper was leaving, I would no longer pine after him.

I did not want to believe the worst in Pel, not after our tentative truce, but he had betrayed me before.

By the end of the song, most of the queen's family had left for the dancing or the food, leaving Marasina and I relatively alone. "Well played, granddaughter," Marasina said to me when no one else was within hearing.

"I didn't much care for the alternative," I confessed, only half paying attention.

"Yes," Marasina said, considering my words. "I believe Valente foresaw an easy victory. He underestimated you. It is a folly I do not plan to make."

I had been watching the dancers, but at her words, my head snapped over to her. "If you do not trust me, why do you want me to be your heir?" I asked before I could stop myself. Marasina could be shrewd. Had she sent the lie to Casper?

"Who said I don't trust you? I simply said I don't underestimate you. You are clever. Cunning."

"And you want that for your heir?" I asked. My deceits had kept me and my brothers alive when we were homeless, but no one had ever been proud of us. I had thought I could resign that part of myself when I became engaged to Casper. My thumb rubbed the place on my finger where his ring used to be. "You don't want one who is noble and honest?" I asked, thinking of the traits that Casper possessed, what made him a good ruler. A king who cared about his people.

Marasina chuckled, a beautiful sound of ringing bells, but tinged with the too-familiar condescension. "You are too young to understand, despite your quick mind, but you cling to human values. In the fay courts, a ruler must be cleverer than her subjects, especially if she is to keep them in check. Valente could never understand that, but I have a feeling you will, with time. Especially as you have spies and tricksters for admirers," she added, looking out at the celebrations.

I followed her gaze, seeing Elrik making his way toward us. I cringed. As sweet as humiliating Elrik in front of the entire court was, I knew I would have to deal with him at some point.

After all, I had agreed to go with him to this revel in exchange for seeing Casper.

And then it hit me.

Elrik had been there, watching us the entire time.

"My queen," Elrik said as he approached, bowing low to Marasina. "And lovely Elenora," he added, giving a smaller bow. The outrage that had been so plain on his face after I tricked Valente was gone, replaced by his usual smug smile that always veered toward predatory.

"Elrik," Marasina said, acknowledging him and giving him one of her stunning smiles. "You must be so proud of our Elenora. She put on quite the show tonight. One would have almost thought her besotted with you." Elrik stiffened at the underlying insult.

Elrik's smile never wavered, but something cold flashed in his eyes, his smile stretching too wide, baring too many sharp teeth. "Time and time again she claims my adoration."

"And so, shall I assume she is what brings you to me?"

"I must admit as much," Elrik answered. He continued speaking with the queen, but his eyes didn't stray from mine. "There is precious little time left of the night, and I would ask my beloved to dance with me. That is if it would suit her and my queen, of course."

"It is perfectly acceptable to me. I have kept my granddaughter away from the dancing long enough if she wishes to partake in the festivities."

"Elenora?" Elrik inquired, reaching out his hand to take mine.

I stared back at Elrik's amber eyes, contemplating my next move, and what his would be. I could not call him out for lying to Casper, not when I knew Marasina would side with any fay, even Elrik, over a human king. And if I outright refused him, if I insulted him once again, then he might take vengeance out on Casper.

I rose and started toward Elrik's proffered hand, but stumbled, falling to the ground, ensuring I did so before he could catch me. I rose shakily to my feet, pulling myself up by my cane, careful to make it appear that my fall was accidental. I waved off the support of nearby fay.

"I wish I could, but perhaps I have overexerted myself this evening. I shall have to decline." He stood for a long time, staring at me, his yellow eyes wide with disbelief that grew into resentment that I would refuse him. I smiled sweetly at Elrik.

Elrik went rigid as a taut bowstring, ready to snap. My heart pounded in my ears, but I refused to show him any fear. Finally, he gave a tight bow, glaring at me all the while.

"Do rest up. I shall check on you later." Without waiting for a response, he turned on his heels and made his way to the palace, shoving aside any faerie that did not get out of his way.

"You certainly have a way with the men of my court. Keep that up, and we'll have them all storming out of here before sunrise," Marasina said, but with a pleased smile.

"I shall try not to scare anymore men this night," I said, but as I did so, I caught sight of Pel, watching everything that had transpired at a safe distance. "Well, perhaps just one more scare," I added, rising and grabbing my cane. "If you will excuse me." I bowed to Queen Marasina before making my way to Pel. I did not want to ask his help, but I was low on options. And if I had to, I could force his help with use of his true name, though I desperately hoped it would not come to that.

18

Lorella was speaking to Pel as I approached. He replied with short answers or curt nods, continually glancing toward me as I drew closer. Lorella finally threw up her hands in defeat, though she smiled when I drew near.

"Congratulations on your win, Nor," she exclaimed, wrapping her arms around me. "I knew you would think of something. You are brilliant." She held me tightly. I hugged her back. Depending how the night went, this might be the last time I saw her, and she had been a true friend to me here, the only faerie family I would miss. I breathed in her smell of gardenia and lavender before gently stepping away from her.

"I always have a trick or two up my sleeve."

"Well done, Nor," Pel said, though he did not move toward me.

"Lorella, mind if I steal Pel away for a moment? I have to ask him a few things about . . ." I considered my words carefully before finishing with, "his brother."

Lorella quirked her eyebrows in surprise, but did not object. I started to lead Pel away when I paused, turning back to Lorella.

"Thank you, Lorella."

"Whatever for?" she asked with a bemused smile.

"For being my friend. And my family. I will always appreciate that." It was the closest I could get to saying goodbye. As much as I knew she cared for me, she was also loyal to her mother, and I couldn't risk Marasina discovering my intentions. I gave her another quick, tight hug before grabbing Pel's arm and forcibly dragging him to a secluded corner of the courtyard. Though my nails dug into his arm, he said nothing.

Once we were out of earshot of other fay, I turned to face him, my heart hammering.

"When was the last time you saw Casper?"

Pel grimaced. "Is this because our queen will not release the kingling?"

"His name is *Casper*."

Pel sighed. "I have not seen Casper since he was sentenced to the Aqueno Prison."

I studied his eyes, desperate to determine if he was telling the truth. He seemed sincere, but I had been fooled by him before. "He told me he would be freed when winter came to Magnomel. Swear that you did not tell Casper he would be freed in winter." I watched Pel, waited for any tell that might give him away, instead, he looked affronted, hurt even.

"Nor, that is a cruelty that not even I would dispense to a prisoner of the Aqueno."

"Someone told him that lie."

"And you already know which of us is willing to sneak into the Aqueno Prison." Pel took my hands, long fingers wrapping around mine. "Compel me with my true name to speak the truth if you do not believe me." He did not move, but his whole body tensed.

The knot in my chest did not unwind, but it eased. Pel had never encouraged me to use his true name, to compel him to do anything, and if he was willing to now, then I did not need to. I could trust him. And he laid the truth out before me. Of course, it had to be Elrik.

"I believe you."

Pel smiled, his shoulders relaxing.

"Take me to Casper." There was no asking in my voice, only a command. The smile slipped off Pel's face as he pulled his hands away from mine.

"Nor, that would be an unwise thing to do," Pel said.

"I don't care."

"By all the sacred magics, Nor, think about what you're asking."

"Think about it?" I snapped. "I have thought about it. There are no plans to release Casper. Queen Marasina is keeping him trapped under a lake."

"And this is Queen Marasina's domain; it is her right."

I leaned in closer to him, so that my lips brushed his ear. I hated what I had to do, hated that I would ruin the small peace we had created, but Pel left me with no alternative. "I can remove your choice."

Pel's hand shot out, and I felt a sharp pain at my wrist. I jumped back, yanking my arm close to me. On my wrist were three lines of scratches. They were shallow, Pel had only grazed my skin with his fingernails, but they were deep enough to draw blood. Thin lines of coppery blood welled up on my wrist. Too late, I looked up at Pel. His fingers had the slightest film of my blood on them.

"You're not the only one with a powerful card to play," Pel said, his voice cold. He held up his fingers. There was hardly any blood on them, but it might be enough. I cursed myself for getting so close to him. I stood frozen, recalling the cold, numbing helplessness of the Magia Sange magic.

Pel stared at me, pain and determination warring across his face. Neither of us moved. Neither of us spoke. Distantly, the musicians played and faeries danced. I waited, not daring to use his name, not risking turning away from him to run. A cold sweat chilled the back of my neck as I forced myself to keep down the rising terror I felt. I had witnessed Pel kill bandits in the woods by forcing them to choke on their own blood.

What if I had pushed him too far?

"It seems we are at an impasse, little *ladrina*," Pel finally said, breaking the silence. I winced at the use of the old nickname.

"You are both fools."

Pel and I simultaneously turned to see Lorella step out from behind a nearby tree. She took in our stalemate, crossing her arms in clear disapproval.

"Were you spying on us?" Pel asked, sounding more astonished than angry.

"Someone had to keep an eye on you two," Lorella said, coming over to us. "And this won't do. Pel, you don't threaten a royal faerie with blood magic, especially not one who is a friend." Pel started to argue, but Lorella held up a hand to silence him. "And Nor, it is the highest humiliation to command a faerie with their true name. *Also,* not something to do to a friend."

"But I need to get to Casper. It is my fault he's a prisoner here, and I owe him that much," I confessed.

"Then we will free him," Lorella said, as casually as if she were commenting on the weather.

"What?" Pel and I said in unison.

"I don't believe it is right to keep someone prisoner for the sins of their father," Lorella said, her face somber. "It wasn't your young king's fault that Soren left us or that he died. And Mother taking her grief out on your king with such a punishment is not right." Lorella held her hand out to me. "And if you are willing to risk freeing him, I shall assist you any way I can."

I reached out and gripped her hand, overwhelmed with gratitude.

"Lorella—" Pel started. He was staring at her wide-eyed, his mouth slightly agape.

"You can help us, Pel, or you can leave, but if you try to stop us, I will wrap you up in a tree," Lorella said.

"I did not expect such rebellion from you," Pel said, though there was an underlying respect in his voice. He dropped his hand, wiping the thin sheen of blood on his trousers. "Very well." He turned to me. "Nor, do you have a plan?"

My plan was rough-hewn, but it was the best I could do. I reminded myself that I only needed to get Casper and myself past the lake. Once we met up with Finn, it would be a quick trek to my waiting brothers and freedom. I swiped a slender knife from the table of roasted meats, hiding it in the folds of my skirt. It was short but honed sharp. That and several hairpins Lorella gave me were the extent of my supplies, but they would have to be enough.

It was decided that Lorella would leave with Corine and Drusia, and Pel and I would depart soon after, meeting her at the part of the lake that could be opened to the Aqueno Prison. A few faeries snickered as Pel and I passed, certain that I clearly had a thing for whichever Magia Sange brother was most convenient, but none seemed suspicious. They likely assumed that Pel and I were planning to do what many of the other faerie couples were doing in the darker shadows of the courtyard, where sounds of kissing and breathy moans could be heard between songs.

Once we left the courtyard, Pel moved swiftly through the meadow, along the thick root pathway that led to the lake. I did my best to keep up, the dull burn of the sitano beginning to make itself known. I pushed through the pain, using my cane for support. Lorella and her maids stood by the edge of the lake.

At our approach, Lorella pulled a piece of sea glass from her pocket and dropped it into the dark water, causing ripples to shimmer along the surface.

For a moment, nothing happened, the lake going glassy as the ripples died down.

But then the churning began, the mini whirlpool that created the strange, dry path through the lake and to the prison. Lorella instructed Drusia to stand watch on the shore by the entrance.

The remaining four of us walked downward in silence, the black water walls as unnerving as they were the first time I came down here. At least this time I was warned when the root path morphed into that of flat stone.

At the first door, Pel cut his palm, murmuring the same incantation Elrik had, his hand pressed against the door. This time Corine stayed behind to stand guard, and the rest of us stepped into the darkness. There was a soft light from the pendant Marasina had gifted me, the Regalia Vive Amulet, the emerald sparks dancing around the golden orb.

When we reached the iron door, I shuddered. This time I could feel my magic dampen, as though it was just out of reach. But I did not need magic to break this lock. I pulled out one of the hairpins and started working the lock.

"You seemed to have a habit of breaking people out of dungeons," Pel said, reminding me of the time he had been locked up in the Rose Palace dungeon.

"Perhaps the problem is that those I care about keep getting themselves locked up," I said, focused on my work, feeling the mechanisms within the lock.

"Those people must consider themselves lucky to have such a resourceful friend," Pel said.

"That almost sounded like a compliment," I said, sparing a glance for him. His features were hard to make out in the near darkness, but I saw a flash of a smile.

"I like you two better when you get along," Lorella said, "but please focus on the door. We have cut a wide path into the lake, and

I'd like to remove it before anyone notices." She tapped her foot until I felt the lock click, and the thick door swung open.

Before I could remind myself of how much Casper despised me, I took the first step to free him.

19

Though I knew what to expect this time, I was still amazed at the strangeness of the Aqueno Prison, with its sheer walls exposing the lake beyond. I stepped into the prison, searching for Casper. I found him asleep on a stone slab, the same tattered blanket wrapped around him. I rushed over to him, my heart aching to see the boy I loved, knowing he no longer cared for me. I did not miss that he wore his signet ring, a glint of gold in the gloom. He had lost weight and was too pale in this eerie prison, but he still looked at peace in his sleep, still looked so handsome. It took all my willpower to resist reaching out to touch him.

"Casper," I said gently. When he did not stir, I repeated, louder. "*Casper.*"

He cracked open an eye, blinking as he woke up. As his eyes focused on me, he woke fully, his demeanor instantly changing to something alert.

"Nor?"

"Yes, it's me. And I'm getting you out of here." I started to pull him up, but he yanked his arm away, scrambling to his feet.

"You can't do that." He focused on the entrance of the prison, his stare fixed on Pel and Lorella, who had both stayed near the entrance, giving us space. "Elrik, why have you brought her back here? I did as you asked."

"Elrik isn't here. That is Pel, along with Lorella. They are friends." *Sort of.*

I tried to reassure Casper. From this distance, it was easy to mistake one brother for the other. Casper continued to stare at Pel as the second half of what he said hit me. "What do you mean you did as he asked?"

"That isn't Elrik?" Casper asked, still straining to see the faeries at the door.

"No, I told you—"

"Where is he?" Casper demanded, frantically looking around as though Elrik might be hiding behind a nearby stalagmite.

"Sulking in his chambers, I suspect. At least, I hope he is. He doesn't know we're here, and I'd like to keep it that way, so let's get you out of here."

I hoped that would be enough explanation to get Casper moving. Instead, he threw his arms around me, wrapping me in a rib-crushing embrace, holding me tight, my head pressed to his shoulder.

I froze, too shocked to move, afraid that this moment would shatter, and Casper would remember he despised me. I closed my eyes, committing this feeling to memory. My face pressed into the rough linen shirt Casper wore as I breathed him in. He no longer smelled of his expensive soap, but rather a musky, briny smell. But I was grateful to have any piece of him, knowing it would not last.

I was not ready when Casper finally pulled away, though he kept his hands gripped on my shoulders, holding me at arm's length. He stared at me, his dark eyes examining every bit of my face. I knew what he saw: unfamiliar golden cat eyes, strange white hair, pointed ears, sharp teeth, and glowing skin. I waited for the disdain I knew would come, waited for the horror to infuse his features. Instead, his face was unreadable, fully focused on me.

"Nor, is it really you?" His hand cupped my cheek, a cool palm on my ignited skin.

"Yes," I answered, my voice little more than a whisper. I wanted to lean into his touch, realizing how desperately I missed it. I swallowed hard, dreading the moment this would all crumble.

I braced myself for his contempt. I braced for further rejection and pain. I did not expect the kiss.

He leaned into me, his lips crushing mine. His lips felt cold as he pressed into me. My heart knew it was being toyed with, knew the agony was coming and I shoved him away. Casper staggered back, looking as stunned as I felt.

"By the Holy Mother, what was that?" I swore, deflecting my pain into anger.

"You are alive," Casper said, which answered none of my questions.

"Of course, I'm alive you fool. I haven't been the one locked in some unnatural prison all this time. I believe it's rotted your brain. Don't think that because I'm here to free you that you owe me some false affection." I rubbed my lips, as though I could wipe away the kiss. "You made it perfectly clear what a monster you think I am."

"I'm sorry, Nor. He gave me no choice."

"He?"

"The one you were with last time, Elrik. The night before he brought you here, he paid me a visit." His face puckered as though he smelled something unpleasant. "He said that I had to tell you I would be freed in winter, that I had to make you want to stay in Magnomel. I tried to refuse, but he said he would hurt you. He told me he would kill you if I could not convince you to stay." Casper bit his lip, struggling with the rest. "I'm sorry, Nor. I didn't know how else to keep you safe."

I stilled, gripping my cane as his words sank in. I had suspected that Elrik had lied to Casper, told him he would be freed in winter, but I had not realized he had gone so far. I wanted to believe Casper, longed to be back in his good graces, and to be in his heart, but it seemed too much to hope for.

"You aren't disgusted by me? By what I am now?"

I held out my palms, exposing the gleaming skin, so far from being human.

Slowly, Casper reached out and clasped my hands. "No, Nor, I'm not."

"But you hate the fay."

"I was a fool to think all the fay are the same. To condemn them all for the actions of some."

"You sound like a politician," I retorted.

Casper chuckled, "Then here is a better answer." Casper drew me in, wrapping one arm protectively around me. "I almost lost you, Nor. Until your visit, I didn't even know if you were alive. I spent weeks down here, convinced Elrik had poisoned you, that you had died. That I couldn't save you, and I would never have you back in my life." He traced a finger lightly down my arm, the small gesture sending butterflies flapping in my stomach. "It was a shock to see how you've changed, but you could have become an ogre for all I care, so long as I have you back."

I pressed my hand against my mouth, too overwhelmed to speak. I wiped away tears that suddenly formed at my eyes, desperate to maintain some composure.

"So you want to be with me?" I felt raw, my heart naked and exposed and already in Casper's possession.

In response, Casper gently released me, going down on one knee as he pulled his signet ring off his finger, holding it up to me.

"Elenora Molnár, I am hopelessly in love with you. Will you marry me?"

Relief and joy flooded over me, leaving me with an elated lightness. I didn't think I could speak without sobbing, I nodded. Casper slipped the ring on my finger. I distantly heard Lorella clap. As Casper rose, I ran my fingers in his hair, locking him to me and pulled him in to a kiss. My lips explored his, which were cold, but soft. I wondered if the sitano in my blood made me run hot or if being in this damp underground prison so long had leeched the heat from Casper. I drew him in tighter, pouring my warmth into him, pouring all my love into him. Kissing me back, he enveloped me in his arms, holding me close to him.

I didn't hear Pel approach until he loudly cleared his throat. Casper and I slowly disengaged, remembering we were not alone. I turned to Pel, heat rushing to my cheeks, as I pressed my lips together.

"I'm sorry, Pel." I didn't know what else to say. I didn't know how to apologize, how to articulate that I cared for him, but my heart belonged to Casper.

Pel shook his head, as if it was not important, though there was a lingering sadness in his eyes. "I've known your heart was elsewhere for a long time." He met Casper's eyes, "She is a rare treasure, you know."

Casper nodded. It seemed the closest the two would get to a truce.

"This is so lovely, congratulations," Lorella said, breaking in. "But I must remind you all that we are still in the middle of a prison escape and should probably leave."

"Right," I agreed, though I was grinning like a fool. Soon, I would have everything I wanted. We would be free, Casper loved me, and I would see my brothers before the end of the night.

I turned, ready to leave the prison.

Standing in the prison doorway was Elrik.

20

"**B**ig brother, what a mess you've made." Elrik leaned against the prison door. "And Lady Lorella, this is almost treasonous."

For the space of a breath, it appeared as though Pel was in front of a mirror, two golden-haired faeries facing each other.

The illusion shattered as the other faerie locked eyes with me, a cold sweat chilling my neck as Elrik's calculating amber eyes raked over me.

"How did you find out?" Pel asked, stepping toward his brother.

"Find out?" Elrik laughed, an incredulous sound, devoid of mirth as he made his way into the prison. "By all the sacred magics, you have an open trail in the middle of the lake!"

"Elrik, I can explain—" Pel started, but Elrik shoved past him and Lorella, his focus back on me.

"My dearest Elenora, why do you insist on causing so much trouble this night?" His words were tight, his whole body taut with barely contained violence.

I could almost feel his cold blood magic, the pleasure he took from controlling me against my will. I stepped back, nearly knocking into Casper. Casper's arms were around me, still strong after weeks in this prison, and a sense of security, of safety warmed the cold within me, reigniting my courage.

"I am not yours." I barely spoke above a whisper, but there was no doubt in my words. "Consider our deal fulfilled."

Elrik froze. His mask of calm cracked, the wild, dangerous creature revealing itself. "This is unacceptable. You humiliate me in front of the court and now I find you in the Aqueno Prison with the human king. I will drag you back to the court by your hair, lock you in a tower, bind you to me with blood magic. Then I will come back and kill your kingling, so you have no one to run to. I will do it all to make you mine. The throne will be mine." Something manic lit behind his eyes, the naked desire for power fully revealed.

Casper's arms tightened around me, but I stood tall, refusing to cower to Elrik's threats, though I knew he meant every one of them.

"I am not yours, Elrik. I never have been, and I never will be."

Elrik cocked his head to the side, surprised anyone would dare contradict him. "I will make you—"

"No. You won't."

Elrik paused, examining Casper's arms around me. His lip curled up in an ugly sneer. "I showed you too much mercy when I didn't kill you the first time." In a swift motion, he pulled a dagger from his belt, the jeweled hilt gleaming in the gloom. Casper tried to pull me away, to put himself between us, but I was not the one in danger. Elrik's focus was entirely on Casper, and by protecting me, Casper made himself an easy target. I heard Lorella scream as Elrik lunged toward Casper, the blade aimed at Casper's heart. I pulled the knife from my skirts, plunging it into Elrik's arm.

Elrik howled with pain, dropping his dagger. There was a long cut on his arm, thick, golden blood pouring out of the wound and soaking the shredded sleeve. Pel rushed over to us, pulling his brother away from me. I kept a tight grip on the knife, ready to stab Elrik again if he came near me or Casper.

"Brother, this stops tonight," Pel said. He released his brother but kept his eyes on the dangerous faerie.

Elrik stepped back, laughing, though the noise was breathy, with hisses of pain as he applied pressure to the wound. "I shall make you pay for that transgression, Elenora."

"You will not lay a finger on her," Lorella said. "She and her king are leaving tonight."

Elrik raised an eyebrow. "Oh, what is the little bastard lady going to do?" He sneered. "You can't go running to mommy. What do you think our queen will do when she finds out you freed her prisoner and allowed her beloved heir to escape?"

"I will deal with that. You will stay silent on the matter. I will pay you whatever you want." Lorella stood tall, her shoulders back and her chin up, not succumbing to any of Elrik's taunts and threats.

Elrik scoffed, clearly trying to seem indifferent, but I could tell he was in pain by the stiff way he gripped his arm.

He leaned back against one of the stalagmites, studying the four of us. "Lady Lorella, anything you offer me pales in comparison to what I shall have with Elenora as mine. She will become queen, and I will rule as king."

"That will never happen," I bit out. "I despise you."

Elrik clucked, "Such a pity. I had hoped to do this the easy way." He sighed. "And I worked so hard to get you to fall in love with me. You have no idea how much planning went into saving you."

"What are you talking about?" I asked, certain I would not like the answer.

"I had to ensure the timing was exactly right for when the curse exploded your door," he said slowly, as though explaining to a child. "I had hoped rescuing you would have elicited more gratitude."

"That was Valente's work—" I started, sensing something was wrong.

"Was it?" Elrik asked, sounding too amused. "Or were you convinced to believe that?"

"But you were with me before it happened."

"For a thief, I thought you would be better at seeing misdirection. I had help." He nodded toward the prison door. "Come in, there is no point in hiding."

In flew Corine, landing besides Elrik. In her hands was a glass orb, red mist swirling inside.

"Corine," Lorella gasped. "What is going on?"

Corine looked up coolly at Elrik, her demeanor vastly different from the faerie I thought I knew. "Do you want me to throw this now?" She held up the orb.

Elrik chuckled. "Not quite yet."

"Corine, what has Elrik promised you?" Lorella asked, her words bitter.

Corine shifted her attention to Lorella, staring at her with utter disdain. "Elrik *sees* me. He values my gifts. Finds me more than a stupid, obedient maid. He has promised to elevate my position at court. Unlike all the Magia Viveralis, he doesn't find me beneath him simply because I can't do strong magic."

"Indeed," Elrik said, gesturing to the object Corine held. "She is most adept at explosions. And most carefully planted one on Elenora's door."

I felt my stomach drop, the betrayal sinking in. I realized how far Elrik would go to achieve power. "And the piro berries, was that you as well?"

"No, my love. Though I wish I had thought of them. Perhaps if I had saved you from near certain death twice, you would be more pliable."

"Where is Drusia?" Lorella suddenly asked, looking around as though the tiny green faerie might be hiding in the prison.

"My simple sister knows nothing," Corine said, smirking. "Elrik ensured that she naps while we tie up loose ends."

"Blood magic," I whispered, horrified that Corine would allow Elrik to use his power on her sister.

"Indeed." Elrik sighed. Addressing Pel and Lorella, he continued, "Unfortunately, I cannot let you leave, now that you know so much, and I can't dispatch you with blood magic, not as this prison is shielded from magic." He pointed to the orb that Corine held. I watched the red smoke swirl around in the glass. "But Corine discovered a way to create a bomb that doesn't need magic."

"We are family," Pel argued, but Elrik waved his hand to dismiss him.

"More's the pity, but it must be done. Unless," Elrik turned to me, "you would care to save your friends."

My heart hammered, even as my body froze. Elrik was not bluffing. One wrong word and he would have Corine blow up the prison. My mouth went dry, but I forced the words out.

"What do you want?"

"You must love me. Be always by my side. Marry me." A cruel smile tugged at his lips. "You will be mine and make me king. Or I kill everyone here." He spoke the terrible words calmly, and I knew he was deranged enough to do it. I realized I had one chance to stop him.

I nodded as I stepped away from Casper, toward Elrik. Casper gripped my wrist. For a few seconds, I faced him, my back toward Elrik and mouthed "trust me." Casper frowned, but released my hand. I crossed over to Elrik, the click-click of my cane against the stone floor the only sound. My other hand gripped the knife, once again hidden in my skirts.

Elrik gave me a wolfish grin as I approached, as though he won some sort of prize. "You may be trainable yet."

I didn't say anything, but moved closer to him, waiting for the right moment.

"Kiss me," Elrik demanded, and I felt a mix of revulsion and a thrill as the opportunity presented itself. I leaned into Elrik. The moment his lips closed on mine, I pulled out the blade.

"Elrik!" Corine yelled at the same time I extended my arm. Elrik pushed me away a second before I could shove the knife into him. I fell on the stone floor, the knife clattering beside me. I started to reach for it—

"Elenora Astira Molnár, I command you to stop."

My whole body went rigid at Elrik's words. I struggled to move, but was immobilized on the ground, unable to even bend a finger. Elrik's sharp grin widened.

"I was wondering if that would work."

Casper rushed to my side, kneeling next to me.

"What did you do to her?" he asked, his voice frantic with worry. I wanted to tell him to get away, but my jaw was locked.

"I used her true name, of course. You see, I had a theory that her given name must be her true name now that she is fay. And what luck that Corine told me about a memory witnessed in Alverdine's home, one of baby Elenora where her parents spoke her true name."

Rage boiled within me, hating Corine for her deception. I hated Elrik even more, my mind aching to attack him, but my body under his command.

"Brother, stop this," Pel said, but Elrik only laughed.

"It is so hard for you to believe that I've won, isn't it, big brother?"

"This is more than a game."

"Everything is a game," Elrik snapped, then calmed. "Elenora, you will come with me. You will do as I command. You shall never humiliate me again. Elenora Astira Molnár come to me. Kiss me as though you love me."

I silently screamed, my mind protesting every moment, even as I rose. I tried to force myself to stop walking, to stop moving, but it was as though my legs no longer belonged to me. I closed the distance between myself and Elrik, my hands already reaching out to him as I leaned up, my mouth ready to kiss him. I silently howled to stop, but my body was not my own. Elrik did not even pull me toward him, rather waited, too pleased, as I was forced to come to him, letting the terrible moments drag out. Unable to control my arms, I ran my hand through his hair, gripping the golden locks and pulling his face to mine in a sick parody of the way I had pulled Casper to me. It was *my* lips that crushed against Elrik's.

Elrik's head was yanked back. I breathed in air, but helplessly leaned toward him again, struggling as strong hands pulled me away. I watched as a knife sliced over his throat. It all happened so fast that Elrik didn't scream, even as golden blood bubbled from the wound across his neck. He fell to the ground, a pool of blood spreading around him. Casper stood over him, my knife in his hand, coated in blood.

Even as Elrik lay dying, my body fought to get to him, to kiss him as I was commanded. As I wrestled against the hands that held me, I silently prayed they would not release me. Elrik's amber eyes stared at me with fading surprise, as though I had been the one to cut his throat. Pel rushed over, holding his brother's head in his lap as Casper staggered away.

"Elenora Astira Molnár, I curse you." Elrik's words were quiet, but clear in the silence of the prison. A cold pressure suddenly washed over me. Elrik coughed up blood, but managed to add, "*Cignamorte tesseranzio desfaire.*" He took a shuddering breath and whispered, "Elenora Astira Molnár, I will it so."

The cold pressure slowly faded, till there was nothing left but a shadow of chill in my bones. My body kept fighting to move toward him, to kiss him even, until his chest stilled and his eyes went glassy. I knew he was dead when I could control my limbs, and I stopped fighting against Lorella. Sensing that I was no longer struggling to get to Elrik, Lorella released me. I slumped to my knees, overwhelmed and numbed.

Pel did not say anything as he silently closed his brother's eyes. He stared down at the body of his brother, the prison quiet, save for my ragged breath. I didn't see Casper approach me, but I felt his hand grip mine.

"You have ruined everything!" Corine screeched above us. I looked up to see the purple faerie flying around the stalactites.

"I will deal with you," Lorella said, her voice even as she flapped her wings.

In response, Corine darted for the door, throwing the glass orb toward the far wall of the prison. The orb shattered against the wall, the red smoke, now freed, exploded in a cloud of noise and dust. Casper threw himself over me.

The last thing I heard were the walls of the prison cracking.

21

Water rushed around us from all sides. I had only a moment to take a breath of air before a wave from the lake collapsed over us. Casper was ripped away from me. I reached out wildly for him, losing my cane in my frantic search. I flailed in the water, desperate to find his hand again, but all I found was water, endless, chilling water. The normally placid lake was a maelstrom of waves, and soon I was tossed and flipped so often I had no idea which way was up. I opened my eyes, but sand stung them, making it impossible to see.

My chest burned for need of air and I had to fight the frantic urge to scream. If I didn't breathe soon, I'd die. Another swell pushed me down, and a sharp pain radiated through my head. I shoved my hands down, feeling a sharp rock and the sandy bottom of the lake. Getting to the surface would be impossible. Black spots started to form around my vision, the need to inhale almost unpreventable.

Desperately, I reached out with the only thing I had left, my magic. I sensed my feeble magic ripped away by another violent surge of water. All except a small knot in my chest. It took all my will to focus on that magic. Weakly, I reached my hand over my chest, surprised to find Marasina's amulet still around my throat. I clutched at it, forcing my power into it, taking every scrap of strength I had and directing it into the amulet before succumbing to the water. A searing heat blazed from the charm, tendrils of it wrapping around my arms and legs, giving me a new rush of strength. My vision cleared. My lungs no longer burned.

I shoved off the lake floor, thrusting my limbs through the choppy water. Even with the viveralis magic, I had to push myself beyond exhaustion. I kicked and swam and even tried flapping my wings to force myself closer to the surface, which I felt rather than saw. The glow of the viveralis token was my only light in the black waters. Even when I was tossed or turned around, with the generations of fay queens around me, I could feel which way led to the surface, as though the magic knew that for my life to continue, I needed air.

My head shot out of the water at last, and I gasped, greedily gulping in air, choking from the waves that crashed around me, getting briny water sucked into my chest along with the precious air. I looked around, trying to orient myself. I was close to the edge of the lake that lined up with the Biawood, away from the Forest Court. My strength was all but gone, and I wondered if I could even make it to shore. Something floated by me, and I reached out, gripping the object in hopes that it would keep me afloat.

To my surprise, it was my pearwood cane. It eased the need to swim as hard, but I had to keep moving. I looked around, trying to find Casper or the faeries, but I couldn't make out anything but the movement of the water.

Praying they made it to the shore, I kicked toward the Biawood Forest. My movements were slow, everything hurt, and each time I raised my arms to propel myself through the water, I wondered if it would be my last time.

I can't give up, I reminded myself, though my head was foggy with fatigue. *Casper needs me. He is just on the other side. He's on the bank. He has to be. We will make it home.*

A few seconds felt like lifetimes before I reached the sandy shore. I collapsed to the ground, wet sand sticking to my skin and hair. I coughed and sputtered, spitting out lake water.

Fighting the urge to lay down, I forced myself to my feet, using my cane as leverage, the need to find Casper wiping out the relief of reaching land.

I searched the waves, but saw nothing but dark, choppy water. Sharp panic seared through me, as I started calling his name.

"Casper! Casper!" I screamed my throat raw, my cries hoarse croaks.

Then I saw them. Further down, Pel was swimming with someone in his arms. Lorella appeared overhead, flying above the lake. She was drenched, but otherwise appeared uninjured from the prison cave-in. She swooped down, helping Pel to heave Casper to the shore. Casper was limp. I raced toward them, the screaming pains in my body muted by my fierce need to get to Casper.

I nearly fell on top of him as I reached them, pushing Pel aside.

"Casper!" I yelled, trying to rouse him. I shook him, hard, as though I could force him back to consciousness.

"Help him," I pleaded to Pel. To his credit, Pel nodded, scraping a sharp stone across his palm, bringing the blood to Casper's lips as I opened his mouth.

"*Annullaris sange,*" Pel said. I stared at Casper's too-white face, his eyes still closed. I prayed to the Holy Family to let Casper live. After several attempts, Pel dropped his hand from Casper's face, shaking his head at me. "I'm sorry, Nor."

"It can't be! Casper, please, I need you to wake up." His lips were tinged blue. "Casper!" I pressed on his chest, praying that he would start coughing up the lake water. "Casper, I can't lose you. Not again."

I beat hard on his chest, afraid I might crack a rib, more afraid that it wouldn't matter.

Casper didn't stir. All the color had leached out of him, all except his blue lips. I pressed again on his chest, needing to do more.

"Casper!"

Nothing. My own heart was cracking, my soul draining away with his life. He had been lost to me for so long. I screamed in frustration and pain. All the fighting, all the scheming to rescue him, and the reward for my efforts was this. *He's dead. I caused his death*, a cruel voice in my head repeated. I tried again and again to shake him, to thump his chest, to breathe life into him. Nothing was working. I thought I might choke on my tears. *He's dead. I killed him.*

"No!" I screamed. "You have to come back to me. You have to!" I pulled at my magic. *Life magic*, I thought desperately. Whatever power I possessed, I would give it all to Casper to save his life. He could have my life if it would buy him another breath.

"*Vive guarriana*," I recited, a healing spell Lorella had taught me.

Nothing happened. The magic I had used in the lake had extinguished my meager abilities.

"*Vive guarriana*," I repeated. I couldn't fail him. Casper needed me. If I didn't save him right now . . . I directed the ferocity of my terror into tearing the magic out of me. "*Vive guarriana. Vive guarriana. Vive guarriana!*"

A small flicker of a buzzing sensation stirred within me. I flung it into Casper's chest where it buried itself and then was gone.

"Casper," I begged, but he lay lifeless in my arms.

Tears stung my eyes, blurring everything.

"Lorella, please help me," I begged.

"Nor, it's too late," Lorella said.

"Please!"

Silently, she held one of my hands. This time, I felt magic pour from her and myself into Casper; it was a warmer, stronger feeling. I focused all my will into seeing him breathe again. I prayed it would be enough.

But even the strong flow of power was a sputtering flame against the downpour that was death. I yanked the amulet from around my neck, breaking the silver chain as I pressed the amulet against Casper's chest, my hand so tight against the pendant I thought it might shatter. "*Vive guarriana.*" This time a surge of warmth swelled within me, as though some hidden reserve of magic and desperation was called to by the amulet. *Not enough*, I thought. I dragged out every last ounce of energy I had, feeling Lorella straining beside me. All my intention was focused on the boy in my arms. The world slipped away to nothing but the magic and Casper.

"*VIVE GUARRIANA.*" As though a dam had been loosened, magic flooded through me, strong and sharp. I felt weightless, yet grounded in the power, as though I were a lightning storm. Its presence surrounded me; a sharp and tangy taste in my mouth and pins and needles up my arms.

I drew the power together, forced every bit of it from me, took everything Lorella could offer, and every flame from the amulet, and directed it all at Casper, shoving the life magic into his chest. The force of it knocked me backward, and I toppled onto the muddy sand, reeling from the impact.

I was suddenly cold, feeling drained and empty.

I scrambled to my knees, crawling back over to Casper. Terrified that it had not worked, I gently leaned over him, my tears splashing on his cheeks.

"Casper?" His eyes were still closed, his pallor still too pale. But his lips were no longer blue. I held my breath, studying him, and saw his chest slowly rise and fall. The joy made me cry harder, relief mixed with exhaustion.

"Nor?" His voice was a croak. Slowly, he opened his eyes. He coughed and promptly vomited up lake water.

"I'm right here." I grabbed his hand in mine, squeezing it too hard in reassurance.

"What . . ." Dark brown eyes stared at me in confusion. "What happened?"

"The prison . . . The lake . . . You nearly—" I wanted to say he nearly drowned, but the words wouldn't come. I knew he hadn't *nearly* drowned. "You swallowed a lot of water."

"Are we free?" Casper struggled to sit up. For the first time, he took in our surroundings, the lake churning from the ruptured prison, the tall trees overhead, and the Forest Court at the center of the lake. He stiffened when he saw Pel and Lorella, though he didn't flinch.

"We will be, very soon," I promised.

"I missed the sky," Casper said, staring up at the night sky overhead, a dark blanket dotted with stars. "And you." Those dark eyes were on me again. I didn't know which I wanted more: to kiss him or beg his forgiveness.

"I hate to be insensitive to your condition," Lorella said to Casper, "but you should leave now if you wish to remain out of my mother's control." Her gaze flickered across the lake toward the Forest Court. "Even if no one from the revel heard the explosion, it won't be long before the destruction of the prison is noticed." Her face paled, and she suddenly went rigid. "Drusia!" Without another word, she took to the air, flying back across the lake.

I watched her go, but the prison entrance had been on the other side, and I lost sight of her. I swallowed hard, praying the little green faerie was unharmed.

"Lorella was right, you should be going," Pel said. He still sat in the sand, drenched head to toe, but only stared at the lake, as though he could see the Aqueno Prison if he looked hard enough.

To my astonishment, Casper put his hand on Pel's shoulder. The gesture was awkward, but his tone was sincere as he said, "My condolences and apologies."

Pel raised his eyebrow, a skeptical look on his face as he turned to study Casper.

"I had to do it to save Nor. And if I am to be truly honest, I would have killed him to avenge Christopher's death." Casper paused before adding, "But I know the pain of losing a brother."

I inhaled sharply. In all the chaos following the explosion, I had been too focused on ensuring Casper survived to truly take in the fact that he killed Elrik. Or that despite my hatred of Elrik, he was still Pel's brother, his family. Casper's words reminded me that Elrik had killed Casper's brother, ordered to by Queen Marasina as revenge for Soren's death. I watched the two young men, both of whom I cared for so deeply, though in different ways. I realized their lives were also irrevocably intertwined. I wanted to smooth things over between them, say something to bridge the distance, but this was between the two of them.

Pel took in Casper's words before staring back at the lake, his gaze unfocused. "I suspect this will hurt more when the shock fades, but Elrik deserved his fate." Pel squeezed his eyes shut, a moment of pain playing across his face before he steadied himself. Returning his focus to Casper, he gave a slight nod in my direction. "Take care of her." His lip quirked in the barest hint of a smile. "She has a tendency to find trouble."

Casper let out a breath that almost sounded like a laugh. "Indeed she does," he agreed, but his voice was warm.

"I am right here," I complained, though something lifted in my heart to see this peace between Pel and Casper, even if it was a tenuous one.

Pel rose to his feet, still graceful despite dripping wet. "You two need to leave Magnomel. Do you need supplies?" He frowned, looking at the Forest Court. I could tell he was worried that provisioning us would cost us time, as well as more chances for him to be discovered aiding us.

"No, we will be fine," I said, certain Finn and the others would have everything we needed. At a concerned look from Casper, I explained that my brother was waiting for us.

"Of course. I should have expected nothing less from the Molnár family."

"But I do have one question," I ventured, Elrik's last words niggling me.

Pel's lip quirked ever so slightly as he asked, "Only one question, Nor?"

"What did Elrik mean? He said something to me, right before," I left the sentence hanging. "Signa mort tess something," I added, stumbling over the unfamiliar words.

Pel's brow furrowed. "That does not make sense. *Cignamorte* refers to the lives of swans, as every creature has some force of life that is unique. But whatever he meant to say, clearly he was not able to finish."

I nodded, feeling guilty to even bring up Elrik so soon. And Pel was correct, his power over me was gone, the power of my name on his lips broke when he died. It was not worth speculating what other schemes he had planned.

Clumsily, I clambered to my feet. I felt stiff and sore, bruises I had ignored while fighting for my life now demanded to be heard. But none of the pains were as frightening as the idea of being caught by Marasina's guards. I reached down, helped Casper rise as I held on to my cane with my other hand.

I took several steps toward Pel, feeling awkward. "I don't know the best way to say goodbye." I fidgeted, uncertain how to express everything to the strange faerie boy I had both hated and loved. "But thank you for saving my life and letting me go." And even though I had no regrets in choosing Casper, a part of my heart ached with the knowledge that I also had to let Pel go.

Pel smiled, and it almost reached his eyes. "Be well and happy, Elenora Molnár." He took my hands, "And know that I will remain your friend." The words seemed to hurt him, though he put on a good show of hiding it. His finger traced the line of my bracelet, the one of gold he had given me. "And I will still come if you summon me." Before I could respond, he kissed me on the cheek, a swift and chaste thing, the light feel of his petal-soft lips on my cheek lasting only a breath before he stepped back. His dragonfly wings flapped several times, water droplets flying off them, before he was airborne and heading back to the Forest Court.

I led Casper into the Biawood. I didn't mind the damp clothes, as the night was warm, but the squish I felt with every step in my wet shoes had me wishing for sturdy, and most importantly, dry boots. But Casper did not complain, and he had briefly died this evening, so I swallowed my discomfort, silently leaning more heavily on my pearwood cane when the sitano made my limbs ache and burn.

I didn't mention that the fay had sharper eyesight than humans. I could clearly see the dark trees and shrubs along our way, where my human eyes would have only seen shadowed silhouettes. It helped not to mistake the outline of a slender tree for an approaching faerie, but I still wanted to jump at every rustle of leaves.

Again, Finn was sitting up in a tree, at the exact same place he had been the two days before. And even better than before, he brought supplies: dry clothes, sturdy boots, along with apples, dried meat, cheese, and a full waterskin.

Casper hungrily eyed the food, and I suggested he eat while I changed behind a tree. Once Casper had also discarded his prisoner attire for something clean and dry, we set back toward Reynallis, Finn leading the way.

The delicious feeling of being dry, along with the food and the sense of impending freedom kept me going, even though exhaustion was not far off. Finn said he found a shortcut through the woods, one that would bring us to Reynallis much quicker.

Indeed, by the early evening of the next day we had reached the strange mist wall that separated Magnomel from the human lands. It was nearing sunset, the golden light disappearing into the white fog beyond. Apprehension about crossing through the wall seeped into my initial relief at making it this far.

I shuddered, recalling the last time we tried to cross the mist barrier, only to be captured by the fay. I tentatively stuck my hand in the mist, the chill damp contrasting with the warm summer air. Casper also eyed the wall warily, though Finn did not seem the least concerned, rummaging through a pack he brought, pulling out three cloaks, throwing one over his shoulders before handing us the other two.

"It is a bit warm for this," I said, touching the thick wool of the cloak.

"Not where we're going," Finn answered, his focus back on his sack.

"How did you manage to cross through the mist without getting lost?" I asked, ignoring his strange comment.

"With this." He triumphantly held up a compass. It was such a straightforward solution, such a non-magical, human solution that I had to laugh.

"Casper, think of the time we could have saved if we had brought a compass." I had expected the mist wall to be filled with enchantments, but I had overlooked the simpler answer.

Casper smiled, despite the dark circles under his eyes. "Next time we are kidnapped, I shall pack a bag first."

"Ready?" Finn asked, extending his hand to me.

"Wait," I said, taking a step back. I carefully cupped the moonstone on the head of my cane, my palms pressed into its smooth, cool surface. I closed my eyes, focusing my will on the stone, and the glamour that lived within the stone. I imagined myself human, my straw-colored hair, chestnut eyes, and tanned skin that never glowed. I thought about red blood in my veins, rounded ears, and teeth that were not too sharp and eyes with round pupils.

As I concentrated on those features, I murmured my true name.

"Elenora Astira Molnár."

I felt a pull of magic from the moonstone, one that soaked into my hands and snaked up my arms, radiating through my whole body. Only when the sensation ceased did I open my eyes. Both my brother and Casper stared at me, eyes wide and jaws slack.

"How do I look?" I asked, hoping I didn't somehow mess up the spell.

"Human," Finn said.

The mist still clung to us, the same unnatural smell of mint and something else filling my nose, but we kept walking. I held Finn's hand, his other holding the compass to his face, keeping us in the right direction. With my other hand, I held my cane as Casper clasped my wrist. It wouldn't do for any of us to get lost this close to Reynallis. Pel's golden bracelet still burned my wrist when I entered the mist, and I knew Pel would be notified that we were here. But I was certain that this time, he would not follow me.

Eventually, the mist lessened around us. Whereas before I could barely see my hand in front of my face, now I could see several feet ahead, see the trees before running into them. At first, the trees were thick with leaves, but as we kept going, they began to lose their leaves, becoming skeletal outlines of branches and twigs, the floor littered with brown foliage.

Soon, the mist was gone altogether. My vision cleared without the strange fog, like a ghostly veil had been lifted. The air no longer tasted of mint, but remained chilled. My breath plumed before me. I looked around in astonishment. It had been summer in Magnomel, everything rich and green, warm and soft. It was as though time had sped forward by several months, landing Reynallis in the midst of autumn, leaves yellowing on trees, the grass brown and dead underfoot.

"I told you that it would be colder," Finn said, taking in our shocked expressions. "You both have been missing for several months."

"So, it is true that Magnomel never sees winter," I marveled.

Casper studied the landscape, his eyes glossy with unshed tears. I gave his hand a reassuring squeeze.

Finn led us to a small hut on the edge of the woods, a warm glow coming from within. Smoke poured out from the chimney, melting into the darkening sky. Finn banged on the wooden door, and I heard a latch click open, heat and light spilling out. My eyes first landed on Devon, my older brother, staring down at me with something like awe before his face broke into a wide grin. I smiled back, my throat suddenly too tight with emotion to speak.

"I told you I'd get them out," Finn said at the same time Jacobie barreled into me, both of us stumbling back at his embrace.

I held him for a long time, relieved and overwhelmed, beyond grateful to have my brothers back. He only released me when Devon complained that we were letting all the cold air in. I reluctantly let go of my little brother, ruffling his hair as I did so. I could swear he grew since I last saw him. But then again, we had all changed since the summer.

Self-consciously, I rubbed my shoulder, confirming my glamour held. My hands only felt my shoulder blades, though I thought I could sense my wings, like water beneath a frozen lake. But as Devon made us tea, and Jacobie pestered me with questions, Magnomel felt far away. Casper sat beside me, never leaving my side, his hand often on mine or his arm wrapped around my waist as though he needed to touch me to confirm this was all real. I snuggled into his arm, resting my head on his shoulder as I let a mug of tea warm my hands.

22

"Constance, it is practically winter," Casper said, gesturing to the window. An overnight frost left icy lacework on the glass.

"Making it all the better to attack. They won't be expecting it."

Casper, Constance and myself, along with Ilana and Flora, as representatives of Glavnada and Faradisia, gathered around the wide oak table in Casper's study. A large map lay spread across the table, small figurines representing potential allies and enemies. We had been home less than a fortnight, but already tensions ran high.

"But it won't be winter there, it is never winter in Magnomel," I pointed out, which earned me an arched eyebrow from Constance.

"And how did you know that in an underwater prison?" she demanded.

I shot Casper a quick glance, one Constance seemed to catch. While Constance had been initially overjoyed to have her brother returned, she had become suspicious of our explanation, doubtful we were telling her the full truth. Possibly because we weren't.

Only Casper and Finn knew that I was fay, masquerading as human. I insisted it was safer that way, choosing not even to tell Devon and Jacobie. I had no intention of ever removing the glamour charm, so I decided there was no need for anyone else to know. Instead, the story we agreed on was that both Casper and I had been held captive in the Aqueno Prison, trapped under the lake till we managed to take down one of the guards and make our escape. We told everyone that I had been poisoned, as I still needed my cane, but left out the true results of the sitano. We relied on the fact that there had been so much chaos during the battle on Casper's coronation that no other human had heard Queen Marasina when she said I had worked with Pel.

"Because it was summer when we left the faerie prison, and then mid-autumn when we arrived in Reynallis," Casper said, exasperated.

"Maybe it was simply an unusually warm day," Constance argued, though she did not question us further.

I exhaled. Once or twice I had let too much slip, small things that I would not have known if I had spent all my time locked away in a prison.

"Perhaps we should take a break," Flora cut in, gently taking Constance's arm. She gave a meaningful glance at Casper and me before adding, "I think we are all a bit tired."

The gaunt look was gone from Casper's face, though the dark hollows beneath his eyes stubbornly remained. Flora was constantly asking after our health, ensuring we got rest, and almost as suffocatingly careful around us as my maid, Annabeth, now was. Though I knew it came from a place of genuine concern, I was uneasy and unused to being so attended to. And right now, I could tell that Casper's fatigue had less to do with his time as a faerie hostage and more with the endless arguments with his sister.

Constance seemed ready to argue, but Flora gently squeezed her arm, giving her a significant look. "Yes, of course," Constance finally conceded.

"I will need to know soon if I should send word home to muster soldiers," Ilana said. "The winter storms make travel in and out of Glavnada very difficult. Perhaps we can finalize this tomorrow," Ilana added before starting for the door. She paused, turning to me. "Which reminds me, Lady Elenora, I recently received a box of sugared peach toffees, a delicacy from my home, and perhaps you would enjoy some?" She smiled, and I swore there was a slight blush to her cheeks as she added, "And maybe your brothers would also like to try them? I shall have the box sent to you." Ilana quickly turned on her heels, leaving the study.

Casper cocked an eyebrow at me. I shook my head. My former nemesis and ice queen had been far too nice to me since we had returned to court. I had a suspicion that the cause of such sweetness was her growing fondness toward my older brother.

Constance returned her focus on Casper. "You should get some rest." She no longer sounded authoritative, but rather like that of a worried sister.

"I feel fine," he grumbled.

She stiffened slightly. "I am not trying to insult you, but I want you to know that it is acceptable if you take the time to recover from such an ordeal. You could travel to the southern palace. Our family always spends winters in Lotanus. It would not be strange for you to do so. You would benefit from the warmer weather."

"Those days were before we had to concern ourselves with the fay at our northern borders. I am staying in Sterling."

"I managed not to ruin our kingdom while you were gone."

"And now I'm back," Casper barked, his annoyance clear.

Constance frowned, but Flora pulled her toward the door. "These two will get more rest if we are out of their hair. Let's go." Constance muttered something under her breath, but let Flora lead her out. When the door finally closed, leaving Casper and me alone, Casper sagged back in his chair. I breathed a sigh of relief, as deeply as my corsets would allow, which did not feel like quite enough air. As grateful as I was to be back in Reynallis, back in the Rose Palace, I had to admit that I preferred the soft, loose clothing the fay chose over human nobility. After crying in relief when Casper and I returned to the Rose Palace, Annabeth wasted no time in ensuring I had enough suitable dresses for the colder months, though all the fine wool dresses also came with heavy, thick petticoats and tight, stiff corsets.

"I thought things would be easy once we returned home," Casper groaned, still staring at the door as though waiting for his sister to burst back in with more complaints.

I made my way to the tea and coffee service, pouring Casper a cup of coffee from the silver carafe, adding sugar and a touch of cinnamon. "I'm certain you would be terribly bored if everything was running smoothly." I handed him the cup before pouring myself tea.

"I would say I could do with some boredom, but after spending so long in an underwater prison, I feel most qualified to say that I understand true boredom."

I paused, the cup close enough to my face that steam tickled my lips. I frowned, studying Casper, not sure what to say. Seeing my expression, he waved his hand as though he could dismiss my worry.

"I only meant that Constance is being so difficult. I will be the first to admit that she did an admirable job governing while I was . . ." Casper paused, "away. But I am back now, and she doesn't need to coddle me."

I snorted. "I would hardly call the endless arguments between the two of you coddling."

"You don't know Constance as I do. She is trying to protect me by decimating the fay. I neither want nor need another war on my hands."

I sipped my tea, trying to think of the right answer. The threat of faerie retribution hung over us ever since Casper and I escaped Magnomel. Each day I wondered if we would see another attack. I thought about it every time I saw the Biawood. "I have no interest in declaring war on Queen Marasina," I tentatively said. "But what if the fay attack again?"

"We have set up more guards along the Biawood, it is watched around the clock. We will not be caught unaware again. I take no issue with building up our defenses, but I do not want humans storming into the Forest Court. There are too many secrets in Magnomel, secrets that need to stay there for your protection." Casper had been staring out the window, but now he focused his attention on me. "I swore I would not lose you again, that I would keep you safe. And I meant it."

I smiled, feeling both warmed and guilty by the lengths Casper was willing to go for my sake. I set my teacup on its saucer and went over to Casper.

"I think your sister might be right, you do look tired."

Casper groaned. "Please, not you too."

But I only gave him a sly smile, carefully taking his cup and setting it on his desk before seating myself in his lap. Casper's look of surprise melted into a pleased expression, his eyes lingering on me as his arms wrapped around me.

"Perhaps you need something to take your mind off the tedium of being king." I gently removed the gold circlet he wore, the one he wore as a prince and still preferred when not required to wear the heavy, ornate crown for public appearances. Putting the circlet on his desk, I ran my fingers over his hair, smoothing the black locks away from his forehead.

He silently watched me, his dark eyes hungry. When I brushed his cheek, his hand came up, imprisoning mine. He turned his head slightly, his lips on my fingers. He kissed their tips, sending goosepimples up my arms. I inhaled sharply, my stomach knotting in desire and anticipation.

I slowly pulled my fingers away, freeing his lips. It was a short-lived freedom as I leaned into him, pressing my lips to his. He tightened his arms around me, securing me on his lap, kissing my lips, my cheeks, and my neck. When I slowed to catch my breath, he whispered my name in my ear, his breath tickling my delicate skin. He smelled of his favorite soap, the expensive scent of cinnamon and cloves. It reminded me of all the other times he had kissed me.

In that moment, the world only existed for the two of us, and I wanted it to remain that way as long as possible.

Our perfect world lasted late into the night, long after the sun set and the stars came out. Long after we had even managed to tire ourselves out with kisses and eventually just sat, entwined in each other's arms, neither of us wanting to break the spell of peace and contentment. I dozed, my head resting on Casper's chest.

When I woke, his study was in darkness, lit only by the light of the full moon. I yawned, shifting slightly, which roused Casper.

"What time is it?" I asked, standing as I massaged a knot out of my stiff neck.

Casper pulled out a gold pocket watch and flipped it open. "It is nearing midnight." He chuckled. "We must have looked utterly exhausted if no one was sent to interrupt us."

I smiled. "I guess there are a few perks to being king." My stomach growled then, loud enough for Casper to hear.

"Shall I ring for something to eat?" he asked, looking pointedly at my stomach.

"I have a better idea," I said, helping Casper to his feet. "Let's go to the kitchens. We can get our pick of what's there and no need to wake anyone this late." Casper grinned, letting me pull him to the door. Once before I had shown him how to take servant corridors to the kitchens, the great rooms filled with the smells of roast meat and baking bread. And I found getting my noble, honorable Casper to break the rules, or at least bend them was surprisingly satisfying.

I was pushing open the door when Casper suddenly fell back as he gasped in pain.

"Casper, what's wrong?"

"Nor, I—" But another spasm went through him, his arms clutching his sides as he hunched over, his body going tight. He tripped, landing on the floor, though he barely noticed, his eyes squeezed tight. I was beside him in an instant.

"Casper, what happened?" I asked, frantic and afraid. His skin was slick with sweat and warm to the touch. My heart hammered as I tried to coax words from him, desperate to know the cause, but it seemed the pain was too intense for him, as his words became garbled the more he tried to speak.

I drenched a handkerchief in the teapot, the tea now gone cold, and pressed it to Casper's forehead, hoping it would provide some relief. I debated calling for help versus staying with him.

"Nor, it hurts," he cried, as he curled into himself on the floor.

"What hurts? What happened?" But he was unable to answer any of my questions. I summoned my life magic, felt the warm flicker in my heart as I sent it into his chest, but it had no effect on his pain. His skin had lost all color, going white as death except for his lips, which were darkening to black.

"I'm going to get help. To get a physician," I said. Casper moaned, but his hand shot out and grabbed mine in a crushing grip. "Casper, I need to get help," I pleaded, but he didn't let go, only squeezed my hand tighter.

Hating myself, I pulled at his fingers, trying to free my hand, all the while my brain ran through poisons, wondering if someone had slipped something into his food, maybe his coffee.

Casper's head shot up and he let out a scream that transformed itself into something feral, a nasal cry that was not human, his neck lengthening as he did so. Blackness filled his eyes, and they shrank. He lost his grip on me.

Casper let out another inhuman noise, the high-pitched whine coming from the back of his throat.

His body was curled up on the floor, but his head was stretching out on a neck that was growing longer and thinner by the second, a sick parody of pulled taffy. I watched in horror as his head shrank, his lips, growing black and hard, extended outward as his nose collapsed into his face. His fingers merged together, and white stubble began to grow on all of his exposed skin, lengthening into long, white feathers that soon covered his body. He gave another scream, and this time I recognized the sound as the call of a bird.

My own cry for help died on my lips as I looked at Casper, or what had been Casper. Instead of a young man, there was a massive swan, as big as the swans that swam in the lake surrounding the Forest Court. He was pure white save for pinprick black eyes and a long black beak. He rose, short, spindly charcoal legs attached to wide, webbed feet. He stood on top of his trousers, his shirt now collapsed around his neck. He bobbed his head wildly, until he managed to free himself of his shirt.

Numbly, I got to my feet, my eyes never leaving the large swan. My mouth was bone dry, and I swallowed before carefully asking, "Casper, is that you?"

If swan-Casper recognized me or his name, he gave no indication. I tentatively stepped toward the creature, all the while trying to keep my voice soft and reassuring. "Casper, it's me, Nor. I don't know what happened, but we will fix this."

When I was less than an arm's length away, the swan raised himself up, stretching his neck as he puffed out his chest. He came up to my waist, but as he extended his wings, he suddenly seemed much bigger, even menacing. He hissed at me, a breathy, angry sound that would have been more appropriate coming from an irate cat. I backed away, trying to rationalize what I was seeing.

Casper stilled, his head swiveling on his long neck from me to the large study window. For a moment, he seemed to be studying the moon. Without warning, he honked again, making me jump. He raised his massive wings till they were nearly vertical to his body before bringing them down, bending them when he needed to raise them again. As he flapped his wings, I could feel the air rushing toward me as he lifted himself off the floor, tucking in his feet. Too late I realized what he intended. I lunged for him, but he was already above me, flying toward the window.

"No!" I cried, as he threw himself at the glass. The window had been closed, but not latched, and swung out upon impact. Casper soared out the window, flying toward the moon, over the Biawood. I rushed to the window, but it was no use. Even if my wings weren't hidden by Alverdine's glamour, I had never mastered the art of flying. And Casper was already becoming hard to spot as he flew further away. There was no way I could catch him on foot.

Helplessly, I watched Casper fly out of sight. It had to be faerie magic, of that I was certain. I thought we had escaped Magnomel unscathed, that we could put it all behind us, but I was wrong.

Unbidden, our last night in Magnomel came back to me, Elrik's curse as he lay dying. I couldn't remember all of the words, but Pel had said it sounded something like a swan's life. I had not thought much of it at the time, too concerned with escape and convinced that all of Elrik's terrible magic had died with him, but what if I was wrong? I had no idea why a curse directed at me, using my true name, had transformed Casper instead, but it was a place to start. I could only hope that Pel would still be willing to help me, even if it meant helping the person who killed his brother.

With no better plan, I picked up a slim knife from Casper's desk, one he used to break the seals off incoming messages. I jabbed my thumb, a quick, sharp pain that resulted in a bead of blood on my thumb. I wiped it over my bracelet, and when the golden thread began to burn, I hoped Pel would be on his way.

23

I spent the next day pacing the palace grounds, wandering through gardens and knocking into people and shrubs since my focus was trained to the sky, scanning it for swans. I was utterly exhausted, having not slept a wink last night.

Pel had arrived shortly after I summoned him, and to my great relief, promised to research swan curses and report back on anything he found, and I could only hope that included a cure. Though I knew my endless walking today would likely not find Casper any sooner, my anxious nerves would not let me stay still for more than a few minutes, even as the exertion brought out the familiar burning in my limbs.

But the gardens were still preferable to the uproar inside the palace. Casper's disappearance was noticed at dawn, sending everyone into a flurry of activity. Constance immediately took control of the situation, directing guards and mitigating the nobles' concerns, assuring them that there was no sign of the fay and it was most probable that Casper had wished for some solitude. The transition back to court life required time, she explained and convinced the nobles that everything was being done, but that it was too early to fear for the safety of their king. Constance personally questioned everyone close to Casper, and I played into her story, lying as I told her that Casper had wanted to go on a ride by himself to have some quiet time to think. I kept the details vague, all the while praying that Pel could find a way to reverse the Chace-forsaken magic that had transformed Casper.

Many of the royal guards were assigned to search for him while others were posted by every palace entrance, instructed to immediately notify Constance the moment he was located. I convinced my personal guard, Sir Yanis, to join those looking for Casper, assuring him I was safe in the palace. In reality, I was hoping to keep the truth about Casper a secret until I could transform him back, and the fewer people who knew about it, the better.

It was late in the day, nearly sundown, when Annabeth finally cornered me in the rose garden. She scurried to me, carrying a thick shawl.

"There you are, milady," Annabeth said, slightly winded, as her breath plumed in the air.

"I was going for a walk," I answered, but I kept glancing at the sky and the Biawood, searching for any hint of a white bird.

"You will catch your death staying in the cold all day." Annabeth wrapped the wool shawl over my shoulders. I wanted to tell her that I was already too warm, the lingering, burning effects of the sitano aggravated by my day's exertions. But the satisfied expression on Annabeth's small, freckled face had me swallowing any complaint.

"Now will you please come inside? I can have supper brought to your rooms."

"I don't know," I wavered, scanning the sky. I had barely eaten all day, my stomach a knot of anxiety, but I did not want to miss Casper should he return.

"Please milady. At least have some tea. And there has been much gossip in the palace today." I cut a glance toward my maid. She nodded gravely, belying how shrewd she had become during her time serving me. "Speculations about the king."

"Fine," I conceded. "One cup of tea. But tell me everything."

Seated in my parlor, I helped myself to not only tea, but also the light supper Annabeth had arranged for me. There were cold meats, soft white cheese, shiny red apples, and small, hot rolls, fresh from the ovens and still warm.

"I almost forgot," Annabeth produced a small jar filled with dark preserves and speckled with yellow seeds. "Yanis sent his family's fig jam for you." Annabeth smiled at the jar as she set it on the table.

"Yanis?" I asked, quirking an eyebrow.

Annabeth colored slightly. "*Sir* Yanis," she amended.

I tucked that tidbit of information away, something to think about after I dealt with the pressing issues. "What talk has there been today?"

"Naturally, everyone is in an uproar over King Casper's disappearance," Annabeth said, quick to change the subject. "And the longer he stays missing, the more whispers there are that he had not simply gone for a ride by himself, or if he had, that something happened to him."

I was reminded of the first time I met Casper. He had been riding in the Biawood by himself and had gotten lost. I gave him directions to the Stigenne Road, but only after I stole his ring. I twisted the signet ring on my finger, wishing I could simply ride into the Biawood Forest and find him lost, but unharmed.

Catching herself, Annabeth quickly added, "I'm sorry, milady, I don't mean to worry you further."

I swallowed my tea, wishing I could confide in Annabeth about what truly happened, but as much as I trusted my maid, I couldn't risk another person knowing the truth.

"No, I asked you to tell me. I know many of the royal guards are searching for him. What else?"

"I overheard that many are certain he was recaptured by the fay. And there were whispers that if the king is not returned soon, Princess Constance will muster forces to attack Magnomel." Annabeth said the word with disgust and shivered at the mention of the fay lands. I didn't correct her. For as beautiful as Magnomel was with its endless summer, the faeries who lived and ruled there could be cruel and cunning.

They aren't all cruel, a small voice in my head reminded me. Lorella was kind and sweet, but also brave and strong, willing to be a true friend. She had risked much to help me free Casper. And Pel, who eventually came through for me, despite our complicated past. The fay were not the evil creatures rumors would have humans believing, and I would have to find a way to reverse whatever dark magic was used on Casper if we were to prevent an all-out war against Magnomel. I wished Casper was here. His skill with political diplomacy was far superior to mine. I hoped that he would return tonight. I had to believe that I had not lost him again, not permanently. Though if he did return, I would need to be the first to find him. I did not want to think what anyone else would do if they found a giant swan waddling through the palace. The most likely place Casper would return to was where he left, I reasoned.

I quickly wolfed down the rest of my supper and dismissed Annabeth, before heading to Casper's study. Despite the chill, I threw the window open wide, leaning out to see the last of the sun's dying light.

Right as dusk was settling in, I spotted a flicker of white burst through the Biawood Forest, flying above the trees. I strained to see, watching in apprehension and relief as it drew closer and I could make out the form of a swan. I wanted to call out to Casper, but swallowed my cry, afraid of what guards might do if they heard me with no king in sight. The swan flew toward the palace, surprisingly graceful for such a large bird. I held my breath, watching as he directed his flight.

When I was certain he was indeed heading toward the study, I stepped back, giving the bird room to land.

In a matter of moments, Casper flew in through the window, landing with far more grace than he had the night before. I watched the bird, wondering if he would hiss at me again. Instead, he took several steps toward me, stretching out his long neck, as if inquisitive. I stared into his beady black eyes, hoping he recognized me.

"Casper, it's me, Nor," I said, feeling slightly foolish speaking to a bird. "Do you remember me?"

The swan cocked his head to the side.

"I don't know what happened to you, but I have a feeling this is Elrik's doing. Pel is doing research for me. I will find a way to undo this," I promised, praying it was a promise I could keep.

The swan waddled toward me. I had no idea if this version of Casper understood what I was saying, but I took some comfort in the fact that he was not hissing. I stayed perfectly still, not wanting to spook him. As the swan approached me, his shiny black eyes stayed fixed on mine. He let out a honk, but the noise was low, almost sad.

"Casper, do you know me?" I asked, searching the swan's face.

The swan extended his neck, till his small, white head was almost level with mine. With painstaking slowness, I lowered myself to the ground, setting aside my cane as I sat.

"Do you know who you are?" I whispered. Tears pricked behind my eyes. I hated how helpless I felt.

Casper took several more steps toward me, his thick, feathered body close enough to touch. He settled himself down, resting the front of his chest on the floor before picking up his feet, tucking them underneath himself. His head reached out to mine, his black beak gently nibbling on my hair. Slowly, I raised my hand, carefully placing it on top of his head. He stilled as I pet him, soft feathers brushing against my fingers.

"I will fix this, Casper," I promised.

He pulled his head back, rubbing it against his wings before he rested his head in my lap. I ran my fingers along his head and back, gently stroking his smooth, white wings as he slowly closed his eyes. I continued to pet him, murmuring reassurances, as my own eyes grew heavy.

⌒ᨆᨆ⌒

I awoke to the feel of something heavy in my lap. Startled, I looked down to see a head of unruly black hair.

I yelped, right as Casper rolled over. *He's human!* He stared up at me with dark, familiar eyes.

"Casper," I exclaimed, joy flooding through me.

"Nor?" His eyes were unfocused as he woke.

Then I noticed that he was not wearing any clothes.

"Casper!" I shot to my feet, the sudden movement dislodging him from my lap. I squeezed my eyes closed, though not before catching a glimpse of his bare, muscled shoulders and firm stomach. I pretended I had not seen more. I heard his head hit the floor. "Sorry."

"Nor, what in the—" he started, but abruptly stopped. "Am I naked?"

"Uh huh." I nodded, keeping my eyes closed.

"And was I—" another pause, this one longer. "Was I a bird?"

"A swan, technically." My cheeks flamed, and I wondered if he could see my blush through my glamour.

I head Casper take several steps. "Um, you can open your eyes."

I cracked open one eye and saw that Casper had pulled an embroidered blanket off one of the chairs, wrapping it around himself. I tried not to admire his bare legs, his muscular calves, telling myself I was only relieved he was human again. I forced a small smile.

"Have I mentioned I admire your daring sense of fashion?"

Casper frowned. "The strangest things seem to happen around you."

That sobered me up. "I'm sorry. Oh, wait." Remembering that I had thrown his clothes in a drawer of his desk, I hurried to retrieve them. I handed him his clothes and quickly turned around, giving him privacy to dress. I stared at the large clock on the wall, noting that it was several minutes until one in the morning.

"I am more decent," Casper finally said, and I turned around. He was dressed, but his cheeks were bright pink. "This is not how I imagined our first night together."

"I didn't see anything."

"Nor, do you know what is happening?" Casper asked.

"Not exactly," I confessed. "But I think it has to do with Elrik's curse." Casper's face darkened.

"But I killed him."

"I know. I don't fully understand it, but Pel is looking into it." Casper pursed his lips at the mention of Pel, but he didn't speak, so I continued, telling him everything that had happened since the night before.

Casper took it all in, nodding slightly. When I finished, he stayed silent, drumming his fingers on the floor.

"You are taking this really well," I said, breaking the silence.

"It's strange. Part of it feels like a dream. I remember falling asleep with you last night, and I remember waking up. But after that . . ." he trailed off, flexing his fingers as though to confirm he still had hands. "At the beginning, I felt feral, as though I was only a wild animal, pulled to the forest. But as the day drew on, I started to remember myself." He reached for my cheek, and I let him, leaning into his touch. "And I remembered you. I had to come back to you."

"I'm so sorry." I closed my eyes, hating the tears that were leaking out. "You always end up in danger because of me."

Casper pulled his hand back, but instead of pushing me away, he held my shoulders, forcing me to look up at him. His expression was serious, his eyes burning, but I sensed the anger was not directed at me.

"Nor, this is not your fault. That Chace-forsaken faerie poisoned you and cursed you, and not even killing him has freed us. Nor, we will—"

But before he could tell me what we would do, he crumpled over, his hands gripping his sides as he once again let out a moan that transformed into a honking cry, one full of agony.

"No!" I cried, but I could only watch, helpless as Casper again transformed into a swan. There was no recognition in his small, black eyes. In a terrible parody of the previous night, swan-Casper again recoiled from me, hissing and flapping his massive wings.

Again, he flew away, out the window as though answering a call from the forest.

24

The next day, as Annabeth helped get me ready, I formulated a plan. Once the sun set, I would go to Casper's study and wait for him. I would summon Pel; hopefully he would have the answer as to how to break the curse.

I wondered if it was similar to a glamour. I would never subject Casper to something like sitano, but Alverdine had said there were other ways to undo a glamour. Then again, would a glamour allow Casper to actually fly as a swan? He said his thoughts were feral when he first transformed.

None of that sounded like a mere glamour.

"Milady?"

I had been staring out the window, scanning the sky for birds, and had missed what Annabeth had been saying.

"What?"

"Which gown would milady prefer today?" Annabeth repeated. I turned to see she had pulled out several dresses.

"Oh, right." I gnawed my lip. In truth, I did not care. Honestly, I would have preferred something from the Forest Court, where even ladies could wear trousers. But as I looked at my options, one immediately caught my eye. I pointed to a gray, raw-silk dress. Annabeth nodded. The fabric had strands of silver woven in, and they shimmered in the morning light. It was a gown Casper had given me, right after his promise to woo me. I had thought him ridiculous at the time, but as Annabeth slipped the gown over my head and tied the silver laces, I felt a bit of comfort to wear something that came from him. Annabeth gestured for me to sit so she could do my hair.

Normally, I enjoyed the sensation of having my hair brushed, but today I sat rigid in front of the vanity, my lips pressed together. I stared at my reflection, unsure if I wanted to love or hate the image that reflected back. Every day since we had escaped Magnomel, I feared that Alverdine's glamour would somehow dissolve, and that I would once again appear fay. At first, I had been relieved to see my flaxen hair and human eyes, but now I wondered if I was only masking my true self. If I could be my fay self, then I could fly after Casper, following him when he was a swan. Well, I could have if I had learned to fly. Not to mention I would likely be arrested as a faerie found in the Rose Palace right after the king went missing.

"The guards will find King Casper," Annabeth said, reading my silence.

I nodded, wishing I could tell her more. There came a knock. Annabeth finished putting in the last of the pins in my hair before answering the door. Sir Yanis entered, flicking a glance over at Annabeth before he bowed to me.

"Lady Nor," he started. I waved off the title, knowing he would never address me as informally as Nor. "Princess Constance has requested your presence immediately."

I raised an eyebrow. "Did she say what for?" Though she and I were on far better terms than when I first arrived at the Rose Palace, she was so preoccupied with Casper and the question of what to do about the fay since our return, that she paid very little attention to me. I doubted she figured out that Casper was cursed, but I remained alert, nonetheless.

"No, milady. Only that you attend to her at her chambers as soon as possible." Sir Yanis grimaced and lowered his voice. "Though if I were to conjecture . . ." he paused, seeming to catch himself. He straightened. "But that is not my place."

"Make it your place," I insisted, impatience and anxiety making me snap. In a more measured tone, I added, "I need my people to be eyes and ears for me when I am not around." I gestured to him and Annabeth.

Yanis relaxed a bit. In a confidential tone, he added, "I think it has to do with the king." That did not surprise me. "She has been questioning everyone who was with him the day before he disappeared."

"Does she think someone kidnapped him?" I asked.

"Oh no," Yanis said quickly. "At least I do not think the princess is accusing any *humans*." He emphasized the last word. "There has been no word from the king and no ransom request. There are whispers that he was retaken by the fay."

In Constance's position, I would probably think the same. I would have to be careful how much information I revealed to her.

I followed Yanis out of my rooms. He walked briskly, and I suspected he did not want to leave Constance waiting long.

As we passed the rooms my brothers occupied, I heard arguing from inside.

"Now is not the time to go gallivanting through the woods." Finn's voice came through the other side of the door.

"I won't be gallivanting in the woods. I don't need you to nanny me," Devon's voice shot back, right as he burst into the hallway. I jumped back to avoid the door. My brother carried a bow in one hand, a quiver of arrows slung over his shoulder. His hair was disheveled, though he was neatly dressed. A brief look of surprise crossed his face to see me right outside their door. "Oh, Nor."

"What's going on?" I asked, stopping to appraise my brother.

"Devon is going gallivanting in the woods," Jacobie said, poking his small face outside the door. I had to suppress a small smirk at the way my eight-year-old brother mimicked Finn's patronizing tone.

"That's right," Finn said, joining Jacobie, his hands on his hips.

"Will you two stop teaming up on me?" Devon growled. He turned to Finn, "It's not like some of us didn't head recklessly into the woods before."

"Devon, are you going into the Biawood?" I asked, loud enough to cut off their arguing. Only my brothers, Casper and I knew that Finn had snuck into Magnomel to find me, and I wanted to keep it that way, especially as tensions were flying high the longer Casper was missing.

Devon turned to me. "I am going hunting, but not in the forest," Devon muttered. "I will stay on the palace grounds."

"He is sad his sweetheart left him," Jacobie said, still standing by the door.

That caught me by surprise. "Your sweet—"

"She is not!" Devon cut me off.

"Who?" I asked.

"Lady Ilana," Jacobie said. I raised my eyebrow at Devon.

"She is not my anything," Devon said, but I detected a note of longing in his voice. "But she did leave this morning for Glavnada."

"Why?" I asked, remembering that the cold weather brewed nasty winter storms in the Netarian Ocean, making a trip to the northern country especially dangerous this time of year.

"Princess Constance decided to launch an attack against the fay, to force them to release King Casper. Ilana's family is close to the Glavnadian royal family. She offered to envoy Princess Constance's message personally." Devon ran his hand through his sandy hair.

I noted Devon's familiar use of Ilana's name, but did not question him about it. Instead, I asked, "Did Lady Ilana tell you that?"

Devon nodded.

"And they kissed," Finn added.

"You two were spying on me," Devon snapped, lunging toward our brothers, but I pulled on his arm.

"Devon, stop that."

Devon stood back. When he seemed less intent on fratricide, I released him.

He sighed. "I need some air." He turned and stormed off.

I faced my remaining brothers. "There is too much going on right now. Try not to provoke him further."

Before Finn or Jacobie could argue, I rejoined Yanis, who had been waiting at a polite distance, though I knew he heard everything we had said. I gestured for him, and we continued to Constance's rooms.

"I was most displeased when I found out my brother was courting a girl named Marietta. When we were children, she used to call me names. But I came to find she is not nearly as terrible now we are grown. She and Evan have two strapping boys."

"Devon is not courting Ilana," I retorted, slightly winded as Sir Yanis took large strides, and I had to use my cane to keep up.

"Of course not, Lady Nor," Yanis agreed, in a flat, professional tone, that told me he did not share my belief. But my brother's possible love life was not the most pressing concern, even if the thought of Ilana and Devon together made me queasy. No, more critical was that Constance was summoning an army against the fay, one to rescue a brother who was not currently held by the fay.

We passed through several corridors, rose-embroidered tapestries hanging from the walls before reaching Constance's chambers. I was escorted into a parlor, a large room with a crackling fire. Chairs and settees were upholstered with thick brocade. Constance was already waiting for me, seated in the largest chair in the room.

"Oh good. Do have a seat, Elenora," she gestured to a chair across from her. I made my way over as Yanis stood back by the door, once again a silent, watching guard. "You shall forgive me for skipping niceties, as there are pressing issues. This is the second day Casper has been missing, and I am forced to conclude that something terrible has befallen him." Though Constance sat with the commanding air of royalty and was immaculately dressed and styled, I could tell how deeply she worried. Her eyes were slightly bloodshot, shadowed by dark circles. Her small hands gripped the armrests of her chair, turning her pale hands white.

I nodded, careful not to give anything away.

"I presume the fay have again taken him, in retaliation for the two of you escaping." She stated these words as though they were merely facts, though there was a flicker of pain that flashed across her face. But she smoothed her face back into a mask of calm authority. "Naturally, I do not blame you, but as the only one who was with Casper during that terrible ordeal in Magnomel, I must ask you if there is anything else you might remember from your time there that could help get him back."

"I am not sure what else there is to tell," I hedged, not wanting to stray from the story Casper and I agreed on when we first returned.

"Don't you want to get him back?" Constance snarled, her cool demeanor cracking.

"Of course I do!" I jumped to my feet. "But sending an army into Magnomel is starting a war. That's not going to bring Casper home." I was breathing hard.

"And how do you know that?" Constance asked, suddenly suspicious.

I snapped my mouth closed. I had been close to admitting that he was not with the fay. Instead, I sat back down. "I don't," I lied. Constance continued to search my face, as if she could pull answers out by examining me. "But I know Casper doesn't want a war."

"Casper isn't here, now. And it's my responsibility to bring him home." In a softer tone, almost to herself, Constance added, "I abandoned him once, I will not do that again."

"When he was in Faradisia?" I dared to ask. Constance gave a curt nod. I knew Constance and Casper had a rocky history as he had spent years as a royal hostage in Faradisia following the Southern War as part of the peace agreement, but I could not let Constance's desire to make amends lead to a new war.

"Did I hear you mention Faradisia?"

Constance and I both turned to see Flora standing by the door. She looked prepared for travel, a thick, white cloak hung from her shoulders, and polished boots peeped out from under a saffron gown. Around her neck she wore a golden locket, bright against her dark skin.

"Flora," Constance said, her breath hitching on the name. Flora smiled, but there was a sadness in her eyes.

As Flora entered the room, Constance rose, meeting her with a tight embrace. A muffled noise came from Constance, one that sounded far too much like a sob. Flora held her tighter, murmuring comforting words that I could not make out. I edged toward the wall, feeling uncomfortable witnessing something so private.

Constance eventually pulled away, straightening. She had regained her regal composure, even as she scrubbed once at her eyes.

"We can send another messenger," she started, but Flora gently shushed her.

"You know that will not work. My uncle will not send aid till he feels the treaty has been rebalanced. He has been insisting on it since he released Casper to return to Reynallis." Flora's voice was soothing, but her eyes were glassy, and she blinked several times before adding, "We should have known we could only put him off for so long."

"But you are not a hostage anymore. King Jovian must be able to see that," Constance countered.

Flora reached out for Constance's hands, squeezing them in hers, even as she sadly shook her head. "This will be the fastest way to get the forces you need to get your brother back."

I swallowed a hard knot of guilt. I wanted to tell them that an attack against the fay was pointless, they didn't have Casper. But what could I say? If I told Constance that her brother was under a faerie curse, I didn't imagine that would stop her from declaring war on Magnomel. My only option was to figure out a way to break the curse before Glavnada and Faradisia could send troops.

Constance and Flora were still holding hands, as though neither wanted to be the first to leave. I took it as my cue to go and I excused myself, promising to tell Constance if I remembered anything that she could use against the fay. She nodded, but her focus remained fixed on Flora. I hurried out to give them privacy.

Back in my own rooms, the day stretched long before me. I was impatient for nightfall, certain that was when Casper would return. And I did not dare summon Pel before he could safely sneak into the palace under the cover of darkness. I hated feeling so helpless and banged my cane in frustration. I wished I had enough magic and the skill to use it to break the Chace-forsaken curse, but my life magic was weak, and though I still had the Regalia Vive Amulet, it no longer glowed, not since I used the power within it to revive Casper on the shore of the lake.

I felt no pull of magic from the orb.

By late in the afternoon, I was nearly rocking with nerves. I stared out my window, the sun low in a gray sky, lengthening the shadows in the rose garden. The garden itself looking more ominous than inviting. It was too late in the year for blooms, and the plants were now bare and thorny.

I wondered if I could get far enough into the Biawood to summon Pel now, instead of waiting till after dark. I warmed to the idea, eager for something to do. Besides, if Pel gave me useful information,

I could relay that to Casper when he arrived. Maybe Pel had even figured out how to reverse the curse.

I pulled out a warm, gray cloak and wrapped it around myself as I headed out of the Rose Palace. If I could break the curse tonight, then we could leave all of this behind.

I stepped outside, the bite of a cold autumn afternoon had me wrapping the cloak tighter around myself as I crunched through the dead grass. I was so distracted that I almost did not notice the sole figure who stood in a meadow near the edge of the Biawood. As I approached, I saw that it was Devon, still hunting, the quiver of arrows on the ground beside him.

Devon did not notice my approach; he was too focused on scanning the sky. He must have seen something, because he pulled an arrow from the quiver and readied his bow. Too late, I followed his gaze and saw the crest of white in the sky, flying above the trees from the Biawood. I cried, breaking into a sprint toward my brother, as he drew back the arrow.

He pointed it toward the swan in the sky.

25

I shoved my brother a moment too late. Devon had already lined up the arrow, releasing it right as I collided into him. The air was expelled out of my lungs, leaving me winded.

"By the Mother's maids, Nor, what was that for?" Devon demanded, but I ignored him, my focus on the sky.

The arrow found its mark in Casper's wing, and even from the ground I heard a cry of pain before the great bird turned around, heading back into the Biawood, descending quickly.

"Chace's chaos," I swore as I started toward the woods.

"Don't bother," Devon grumbled. "That bird will probably fly too far into the woods to catch."

I ignored Devon, and he muttered something about how I was acting like a fool, before he turned back to the palace. It was not long before I found a trail of blood, dripping on tree leaves and the dirt below. I prayed the injury was not serious. Ahead, I heard the furious cries of a wounded bird. I pursued the sound until I found Casper.

One large wing was extended, Devon's arrow still embedded in the flesh of the wing, turning his snow-white feathers red with blood. I tried to approach, but Casper raised himself up and hissed at me, a clear warning not to come any closer. I raised my hands and took several steps back.

"It's only me. I won't come closer if you don't want me to," I said to the swan. Casper studied me with his tiny, jet-black eyes, but I couldn't tell if there was recognition there. I sighed, knowing that I would need to wait here until midnight. I wrapped my cloak tighter around myself as I sat against the trunk of a large hickory tree, keeping my eyes on Casper, ready to jump up and follow him if he should take off again. Several times he attempted to fly, but only managed a few flaps of his wings before the injury caused him too much pain. He eventually gave up, tucking his head into his good wing, the other one spread limply on the ground. I ached to help him, but whenever I approached, I was greeted with a hiss.

As the hours drew on, I noticed a change in his demeanor. He was more alert, his small eyes focusing on me. Casper had said he felt more human as the day progressed, and I hoped his attention was a sign he was remembering me.

I carefully moved toward him, crawling on my hands and knees to avoid startling him. Casper took a step back, and I stilled. But this time, he did not hiss.

I sat only a few paces away from him.

I waited.

The sun was dipping into the horizon, shadows in the forest blending into the darkness of night when Casper moved again. I had been breathing into my hands, rubbing them together for warmth, but I froze when I saw him stand, despite the growing cold. He took several waddling steps toward me, close enough that he was nearly in my lap. I felt the brush of feathers as he settled down next to me.

"Casper, it's all right. You are going to be all right," I cooed, my voice soft and coaxing.

Casper reached his long neck toward me, until his head nuzzled my hand. Tentatively, I stroked the top of his head, starting at the ridge above his beak and gently dragging my fingers across the soft, stubby feathers on the crown of his head. He closed his eyes, and made a low, guttural noise, a soft grunting.

I continued that way for a long time, ensuring he felt safe with me, as the evening stretched into night. Eventually, I reached out my hand to pet the longer feathers along his back. When he allowed this, I carefully touched his injured wing.

"I am going to heal you," I said. Casper stared at me, and then nodded, a graceful bobbing of his head that I hoped meant he finally understood me.

I held his wing with one hand while I gripped the arrow with my other. I gritted my teeth, preparing.

"I'm sorry," I said as I yanked the arrow out of the flesh of his wing. Casper let out a loud honk of pain, flapping his large wings as I tumbled backward, the freed arrow clutched in my hand.

Dropping the arrow, I waited for Casper to settle down, knowing I could do nothing while he paced and squawked. When he finally stopped, he met my eyes before extending his injured wing. He stilled, and I took that as permission to approach him. The wound itself was small, but deep, a ragged puncture in his skin. Blood flowed from the injury, and I could see the shiny, red muscle between feathers and skin. My heart tore to see him in pain, and I desperately hoped my magic would be enough to heal him.

Gently, I placed my hand over the wound. Casper let out a squawk of pain but managed to stay still. I tried to ignore the blood that flowed over my fingers, the copper smell in the cold air. I closed my eyes, exhaling as I focused on my magic. It was harder to find with the glamour in place, covering my true self like a gossamer cloud, but I pushed through, feeling the familiar warmth of the life magic in my heart. I drew it out, pulling the magic down my arm and pouring it into Casper's wound. The buzz of power grew stronger, from a faint pulse to a steady flow.

"*Vive guarriana*," I whispered, directing the magic to heal his wing. I pictured his wing intact, the hole closed and the skin smooth. The longer I worked, the harder it became. Sweat beaded on my forehead, and my limbs felt heavy, but I forced myself to keep going. When I felt the smooth skin under my fingers finally knit together, I pulled my hand back, studying his wing. The wound was closed, a pink, puckered scar devoid of its feather coverage, the only indication that he had been hurt.

I sat back, exhausted and breathing hard. I no longer felt the warmth of magic, and my arms and legs were starting to ache and burn. But I didn't care. I was satisfied to see Casper's healed wing.

The moon was high in the sky. It was full two nights ago, and this waning moon was still large and bright, giving me plenty of light to see Casper. He was more at ease now. He settled back down, tucking both wings by his side.

"Well done." Out of the shadows, Valente stepped into the clearing, slowly clapping his hands. I jumped to my feet, causing a startled Casper to squawk in protest.

"What are you doing here?" I asked, a chill running through me that wasn't from the crisp autumn air.

Valente crossed his arms and studied me; his white curls bright in the moonlight. He wore no armor, but rather a dark green tunic and trousers and tall black boots that blended into the forest.

"I could ask the same of you. Disappearing the way you did. And here I find you glamoured to look human." He sneered in disgust. "It's disgraceful."

"I don't want to be heir. You can have it."

Valente scoffed. "That's not the way things are done. You should have forfeited the challenge if you didn't want to be heir." He took several steps toward me. Casper hissed in protest, but I settled my hand on his head, not wanting him to get involved. "What a protective pet you've found."

"I'm warning you, leave him alone," I snapped. My heart was racing. I was unarmed, having dashed into the woods without bothering to take a weapon. It was only a matter of time before Valente saw through my bluff.

Valente smirked. "I wonder if your swan can be taught to wear a crown." I glared at Valente, but he only looked amused. "I have many eyes and ears at the Forest Court. And it did not go unobserved that Pel was researching swan curses."

"You can't have him back," I said, stepping between Valente and Casper, ready to tell Casper to fly the moment Valente attacked.

Valente chuckled. "And where would we put your kingling? You blew up our prison."

"That wasn't me," I started, but Valente waved off my explanation.

"I don't care. And I'm not here for the swan king." His face soured. "I'm here for you."

"I'm not going back," I said, though I felt trapped. I couldn't outrun Valente and doubted I could so easily outwit him a second time.

"I'd prefer it if you never returned to Magnomel."

Fear spiked through me. "Are you going to kill me?"

"I wish I could." Valente sighed. "But have you forgotten the terms of our challenge? I swore that I would not allow any harm to come to you, either by hand or by my knowledge."

"Then why are you here?"

"Mother is furious. One of her subjects is dead, another is missing, her prized prisoner is gone, the entire Aqueno Prison blown up, and her heir has run off. Did you think there would be no repercussions?"

"What is Marasina planning to do?"

"She is weighing her options. I think you have her baffled. The idea that an heir of Magnomel would give it all up to live with humans is beyond ridiculous." Valente smirked. "Turns out you do take after your father. But she is a decisive ruler. I imagine she will muster her army soon, to bring you back by force if you don't return and explain yourself. She is most adamant that she not lose you as she lost Soren."

"And you came here to warn me?" I asked, unable to keep the skepticism out of my voice.

Valente grimaced but nodded. "If I believe you are in danger, it is part of the terms of the challenge that I aid you. Even if I despise you."

"I can't return, not yet." My mind was reeling, trying to figure out how to pacify the Faerie Queen. "I need more time. Can you convince her to stall the attack? Tell her I will come and explain when I am ready." I held my breath, still not ready to believe Valente would actually help me.

"Very well," Valente said, reluctantly. "I will do what I can. But I advise you not to take long, Elenora. Queen Marasina has limited patience."

Without waiting for my reply, he spread his wings and took to the air, flying back toward Magnomel.

When Valente was no longer visible in the dark sky, I breathed a long sigh of relief, dropping to the ground. The adrenaline seeped out of me, and I was left exhausted by the encounter.

"Well, that was unexpected," I said to myself.

Casper lifted his head, seeming to acknowledge my words. We sat in silence for several minutes, watching the sky. Part of me was still afraid that Valente would return.

I was ready to head back to the relative safety of the Rose Palace.

"Casper, can you fly?"

He flapped his great wings several times, testing out the healed one before bobbing his head at me. I took that as a good sign.

"Can you meet me back in your study?"

In response, Casper bobbed his head at me before taking off, flying above the trees and back toward the Rose Palace. Wishing I could use my own wings, I sighed, picking up my cane and starting the longer journey on foot.

By the time I reached Casper's study, it was close to midnight. My legs ached, the burn in them worse from the exertion. Casper was already there, and he shook his head at me, as if to ask what took so long.

"I don't have wings like you," I griped, as I pulled out his shirt and trousers from the drawer in his desk, laying them out for him. "At least not ones I can use."

Casper waddled over, inspecting the clothes with his beak. He nuzzled his head into the shirt, as though trying to put it on, but only managed to get stuck in the fabric. He lifted his neck, the shirt draping over his head, and honked loudly, jerking his head back and forth to remove the shirt. Despite the dire situation, he looked so comical, I had to stifle a laugh.

"Hold on. I will save you from this malevolent shirt," I said, catching the edge of the garment and gently pulling it off him. "No mere cloth will vanquish me," I added as I tossed the shirt next to the trousers. Casper stared at me like he was not amused.

"Probably for the best you wait till you have arms to get dressed," I told him as I sunk into a nearby chair. I felt my fatigue more acutely once I stopped moving. "I need to summon Pel." Casper let out a honk that sounded like annoyance. "He might have information on how we can break the curse." Casper let out another short honk but waddled behind his desk.

I pulled a hairpin from my braids and jabbed my thumb, rubbing the small bead of blood across my golden bracelet. When the familiar burn of the heating gold scorched my wrist, I clamped my mouth closed, not wanting to alarm Casper. I almost welcomed the pain, eager to know if Pel had answers.

As the burning heat faded from the bracelet, I relaxed back into the chair, feeling intensely drowsy. Besides the physical and magical exertions, I had not slept much in the last two days. I closed my eyes, telling myself it would only be for a moment.

I opened my eyes to three faces gazing down at me. I yelped, startled, as I focused on Pel, Lorella, and Casper. Casper was again human. I jumped to my feet, grabbing hold of him to confirm that I was not dreaming. His arms felt real enough under his shirt. I held on to them a moment longer, unable to stop myself from enjoying the feel of muscles as he stood so close to me. I reluctantly released him.

"You are a sound sleeper for a thief," Pel said, with a slight quirk to his lips.

"You never told me you snore so loudly," Casper said, a look of mock concern on his face.

"I do not." I punched him in the arm, then immediately realized my mistake. "I'm so sorry. Is that the arm that was shot?"

"You were shot?" Lorella looked over, horrified.

"It is." Casper rolled up his sleeve. There was a round scar, shiny and pink, but the skin looked healthy. "But you seemed to have fixed it. I didn't know you could do that." I couldn't tell if it was awe or fear in his voice.

"I taught her healing magic," Lorella piped in.

Casper inclined his head toward Lorella. "Thank you for that. Nor saved my life in the woods today."

I tried not to gape at the scene before me. I would never have imagined Pel and Lorella at the Rose Palace, much less seeing them with Casper and for him to be thanking a faerie. But perhaps I was underestimating my love and my friends. I felt a warm surge of gratitude.

"Thank you for coming," I said to Pel and Lorella, swallowing down a wave of emotion. I wanted to know what Pel had discovered about the curse, if Lorella knew something as well, but I forced myself to wait, instead I asked Lorella, "What happened after we left? What happened to Drusia?" For Aloisia's sake, I hoped the little green faerie had not been caught in the flood.

Lorella smiled, but there was sadness in her eyes. "Drusia is well. She was not close enough to the bank when the lake flooded." Her brow furrowed. "She is safe, but she is heartsick that her sister betrayed us."

"And Corine?"

Lorella shook her head. "I do not know. She did not return to the Forest Court. She was either caught in the flood or escaped and went into exile. It stings to know she lied to me, but I still hope that she made it out alive." Suddenly realizing what her words might mean to Pel, she shot him a worried look. "I'm sorry, I didn't mean—"

Pel waved away her concern.

"Elrik got what he deserved," Pel stated, but his words were flat, as though he had pushed away any emotion. The four of us stood in awkward silence, unsure how to move forward. Finally, Pel spoke, "But we did not come here to rehash that night. There is much we must tell you about the curse. Lorella may have discovered its origin."

"And there is not much time," Lorella said, looking at Casper. "How long do you stay in your human form?"

"I'm not certain—" Casper started.

"One hour," I interjected. "Between midnight and one in the morning."

Lorella nodded. "That confirms it."

"Please," Casper said. "Tell us what you know."

"Does *cignamorte tesseranzio desfaire* sound familiar?" Lorella asked.

"Yes, that was what he said." I nodded. A cold shiver ran through me, remembering Elrik's dying words.

"It's the swan song curse," she said.

"We had determined that transforming into a swan was part of the curse," Casper said. He kept glancing at the clock, and I knew his courtly manners were at odds with his impatience to know the cure.

"But why wasn't *I* the one affected?" I asked. *Did I accidentally transfer the curse to Casper?* "Elrik cursed me, he said my name." In a whisper, I added, "My true name."

"Did you know swans mate for life?" Lorella asked, looking between Casper and myself.

"I don't see how that is relevant," I said.

"It is a critical part of breaking the curse," Lorella answered.

Casper went pale. "Please don't tell me I have to mate with a swan."

Pel laughed until Lorella swatted him. "No, King Casper. That is not what I was implying. But the swan curse affects the one who is most loved by the person who is cursed."

Oh. All eyes settled on me, and I felt myself flush with embarrassment. I closed my eyes, wishing I could turn invisible.

"I'm sorry, Casper."

"I'm not angry," Casper said.

"You're not?" I cracked open one eye, surprised to see Casper was indeed, not angry, but rather staring at me intently, his lip slightly crooked up, almost smiling.

"Well, not at you. I might even consider myself flattered that I am the one . . . that it means you love . . ." Casper's sentence sputtered out, and I realized he was as flustered as I was. "Or I would be flattered if I did not have to be a bird twenty-three hours a day."

I wanted to kiss him, to assure him that he was the one I loved the most, but I saw Pel had gone rigid, though he did not say anything. Instead, I turned back to Lorella.

"How do we break this curse?"

She shook her head. "Unfortunately, *we* cannot. As the one cursed, you and you alone must break it."

I took Casper's hand, and he squeezed mine back, a warm, familiar grip. "What do I have to do?"

Lorella furrowed her brow. "The texts I found on the swan song curse are not entirely clear on that. It is a very old curse, not one used frequently. Elrik was into some very dark and old magic. But the closest I could come to a translation was that you must silently cover your love in a piece of you." I raised an eyebrow, but before I could voice my confusion, she added, "But Pel found a few records of the curse in our histories."

Pel looked solemn. "There is a record of a fay woman who was spurned by her lover when he fell in love and married another. The spurned faerie cursed her former lover with a swan song. The fay man made a cloak for his wife, who was now cursed to transform into a swan. But making the cloak was not enough. To imbue it with his life, he soaked the cloak in his blood. Once he draped the cloak around the swan that was his wife, the curse was broken."

I swallowed hard, horror rising in me. "Could I perhaps cry on a cloak instead? Maybe spit on it?" I tried to laugh, but my throat was too dry.

"This is too dangerous. Is there another way?" Casper asked, stepping closer to me. I tried to relish the feel of his protective nature, but I doubted the faeries had an easy shortcut. All fay magic came at a price.

Pel smiled, his sharp teeth visible in the moonlight. "There is not, but I believe Nor already has all the materials she needs for this garment." He gave me a knowing look. "You have a room full of gold thread that you already paid for in blood."

Casper inhaled sharply. He knew I had worked with Pel to transform the straw into gold, but I had glossed over the details of how Pel needed my blood to do so. At the time, Casper was so furious with

me, that I did not think such a detail was important. I braced myself
to explain, but then saw that we had only a few minutes before our
hour was over.

"Casper, I promise to explain later. But we do not have time tonight." I pointed to the clock. We had three minutes. Casper's lips
narrowed into a thin line, the displeasure on his face was plain, but he
gave a curt nod. "I'll make a cloak out of the gold thread," I confirmed.
"What else do we need to know?"

"You must be silent from when you start your work until the curse
is broken," Lorella said. "Or you risk the curse becoming permanent."

"Fine," I said. I would deal with that challenge soon, but right
now we needed all the details of the curse. If I could not speak, then I
could not explain anything to Casper. "And what else?"

"You only have till the new moon," Pel said.

"The new moon, that's in less than two weeks," I said, running the
numbers in my head. "Why couldn't this be a curse until the next full
moon." I sighed. "But I can make that work. How long can it take me
to make one cloak?"

"And Nor, there may be other challenges, ones we cannot fore-
see," Pel warned.

"I will manage," I promised.

"Nor, here." Casper ran over to his desk, pulling out a drawer and
dumping the contents on the ground. Before I could ask what he was
doing, he pulled out a panel of wood, a fake bottom I realized. He
reached into the actual bottom of the drawer and pulled out a large,
brass key.

"Much of the gold is still in the tower. The tower is never used,
so it seemed a safe place to store it." He reached toward me, offering the key. "Please—" he started, but his words were cut off as the
clock chimed the hour. He let out an agonized cry, the key dropping
from his hand as his arms sprouted white feathers and morphed into
wings.

I watched, helpless, as the curse took hold of him. Once a swan, he wasted no time escaping out the window, wide wings carrying him into the night.

I reached down and picked up the key from the floor.

26

Knowing it would not be safe for two faeries in the Rose Palace, Pel and Lorella departed soon after Casper flew off, promising to do additional research to see if anything else could be discovered about the curse.

I advised them to be careful, relaying Valente's warning.

Once I was alone, I allowed myself a few seconds to breathe, trying to calm frayed nerves and quiet my anxieties. The situation was not good, but at least I had a plan.

All I needed to do was sneak into a tower, silently weave a cloak, and put it on Casper before the new moon. Laid out in such simple steps, breaking the curse almost seemed easy.

I lit a candle, carefully placing it into a small lantern, before opening the study door.

I expected an empty hallway at such a late hour and nearly cried out when I saw someone crouched by the door. I jumped back, my eyes adjusting to the dark corridor, as I recognized the figure.

"Finn, for Aloisia's sake, what are you doing here?" I hissed. I scanned the hall, in case Devon or Jacobie were with him, but I saw no one else.

"I should be asking you what is going on." Finn rose, no longer trying to hide. Instead of looking sheepish at being caught, he seemed excited.

"Nothing," I said instinctively.

"Nothing?"

"Nothing that involves my nosy younger brother." I tried to stare down at him, though to my chagrin, Finn had grown during the months I was gone and was now slightly taller than me.

"Faeries and curses? I think you've gotten in over your head, Nor. You should consider asking your family for help."

"How much did you hear?" I asked, stalling for time as I tried to think of how to explain this to my brother without having to tell him anything.

"All of it." Finn puffed out his chest, and I realized he was proud that I had not caught him eavesdropping until it was too late.

"Chace's chaos," I swore. "You cannot tell Devon or Jacobie." Devon would only worry, and Jacobie was too young to be trusted with such a secret.

Finn looked hurt. "You should know you can trust me, Nor. I haven't told them you are, you know—" Finn flapped his hands, in a way to invoke the image of a faerie, though in truth, it mainly made him look like a chicken.

"Yes, fine," I snapped, clamping his arms to his sides to stop his faerie parody.

"Let's go to the tower," Finn said, squirming out of my grasp.

"There is no 'we' on this task. This is my responsibility. Go back to bed." I started down the hall, hoping Finn would obey. Instead, he fell into step alongside me, his long legs easily keeping pace with my smaller steps. Even with the use of my cane, I felt too tired to move faster. Frustrated, I whirled on him. "If you are so good at eavesdropping, then you know that I am the only one that can break the curse. I don't need your help." I hated myself for my stinging words, but it was better that I hurt my brother's feelings than allow him to put himself in danger.

Finn only crossed his arms, tilting down his chin so he could stare up at me, defiance showing in his brown eyes. "I heard the rules, all right. I'm not an idiot. You must weave the cloak yourself. But did you think that having someone else in the palace who could watch your back might be a good idea, especially since you won't be able to speak? Someone who can fetch your meals and make excuses as to why you are sequestered in your rooms all day?" Finn dropped his arms to his sides. "We are family. You aren't supposed to be the only one taking care of us. Let me help you."

I stared at my brother, not sure if I could speak for the lump in my throat. I was not the oldest, not even the smartest, but I was cunning and clever, willing to be deceitful if that meant keeping me and my brothers safe and fed. I could lie and cheat with a smile, and so, I had decided it was my responsibility to keep my family safe. I had not thought about it going the other way.

But here was Finn, insisting on helping me when I would be at my most vulnerable. I would not be able to make up pretty lies with a vow of silence.

"This is going to be dangerous," I warned.

"I live for danger."

I playfully punched my brother in the arm. "You live for apple tarts and libraries."

"Yes, first apple tarts and libraries, but then danger." Finn gave me a serious look. "Come on Nor. I can help you."

"Fine," I grumbled, trying to hide a sniffle with a cough. "But if you do something stupid and get yourself in trouble, I will never forgive you."

Finn only smirked. "You love your brothers far too much to never forgive me."

I looked up at him. "In that case, if you do something stupid, I will use your favorite books as saucers for my teacups and ring them all with tea stains. I recall you are especially fond of a boring philosophy tome."

Finn gasped. "You would desecrate the works of Alonzo Chartons? You monster."

The mock look of horror on Finn's face had me stifling giggles on our journey. It was a much-needed moment of lightness that vanished when we reached the tower's stairs.

"Are you certain?" I asked my brother. He nodded. I wished I felt his conviction. My voice was my greatest strength, melting people's skepticism when I ran schemes, distracting them when I picked their pockets, convincing them the water I was selling had magical properties. My body was weak from the sitano and my magic was little more than a trickle, but I knew the power of words, of being able to argue and convince.

But Casper needed me.

For that reason, I took a deep breath and started up the tower's winding stone stairway. Progress was slow; the thick, roughly cut stairs were steep and the narrow stairway, with a width of only my arm-length, was dizzying. I had to take several breaks, leaning on my cane, waiting for the burn in my legs to die down to a manageable simmer of heat. Finn said nothing, but patiently waited every time I paused.

When we finally reached the top of the stairs, I pulled out the bronze key. I had a flash of memories from the last time I was here, when I was a con artist, sentenced to transform straw into gold or atone for my crimes. I had Pel's help that night, but this task I would have to do on my own. With a silent prayer to the Mother, I fitted the key into the lock and twisted it. When the lock clicked, I pushed the heavy door open, revealing the small room.

Finn gasped as the lamplight reflected on the heaps of golden coils, piled throughout the small room. Some of the gold had been removed, but much of what Pel had created remained, a locked and hidden treasure. The room looked more or less untouched from that fateful night; the bloody rags and broken shards of pottery had been removed, but the cot, chair, and the spinning wheel with matching stool remained, each coated in a light layer of dust. As Finn stared open-mouthed at all the gold, I walked around the edge of the room, careful not to touch the gold. I lit the candles in the wall sconces, evenly spaced around the tower, all except for a missing one. That sconce I had pulled off the wall in an ill-fated attempt to climb down the tower. I inhaled, grateful the smell of blood had not clung to the room. Instead, I smelled the fresh, cold, night air, brought in from the opening in the stone wall that served as a window.

"You made all this?" Finn asked, reaching over to pick up a glittering coil.

"I only helped," I said, stifling a slight shudder, remembering the cost of so much transformation and greed. *This gold is made of my blood.*

"How are you going to weave it?" Finn asked, examining one of the spools of gold thread.

I stared down at the gold, willing an answer. In my rush to reach the tower, I had not taken the time to figure out how I would actually create the cloak. "There has to be a loom somewhere in this palace."

Finn frowned. "And how would you get a loom up those stairs? You certainly don't want to bring all this gold to a weaver and ask to borrow their loom. That might raise suspicions."

"I know," I snapped, frustrated that Finn was correct. The last thing I needed was to be caught carrying loads of gold out of the palace, especially when I would not be able to speak to defend such actions.

Finn ignored me, his focus still on the thread of gold he held. He wrapped the gold around his fingers, creating a simple slip knot, while leaving a loop of thread instead of pulling it tight. He pulled a length of thread through the loop, creating another loop. He did this several more times, creating a small chain.

"What about finger weaving the cloak, the way Mother used to make wool blankets?"

I studied the golden chain, remembering how our mother would take fat balls of wool yarn and create blankets by crafting such linked chains. After the initial row, she would double back, pulling through more thread to create a second row of loops, each connected to the ones next to it. With thick yarn, she could make a blanket within an evening. The fine gold thread would take me much longer, but it was a method that did not require a loom. I could do it all here in the secrecy of the tower. I smiled.

"Finn, you might be brilliant."

Finn beamed, undoing the small chain. "Yes, I know."

I felt invigorated as I surveyed the piles of gold. If I fully dedicated myself, then the cloak should only take me a day or two, which would break the curse long before the new moon. And once Casper was human again, he could stop the war Constance was planning.

"Want to get started in the morning?" Finn asked, already heading toward the door.

"I think I shall start tonight," I said. Finn frowned, but I continued. "The sooner I start, the sooner I finish."

"You still need to sleep and eat."

"I could not possibly sleep right now. But you should get some rest. And you can bring me breakfast in the morning." Remembering that I would not be able to speak until the cloak was done and on Casper, I added, "Thank you."

Finn shook his head but did not argue with me. "I will see you in the morning."

After Finn left, I settled myself on the stool, ready to spend the rest of the night weaving gold. I picked up a coil of gold, running the smooth thread across my palm. I wrapped it around my fingers, but as I pulled the thread through to create the slipknot, something sharp bit into my thumb and forefinger. I dropped the thread, swallowing down a cry of pain as I drew my fingers up to examine them. Several scratches were on the pads of my fingers, deep enough to draw fine lines of blood. I looked down, wondering at the cause, when I noticed the change in the gold thread.

Instead of smooth thread, the gold had transformed into a thin vine, studded with small, sharp thorns. I ran my finger across the vine, feeling the tiny sting of the thorns. It was impossible to pick up the vine without the thorns cutting into my hands. The thorns were tiny, but sharp as blades, and though the cuts were not deep, they stung.

Baffled, I tossed the vine away. I chose another coil of gold, but as I was readying the knot, again, the thread transformed. I watched as the thread grew sharp nettles right as I began my work. My stomach turned, a mounting sense of unease as I picked another spool of gold, ignoring the tiny cuts on my hands as I tried to start weaving. The moment I tied the first knot in the thread, it transformed, sprouting horrible little barbs.

I tried to start weaving with several other threads, and every time I began, thorns protruded from gold. I held the final one, pressing my lips together in a tight line to avoid screaming in frustration. I blinked back pressure behind my eyes. Even from beyond the grave, Elrik was able to hurt me. I had been a fool to think his dying curse would be so easy to undo.

I tried to summon my life magic to heal my fingers. When I concentrated, I could feel a dull pulse of magic in my chest, but without the ability to use the words Lorella taught me, I couldn't pull the magic down into my hands.

My fingers were stung, scratched and bloodied. Pel's warning came back to me, the one he told me when I asked that he transform the straw in this tower into gold.

"You do know all magic comes at a price."

I could almost hear his voice, the warning he wished I'd heed. But instead, I told him I would pay any price. I studied the barbed gold resting on my palm. To break the curse, I would have to pay in pain. I tried not to dwell on how many piles of thorny gold I would need to weave, instead, I focused on Casper, the utter faith he had in my ability to break this curse.

Gingerly, I picked up the knot, pulling a loop of the golden vine through it, doing my best to ignore the sharp sting as the thorns bit into my hands. Even when my fingers were so bloodied that drops leaked onto the woven cord, I kept working, finding a grim satisfaction when I finished the first row of knotted loops, the hem of the cloak that would save Casper.

I took a deep breath and began the process all over again.

27

Finn was horrified when he came to check on me the next morning. Bearing a platter with a pot of tea, along with fresh bread, cheese, and apples, he nearly dropped it when he took in my sight.

"By the Mother's maids, Nor, what happened?" he asked, promptly setting down the tray to examine my hands.

I was about to tell him I was fine, that I was only scratched, when I remembered the rules of the curse, and clamped my mouth closed before I could speak and ruin any chance of saving Casper. Instead, I shook my head, pulling back my hands as I gestured to the beginning of the cloak. I had only managed several rows of weaving during the night, the work painstakingly slow with each twist and pull scraping my fingers, but at least it was a start. Finn picked up my work, yelping as he felt the tiny barbs.

I wiped my hands on the inside hem of my dress, trying to conceal the blood, before I greedily poured myself a cup of steaming tea and added in heaps of sugar. Even with my own thick cloak wrapped around me, it had been a cold night in the tower. The liquid warmed my belly, but also sent more feeling into my numb fingers, the multitude of scratches making themselves known.

Finn stared, befuddled, at the beginnings of the golden cloak, until I showed him how every time I added a new golden thread to my work, that thread grew thorny.

"I don't like this, Nor," Finn said, reaching to take my work. I shook my head, and unable to speak, drew the woven gold closer to me, refusing to let him take it.

Eventually, he gave up. Or so I thought.

He returned a short time later with gloves, but I found that my fingers could not manage the intricate work of weaving in thick leather gloves, and thin, linen gloves did not provide protection. After that, he tried salves, but I could not keep any on long enough, as they rubbed off on the golden strands. He finally accepted what I already knew, this magic required a price.

Finn continued to bring me meals, blankets, and updates from the rest of the Rose Palace. The news only became more dire with every passing day. Constance was convinced the faeries had recaptured Casper, and she was preparing a full attack on Magnomel. Flora and Ilana had both left for their home countries to provide aid for Reynallis, and it was a matter of weeks, if not days, before the armies of Faradisia and Glavnada joined the Reynallis forces. If Casper did not return soon, there would be no way to stop an attack.

For my part, I tried to work as quickly as possible, feeling the pressure building around me. The work was so much slower than I hoped, taking me hours to do what I could have achieved in minutes if I was weaving yarn. The pads of my fingers were cut and bloodied, but I did not dare let myself stop, afraid I would run out of time. I spent days in the tower, silently weaving, pulling, and looping the cursed gold.

Every day, I took a short break to ensure I was seen around the palace to prevent rumors that I had also disappeared, but even that proved difficult. Finn would let me know when Devon was out hunting or Constance was holding court, then I would make rounds to be seen, but only at a distance. I would ride Chance, my large black and white stallion through the royal gardens or hurry down hallways that I knew were clear of those who knew me well. I would rush, clear I had a pressing appointment to avoid anyone attempting to speak to me. And if someone tried, then I could only hope that the fact that I ignored them came off as arrogance.

I had no idea what lies Finn created to excuse my absence from the palace the rest of the time, but I suspected they would not hold up much longer from the anxious way Finn peered at the golden cloak every time he brought me food or the nervous way he tapped his foot. I wanted to tell him that I was working as fast as I could. Instead, I put my frustrations and my anxieties into my weaving.

Eventually, a coarse gold fabric began to take shape. My work was clumsy, some knots too big and others pulled too tight, making the fabric stretch and pull in unflattering ways, but I did not care. It was satisfying to see that my pain and labor were creating something. And in a rough way, the fabric I created was almost beautiful, glittering and wild.

The only true break I gave myself was between the hours of midnight and dawn. Early on, Casper would fly into the tower well before midnight, sometimes as early as sundown. He would settle into the small room, burrowing his head in the soft down of his feathers, sleeping till his midnight reprieve from the curse. I had crept into his study the first night, gathering his clothes and taking them to the tower.

Once Casper transformed into his human self, he insisted on washing the blood from my hands, a deep furrow in his brow showing his concern, though he did not speak of it. Instead, he held me in his arms, the temptation of his embrace too sweet for me to resist. It was the only time I let my guard down, allowing myself to savor the few precious moments we had together. Almost nightly, the exhaustion overtook me, and I fell asleep in his arms, only to wake up hours later, alone and laying on the thin cot, knowing Casper had carefully moved and covered me in my wool cloak before the curse took him away again.

But as the new moon drew closer, I could sense the curse trying to claim more of him. He was restless as a swan, pacing and even hissing, as though he hated the confines of the tower. One night he did not show at all, and I was terrified something happened to him, until the next night he explained he had been too far in the woods to fly back before midnight. Each night that passed reminded me that we were one day closer to the curse being permanent unless I finished the golden cloak. I reminded myself of that every time my fingers stung or bled, every day that my limbs ached from hours in the cold room, or my eyes went blurry from fatigue.

And it worked.

Two days before the new moon, I finished the cloak. I pulled the last thorny thread through the last loop before tying off the end, laying out the cloak on the stone floor as I sucked on my bleeding fingers. But seeing the sparkling garment spread out and finished made the pain in my hands feel worth it.

It was midafternoon, and weak sunlight glittered off the cloak, making my rough weaving and the barbed garment look finer than any noble's attire. I wanted to laugh, a sudden lightness overtaking me, knowing the days of worry would now be ended. This time tomorrow, Casper would be human for good. Not wanting to make a sound, I did not trust the curse to tell the difference between laughing and speaking, I simply grinned, admiring my handiwork.

I stretched, my limbs stiff from the chill and sitting for so long. I looked out the window, suddenly eager to leave my self-imposed prison. The rose bushes were bare this deep into autumn, but it was still a sunny day. I had hours before Casper would arrive, and a brisk walk through the gardens sounded wonderful. Finn had told me that Devon and Jacobie were fishing with a group of noblemen and Constance was in meetings all day with advisors. It would be the perfect time to get a breath of air and still be back long before Casper arrived.

I wrapped my gray cloak around my shoulders and picked up my pearwood cane, almost skipping out of the tower. I carefully locked the door, slipping the brass key into my pocket. I was sore by the time I made it to the palace grounds, but it was worth the aches to feel as free as I did out of the tower. I crunched through dead grass as I headed to a small grove of apple trees. Though we were past peak apple picking season, a few bright red apples still clung to the trees. A juicy apple would be the perfect reward for finishing the cloak. My mouth watered as I plucked the biggest, glossiest apple I could find, biting into its white flesh, savoring the sweet, tart juice.

As I headed back to the Rose Palace, I thought about how pleasant it would be to go apple picking with Casper. I wondered if he had ever picked his own apples, or merely asked servants to do it for him. More importantly, the apple grove was far enough from the main grounds that we would have some measure of privacy. Away from prying eyes and without the constant threat of faeries or war would be the perfect place to get lost in kisses. I wanted to feel his lips on mine, both his soft, gentle kisses and the deeper ones, the hungry, eager kisses after he pulled me close to him.

"Nor?"

I had turned the corner, close to the entrance of the Rose Palace and had been too distracted to see who was approaching. Only a few paces away, Devon stood, worry etched into his face, brows knitted in concern. Jacobie stood beside him, along with a dozen other noblemen. All eyes were on me.

Chace's chaos, I thought, realizing they must be returning from fishing. I quickly nodded in acknowledgement of my brothers, before turning on my heels, back the way I had come. I hoped Devon would not follow me. If he felt insulted now, I could make it up to him later. Tomorrow, this would all be over.

"Nor, are you angry with us?" Jacobie asked. The hurt in his voice momentarily stopped my feet. I yearned to turn back to him, to scoop him up in my arms. But I could not risk it, not when I had to remain silent. I forced myself to keep walking.

"Nor, why are you ignoring us?" Devon said. I heard him following me. I started to walk faster, knowing I would need to break out into a run if he continued to pursue me. I stomped my feet, as though upset with them.

"Nor, stop this." Devon was right behind me, grabbing my arm to turn me toward him. "Nor, please talk to me. You have been avoiding me for days." Devon stared at me, and I saw pain in his brown eyes.

I wanted to apologize. Instead, I twisted my arm, forcing Devon to release me. I began to sprint toward the Biawood on the far side of the palace grounds. I was slower than my brother, but I might be able to make it to the woods before he caught up to me.

"Elenora Astira Molnár, you should be ashamed to treat your family in this way."

Devon's voice rang out across the grounds, but it was the first three words that hit me. As strong as if he had rammed into me, I was knocked off my feet. My cane rolled along the grass and the hairs on the back of my neck prickled. It felt as though threads were coming loose along my skin, an odd sensation, as tiny strands all pulled to the moonstone on my cane. As I struggled to my feet, I heard the back of my dress rip, my dragonfly wings emerging from my shoulder blades.

I glanced down at my hands, the skin a glowing copper. I looked up at my brothers; the horror on their faces mirrored every noble surrounding them. I wanted to explain, to tell Devon and Jacobie it was still me. I wished I had told them when I had the chance. Devon's eyes bore into me, and for a fleeting moment I thought he might be able to see the truth.

Around him, nobles began to pull out swords and yell, ordering the guards to seize the faerie. I waited for a breath, praying that he would tell everyone to stand down. Instead, his eyes darkened, and he reached for his own dagger.

I turned and ran. Becoming a faerie had not made me any faster, and I silently cursed my useless wings. I sprinted toward the Biawood, but only made it a few steps before someone slammed into me, knocking me to the ground. I fell, air rushing from my lungs. I struggled to catch my breath, trying in vain to get away. A royal guard yanked me to my feet, bringing me face to face with Devon. Pure hatred burned from his eyes, frightening me in ways my brother never had before.

"What have you done with my sister?"

As I struggled against my captor, my mind processed his words. I opened my mouth to clarify, to tell him that I was his sister, not some faerie imitating her, but as the words were on my lips, I snapped my mouth closed. If I explained myself now, I would be dooming Casper. Devon stared at me, his sneer growing with every second I denied him an answer. He tensed, a way I recognized before he started a fight, and for the first time in my life, I was afraid my brother would hit me.

Instead, he addressed the guard. "Lock it up somewhere secure. I will notify Princess Constance that a faerie has been captured. One that magicked itself to look like Lady Elenora." Devon turned back to me. "The Princess is not happy that your kind took her brother. She has ordered that any faerie caught in Reynallis is to be put to death." And then he spat in my face before storming back to the palace.

28

The dungeon was colder than I remembered, though just as foul. After guards threw me in a cell, I assessed my options, but my future looked bleak. The only other time I had been to the dungeon was months ago, when I had snuck in to rescue Pel. That night I slipped by a sleeping guard and picked the lock to Pel's cell. I would not be so lucky this time. Perhaps because of Pel's earlier disappearance, security was much tighter during my imprisonment.

Royal guards had manacled my wrists together, making it impossible for me to reach my arm through the bars to pick the lock. And even if I could manage the lock, the guard on duty was not as lack as the one stationed the night I had freed Pel. This guard, a burly man with a thick beard, regularly paced along the narrow hallway that divided the cells. His frequent trips past my cell also kept me from using Pel's bracelet to summon him. Even if I managed to summon Pel, he would likely be caught. I watched the torchlight flicker on the rough stone walls and tried not to gag on the smell of rot and stale urine that permeated the dungeon. I could feel the iron in the bars of my cell numbing my magic, but my magic was such a small thing, that I barely registered it over the chill I felt. I shivered, wishing I still had my cloak.

I tried to come up with a plan, something clever that could get me out of my predicament. If I only had parchment and ink, I could explain the curse, could write out details that only I would know, things that would have to convince my brother and Constance that I was not some dangerous fay out who betrayed them. I could instruct them to get the golden cloak to Casper.

I could not yell for the guard, could not risk speaking at all, but if I got his attention, then maybe I could find a way to show what I needed. I banged the manacles on the bars, the collision of metal on metal echoing through the dungeon. Several prisoners shouted at me to stop, but it drew the attention of the guard, which was all I cared about. When the man approached, I tried to mime writing. However, the movements looked erratic with my wrists bound up in iron.

"You won't be putting no spell on me," the guard said, mistaking my gestures. He pulled an iron horseshoe from a string around his neck, holding it out in front of himself like a protection charm. I shook my head, but he mistook that too, backing slowly away from me, never setting down the horseshoe.

Tired, I eventually gave up, sitting in the meager pile of damp straw that was meant to be a bed. I had never felt so defeated before, not even when I was locked in the tower room and tasked with spinning straw into gold. Even then, I was able to make a plan. Now, I had nothing. I ran through my options again and again, hoping to find something that would work. I might be able to explain, might be able to convince Devon and Constance and everyone else that I was still myself, though transformed. It might be enough to save me. But it would doom Casper to remain a swan. But what would happen to me if I stayed silent? Constance had decreed that all faeries caught in

Reynallis would be put to death. I fumed, hating how close I was to breaking the curse, but so far from doing it.

"Shift change, gotta take over."

"What?"

"I told you, your shift is up. But if you want to stay here all night, I'd be happy to give you my shift." I recognized the voice as Sir Yanis, but it seemed too good to be true.

"Ain't no one want dungeon duty, 'specially with some Chace-forsaken fay," I heard the other guard say, shuffling to his feet. "Good luck with that." I listened as the guard's footsteps faded away.

There was no sound for a while, but then faint footsteps sounded, and I could make out two people coming toward my cell. I stood, not wanting to be taken unaware by whoever was now in the dungeon. Yanis came into view, flanked by another figure wearing a hooded cloak.

"Nor, by all the Mother's maids, what happened?" Finn asked, pulling off the hood.

I smiled for the first time since my glamour broke, delighted to see my brother and Sir Yanis. I could not have asked for better allies right now than the person who knew I was fay and my guard, who hopefully had the guards' ring of keys. I couldn't explain, so I did what I could to gesture to the lock on my cell door. I managed to get the point across, despite my shackled wrists.

"I need something more to convince me that this is indeed Lady Elenora," Sir Yanis said to my brother. I noticed that Yanis did not seem pleased or even relieved to find me. Rather, he studied me with intense skepticism.

"Sir Yanis, I swear this is Nor," Finn insisted.

"That is what you told me to convince me to go along with your unorthodox scheme, Lord Finn," Yanis said, his eyes sweeping toward the entrance of the dungeon as though afraid of being discovered. "And I promised only to bring you down here. I cannot risk the safety of our kingdom on the chance that you have been fooled by a faerie."

"I know my own sister!"

I nodded vigorously, fighting the urge to scream. Yanis was the most honorable guard I knew. He had thrown himself in danger during the faerie attack at Casper's coronation, and I knew he would die protecting me and Reynallis. But I also knew he viewed his role as royal guard as something sacred, and I had never seen him bend the rules, much less break them. Finn must have gone to great lengths to convince Yanis that there was more to Devon's story for him to do something as unlawful as this. But I had no way of proving that I was myself, and not a faerie spy. His next words were even more damning.

"Everyone knows that the lady has not been herself. Annabeth confided in me her own concerns about Lady Elenora. She noted that her mistress had been almost entirely absent this last fortnight, right around the same time King Casper went missing."

I groaned. Naturally, my maid would be worried that I had barely spent any time in my rooms. Annabeth was attentive, and a wonderful confidant, but I had been in such a hurry to begin work on breaking the curse that I had not thought to enlighten her to my plans. And once I began, I avoided Yanis and Annabeth, knowing my silence would raise suspicion. I wished I had confided my plans to both of them when I still could speak.

"She cannot speak because she is breaking a curse," Finn insisted. I nodded in agreement, but Yanis looked at Finn with so much pity that I felt my hope slipping away.

"This creature may have told you such things to gain your trust," Yanis said, trying to steer my brother away from my cell. "Faeries can be tricky like that. But wishing this was Lady Elenora doesn't make it true."

Finn yanked his arm away from Yanis. "Nor, tell him who you are."

I shook my head. Finn knew I could not speak.

But Finn only grew more desperate, grabbing on to the bars, his knuckles turning white. "Nor, I know you wanted to save Casper, but it's too late. I can't get you out of here if you don't prove who you are. No one believes me. Even Devon doesn't believe me." Finn began to cry, sobs he tried to swallow down, that cut into his words. "There is a pyre being built outside. They will burn you in the morning. Don't you understand? You will die if you don't speak!" Yanis tried to pull Finn from the bars, but Finn snarled at him that he wouldn't leave me. My clever, bright brother looked so much younger than thirteen in that moment. He was a fragile, young boy, and I was breaking him.

My stomach was a pit of ice. Even with Devon's words, I had not thought I had so little time, had not imagined that Constance would sentence me to death so quickly. She was hard and stubborn when she needed to be, but she also cared about fair treatment.

Or she had before Casper and I had been captured. Perhaps she felt pushed too far by the fay and decided killing a faerie would send Queen Marasina a message. I hated that I could not explain how wrong she was. If she killed me before I got the cloak to Casper, she would doom not only me, but her brother. I could not believe that only this morning I was admiring my work, a strange and thorny golden garment that would set Casper free. Now I had to choose between my life and his.

Or did I? I didn't have the cloak, but I had the tower key and the one person in all of Reynallis who also knew how to break the spell. I could only hope there was enough time. I dug into my pocket, no easy feat with the manacles, but managed to pull out the heavy brass key. I leaned into the bars, offering it to Finn, praying he would figure out what to do with it. He stared at the key, his eyes still wet with tears. For a terrible moment, I thought he might refuse to take it. But eventually his fingers wrapped around the key, though he shook his head. I tried to plead with him with my eyes, convey everything that I could not tell him.

"What is that?" Yanis asked, staring at the key with some suspicion. I had a horrible fear that he would take the key from Finn, confiscate it as a dangerous fay artifact. Seeming to sense the same thing, Finn held the key close, protecting it with his body.

"This is the one thing that can prove my sister is innocent."

Yanis looked between me and the key, a conflict of duty and conscience. Finally, he took a step back. "If you are so certain Lord Finn, I suggest you hurry. I cannot release a faerie, but if there is even the slightest chance you are correct, then you better prove it to Princess Constance."

Finn nodded. He took several steps toward the entrance of the dungeon before he turned around, coming back to stand in front of my cell. I waved my arms for him to get going, not wanting him to waste precious time. I had no idea if it was close to midnight or even after, and every second Finn spent here was one more second closer to missing Casper's visit to the tower. But Finn refused to leave.

"Nor, I will do everything I can to get the cloak to Casper, but if I fail, you have to promise to speak, to defend yourself. I can't lose you."

I swallowed the lump in my throat, not wanting my brother to see me cry. I nodded, knowing it was the only way to get him moving. I watched him go, hoping it was not the last time I would see him.

I paced my cell, the dull burn of the sitano preferable to sitting still. Time dragged, and any amount of hope I had that Finn had broken the curse withered and died. I pulled at my magic, trying to feel its pulse. After some concentration, I felt the familiar warmth in my heart, the pulse of energy. I tried shooting it down my arms and into the manacles, and though I felt the wave of power surge down my arms, it merely pooled in my fingers, giving them a strange buzzing feeling, but nothing more. The iron in the manacles made it impossible for my magic to extend beyond my body. I gave up, exhausted and defeated. I silently cried, knowing how much was lost.

But even if Finn did not find Casper, there was still one more night before the curse became permanent.

29

When two guards came to collect me, I knew I had run out of time. Yanis watched me as I was dragged out of my cell, his wary eyes making it clear I had not convinced him.

As I was taken outside, the blinding light of the morning hit me as my lungs filled with cold, fresh air. I tried to stop, to adjust my eyes and savor the air while I could, but the guards kept marching me forward, toward the same place near the apple grove that I had been only the day before when Devon broke my glamour. There was a crowd of people from the palace on the greens, servants, guards, and nobles, the poorest and the richest alike, all standing, waiting for me. They hollered as I was led by, calling me an abomination and brandishing iron in my direction.

As I blinked for my eyes to adjust to the light, I saw the stake. My heart spiked, a sharp rush of fear and adrenaline flooding my veins as I took it in. A tall, wooden stake had been erected, surrounded by a short platform, built out of rough wood and packed with dried straw and branches. Two of the royal guards stood close to the platform, each holding thick torches. The fire of the torches reflected in the eyes of the guards. My mind played out my worst memories, all involving fire. The burning of my village in the Southern War. I was eleven, escaping into the night as everything I loved went up in flames, soldiers killing my mother and sending me and my brothers crying into the woods. I remembered the taste of ash and smoke. The jeers and yells of the crowd melted into the victory cries of soldiers.

I wanted to fight the guards, to put up some sort of struggle, but the sight of the stake paralyzed me. Even as my mind screamed for me to move, my limbs went slack, the primal terror of knowing I was about to die overwhelmed me, a strange numbness making me almost feel like I was floating out of my body.

The guards hoisted me onto the platform, shoving my back against the stake, crushing my wings behind me. I tried not to think about the guards, instead scanning the crowd for my brothers. I could not find them, and wondered if they were here, lost amongst the crowd. Would Finn have the cloak, was he searching for Casper now?

The guards removed my manacles as they roughly yanked my arms behind me and the pole, tying my wrists together on the other side. Rough straw scratched along my legs, and I wanted to cackle, to laugh hysterically, madly, at the idea that straw would be the reason for my downfall after all. I had no faerie to save me, but as I thought of Pel, I realized his bracelet was no longer covered by manacles, but rather pressed into the rough wood. I pulled my wrists along the side of the stake as much as I could with them bound. There was slight movement, nowhere near close enough to free myself, but enough to scrape my wrists along the rough wood, sharp splinters stabbing into my skin, I rubbed at the wood harder, struggling to draw blood. My skin was raw when I felt the bracelet go hot, the indication the magic was activated. I stared into the sky. I knew Pel could not possibly be close enough to save me, so I looked for a white speck, for a swan in the sky.

"Your kind cannot save you now!" A sharp voice brought me back, and I leveled my gaze on Constance, making her way toward me as the crowd parted in deference to her. She was dressed all in black, a velvet cape trailing down her back. Her eyes burned with hatred.

I desperately wanted to tell her who I was. I strained again to scan the sky. I thought I noticed movement, but the day was cloudy, and I could not be certain.

"There is no point hoping the fay will be coming." She gestured to the guards all around us. "I have set many of the guards to watch the forest and the skies, to sound the alarm if any so much as think they see a faerie. I did all this when your queen kidnapped my brother . . . twice!" Passion filled her voice, and as she approached me, I could see her eyes were bloodshot, as though she had been crying all night.

"But I had not expected a changeling." As she spoke, the crowd gasped and shouted. "We had not figured that the faeries would be so devious as to send King Casper back with one of you, to spy on us humans. For the crimes of impersonating a noblewoman, espionage against Reynallis," here she paused, building up her anger as she added, "and most heinous, kidnapping King Casper, I sentence you to death!"

I shook my head, desperate to deny the accusation. But Constance had proof right in front of her eyes. I expected her to gloat, to shame what she believed to be a fay spy, a threat to Reynallis. Instead, her eyes widened as she got closer to me, the anger mixed with something that might have been fear. The two guards with torches approached the platform.

Constance held up her hand, stopping the guards. "But I can be merciful. I will spare you if you tell me where my brother is. Where have you taken him?"

I nodded my head up, trying to indicate the sky, even as I knew I was doomed. Constance studied me, appraising my silent gestures.

"I will do more than simply spare you. If you return my brother, then I shall free you as well." As Constance's eyes bore into me, I sensed she was telling the truth. There was urgency to her plea, and I realized the fear was not of the fay, but for her brother. I raked my eyes over the clouds, wishing beyond hope to see a faerie or a swan.

And then I saw him.

A sleek white silhouette far up in the sky, but beyond doubt one of a swan. I had no idea how Casper had known to come back, he never had in the mornings before, but I prayed he would not turn back to the woods.

Small hands gripped my chin, Constance forcing my head down to look at her. Her eyes were frantic, though she kept her voice even.

"I don't want to kill you," she said, her voice softer, exposing the truth in her statement. "I have never killed anyone, and I do not wish to start today. I have lost everyone I love. I will not let you take my brother." Her voice cracked as she added, "Please, tell me if he is alive."

The pain in her voice pulled at my heart. If I was not terrified for my own life, I would have pitied her. For a moment, Constance looked like she would break down as she misconstrued my muteness as confirmation that Casper was dead. The hard shield was back, Constance's face a stony mask.

Something glinted in my peripheral, catching my eye. Someone ran toward us from beyond the far side of the palace, too far to make out, but the pale sunlight shimmered off something they carried, something . . . gold. I struggled against my binds, desperate to buy Finn and Casper more time.

Constance's voice filled with iron as she added, "But I swear by the Mother and on my own mother's grave, I will kill you this morning if you do not tell me what has been done with my brother."

I ground my teeth with the desire to tell her, to prove how wrong she was. Casper was close enough to circle the peaks of the towers, his massive wings gliding in his descent. I looked between Constance and the sky, willing her to see, to understand.

"Fine." She pressed her lips in a tight line, stepping away from me. She nodded toward the guards. "Let the faerie burn."

In unison, the two guards lowered their torches to bundles of dry straw shoved in between planks of the platform. The straw lit instantly, bright orange flames devouring the quick-burning straw and catching on the wood planks, the fire going pale yellow as the planks burned. I could already feel the heat, watching helplessly as flames leapt toward me, blurring the air around them.

Panic threatened to undo me. I bit my lip to keep from screaming and instead focused on the blood I tasted as my teeth cut my lips. With great effort, I closed my eyes, turning my thoughts inward. I concentrated on my magic, reminding myself I was a Magia Viveralis. I smelled smoke, heard the crackling flames, the warmth growing uncomfortably hot. My legs and chest began to sweat. I only needed to keep myself alive till Finn got the cloak on Casper, I reminded myself.

Vive guarriana, vive guarriana, vive guarriana. I silently chanted in my head, willing a pulse of magic in my heart to grow.

As sweat rolled down my forehead, I felt the first stirring of magic in my chest. I nearly cried in relief, but the smoke was growing thicker, making anything more than shallow breaths impossible. I built the power in my core, expanding my magic until my entire chest tingled with the buzzing sensation.

The heat around my feet spiked, and I felt them blistering. I shot my power into my limbs, all my concentration keeping the buzzing, pulsing magic flowing in my veins, running through my skin, protecting me.

The heat of the fire diminished, though smoke still thickened around me. I risked cracking open my eyes. The flames had not subsided, rather the conflagration surrounded me, flames licking up my feet and legs. Instead of excruciating pain, I only felt warmth. My skin was also intact, glowing bright copper, even as white-hot fire danced between my toes. Feeling a ray of hope, my concentration slipped, a slight hiccup in my control, and in that brief moment, the pain of the fire ripped over my leg, blistering and burning skin.

I screamed but managed to draw my magic back over myself. The pain eased, but the strain of forcing so much magic through me intensified with every passing second. My eyes stung from the black smoke, and the thickening air made breathing a chore. I coughed, tasting hot, chalky soot.

I focused on my magic. It was the only barrier between me and an excruciating death, but as I drew on my last reserves of strength, I could feel it depleting, draining out of my body. I felt my heart empty of my magic, even as I strained to push the last remnants of my power through my limbs.

Though my vision was blurred with tears and smoke, I saw a magnificent, giant swan flying through the flames. The bird's beak struck at the ropes around my wrists, its long neck bobbing in and out of the flames.

It worked on the ropes until a bright sheet of gold was thrown on the swan, covering it as beams of light shot through the cloak. There was yelling beyond the crackle of fire.

The swan was transforming, turning lean and human. I watched as white feathers shed from the swan, replaced by arms clad in gold. For the length of a breath I smiled, at peace in the knowledge that Casper had been saved.

But as I exhaled, I felt the last of my power slip out of me. The moment I had no magic left, the fire ate me.

Scalding heat enveloped me, boiling me alive. I screamed, scorching my throat with burning ash. My skin blistered and cracked, as fire drove up my legs, along my sides. My delicate dragonfly wings tried to seize up as the fire destroyed them. My face felt like it was melting, my nerves exposed and raw, howling as the fire destroyed me.

My world was an agony of dying, of peeling skin and sizzling, exposed muscles. I screamed and screamed, cooking alive, as I choked to death on black clouds.

A bright flash of flame became a sword of gold, held by an angel, that slashed through my bindings. The angel had Casper's face. His lips moved, but I couldn't hear anything he said. I felt outside myself, barely conscious. I didn't think I had much time left in this world, certain I was looming at death's door, but at least Casper was freed.

He grabbed me, pulling me out of the flames. I cried, his touch shattering my exposed nerves. My sight went completely white and then black, as I was picked up, the ground gone beneath me. The heat dimmed, feeling no longer external, but coming from my own damaged body. The air was again breathable, though I was ravaged from the inside every time I took a breath. I tried to open my eyes, but I remained in darkness. My face hurt too much, and I could not be sure if I still had eyelids or eyes. I wondered if I was dead or blind. Casper was carrying me, and all I could do was whimper, every step sending shooting pain throughout my entire body. Distantly, I thought that if I was dead, it should hurt less.

It was my last conscious thought.

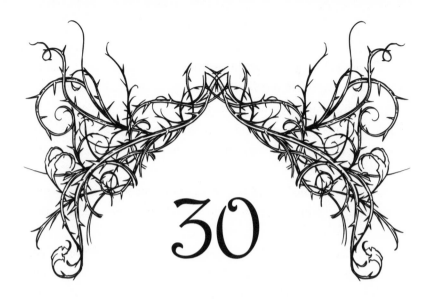

30

I awoke to see Annabeth leaning over me, dabbing a cool cloth to my forehead. I was in my bed, though I had no memory of how I got there. Seeing me open my eyes, Annabeth squeaked, almost jumping away from me. I could see her uncertainty now that I was awake.

At least I can see.

"Am I dead?" I asked. My voice was raspy, my throat stung, but less than I would have imagined. My entire body ached, but I was in no severe pain. I attempted to sit up.

Seeing my struggles, Annabeth suddenly burst into tears, crying even as she tried to help me sit. "It really is you, milady. I am so, so sorry." Annabeth was apologizing and sobbing, the cries turning into hiccups.

"I will take it from here." Casper was suddenly beside the bed. In a kind tone, he suggested Annabeth fetch me some tea. She bobbed a quick curtsy before hurrying out of the room. Casper gently propped pillows behind my back.

Even as daylight streamed in from the window, there was no sign Casper would transform into a swan. I greedily drank in his every detail, elated beyond words to see Casper human again. His black hair was disheveled and there were shadows under his eyes. I reached up a hand and touched his cheek. I smiled, feeling the stubble on his face.

"You're human," I said before I began coughing again. Casper poured me a cup of water from the pitcher, helping me carefully swallow several sips.

"Thanks to you, my love." Casper clasped his hand over mine, gently kissing my fingers. His eyes darkened as he squeezed my hand. "I was terrified I had arrived too late. Everyone in the Rose Palace save for your brother owes you an apology." Casper's lips turned down in a grimace. "I wanted to throw every single person in the dungeon for what they did to you."

"I hardly think the dungeon has room for everyone in the Rose Palace," I said, though I secretly felt pleased by his fierce concern.

"I'm serious, Nor. I don't know what I would've done if I had lost you."

"I felt the same way when I thought you might be a swan forever," I said in a rough whisper. "But I am too happy to see you to think about vengeance. Besides, they could not have known."

"You are being exceedingly generous considering my sister tried to execute you."

I couldn't hide the shudder; the memory of being tied to a stake would haunt me.

"Why don't I hurt more?" I had been certain I was dying in the fire, convinced my body was destroyed.

But I felt little pain now.

I looked down at my arms. My burnished faerie skin was intact. I could make out faint scarring, light markings that were nowhere near as terrible as they should be.

Casper nodded toward the door that led to my parlor. "Pel and Lorella arrived soon after I got you out of the fire. Pel said you had summoned him."

"Are they safe?" I asked, suddenly fearful that the laws against faeries put them in danger. I threw off my quilt, about to seek them out, when Casper put a gentle, but firm hand on my shoulder.

"You need to stay in bed. The faeries are under my protection. I explained everything that happened to us to Constance and the rest of the court. From our capture, to you being the Magnomel heir, to Elrik's death. And while I cannot promise that everyone is entirely comfortable with the fay, they understand that no faerie is to be harmed in the Rose Palace, or in any of Reynallis."

I looked down at my hands, my skin clearly not human. "I imagine Constance was most surprised," I deadpanned.

"Well, she—" Casper started, but was interrupted by Constance herself striding into my room.

"Yes, I *was* surprised," Constance said, her tone brisk. "I instructed Annabeth to notify me the moment Elenora was awake." She faltered then, as she took in my appearance. "Is there a way to reverse this?" She gestured toward my wings. "We can have the finest physicians—"

"No," Casper cut her off. "This is who she truly is. There is no need for her to change anything." I nodded, grateful to not have to explain.

Constance's breath hitched slightly, as though she wanted to speak but was uncertain of what to say. "It will be hard for a faerie in Reynallis." Before I could respond, I noticed Constance's eyes going glassy before fat tears began to roll down her cheeks. She squeezed her eyes closed.

"Elenora, I am so sorry. So deeply, gravely sorry." Constance finally opened her eyes to look at me, though her hands knotted together in front of her. I had never seen such an outpour of emotion from Casper's sister, and it rendered me speechless.

Constance wiped at her eyes, even as tears still ran down her cheeks. "I've always hated the fay. And since they murdered our older brother, I took that as a sign they were all wicked. But I almost had you killed. And you would have died if not for Casper and Finn. And it would have been my fault. I am so sorry. I thought I was protecting Casper, but I had it all wrong." Constance broke down crying, her breath uneven between sobs.

As I gave her time to weep, I realized I was more like Constance than I ever thought possible. When she calmed down to the point of an occasional sniffle, I reached out and clasped her hand. Though she didn't withdraw it, she held my hand with caution, as though I might break.

"I forgive you," I said.

Constance studied me, her eyes red and puffy. "How can you forgive me? I watched the horrors of that fire . . ." she trailed off. I knew I would be haunted by the memory of that terrible day, but I was weary of vengeance. I wanted hope instead.

"Because I understand what it means to do anything to protect your family. And because I want us to focus on the future. One where there can be peace between humans and fay."

"Thank you, Elenora." Constance's words were little more than a whisper, but she gave me a watery smile.

"And I will heal thanks to Pel and Lorella. It's a wonder they arrived so quickly," I mused.

"They were close by, knowing that the time was almost up to break the curse. Lorella came with Pel and she used her magic to heal you," Casper said.

I looked down at my hand, Pel's gold bracelet still wrapped around my wrist, undamaged by the fire. "I have never been so grateful that he tricked me with an unremovable bracelet. I was lucky to have gold I could never spend." I fully took in Casper's attire. "And speaking of gold, what are you wearing?"

Casper looked down at his clothes, almost sheepishly. He wore an outfit of pure gold, as though someone had used spools from the tower to construct the fitted trousers, the fine tunic, and calf-length boots. Unlike the cloak I had woven, the fabric was fine and smooth, resembling liquid gold. The only thing marring their perfection were the detailed accents, what might have been white feathers sewn into complex patterns on the tunic and up the seams of the boots. The feathers were covered in ash, many blackened or burned off entirely. Around his waist was a belt that also might have been made of swan feathers, but only a few stringy plumes remained.

A gold sword rested on one of my chairs, with a thick, golden cloak draped over the side. It was not the thorny, wild thing I had created, rather it was piled in rich folds, another cluster of destroyed feathers forming what would have been rich trimming if the plumage had not been burned.

"When Finn threw your cloak on me, it transformed, even as it was transforming me. I became human and the cloak became fine gold, smoothing around me and turning into this." He gestured at his clothes.

I recalled my golden angel and smiled.

"I might have ruined your lovely new outfit," I said, reaching out to stroke one of the few surviving feathers, a half-burnt thing embroidered into his tunic.

"Perhaps I should get cursed again so you can make me another one," Casper said with a smirk.

"Don't you dare," Constance snapped, regaining some of her composure. The look of horror on her face was enough to make me laugh.

I plucked out the feather, letting it float to the ground. "If you are still wearing this," I tried to do the calculations in my head, "then how long have I been out?"

Casper's face grew serious. "Two days. It took a lot for Lorella to heal you, and then we all had to wait." Casper laced his fingers in mine, as though needing to physically touch me to assure himself I was alive. "I did not want to leave your side."

I looked down at our interlaced fingers and smiled. I noticed his signet ring was still on my finger, the imprint of roses unscathed by the fire. I ran my thumb over the ring, before tracing the lines of his fingers. There was so much work to be done, so much to fix, but for the moment, I was content to be right here, close to the one I loved, feeling safe and protected.

After three days, I was deemed rested enough to leave my bed. At least, I deemed myself so. Despite my reassurances, Annabeth was beside herself with guilt at having not realized who I was and seemed intent on making up for it by ensuring I had constant care and a steady supply of pastries, all hot and fresh from the kitchens. While I enjoyed the idleness the first day, by the second day, I was restless, and uncomfortable with all the apologies.

Annabeth was not the only one eager to make amends. Sir Yanis was first, followed by a very repentant Devon. He oscillated between begging my forgiveness for his part in my arrest and chastising me for hiding both the fact that we are half fay, and the curse from him. Finn made the problem worse by being far too smug about knowing the truth, at least until I finally threw a pillow at his head. But I did not mind my brothers' bickering. I was too happy to have our family back together.

I spent most of the second day in bed as Finn and Devon played cards and Jacobie snuggled in bed with me, every now and again asking if he could have wings like me. The first time he asked, I exchanged a silent look with Finn and Devon. At some point, my brothers would have to deal with the knowledge that they were also half fay, but that discussion could wait. For now, I distracted Jacobie with the promise of a pear and almond tart if he could find Annabeth to fetch one from the kitchens. By the third day, I could no longer stand my confinement. There was too much that had to be set right, and I wanted to be a part of it, especially if I could do anything to bridge the divide between faeries and humans. When Casper confided that there would be a council to determine the next course of action, I refused to miss it.

Annabeth realized I was leaving my rooms, with or without her help, so she set to work, preparing my bath and laying out fresh towels. As I dried off, I noticed the gown she pulled, a velvet dress of deep teal, trimmed with shimmering cream ribbons. The dress was unfamiliar. I ran my hand over the soft velvet before picking it up. The back of the neckline had a deep plunge that would reach to my mid-back.

"Annabeth, where did this gown come from?"

"I had it made, milady," Annabeth said, carefully studying her toes. "I thought you would like a gown that can accommodate your wings. I did not want to disturb you with such things when you needed rest. I also thought the color would be nice with your new skin, I mean, complexion." Annabeth peeked up at me, biting her lip. "I hope I did not presume too much, milady."

I found it hard to speak from a wave of emotions. Though many people asked after my health, wishing me a full recovery, most of them skated around the fact that I was now fay. I had begun to feel as though it was something shameful. I threw my arms around Annabeth, embracing the small girl in a tight hug. Annabeth stiffened in surprise and I was certain I was breaking all the rules of decorum. I released her, scrubbing at my eyes so I wouldn't cry.

"Thank you for seeing me," I whispered.

"It is my job and honor to serve you," Annabeth said, with a dismissive wave of her hand. But as she tied the laces of my new dress, she smiled. "Your wings are lovely things."

I stared at myself in the mirror. Annabeth had been right about the color, the dark blue-green velvet perfectly complemented my glowing copper skin. I extended my wings, their opalescent surfaces reflecting the light. My white hair had been cropped after much of it burned, but there was enough to frame my face, though the points of my fay ears poked out. Annabeth secured a dainty tiara on my head, one studded with pearly moonstones. It was a gift from Constance, one she had given me when my pearwood cane had been recovered and returned. I told Constance that the moonstone in the cane used to belong to my father, and we spoke at length about our families, especially those who were no longer with us.

Before she left, she squeezed my hand and told me that she was looking forward to us being sisters.

Annabeth dusted my eyelids with a fine golden powder that, instead of hiding the gold of my eyes, made them even more prominent. Though I was not entirely accustomed to seeing myself as fay, for the first time, I realized I was not disgusted by what, *by whom*, I saw reflected in the glass. I might no longer look human, but as a faerie princess, I was beautiful.

As I seated myself at the large, round table in Casper's study, I noted the advisors Casper had chosen. In addition to Constance, Devon and Finn, Pel and Lorella were in attendance. Since the Southern War, I had believed nobles cared only for themselves, but Casper had faeries and commoners at his table. Perhaps he truly could be a different kind of king.

"I thank you all for your time," Casper said, addressing us. "It would be an understatement to say that much has happened since my return, and our actions in the next few days and weeks will dictate the future relationships of Reynallis with her neighboring countries. Before I bring in a bunch of yelling nobles, I want to strategize a plan with those most closely involved."

As Casper let his words sink in, I realized I was seeing yet another side of him. He was not the imperial, grand monarch nor was he the charming boy, rather, he was a dedicated leader, a caretaker of his country. He did not need an elaborate show or ceremony to command the respect of those closest to him.

"Relations with Magnomel have not been good, but I do not want to start my reign with another war, not if there is any way it can be avoided. The damage from the Southern War is still felt by our most vulnerable citizens." Casper glanced at me as he added, "I have my betrothed to thank for opening my eyes to that fact. It took a thief to make an honorable king," he said, winking at me before turning his attention back to the rest of the attendees. "There are poor villages in the south that have never been rebuilt, people who are still going hungry years after we stopped enforcing rations. A war against Magnomel will only further delay aiding our southern cities and bring the same fate to our towns in the north."

"Peace is a noble goal, but what of Queen Marasina? We have no way to trust her," Constance said. She considered her next words before adding, "I was wrong to think that all fay are evil. I have learned much from new friends," she nodded at Lorella, "but even as I recognize my ignorance, we cannot ignore that Queen Marasina ordered an unprovoked attack on the Rose Palace during your coronation. Good lives were lost in that battle in addition to her capture and imprisonment of you and Elenora."

"I am genuinely sorry for my mother's actions against the humans but starting a war against us will only lead to further bloodshed." Lorella spoke softly, but without any hesitation.

"And if your mother decides to attack again?" Constance countered.

"She will not."

"How can you be certain?"

"Enough!" Casper said, using his commanding voice. Both Lorella and Constance closed their mouths, sitting back in their seats and glaring at each other. "We may already have a solution to peace with Magnomel." All eyes fixed on Casper, expectantly. He took my hand. "An alliance by marriage."

For a long time, no one spoke, taking in Casper's words. He squeezed my hand, and I returned the gesture. As I watched the people around the table, I dared to glance at Pel, afraid this reminder would cause him pain. Rather than upset, he looked pensive, and whispered something to Lorella, who nodded.

"That is not a terrible plan," Lorella finally said, breaking the silence. "Public violence toward one's kin is considered highly disgraceful. It would be unheard of for royal fay to commit such an act."

"But Valente tried to have me poisoned," I countered. My confidence in such a straightforward strategy dipped as I remembered my uncle's attempt to assassinate me. Even if he owed me loyalty now, Marasina was under no such obligation.

"Yes," Lorella conceded, "but he did not do it himself. It would have been a very different matter if *he* had given you the piro berries. That would have been far more dishonorable."

"A strange sort of honor," I grumbled, but I had to concede that Valente did abide by a moral code. He had gone to the trouble of warning me in the forest that Marasina would demand my return eventually.

"Strange or not, it is the way of our people. And if Nor is queen of Reynallis, I cannot see a way my mother would view open attacks on Reynallis as anything other than overt violence toward her granddaughter. She may not like it, but the honor due to living kin outweighs revenge for the dead."

"We can inform the queen when we return to Magnomel," Pel said, glancing toward Lorella, who nodded.

"I will go. I should be the one to tell her," I said.

"What?" Devon and Casper said in unison. Chatter broke out, Casper and my brother both making arguments as to why I should never return to Magnomel.

"It's the honorable thing to do," I said. "Which may be a surprise coming from me." Finn snickered and Devon elbowed him in the ribs. "But it is true. Because of humans, Queen Marasina lost a son, and if I never see her again, she will view humans as taking her granddaughter away as well. She might not openly attack Reynallis, but she will only resent humans more, and a bitter peace is not a lasting peace." I paused before adding, "And I promised Valente that I would go back and explain."

"Is there any way I can talk you out of this?" Casper asked. His grip on my hand tightened, and I could see the shadow of fear in his eyes.

"No, you cannot." I placed my other hand on his, trying to reassure him. "But I will be fine. I know that Queen Marasina cares for me in her own way. And whether I like it or not, she is family, and I've lost too much family to lose any more."

"Then I shall not stop you." And if Casper felt anxiety at my decision, he did his best to hide it.

"Excellent! I'll come with you," Finn said.

"You will not," Devon said.

"Why not? We're family too."

"Because it's dangerous." Devon glared at Finn.

"Come on, I've already gone into Magnomel twice, and I was fine."

"I'm not certain that is a good idea," I said. "You still look entirely human, and while Alverdine could remove your glamour, that is a big decision." I raised my hand before Finn could argue or Devon could agree. "But regardless, you are right. You and Devon and Jacobie are all her family and deserve to see her as much as I do."

"You two are incorrigible," Devon said, but I knew we had him. He rarely got his way when Finn and I both agreed on something.

"Now that our strategy for relations with Magnomel is," Casper glanced between my brothers and me, "*mostly* decided, we must take immediate action to de-escalate war preparations, starting with sending messengers to Glavnada and Faradisia to halt the request for reinforcement armies. Lady Ilana and Lady Flora should also be invited back as guests to the Rose Palace, should they wish to return."

"I can go to Glavnada," Devon quickly offered, drawing the eyes of everyone in the room. "What?"

"Eager to see Lady Ilana?" Finn goaded.

"No, that's not it," Devon said, but the flush of red creeping up his neck told a different story. "Though she is a wonderful girl, err, woman, umm, lady." He cleared his throat. "Sailing to Glavnada sounds far better than venturing to Magnomel, and I know there is no talking either of you out of heading there. Better I take Jacobie with me, to keep him safe."

"And so you can see your lady love?" Finn added in a very loud whisper. Devon punched his arm. Those around the table politely muffled snickers and hid smiles at my brothers' antics, all except Constance, whose face had become forcibly blank.

"Delighted to see that matter is addressed," Casper said. "That only leaves notifying Faradisia. Constance, I was thinking you could lead the retinue to the south."

"Flora can't come back," Constance blurted out. Cracks formed around her stony expression, as she blinked rapidly to keep her composure. "Even with the war called off, Flora was only allowed to stay in Reynallis as a royal hostage. King Jovian has been eager for Flora to return since you were released to take your place as king. He would see it as an insult to Faradisia for us to have her here with us when you are no longer there."

"Perhaps you can convince King Jovian that Flora's invitation back to our court is one of an honored guest, not a royal hostage?" Casper spoke softly to his sister, but she shook her head.

"He interprets a royal guest as an unofficial royal hostage, I am certain of it." Constance wiped once at her eyes and pressed her lips together in a tight line.

"What if she was not returning as a hostage or guest, but rather to fulfil a different sort of contract?" I said, an idea starting to take shape.

"Such as?" Constance asked, though she looked doubtful.

"If a marriage with the Magnomel heir can cement a peace between kingdoms, perhaps a marriage with the niece of the Faradisian king would also ally our two countries." I looked intently at Constance, waiting for her response.

Constance lit up, a hopeful smile spreading over her face as she practically jumped to her feet.

"Elenora, you might be brilliant." She turned to Casper. "I shall start preparations for my trip immediately." She hurried out of Casper's study, her velvet skirts swirling around her.

Casper grinned as he watched his sister scurry away. "Thank you, Nor. I do not believe I have ever seen her so excited."

I kissed his cheek. "Being reunited with one's love is a pretty thrilling thing."

31

The flakes of an early snowfall melted off our travel clothes as we
rode out of the mist barrier and into the eternal summer of Magnomel. Though the air was balmy, smelling of new leaves and sunshine, I kept my cloak on.

Casper had given me the golden cloak, the ruined feather trim
replaced by velvet, as a token to keep close to me after I persuaded
him not to join me. I believed that I could reason with Marasina, but
I was also not willing to tempt fate by bringing her the Reynallis king.
Casper was reluctant, but eventually saw the reason of it, especially as
there was no one to rule in his place with Constance on her way to
Faradisia.

"This is so much faster by horse," Finn said, pocketing the compass he had used to navigate through the mist.

"It is still faster to fly," Lorella said. She and Pel had agreed to
escort us to Magnomel, and I hoped that having her support would
help me convince Marasina to choose peace.

Finn openly stared at Lorella's wings, and I could almost hear the gears in his mind at work. "If I asked what's-her-name to remove my glamour—"

"You mean Alverdine?" I interjected.

"Yes, Alverdine. If I asked Alverdine to remove my glamour, would you teach me how to fly?" Finn looked at Lorella with bright eyes.

Lorella smiled at Finn. "First, be sure you remember her name or she might turn you into a toad." Finn's mouth dropped open in horror, but Lorella giggled. "I am only kidding. And of course, I would. Now, the first thing I would teach you would be how to master your wing movements." She continued explaining the mechanics of faerie flight, with Finn hanging on her every word. While I was genuinely pleased to see a friendship forming between Finn and Lorella, I couldn't help but feel a stab of jealousy that I had never had the luxury of time to learn how to fly. I carefully fluttered my own wings back and forth, slow enough not to spook my horse. I could move them at will, but it was a far cry from flying.

"I still can teach you to fly, if you like." Pel had pulled his horse up to mine and was studying me.

"Will you get out of my head?" I asked, but I smiled ruefully.

"I cannot help it if we think alike. I've always told you we are similar, you and I."

"Maybe," I conceded, unsure where the conversation was going. I hoped he knew better than to ask me to stay with him.

"And I am realizing that is the reason we would never work."

"Oh?" I knew Pel was willing to let me go. He knew I was betrothed to Casper, but I had not expected such a blunt acknowledgement.

Pel gave me a slight smile, though it was tinged with sadness. "I shall always care about you, Nor, will always be a friend when you need one. But I know now that I cannot be more for you. You and I are like identical puzzle pieces. We are so similar, but we do not fit. We know how to lie and cheat and survive, but being together would only keep us that way."

"I'm sorry," I said, unsure how to articulate exactly how I felt.

Pel dismissed my apology. "I don't say this to make you feel bad. Your king may be a different kind of person than you, but the two of you fit. Seeing you with him at the council meeting, you work together, using each other's different strengths and abilities to reach your goals. And if one of those goals is peace between Reynallis and Magnomel, I would not be so dishonorable as to disrupt that."

"Thank you." I wanted to say more, but again, my words failed. I felt freer, released from the guilt of not choosing Pel. But there was also a part of my heart that ached, knowing he was letting me go, even as I wanted him to.

I knew it was selfish of me, so I kept it to myself.

"I think the two of you will have a good life together."

Pel and I sat in silence for a while as Finn and Lorella rode ahead of us, discussing everything from flying to the library in the Forest Court. As Pel watched Lorella, something seemed to soften in his face.

"She likes you, you know," I said, keeping my voice low enough so only Pel could hear me.

Pel smiled, his eyes still on Lorella. "I might have started to notice that."

"Lorella is a good person."

"I know."

"A really good person. Far better than you or I."

"So, like your kingling?" Pel started, but corrected himself, "I mean, like your king?"

"Yes, like Casper. Both of them are far too good for the likes of us."

"Then what are we to do?"

"Be the best versions of ourselves to show them that they were not fools for choosing us." I smiled as I rubbed my finger over Casper's signet ring. "Possibly even give up a life of deceit and trickery for them." Pel sighed dramatically and I chuckled. "At least most of the time."

"Valor and honesty," Pel mused. "It would be an interesting change of pace."

"Such a change," I agreed with a smirk. "And also know that Lorella is a dear friend, family even. So be mindful that you treat her well."

"By all the Mother's maids, you live here?" Finn exclaimed when the Forest Court came into view. Even I could appreciate the beauty of the sparkling lake and living tree palace.

"Indeed we do," Lorella said, smiling. "If our peace talks go well, then I would be delighted to show you around. We have the most impressive—"

"Library," Finn interrupted. "I want to see the library."

As Pel flew over the lake to retrieve a glass boat for us, I watched the swans, large and graceful, peacefully floating along the water's surface. I thought seeing swans would terrorize me after the curse, but instead, I felt oddly fond of the birds, as reminders of Casper.

The faeries in the meadow and by the shore began to take notice of us as we settled into the glass boat, making our way to the Forest Court. Finn could not decide if he was more fascinated by the watching fay or in trying to figure out the magic behind the glass boats as our craft conveyed us across the lake. I saw no fear in Finn's eyes, only a wild excitement, an eagerness to learn everything about this new world. He plied Lorella with questions, as I surveyed the faces of watching fay. Queen Marasina was nowhere in sight. I assumed she would be in the courtyard, being told of our unannounced arrival.

Only one faerie flew out to greet us. A whirl of shimmering green descended from one of the palace balconies. Drusia swooped down to the edge of the lake, practically hopping with excitement to see us. She bowed deeply to Lorella and me and fell in line behind us as we made our way across the meadow. I appreciated her support, though I couldn't help noticing that Corine was nowhere to be seen. But my brief wonderings as to what had happened to Elrik's ally ceased the moment we stepped into the courtyard.

Fay filled the grassy area, clustered around trees and by the sparkling waterfall, but it was the thrones under the massive willow tree with the cerulean blooms that held my attention. Queen Marasina sat on her throne, the other empty, with the noble fay surrounding her. Her children, including Valente, sat closest, their pale hair and bright blue eyes silently taking us in. I felt a stab of fear to again be so surrounded by the fay, but I forced myself to keep going, reminding myself that I was also fay, and the granddaughter of their queen. As we approached, I pulled out the pendant I wore, letting the Regalia Vive Amulet drop heavy around my neck.

Queen Marasina studied us as we drew closer. She was a dazzling sight, dressed all in silver, including a woven crown and a jeweled dagger. Her hair was loose, almost melting into her dress. It made her sharp sapphire eyes stand out as she silently waited for us to approach her.

I thought about the different sides of the Faerie Queen. She was the fierce warrior, the leader of an attack that still gave me nightmares. But she was also a mother, still grieving for a dead son. And she was a cunning queen, carefully ruling over her faerie subjects. I wondered which version of Marasina we would be met with today.

We bowed low when we reached Marasina, all of us waiting for her to speak.

"You surprise me, granddaughter," Marasina finally said, her voice the only sound in the courtyard as the other fay stared at us. "After freeing my prisoner, destroying my prison, and causing the death of one of my subjects, I had not imagined you would be returning to us."

"Elrik wanted to control me; he would have used my true name to turn me into a puppet for his use."

"I said you caused his death, not that it was unwarranted," Marasina said, so coolly it sent shivers down my spine. "And is that the Regalia Vive Amulet? But it has been drained of all its power." Marasina narrowed her eyes. "Shall I add desecrating a royal heirloom to your list of offenses?"

This is getting off to a wonderful start, I thought. "You did gift it to me after the challenge. Doesn't that mean I could do with it as I pleased?" I heard Lorella's sharp intake of breath, but my gaze remained on the queen.

"That is true," Marasina reluctantly admitted. "But I had not anticipated you would draw generations of power from it. The strength of will alone had to be incredible. What did you possibly do with so much power? Grow a forest in a desert?"

"I brought King Casper back from the dead. He drowned when the Aqueno Prison flooded." I saw no reason to lie, though murmurs broke out amongst the fay.

Marasina raised an eyebrow. "Not even the most powerful of the Magia Viveralis could have returned a soul to life after they crossed over, and you are certainly far from powerful." Her words sounded more like fact than insult, so I only nodded. "But to pull from the Regalia Vive Amulet, to use the magic of your ancestors, that was a clever move." Marasina considered me for a moment before adding, "What you lack in strength of magic, you make up for in cunning and sheer determination." Her mouth twitched slightly, almost into the hint of a smile. "For you must have some skill to have my best spy and my own daughter supporting you."

"I do my best," I acknowledged, before glancing at Pel and Lorella. "And I am fortunate to have good friends to back me up."

"I imagine you have come back to resume your position as heir, now that you have experienced the intolerance of humans." As Marasina spoke, I could see Valente's face tighten, though he remained silent.

"No, I have not," I said. Marasina's mouth formed a silent "oh?," but I kept speaking. "I have come to sue for peace between the fay and the humans, and to introduce you to one of your grandsons." I stepped to the side, allowing Finn to draw up beside me. Finn gave Marasina another deep bow. "Queen Marasina, please allow me to introduce my brother, Finn Molnár."

"Come here, boy," Marasina commanded. Finn took a few tentative steps toward the queen as she studied him. "I can almost see the resemblance, though your human features get in the way."

"Thank you," Finn said, his voice somber.

"It is rare for a human, or even a half human to enter Magnomel of their own volition these days."

"As Nor said, we want peace. And I support my sister and wanted to meet my grandmother." Finn considered for a moment before adding, "And I heard you have the most incredible library."

Marasina quirked up her lips. "Your father loved books too. He was always reading, and he would keep a spare book nearby for when he finished whatever his current book was." Marasina pointed to windows high up in the palace tree. "The grand library is right over there. I can have someone show it to you. As Soren's children, you and Elenora shall be welcomed at my court, even if you keep that human glamour." Her face soured slightly.

"Thank you," Finn said, his gaze fixed on where the library was.

"But a treaty of peace with humans is asking too much."

"Do you really want more bloodshed between us?" I asked.

"It is because of humans that I lost my son."

"And it will be because of your stubbornness that you will lose your granddaughter," I said, feeling desperate to make Marasina see reason. I stared into her blue eyes. "If I have to choose between you and Casper, I will choose him. Please don't make me choose."

Finn gave a final, wistful glance at the library before holding my hand in solidarity. "And I stand with my sister."

Marasina's brows knit in displeasure as she took in our defiance. But I never knew what her response would have been, because Valente took that moment to step forward.

"If Princess Elenora sides with the humans in a war, I will have no choice but to fight by her side." Valente's words were flat, though his nose wrinkled in disgust.

"Why would you—" Marasina started, but stopped herself, understanding dawning on her.

"Because I swore loyalty to Princess Elenora after the challenge," Valente reminded her. And though he looked like he was swallowing something bitter, he did not flinch away from his vow. "By the magic in my blood, I vowed to never allow her harm by my hand nor by my knowledge." His cold, blue eyes met mine and he gave a slight nod, indicating that he would honor his promise, regardless of his feelings toward me.

Marasina sat back in her throne, studying Valente and me for a long time, her serene face unreadable. The silence in the fay court crackled with anticipation.

"It seems that you have outwitted even me, granddaughter," Marasina finally said, the full weight of her gaze resting on me. "You give me the impossible choice of choosing between revenging my dead son or losing my living one."

"I know my father would have chosen family," I said, thinking of my father's fierce love.

"I am not pleased to be put in this position," Marasina said, and for a terrible moment, I worried her wrath would undo all our efforts for peace. Her eyes cut to Valente, as she reached an internal resolution. "But I will not lose more of my family to my own reckless actions.

I shall agree to a peace with your king, so long as no harm comes to my kin in his domain. But if you leave here to be with your human king, then I strip you of your position as heir, and it shall be bestowed on Valente."

I bowed, trying to hide the flood of relief I felt. "I understand." Straightening, I met Marasina's eyes. "And thank you."

I turned, about to take my leave of Marasina and the Forest Court, when she called my name. I pivoted back to face her.

"You should know, that even though you are no longer heir, you are still a princess of this court. You and your brother—"

"Brothers, actually," I corrected. Marasina raised an eyebrow. "I have two others, but they did not join us."

"You and your *brothers* are still members of this court and welcome to visit the Forest Court at any time." A shadow of sadness clouded her face. "I do not wish to make the mistake I made with Soren for a second time. I would like to know my grandchildren."

I smiled. "I think that can be arranged."

Finn nodded eagerly beside me. "There's still the library I need to see."

Marasina smiled. "Indeed, and it is a vast library."

"Well, now you will be stuck with Finn," I joked, but the delight in Finn's eyes told me that I might not be too far from the truth.

32

Thank Aloisia for the peace between Reynallis and Magnomel, for I could barely handle the stress of wedding preparations over the next few months, and the wedding was not even my own. The decisive, no-nonsense Constance I thought I knew became someone who spent weeks fretting over flower arrangements and dessert options. I would have found the obsessing annoying if it was not blatantly obvious that her true desire was to give Flora a perfect day to start their married life. That made it cute, at least most of the time. I still found myself hiding in Casper's study on more than one occasion to avoid Constance demanding my opinions on table decorations or which set of crystal goblets to use, only for her to completely ignore whatever I suggested. Flora was the only one who could calm the princess during the whirlwind of preparations, still managing to remain her sweet self throughout it all.

But despite the chaos, there was a joy that permeated the air of the Rose Palace, perhaps even all of Sterling. Excitement for an upcoming wedding combined with the sweet relief of peace. News of peace with the fay traveled fast, even if there was initial skepticism. But slowly, the people of Sterling began to see that peace was feasible. At first, there was simply gratitude that there were no more border skirmishes, and the fear of fay slowly started to ebb as the raids ceased and children who had been stolen by the fay were returned. Eventually, the borders even opened to the brave human or curious fay who wanted to see what lay beyond the mist wall.

Closer to home, I was learning to love myself as the humans around me came to accept my new form. Though Casper ensured my safety immediately after the curse was broken, for weeks I endured poorly disguised stares and whispered murmurings. But with time, the strangeness of having a faerie amongst the court wore away, and my appearance was no longer a novelty. Some people took no time at all; Annabeth and Yanis immediately showed their loyalty. To my surprise, Lady Ilana was one of the first nobles to accept me when she returned to the Rose Palace. Oddly, I found her salty comments on my gowns comforting, as she treated me exactly the same as before I became fay. There were some in the court who refused to accept me, who probably never would. Their rejection stung, but I reminded myself that there were those who loved and respected me for who I was, and their opinions I would value a thousand times more than the people who clung to their ignorant, prejudiced views of the fay.

The day came when I no longer missed my human form as I looked at myself in a mirror. I still required my cane, and my bones still burned subtly if I overexerted myself—a permanent effect of the sitano—but it did not stop me from living my life, and the moonstone on my pearwood cane reminded me that I had a piece of my father always with me. My white hair and pointed ears became familiar, and I could see the beauty of my glowing, copper skin and golden eyes. It helped that Casper looked at me with the same adoration as when I looked human. He even took great pleasure when he discovered how sensitive my wings were. He would hold me close, gently running a finger down the length of a wing, his touch as light as a feather. Whenever he did that, my entire body would ripple with delight. He would smile, calling me his beautiful faerie princess.

I met regularly with Queen Marasina, in the beginning to ensure she kept to her word. While she allowed my visits, she was initially frosty, still sore I had tricked her into a ceasefire. But she warmed up, in no small part to her delight in Finn, who was a frequent visitor to Magnomel, enthusiastically devouring books in the great library and listening with rapt attention whenever Marasina would tell him the history of the Magia Viveralis.

Finn and Drusia became fast friends, and they could often be found eagerly chatting about everything from ancient faerie lore to the best kinds of cherry pies. I was especially grateful that Drusia had found such a good companion in Finn, as Corine never returned to the Forest Court. Marasina issued an official exile on her, punishable by death should she return. While I had no love for the faerie who tried to blow us up, I knew Drusia took the hit hardest. Seeing her open up to Finn, smiling and sociable, warmed my heart. Finn was considering moving permanently to the Forest Court and removing his own glamour, with the help of Alverdine's skill and not sitano, but Devon insisted he wait till he was sixteen.

Though I would have never imagined this path for my life, I could not have been more thankful.

It was the first day of spring, the start of the Spring Faire, and a beautiful day for a wedding. I sat in the front pew of the cathedral, staring at the impressive floor-to-ceiling stained glass. It had depicted roses before I destroyed it as a means of escape when the fay attacked during Casper's coronation. Casper had the stained glass replaced with roses and swans, the milky white glass of the swans a striking contrast against the red glass of the roses. When I asked him about his choice, he told me that he never wanted to forget what we had overcome together.

I smiled, smoothing down my skirts as I waited for the music to begin. Annabeth had developed a special talent for ordering and customizing dresses that were practical and functional for my faerie form. Today I wore an iridescent silk gown the color of moonstone that matched the gem in my cane and made my copper skin look even brighter against the pale fabric. Behind me, I could hear Jacobie fidgeting before Devon shushed him. I turned to give them a quick smile. Devon, Finn, and Jacobie were all dressed in green and gold. Next to Devon sat Lady Ilana, looking as elegant as the first day I saw her, though some of the ice in her demeanor had since thawed, and I noticed her hand resting subtly on top of Devon's. I shook my head, not wanting to consider Ilana as a potential sister-in-law, though the idea was not as horrid as I would have once expected.

The music began, the first notes from the massive organ ringing out from long pipes and filling the cathedral. The congregation quieted, voices hushing each other as everyone twisted in their seats, charged anticipation of seeing the royal brides. The massive doors were pulled open, and Constance came into view, Casper by her side. As they slowly walked down the aisle, the swish of gowns and scrape of chairs echoed throughout as everyone rose to their feet in honor of their king and princess.

Casper was magnificently dressed in red and gold, with the intertwined roses of the Famille De Rose crest embroidered on his tunic. He wore his ceremonial crown, the bejeweled and sculpted one from his coronation. The large ruby on top of the golden arches of the crown winked in the morning light. And while he looked regal, even his grand attire paled compared to the splendor that was his sister. It was a tradition for a noble couple to wear their betrothed's colors at their wedding, as a show of commitment to the new partnership. Couples often gifted each other their wedding clothes, which Flora and Constance had done. So instead of the Famille De Rose red and gold, Constance shone in the orange and white of the Domus Ante Solis family.

I had been skeptical of how Constance, with her pale skin and black hair, would wear such colors, but my imagination had been far too limited. Flora had commissioned a stunning gown from Faradisia. The bodice was snow-white silk, richly embroidered with seed pearls that shimmered in the light and complemented the pearl and diamond tiara that was set into Constance's raven curls. The gown was dip-dyed for an ombre effect, where the white melted into deepening yellows and oranges along the length of the skirt, reminding me of a radiant sunset, the rich colors infused with gold and copper threads, the edge of the skirt shifting to a deep russet, almost as black as night. The dress seemed to glow with its own light, and that light was matched by the beaming face of Constance. I had never seen her so beautiful nor so happy. As they reached the front of the cathedral, Casper kissed Constance on her cheek before leaving her in front of the waiting Father Geoffroi.

I smiled as Casper joined me. He interlaced his fingers with mine, giving them a subtle squeeze. My heart fluttered to see my charming love looking so handsome, especially with the joy that was clear on his face. We turned back toward the door, eagerly awaiting Flora.

Murmurs and gasps of delight were heard as the next song began, and Flora entered the cathedral, her uncle and King of Faradisia, King Jovan, escorting her. Constance had gifted Flora a dress of garnet silk unlike any gown I had ever seen. The bodice and sleeves were overlaid with delicate gold lace, and a braided golden belt cinched her waist. The voluptuous skirt consisted of hundreds of layers of red silk "petals" that moved and shimmered with her every step. Each petal of the rose skirt was edged in gold, and Flora had dusted golden powder into her hair, which was ornately braided with gold beads and ruby chips. The gold lining her eyes was bright against her dark skin. Her sweet, serene smile became a full, radiant grin as she saw Constance waiting for her.

Once they reached the altar, King Jovian kissed her cheek before taking her hands and pressing them into Constance's. He then made his way to the pews, and everyone took their seats as the ceremony began. Father Geoffroi spoke of love and the couple's commitment to each other, blessed them by the Mother, and dabbed oil anointed in Aloisia's name for wisdom and faithfulness. Constance and Flora stared into each other's eyes as though they were the only souls in the cathedral, instead of the hundreds who watched on.

When it was time for them to kiss, I found myself wiping a tear away from my own eyes.

"You know, we're next," Casper whispered to me.

"I was hoping with one royal wedding this year, we might be able to get away with eloping," I whispered back.

"Not on your life. I want to show the entire kingdom my bride."

And for once, I had no witty retort for him.

"Nor, I have something for you." Casper and I were sitting in a corner of the ballroom. Casper had suggested we take a break from dancing when I confessed that my legs were starting to ache. He had fetched me a goblet of fine Faradisian sparkling wine, as the two of us relaxed on cushioned chairs, watching the festivities. The sun had long since set, but no one seemed ready to give up on a night of celebratory feasting and dancing.

I raised an eyebrow at Casper. "Why did you get me something for your sister's wedding?"

"This is not because of Constance's wedding." Casper grinned, a mischievous look in his eyes that I always found utterly adorable in my charming, noble king. Casper pulled me to my feet, and the two of us slipped out of the ballroom.

After a few minutes I realized where he was leading me.

"Why are we going to your study?"

"Because," he said, opening his study door and ushering me inside. "I wanted to give this to you on our anniversary."

"Our anniversary . . ." I started but trailed off as realization dawned on me.

"It was at the last Spring Faire that we met."

I smiled, thinking not so much on that day, but rather all that had happened in the life-changing year between then and now. "And you want to celebrate the day I swindled and lied to you?" My surprise was evident, and Casper chuckled softly.

"I want to celebrate the day we met, because it was all worth it to have you in my life." He leaned closer to me, trailing a finger up my wing, making me shiver in delight.

"Well, in that case, you're a day late," I said, smirking.

"What? Am not. I clearly remember the Spring Faire."

"Yes, but we met the day before." I gave his cheek a quick kiss. "I stumbled into a lost young nobleman in the woods the day *before* the Spring Faire. A foolish one at that. I managed to steal his ring before directing him back to Sterling."

Casper pulled my hand to his lips, kissing his signet ring on my finger before letting his lips trail up my knuckles. "My apologies, I will have to make it up to you." He looked up from my hand, meeting my eyes with a wicked gleam that made my heart pound and my breath catch in my throat.

"I'm sure you shall think of something," I said.

"I will start with this," he said, suddenly pulling away and reaching into a drawer in his desk. He drew out a thick leather book, placing it on the desk. The book was huge, as long as my forearm, and "MAPS" was embossed on the cover. "Open it."

Carefully, I opened the book. Inside were large maps, beautifully illustrated and meticulously drawn out. There were detailed ones of Reynallis, Faradisia, Glavnada, and rough outlines of Magnomel, though many pages were blank, save for the title Magnomel at the top, as though they were waiting for a cartographer to discover the landscape beyond the borders of Reynallis.

"This is beautiful," I said, taking in each exquisite page.

"Here," Casper said, carefully flipping back to an early page I had missed. "Read this."

Inside was an inscription, written in Casper's own elegant hand.

To my dearest Elenora,
    From gold spun to a curse undone,
    Our journeys together have only begun.

I looked up at Casper, the questions in my eyes met with his loving smile. "Journeys?"

"I thought you might wish to do some traveling before we wed."

"Anything to delay planning another wedding," I said with an exaggerated sigh. More sincerely, I added, "Where did you have in mind?"

"Everywhere. We can see Faradisia and Glavnada. We can travel the world before settling down to rule. Constance has proved herself a capable leader and can rule in our stead while we are away."

"I think I would like that," I said, warming to the idea of such an adventure with Casper.

"And there is more I want to do in Reynallis," he said.

"Oh?"

"You were right, Nor, as you usually are. We need to go out into our country to help our people. Because there is peace with Magnomel, we now have the resources to truly focus on rebuilding Reynallis where she hurts the most. We can go to the south, repair what the Southern War broke. Make our country better than it ever has been, seek out what our people need. You have been the voice of the common people to me, reminding me that we need to aid our whole country, but especially those most vulnerable."

His dark eyes were eager, if a bit uncertain when I did not respond, suddenly too overwhelmed to speak.

He continued. "I know it will not be easy. There is lasting damage from the war and it will take time for our people to understand that the fay are not to be feared. News of your true form has permeated through Sterling, but not all of Reynallis. Some might take issue with our future queen being fay, but I believe we can show our country that there is a better way to live than a life filled with prejudice and fear, if you are willing to go with me."

I nodded, my eyes brimming with happy tears. "And the blank pages?" I asked.

Casper looked a bit sheepish. "No human has created a comprehensive map of Magnomel. We only have false ones filled with superstitious imaginings. We can travel there, open communication, and fill in the blank pages. The more ignorant prejudices we replace with truth, the more we are likely to ensure a lasting peace." He paused before adding, "And you deserve to know more about where your father was from."

I wiped my eyes, startled by his willingness to return to Magnomel on my behalf. I carefully closed the book. "This is the second-best gift I have ever received," I said, my voice choked with emotion.

"Only the second best?" Casper's voice was light, but I detected a hint of genuine disappointment.

"Yes," I said, taking a step closer to him and looking up into his dark eyes. I breathed him in, the familiar spicy scent of cinnamon and cloves that I loved. I lifted my hands to his face, carefully cupping his cheeks in my hands. "The best gift was when a prince promised me his hand in marriage if I gave him a room of gold." I pulled his face down to mine, and whispered, "And after many trials and challenges overcome, he gave me a happily ever after."

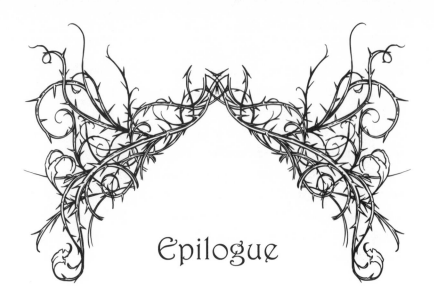

Epilogue

"**I**f I die, I am going to haunt both of you," I said, looking between Pel and Lorella.

I gazed out the window from the room in the tower. Far below, my friends and family stood, along with most of the court, all eagerly waiting and watching. Word had spread throughout the Rose Palace that their future queen had learned how to fly, and it seemed no one wanted to miss my display. I, however, was feeling a bit queasy this far from the grounds and started to question why I had been so brazen as to promise to fly from the tallest tower.

"You have been doing wonderfully in our lessons at the Forest Court," Lorella said. "Simply think of this as our next lesson."

"But we never started a flight so high up," I countered. Far below, I could see Casper waving up to me, cheering me on. Beside him stood my brothers, Ilana, Constance, Flora, and I could even make out Annabeth and Sir Yanis. They all looked far too small from this height and my stomach gave an unhappy flip.

"Nor, would it make you feel better if I said it is very unlikely that you will forget everything we've taught you and plummet to your death?" Pel asked, unable to keep the smirk off his face. I shot him a look. "If you do, I'll say something nice at your funeral," he added.

I grumbled as Lorella scolded Pel. But her admonishments melted away as Pel took a step toward her, under the guise of having a better view of my flight. I did not miss the way he put his arm around her, smiling as he pulled her close to him. Nor did I miss the way she beamed as he did so. It made me happy to see them both so smitten with each other.

"We have taught our little chick well, it's time to throw her out of the nest," he said, but his voice turned surprisingly sincere as he added, "Nor can do anything she puts her mind to." He winked at me. "You can do this."

I nodded, hoping my smile hid the fear I felt. I had managed to fly before, but never starting from such a height. Lorella promised that it would be simple once I tried it, but that seemed an easy thing to say from someone who had flown since childhood. I looked down, blowing a kiss to Casper, which he pretended to catch. Then I looked up, ignoring the ground far below as I focused on the bright blue sky, the plump white clouds, and the freedom that lay before me.

I inhaled deeply, closing my eyes as I remembered my training. Beginning with my shoulder blades, I tightened my muscles, feeling the tendons activate past my shoulders and into my wings, which had grown stronger over my months of training. I flapped them several times, feeling the breeze they created as I reminded myself that I knew how to work my wings.

I stepped out of the window.

For a terrible, weightless moment, I fell before I could pump my wings fast enough. I kept my eyes squeezed tightly shut, focusing on the systematic movements of pressing my front wings forward and then the back wings, feeling the air flow between them. It became a sort of dance, and soon I felt the familiar control, the moment my body remembered the feeling of flying from all my practice lessons, and I was rising in the sky.

I opened my eyes, the anxiety morphing into elation as I soared up above the royal grounds. I whooped with excitement, feeling the wind against my face, running through my hair. I turned my attention downward, gliding down on shimmering wings till I was mere feet above the heads of the crowd. Using the momentum, I shifted up, my wings cutting through the air as I looped and spiraled. I flew above the tower, enjoying the stunning view of Sterling spread out before me. I grinned, excited to travel the lands with Casper, visit all the places I could see from this vantage, as well as so much more.

As I soared through the air, ready to take on my next adventure, I felt free.

About the Author

Brandie June loves storytelling in all formats, whether she is marketing animated movies or writing fantasy novels. She spent most of her early life onstage, or at least as close to the front row as she could get. Initially an actor, she got her B.A. in Theatre from UCLA and branched out into costume design and playwriting.

She developed an interest in marketing and returned to UCLA to get her M.B.A in Entertainment Marketing. When not writing, she promotes kids' movies and anime as a marketing director of family entertainment.

She has published several pieces in anthologies, was a finalist for The Writers of the Future Award, is a member of Science Fiction and Fantasy Writers of America, volunteers with YALLWEST, and was a staff member of the Greater Los Angeles Writers Society. She loves speaking at writing and book events and has spoken at San Diego Comic-Con@Home, WonderCon, West Coast Writers Conference, SFWA Nebula Conference, The Book Fest, LosCon, BayCon,

Creative Writing At Pacific, Southwest Manuscripters, and the Las Vegas Book Festival.

Her debut novel, *Gold Spun*, is a fresh retelling of the Rumpelstiltskin tale through the miller's daughter's POV. Except now the miller's daughter is a con artist and Rumpelstiltskin is a mysterious faerie with a dark secret. *Curse Undone* is the second book in this duology.

You can find out more about her at
www.brandiejune.com
and follow her on Instagram at @thebrandiejune
and on TikTok at @brandiebooks.

Acknowledgments

Wow! We made it to a sequel! First and foremost, my thanks to you, the reader. Thanks for taking a chance on a new author and all your patience after I left you hanging at the end of *Gold Spun* while I was writing *Curse Undone*. I hope you feel satisfied with the conclusion of Nor's story.

A million thanks to Sue and her fantastic team at CamCat books. It has been an utter delight to work with all of you! Maryann, this cover is stunning. Laura, thanks for all your marketing efforts. Bill, I appreciate all your help. Helga and Bridget, I'm so lucky to have worked with such great editors who really got Nor and helped me conclude this story. And my immense gratitude to everyone in my writing tribe. Every friend who's cheered me along in this crazy writing adventure. You guys are the best. Thanks to Craig for giving me support when I needed it and space to write. Much love to my fur and feather babies. My pups Buttercup and Nor graciously sleep in the office while I write and Puck, my baby bird, is a great shoulder buddy.

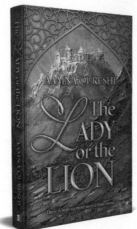

CamCat
Books

VISIT US ONLINE FOR MORE BOOKS TO LIVE IN:
CAMCATBOOKS.COM

CamCatBooks   @CamCatBooks   @CamCat_Books